Between Earth And Arcturus

James Prescott

ACKNOWLEDGMENTS

Many thanks to Natalya, who encouraged me to get this into print, and to Devis, who created the music for the audio podcast of this novel on www.workingthegalaxy.com. A special thanks to all of my talented friends in the South Bay Writers Group who critiqued the book.

CHAPTER 1

Commander Aguire thought about his captain's transfer to a new ship. It seems everyone who's like family to him eventually goes away. He glanced sideways at Leroy Donno, who had a rare smile on his normally somber face. Aguire's mood dipped a bit lower realizing that someday Donno might go away, too.

"You blew a year's pay just to impress women, didn't you?" Donno's smooth southern drawl nudged José Aguire's attention back to the Kansas highway where the snowy prairie rushed by at 200 kilometers per hour.

"So, I bought a car." Aguire answered, toying with the tint controls for the windows, alternately dimming the glare from the snow, then returning it to brilliant white. "Loosen up, it's time to celebrate."

"Your promotion isn't official yet." Donno's smile stretched into a real grin. "But okay, I can see it's hard to wait."

"Right." Aguire grinned back at the Lieutenant Commander, his buddy since pilot's school, before the war.

Donno pointed ahead. "Let's stop at McConnell before heading back to New Wichita and see if I'm gonna get transferred to Poluka's new ship, or get stuck as your first officer, Captain Aguire."

"Captain." A grin brought out the chiseled dimples on Aguire's lean face. "I'll be a friggin' captain the next time I board the Livingston, and of course I'll get stuck with you as my first officer. You don't think Poluka wants a bum like you, do you?"

"It doesn't work like that anymore, buddy." Donno shook his head with a sad, practiced expression. "The old Federation let captains choose their crew, but the New Fed changed all that. The politicians have as much say-so as the captain does."

"Are you sure?

"They told us in the repatriation class we had to take. There've been lots of changes since the old Fed got wiped out. I hear things are really bad in Europe."

To Aguire, Europe meant memories Madrid. He could almost picture faces from the orphanage. He hasn't seen those guys since he joined the Navy, and his old amigos went into the Army. He should call them. He always plans to call them. This time he will. Maybe they can meet before he leaves again.

The car dropped them off at the admin building of the Exploration Corps Annex at the McConnell Spaceport and then parked itself nearby.

Aguire lazily strolled behind Donno to the lobby. His buddy was wearing the powder-blue uniform of the Corps, but Aguire was enjoying the civilian clothes a pretty sales-girl chose for him yesterday. He learned that letting a woman pick clothes for him was a good start for seduction. In fact, he spent last night in her bed.

He'd always been popular with the ladies in America and Mexico, more so than in his native Spain. They liked his strong, masculine face with straight black hair slicked back, away from his face. When he was a teenager he looked older, making it easy to lie about his age and join the Navy a year early. Now that he was thirty-two, he still looked like he was in his twenties, and sometimes, like when on planet-leave and away from his responsibilities, he acted like a teenager.

The lobby was empty except for a cadet playing computer games at the receptionist's desk. Etched into the granite wall behind the desk was the emblem of the Exploration Corps, the symbol of his life for the last four years.

The cadet lurched to his feet and stiffened to attention which struck Aguire as an overreaction to their arrival.

Just then Aguire recognized the sneering voice of Gary Fisher coming in the door behind them. "So, Aguire, I heard you were back."

Despite years of seniority, Fisher was stuck at the rank of commander, having absolutely no aptitude for leadership. Unlike most in the Corps, Fisher never saw combat in the military. In fact, Aguire suspected if Fisher ever were in a battle, one of his own people would blow his head off.

There's a cheery thought: Fisher without a head.

Fisher flashed his toothy grin and held up a sleeve, displaying the four gold stripes. Aguire's smile vanished.

"That's right, Aguire. I'm an admiral now, and I'm looking forward to seeing you back in uniform, Commander."

Aguire's tongue came back to life. "An admiral? How?"

"The New Federation," Fisher said, "recognizes faithful service, and gives credit to the deserving. I understand Captain Poluka's getting the new ship, in which case I'll have some influence about the reassignment of his officers. I'll see about getting you transferred to my office." Fisher laughed and swaggered onward into the building without looking back.

Donno made his inquiries about assignments, but nothing was posted yet. Aguire was quiet when they climbed back into the car and continued to New Wichita.

Something was very wrong on Earth if Gary Fisher got any kind of promotion. But if he jumped from commander to admiral then the universe just took a turn towards insane.

"I gotta visit my mom in Atlanta." Donno said. "Drop me at the station. I'll catch the next bullet train."

"Yeah, say hello for me, okay? You were right. There have been a lot of changes. How could the Corps do something as stupid as making Fisher a damned admiral? That asshole shouldn't even be in a uniform."

"I thought you heard. Everybody in HQ is talking about it, though not too loudly. Fisher came out on top when he backed up the coup with information that led to the slaughter last year. He knew the secret location where the President's people were meeting, and passed it on to…well…to the people who're now our new government. He even got his own admiral killed, and he's real proud of himself for that. Seems the New Fed appreciates it, too. There's the train station. Listen, I'll bring back one of my mom's pies for you if baking is still legal."

"Thanks." Aguire forced a half-hearted laugh while the car hovered at the curb, and Donno got out.

"I'll see you in a day or two." Donno called over his shoulder and ran to catch the next bullet train to Georgia.

Aguire told the car to take him home, which the car recognized as the hotel.

From a window in his suite, Aguire looked down on the street where his car was parked, drumming his fingers on the windowsill.

A group of college-age women, tourists judging from the cameras they carried, stopped to admire his car. He chuckled when they took turns leaning on the luxury vehicle in sexy poses while the others took pictures.

"That's right, girls," he whispered. "One in a million can afford a car like that. It's a sign of success, and I worked hard to get there."

Turning away, he leaned on the wall, not noticing when the women moved on. His eyes panned the room that seemed larger when he first rented it. Spacemen aren't supposed to be claustrophobic, but damn if this room didn't feel like a cage.

Seven years in the navy, most of it fighting rebels on the moons of Jupiter, then almost five more in the Exploration Corps brought him to the brink of getting his own command.

"I worked hard, damn it." He clenched his fists, and paced the floor, unable to stop thinking of the gold braid on Fisher's sleeve. An admiral. They made him a goddamned admiral!

He stopped pacing when the com console caught his eye.

"I need to talk to Poluka."

He pounced on the console's call button and asked to be connected to Captain Paul Poluka. The screen indicated he was calling to California. Perhaps Poluka was at his father's farm.

An elderly man's face filled the view-screen.

"Hello. What can I do for you, young man?"

Aguire was so accustomed to being called "Commander" or "Sir" he almost looked around to see if a young man was behind him.

"Hello," the white-haired man repeated, "Are we connected? Damn, I miss telephones."

The old gentleman had a harsh, sort of impatient voice.

"Yes. Hello, sir. My name is Commander José Aguire. I'm trying to reach Captain Poluka."

The old man was silent for a moment, staring with his bright green eyes in a way that made Aguire suspect that he hadn't been understood.

"Paul? Yes, he's here, but he's having supper just now. Maybe he could call you later."

"That'll be fine. Thank you." The screen went blank and Aguire began to relax. The Captain will know what to do. If anyone knows how to handle admirals, it's the man that Aguire tried to emulate for the last ten years.

Poluka had a knack for finding creative solutions to impossible problems, yet Aguire always had difficulty veering from the narrow path of tried and tested regulations that governed everything from how to brush your teeth to how to nuke an enemy.

He lay down on the bed with his hands behind his head and asked the ceiling, "Where would I be without the Corps?"

He never liked thinking about where he came from, but sometimes he just couldn't help it. He barely remembered the day his father died. Three years later, when he was nine, his mother died, too. He stayed in a Catholic orphanage for a while but later ran away, joined a gang, and lived in the streets of Madrid. The Navy turned his life around, giving him a career and purpose, providing a sense of order that he never knew before.

When the Jupiter War ended Aguire transferred from the Navy to the Exploration Corps, keeping his rank and rate of pay. His sense of duty, first to the Navy and now to the Corps, kept him focused on making his career not just what he did, but who he was.

On planet-leave, however, Aguire knew how to have a good time. His zest for partying was legendary and once got him expelled from Mars with orders not to return.

The com console chimed, and Poluka's round face appeared. "Commander, how are you?"

"Hello, Captain. I hope I didn't interrupt anything."

"Nothing I can't do later. What can I do for you?"

"Sir, Gary Fisher is an admiral now—if you can believe that—and he says he's going to get me under his command. Could that happen?"

Fisher's name brought a sour grimace to Poluka's bland features. Like so many others, Poluka dealt with Fisher at the end of the war when soldiers were transferring into the Corps and Commander Fisher was working a desk in the capital city, making things as unpleasant as possible for everyone.

"I'll be honest with you, José. It's not entirely up to me. I'm not sure what I can do."

CHAPTER 2

Lynda Stokes noted Aguire's dismay on com screen, but Paul Poluka reassured him, "Don't worry. I'll make some calls and find out if there's anything to it.

"Thank you, Captain." Aguire said.When the call ended, Lynda's father turned from the dinner table and snorted, "So, if you do nothing, that bastard Fisher may solve our problem for us."

A flash of offense appeared on Paul's meaty face and Lynda muttered, "Papa! He's Paul's friend."

"Of course," G.J. Stokes continued in a more sympathetic tone. "It was a bad joke. Nobody should get stuck under Fisher, but really, Paul, you can see that Aguire doesn't fit into our plans."

"I'm not going to leave Aguire under Fisher's command, G.J.," Paul said. "If he doesn't come with us, then I'll see to it he gets command of the Livingston, which is what he wants and expects anyway. But I still think Aguire should be my first officer on the Hanno."

Paul was being unreasonable. He'd been in a bad mood ever since arriving at the Stokes estate in Napa Valley and Lynda thoughtlessly joked about how his shadow looked like a bowling pin. She'd never guessed he could be so sensitive about the weight he'd gained since she last saw him three years ago. He still looked good in his dress-gray uniform; still the surrogate big brother she needed since her own brother Gentry disappeared in the Zone a decade ago.

Her green eyes shifted to her father. Has Papa changed much in the last three years? His hair was white now, instead of salt-

and-pepper, but his bright green eyes still had a gleam that betrayed his sharp mind.

She knew she'd changed, going from eighteen to twenty-two she finally developed some feminine curves that she'd waited so long for—longer than other girls.

Now she realized that Paul hadn't said anything about how she looked, and it annoyed her.

Paul sat down at the dinner table while her father drained the last drops from the wine bottle into Paul's glass, saying, "Lynda's gone over Aguire's records, Paul. In fact, she's gone over the records of thousands of officers to see who might be a threat to us, and José Aguire got a very bad score."

"Score?" Paul scowled. "This isn't a game. And how can anyone go through thousands of personnel records? Did you just have a computer read them, Lynda, or did you actually study any of these people?"

Lynda scooped up another bottle of wine from the bar and gave it to Paul to open.

"Actually, I did some of both," she told him. "In Aguire's case I read all his records and I agree with the computer—he'll never choose to commit treason against the New Federation. Instead, he'll have us arrested."

"Not Aguire." Paul fairly shouted, then caught himself and continued more calmly. "You can't tell anything just from records. You've got to meet the man. Get to know him, like I do."

"You've got to appreciate how serious this is, Paul," G.J. said. "The old government was bad enough for us to abandon everything we have on Earth, but this New Federation is worse. This crowd can arrest you at breakfast and pass a death sentence before lunch. Lynda and I reserve the right to veto any officers you choose for the new ship."

"Tell me, Paul," Lynda said, "when you were in deep space and heard about the fall of the old Federation, what did you do?"

"I immediately returned to Earth to preserve the illusion of loyalty, and also because I knew we couldn't wait any longer. I used those five months to speak with each crewman and get a feel for how they might accept turning renegade."

"You talked to all of them?" Lynda asked.

"Well, no. I already knew some wouldn't go along with it."

"Did you talk to Aguire?" Lynda asked.

Paul looked down at the table. "No, but you need to meet him."

"Maybe we will. Papa will be teaching your new crew at the Academy, and I'll be helping him." She looked at her father and saw he approved of where she was leading. "Tell Aguire that it's not certain yet what his future will be, but that he should take the training anyway."

Paul nodded slowly, his right hand touching his collar, fingering his captain's insignia.

"Yeah, um, in the meantime, someone else will have to get the promotion he was expecting."

CHAPTER 3

A month went by before Captain Poluka called and asked Aguire to pick him up at the McConnell spaceport.

Aguire drove east through New Wichita and into the wide-open prairie, where the rusty ruins of Old Wichita grew out of the horizon on the left. McConnell, shiny and new, was dead ahead.

McConnell was like a small city, mostly for commercial service, but with sections reserved for Army, Navy, and Corps use. Aguire told the car to go park itself and went into the civilian side.

Halfway to the arrivals terminal, he saw a public com console and remembered he wanted to call an old friend. Eleven years ago he'd joined the Navy. His buddies from the orphanage joined the Army, except one who stayed in Madrid and might know where the others were. Aguire had lost track of them, and the new com system couldn't seem to locate them.

He punched a search into the com and waited...and waited.

Maybe the com was broken or the system was down.

"Aguire!" A man's voice barked at the back of his head and spun him around to find Mike Sullivan, a spaceport police officer, right behind him.

"Hey, Sullivan, what the —"

"Get away from the console, Aguire." Sullivan reached past him and punched the cancel button. Something in his tone prodded Aguire to move without asking questions. The cop's eyes darted around the bustling spaceport. His every movement was tense, as if some inevitable catastrophe was overdue. A dozen steps from the machine, they stopped and faced each other.

"I don't know what you're doing, Aguire," Sullivan said, "but don't do it again."

"What the hell, Sullivan? I was looking for an old friend.

What's going on, amigo?"

"I got a call," Sullivan gestured at the radio clipped to his collar, "to see who was using this console. Whomever you were searching for is bad news. The last time this happened I found my kid's piano teacher trying to make a call. Like a good little cop, I reported what I saw. An hour later she was arrested by federal goons and hasn't been seen since."

The policeman squeezed his radio and said, "Sullivan here. There was no one at the console when I arrived."

"Understood. Hey, Sullivan, the cameras aren't working again. See if you can fix it. Dispatch out," a voice replied.

"What the hell's going on, Sullivan?" Aguire demanded.

"It's the New fucking Fed, man." Sullivan scanned the faces around them, not like he used to, not like a cop doing his job, but more like a soldier in enemy territory. The people walking by avoided him, not making eye contact. "I'd quit this job, but you know how many kids I've got? Mouths to feed, you know?"

They didn't talk long. Sullivan continued his rounds, and Aguire needed to meet Poluka.

At the terminal, Poluka was collecting his baggage. Aguire pressed a button on his car key, and the car met them at the nearest exit.

Aguire got a couple of beers from the back seat and handed one to Poluka on the way to Poluka's suite, which was one of many old houses the Spacemen's Association owned between New Wichita and Old Wichita.

"It's a gloomy view." The captain nodded at the distant ruins of Old Wichita which seemed just a few steps away on the snowy plain.

Rebel generals formed the Federation there forty years ago, after what had been called the Last War. Now, that Federation was gone, too. The clamor of war echoed in Aguire's memory, not this Last War but the more recent Jupiter War, where he'd first met Captain Poluka.

"Here's to peace." Aguire raised his beer.

"Peace." Poluka raised his bottle and took a swallow. "They passed over you. I'm sorry."

"Yeah." Aguire grimaced. "Turner commands the Livingston now, but I can continue as first officer—under Captain Turner."

Poluka frowned. "Turner's a good man, but you should have

got it."

"It'll take years waiting for another ship as Turner's first-officer, but I sure as hell don't want to get stuck working for Admiral Fisher."

Poluka frowned at the bleak landscape. "You may not get assigned to my new ship. It's not just my decision."

Aguire groaned and mumbled, "Things sure have changed."

Poluka pulled his gaze away from the prairie and studied Aguire. "What do you think of all the changes, Commander?"

"At first, I thought it wouldn't make much difference." Aguire shrugged. "You know, a new system, a new calendar, a Senate. Big deal. But everybody's scared. I liked the old way better."

"Having a Senate is the only improvement that I can see," Poluka said. "That new calendar business was a mistake. The idea was to get rid of religious holidays. It's no secret that Batastia blames religion for most of the world's problems."

"Batastia? The vice president?"

"Yeah, the President is just a figurehead. Vincent Batastia runs the show."

"That explains the trouble when I tried to buy Christmas decorations."

"Eh? You got in trouble?"

"Yeah, some of our officers wanted a holiday party with some local girls. We've done it before and it always gets us…um…."

"I understand what it gets you, José. I know the kind of women you invite to parties, but how did you get into trouble?"

"The stores aren't carrying anything for Christmas. It made them nervous just hearing the word Christmas and they tried to get me to leave, so I made a stink about it. They called the cops."

"You got arrested?" Poluka seemed oddly pleased.

"Well, I got an order to appear in court for disturbing the peace."

He was embarrassed now. He once got in trouble during a stopover on Mars. Poluka had been furious.

"How will you keep it off your record?" Poluka asked.

Aguire took a deep breath. "I'm not going to. This is a matter of principle. I'm not religious myself, but the government can't dictate what people believe, right? I mean…where will it stop?"

The car entered a neighborhood of rustic houses on huge lots, slowing to navigate through rural, snow-covered roads.

"When's the new ship getting commissioned?" Aguire asked.

"Soon. They won't let me choose my own crew, but I get to pick the first mission. I'm going to investigate the Zone, and then Arcturus."

"The Zone? It's about time. Didn't your brother's ship disappear there?"

"Yeah. Like every spacecraft going that direction, he never returned. Hundreds of robot probes have vanished attempting to reach Arcturus." Poluka was getting excited now, gesticulating as he spoke. "The Himilco—my brother's ship—was equipped with the very first Stokes Tube, but she was a tiny ship cobbled together on a shoestring budget. She might have made it, but she didn't, and we still don't know what's out there to be afraid of."

"Your new ship can do it?"

"Exactly. Think of it, Aguire." Poluka pointed at the sky. "We've explored star systems hundreds of light years away, except in the direction of Arcturus, which is only 36 light years from where you're sitting, and all because of the Zone, the mysterious region of space that scares the snot out of most spacemen. My new starship, the Hanno, will be the first to make it there."

His love of discovery was something they had in common. For explorers, it's being first that counts. Nobody cares who got there second.

"The government agreed to Arcturus for the first mission?"

"For simple self-interest, I can assure you. Construction of the Hanno was practically complete when New Fed took control. Otherwise, they'd have scrapped the whole project. So, they got a very expensive starship with experimental engines that some people think won't work right. They took a gamble, after a little persuasion, because there are still powers who aren't part of the New Federation, independent worlds, fortune hunters and so forth. If someone else gets to Arcturus first, it'll damage the prestige of the new government as well as cloud any legal claim to Arcturus. The Alpha Virginus system is a likely candidate. They're in a good location to simply go around the Zone to get to Arcturus. If the Hanno is a failure and never returns, the New Fed can say it was a project of the old government and their hands were tied, but if she makes it, well, that would be something."

"So, we've got idiot politicians making a scientific decision,"

Aguire concluded, "and we like the decision, which was made for all the wrong reasons."

"Beautiful how that works, isn't it?"

The car stopped at a house with a big, covered porch and deer tracks all over the snow. Nearby pine trees lent a delicate scent to the crisp winter air.

Some of Poluka's stuff was already there, hastily dropped off when they returned to Earth. Trinkets and artifacts from bygone times lined the bookcases and shelves. A meter-long model of a wooden sailing ship sat on the kitchen table.

"You finished it," Aguire said, referring to the model.

"Almost. It needs paint now."

"I can imagine you on an old ship. When will we know something about my next assignment?"

"In the next few weeks. Training starts soon. Even if you don't know your status, you should take some classes. Maybe it'll help convince people that you should be on the Hanno."

CHAPTER 4

Elisa Santino loved the Exploration Corps, but after the violent takeover she got shuffled around until she finally ended up working for Admiral Fisher, and the only way out was to resign. If she had to quit the Corps, she might as well make herself rich first.

There were deep, dark secrets surrounding the construction of the new starship. She told no one she'd discovered Gentry Stokes Jr. and Captain Paul Poluka were up to their necks in some kind of sneaky business. Stokes used all his connections—even among his competitors—to hide the real design of the starship. She figured he would pay for her silence.

She got to her desk before sunrise—hours before anyone else—but kept her computer switched to keyboard instead of voice, so anyone who might be around wouldn't hear how she hacked into secret files.

At six-thirty, her coworkers began trickling into the Department of Design Review. Elisa closed the files she'd hacked into after copying the interesting parts to a button disk. She looked up, smiled and said "good morning" to each person as they came in.

Most didn't know much about her, except that she was good at office work and very pretty. Her looks sometimes gave her an edge, which she took full advantage of, but her height—only 147 centimeters—and her petite 50kg body made her seem childlike, which caused people to not take her seriously. In most cases concerning her career, it wasn't helpful.

At five minutes before seven, the son of a bitch arrived. He always showed up 35 minutes earlier than scheduled, and this always surprised the newcomers, which was the whole point. When he barged into the room with that meaningless grin on his pasty white face, the new clerk named Julie almost screamed.

Everyone knew Fisher was trying to get Julie into bed. He'd tried with Elisa, too. In fact, he tried it with most young women whom he outranked. That's what got Elisa demoted from lieutenant to ensign; she refused to spread her legs for the disgusting son of a bitch. Not that she had anything against sleeping around—she did her share—but never with creeps like Fisher.

"Admiral," Julie gasped, "we weren't expecting you so early."

I was, Elisa thought.

"Uh-huh," he grunted absently as he whisked around the office to see if anyone was late or goofing off. He loved catching somebody at something. It was his idea of power: his power over his people.

After completing a loop around the office, he left for the cafeteria. Julie sighed with relief when the door swung shut behind him. Julie needed something to do, something to keep Fisher from pestering her.

"Julie," Elisa called softly. "Could you give me a hand with something?"

Relief erupted from the young girl's face. "What can I do for you, Ensign Santino?"

She had a sweet face and was petite like Elisa, but not so short. Fisher went for the small women, especially the young ones. Elisa didn't know for sure what a date with the son of a bitch was like, but she'd heard rumors about one girl who had to go to the hospital after a night with him. She moved to another city the very next day and changed her name so Fisher couldn't find her again. Elisa never heard of a woman seeing him a second time.

"I need you to check some files." Elisa explained. "Look for subcontractors who worked on the Hanno and got paid twice for the same job or materials. It happens sometimes."

"I can do that," Julie responded with an angelic smile.

"Sure you can. Use my computer. It's all set up."

Fisher came back with a cup of coffee in one hand and two donuts in the other. Elisa silently prayed his addiction to caffeine and sugar would lead to a heart attack—or at least a stroke.

"Ensign Santino." Fisher loudly emphasized her reduced rank. "I expect the Hanno report finished by noon. I have a meeting with the president's cabinet today."

"It will be ready before then, Admiral." She always called him Admiral instead of sir because, in her mind, sir indicated respect.

"It better be accurate and complete."

"It will be, Admiral." How would you know the difference, you son of a bitch?

"It better be."

You said that already, asshole. "Yes, Admiral."

Fisher moved around the desk to look over Julie's shoulder at the computer screen. "What are you doing?"

The young woman paused but didn't turn to face him. "I'm checking financial records, sir."

Elisa added, "We're looking for signs of fraud."

The Admiral hovered about a moment longer, fidgeting, as if trying to think of something to say, before finally going to his office.

"Ensign Santino?" Julie whispered when he was gone.

"Call me Elisa. He's like that with all the new girls. He was probably going to have you do something that involved working closely with him, but the thought of finding evidence of fraud distracted him. It'd mean having power over someone else."

"Is that what he wants? Power over everyone? Over me?"

"Listen, he doesn't have as much power over you as he'd like you to believe. You're a civilian. Just refuse, and there's nothing he can do."

"He could fire me."

"There are better jobs and better bosses. If I were you, I'd just quit and file a complaint, but don't tell anyone I suggested it."

Julie became absorbed in her task, unaware that Elisa already did this research weeks ago and covered up everything she wanted to remain hidden. The secret transactions of Stokes Industries would only be valuable if they stayed secret.

Admiral Fisher returned at noon in his dress-gray uniform.

"How do I look?" he asked, standing straight, shoulders back.

"Very nice, Admiral," Julie said.

Like a jackass in a uniform, Elisa thought.

"Where's my report?" he demanded.

His report—as if he'd done any work on it. Elisa handed him a button-disk, knowing how he'd react.

He looked at it, and rolled his eyes in disbelief.

"You should know, Ensign Santino, that for a meeting like this, I need it printed on paper."

"Of course, Admiral." Elisa handed him a large envelope. "Here's the printed report."

He took the envelope and made an exaggerated show of hefting it to check the weight.

"How many copies?"

Elisa hesitated. He had her. "Five copies."

He rolled his eyes again. "Five? I need six or seven, Ensign. You should have known that. I thought you were trained. Well, I don't have time now. I'll have to see if the vice president's secretary can make more copies for me."

She was gritting her teeth by the time the son of a bitch finished scolding her in front of everyone. When he finally left, the reduced tension throughout the office was almost palpable. Most of her colleagues would have a long lunch to celebrate the admiral's absence.

Elisa spent her lunchtime in the office, taking advantage of her coworkers' absence. The admiral slipped up when he mentioned the vice president's secretary. It meant that the meeting was not quite what it seemed. He'd be seeing Vincent Batastia, the new vice president and the architect of the New Federation, who was also the scariest thing to happen to the planet Earth in a long time.

Elisa went to the admiral's office and hacked into his protected files. This last year had taught her a lot about the complex networks of information that were going to make her rich, and she'd gone to a lot of effort to discover all of Fisher's most secret passwords.

In a file of archived correspondence she found that Fisher was working closely with a Navy admiral named Higgs who was guiding the son of a bitch up the ranks of the political insiders. There were vague references to new government programs dealing with redistribution of wealth, and—what the hell? — forced relocations? She didn't like the sound of that.

There was also one mention of The Blacklist, which Elisa wanted to find out more about. There were several comments from Fisher concerning "the perks" which were available to the most privileged insiders. Fisher's references to perks came across like a dog begging for a treat, and Higgs's responses promised that Fisher would soon qualify to enjoy such privileges.

It was too much to read during lunch. She'd take it home to study later. She went through an elaborate procedure of creating a mirror archive that the network recognized as legitimate, and copied everything into it before redefining it as a deleted archive so that it would slip through the security protocols and allow her to copy it to a button disk. She broke several laws getting the job done.

By the time people returned from lunch she was back at her desk reading a magazine about beach houses in Croatia. She might get one of those, after taking what she knew to Gentry Stokes Jr., and extorting a piece of the Stokes family fortune from him. The thought of retiring with both her youth and a lot of money sent a tingle of anticipation through her tiny body.

CHAPTER 5

Navy Admiral Wolfgang Higgs watched the Exploration Corps admiral strut through the West Point spaceport. He enjoyed watching people and figuring them out.

He now understood it was his own vanity that misled him about his protégé; a perverse dolt like Gary Fisher can only rise so high before he can no longer keep up with real leaders. Fisher was as high as he could ever get, and perhaps too high.

"Admiral Fisher," Higgs called out from the cocktail lounge where he waited.

Fisher came into the lounge with that toothy smile of his. He was a reasonably handsome man, twelve years younger than Higgs, and looked excellent in an admiral's uniform.

Higgs was jealous. When Higgs was given his position after the coup, he had to get a uniform made for his extra-large girth and always felt he didn't look military enough.

"Admiral Higgs," Fisher said with the tight jaws that Higgs had learned were a sign he was trying hard not to stammer, "I expected to see you at the Capitol."

"I thought it best to meet you early and review a few things before the meeting."

The dolt nodded several times with a raised-eyebrow 'oh, yes, of course' expression, meaning he didn't have a clue what they should talk about.

If it had been anybody else, Higgs would offer him a drink and chat for a bit before going downtown, but he'd chatted with Fisher before and saw no need to try it again. He pushed away his half-finished whiskey and dropped a generous tip on the table. They went out to Higgs's waiting car.

"You've done well with your new responsibilities, Admiral," Higgs said as the car got moving. "I know the financial side of things isn't the usual business of your department, but we have a keen interest in Stokes Industries and want to know everything about their business practices."

"Yes, sir. I've got a pretty good overview of the whole operation concerning this particular starship."

"Of course, but what we really need is information on the company's vulnerabilities, especially anything that might be used as leverage on Stokes himself. You can send everything you've got to the attorney general."

The puzzled expression on Fisher's face made Higgs impatient, but he merely explained—again, "The new government will eventually be like the old Corporate State, but with all the little problems fixed so everyone would stay happy. To do that, everything happening among the corporations must be monitored."

Higgs put it in the simplest terms possible. It was a risky thing to admit while—after forty years—most of the world still despised the Corporate State and would willingly fight another war to stop it from coming back.

Higgs was a scholar of history and understood where things had gone wrong. It would be done better this time, and would only be an intermediate step leading to an even better, perfect system that will last forever. It was his dream.

There was actually a lot more to it, but he wasn't about to start educating Fisher on the finer points of designing a new society, especially because Fisher wouldn't fit into the new society. What Fisher would fit into were some nasty plans Batastia had going, many of which Higgs wished weren't necessary.

While they talked about expanding the responsibilities of Fisher's department to deal with political issues, the car slowed to pass through the warehouse district. Higgs chose this route to see Fisher's reaction.

"Look at these people." Higgs indicated shabbily dressed men standing along the street. "They're always here, waiting for someone to stop and offer them work for the day, odd jobs and such. They come from outside the city where they live in crude huts."

"Mm...primitives," Fisher sneered. "We have them in Kansas too. They're called grasslanders there."

"Yes. They're called swampies here, because they live on the little delta islands. The ones in the Rocky Mountains are called stonies—short for stone-age, I suppose. There are more in South America, Europe and Asia, too...holdovers from the bad times following the Great Disaster. In 500 years they haven't progressed enough to join the rest of the world."

"They should be arrested," Fisher said, "and forced to learn some useful skills."

This was the response Higgs had hoped for.

"Well, there is a plan, a sort of a pet project of mine. I don't think there's much we can do with the adults, but the children could be...rehabilitated...for their own good. The vice president hasn't warmed to the plan yet, but I think he will once I clarify the benefits."

A waifish girl of perhaps fourteen years carried a basket of fruit for sale. A faded yellow skirt and a ragged, oversized shirt hung on lean, wiry limbs that came from walking miles each day in her homemade sandals. Her face was innocent, pretty, and friendly.

Fisher's eyes raked her body and he laughed, "I could think of something that one would be good for."

Higgs was disgusted. "Tell me. What's your conclusion about the new starship? The paper trail of how the Hanno is being funded seems to run in circles, which is typical of the old government's bookkeeping."

They discussed his concerns until arriving at the Capitol. Before the Great Disaster there was a university about 400 kilometers northeast of the old United States capitol. Through the perseverance of the faculty and students, the school survived the worldwide calamity, becoming a center of law and order for the region as nation-states began to reappear in the twenty-fourth century. Today, it was the capital city of Earth and, essentially, the galaxy.

The Capitol building was originally made of stone blocks taken from ancient ruins, but was gradually remodeled with modern materials and white columns and gabled windows: A grand mansion.

Statues from before The Disaster decorated the north and west gardens like a macabre tribute to an almost mythical era. Monuments from modern times lined the avenue leading from the public entrance on the south side.

Admiral Higgs was deep in thought as they walked through the rose garden to the main building. Fisher gawked like a tourist at the elegance of the place until they met an attractive young woman who directed them to the elevator.

Inside the lift, Fisher whispered, "Is she one of them?"

"Eh?" Higgs turned and raised his eyebrows. "Is who one of what?"

"That girl. Is she…one of the perks?"

"Oh, uh, no. She's just an intern. Really, Fisher, you shouldn't get preoccupied with the perks."

Higgs watched with veiled amusement as Fisher blushed scarlet.

"Oh…I'm not p-p-preoccupied. I-I was just wondering. That's all."

Fisher briefly met Vincent Batastia once, but this was his first visit to the office of the most powerful man in the galaxy.

Higgs explained to Fisher just after the coup that vice presidents were almost never assassinated. Therefore, it was prudent to have an expendable figurehead while leaving the real power in more capable hands. The right hands. Batastia's hands.

The New Federation's president, Arnold Garane, was once a professional actor. The press adored him, at least for the moment, but the real power was Vincent Batastia, a man virtually unknown to most people until recently. He was the center of the Inner Circle, a discrete group of businessmen that Higgs was part of and Fisher aspired to join.

Higgs worked for TerraPharm as a drug industry lobbyist when Batastia recruited him for something he'd always dreamed of doing: rebuilding civilization into a perfectly designed empire that would last forever.

Batastia had a persuasive, old-fashioned charm that spoke of generations of wisdom distilled into a patriarchal figure of bold vision which touched Higgs's yearning for great achievements. Only the rarest of men at the right moment in history could lead mankind away from the shortsighted policies that keep the human race from becoming gods. The time was now and, Higgs believed, Vincent Batastia was such a man.

His belief in Batastia was eroding, however. It started with the plan to take over the government. They looked at every possibility and simply couldn't find a way that didn't require the deaths of not only the old government leaders, but also hundreds of innocent people. After it actually happened, the body count turned out to be nearly five thousand. It weighed heavily on Higgs, but he became more comfortable with it as he settled into his new position. What still disturbed him was that it never seemed to bother the original members of the Inner Circle.

Such men were in today's meeting. Batastia himself led the meeting from his gigantic, polished walnut desk. Attorney General Alexei Volk stood slouching by the window with his hands in his pockets, half turned so he could watch the room with his left eye and look outside with the other. Volk was a predator.

Chief of Staff Heinrich "Crush" Skor sat at Batastia's right hand. He had a shaved head with old scars, and he never smiled. When Higgs first tried to find out more about the man, he ran into a dead end. Skor had no past except for being Batastia's long-time acquaintance. No one ever talked about how he got the nickname, but Higgs knew 'Crush' kept a sledgehammer in his office.

The Secretary of the Treasury, like Higgs, was recruited from private industry.

"Ah, Admiral Higgs." The vice president smiled warmly, transforming the fine wrinkles around his eyes into deep canyons. He was in his sixties—perhaps even seventy—a product of the old Corporate State that ended in the worst of wars. So many were displaced and changed their names that people like Batastia had to be forgiven for not knowing their own birth dates. "My golden boy, how do you like being head of the Navy, eh?"

"I couldn't be more pleased, Mister Vice President."

"And here is our Admiral Fisher, our hero." Batastia turned his dark eyes toward Fisher who was grinning like an idiot. The words were accurate enough—Fisher received a medal for discovering the time and location where the previous government could be ambushed—but Higgs detected a subtle disdain in how Batastia said it.

The Secretary of State, another long-time friend of Batastia's, came in with his nineteen year old son who was being groomed for some future position.

A general—the new head of the Army—followed them. Some referred to him as Higgs's counterpart, which Higgs graciously tolerated.

There would be no public record of this meeting. Official meetings were with President Garane and resulted in nothing beyond good press, which also had its value. Four more politicos arrived and the business of building a new world began.

First on the agenda was money. The Secretary of the Treasury gave a good overview on the distribution of the planet's wealth, with suggestions on how to get hold of a lot of it. This dovetailed nicely with a discussion on corporations.

"Big stockholders," Batastia said, "must be made to understand that it's crucial to stand united with the New Federation. They will have a voice in some things, but overall strategy must come from this office, otherwise corporate leaders will treat their positions as mere jobs rather than designers of a world that will come to fruition when their grandchildren are in charge."

"Precisely the point I made in my master's thesis," Higgs agreed with delight.

"Yes, Wolfgang, I remember reading it," Batastia said. "But to make it a reality, we must still overcome many challenges, such as the general population. As a scholar of history, as I am, you realize the old Corporate State lost control of the masses because they didn't bother tracking trends outside of the corporations."

"Well," Higgs enthusiasm was building momentum, "the State never really had much control to lose."

He saw the flicker of offense on Batastia's face, and furiously backpedaled.

"No, no, what I actually mean is that there were too many people who chose to live outside the system. They didn't participate in what was the legitimate commerce and productivity. Much has changed since then, but there are still many who fall into this category."

His mentor's face softened and nodded. "Of course. You are referring to the primitives. What are they called around here, swampies? In Europe, people call them landstreicheren. You've been gathering them, I believe, and putting the land they occupy to better use, yes?"

"Ah…yes. I've worked out an arrangement with the governor of North America to take custody of the children of primitive families, starting in the Rocky Mountain region. The children will be raised as wards of the North American State, and taught to be productive model citizens under the New Federation. When they become adults, they will be integrated into society and help us steer the public in the right direction."

"I understand, Higgs." Batastia sat back with half-closed eyes. "They can also be our eyes and ears for any sign of conspiracy."

"Yes, I suppose that would be another benefit. If it works in the mountain area, we can expand the program to other regions."

"My sources tell me it is working even better than you describe," Batastia said to Higgs's delight, "except for the leftovers."

"Eh?" Higgs was puzzled. "Leftovers?"

"The parents of all these children. You've got over a thousand kids in your special training, but the parents are camped at the gates of your new school making trouble and smuggling messages to the children."

"Oh, that. Yes, I'm studying what might be…"

"Consider it solved." Batastia rocked his chair forward and slapped the desk with a meaty hand. "I approve of your plan, Higgs, and I have arranged for the troublesome primitives to be moved elsewhere. Let's not speak of it now, but rather we will turn to a different issue—our new starship."

Higgs was flustered—not quite sure what just happened—but, consummate actor that he was, managed to smile and bow his head as if accepting a gift from his patriarch.

He looked at Fisher, expecting the man to say something intelligent, but was disappointed. Fisher was out of his league, overawed by the figures of power and authority that surrounded him.

"Admiral Fisher?" he said, hoping to break the spell and keep his protégé from making them both look ridiculous. "Your department has done exhaustive research on the Stokes Industries starship design?"

"Yes, t-that's right. I have a report." He opened the envelope and pulled out a sheaf of papers.

"Yes, of course, Admiral…" Batastia glanced down at something scribbled on his desk blotter "…Fisher, but we just need the conclusion. Is the Hanno everything that Stokes claims, or a waste of money?"

Fisher fought the urge to squirm when all eyes turned to him in expectation.

"Well, the bottom line is, the Starship Hanno is unsafe. Every expert in the field has serious doubts about Mister Stokes's theories."

"You say that it is unsafe?"

"Yes, sir. The moment the new engines are switched on, the entire crew will be subjected to dangerous energy fields."

"Fatal energy fields?" Batastia asked with his eyebrows raised, forming an upside-down V shape in the middle of his forehead and producing lots of wrinkles above them.

"Yes. They may survive once, but they would certainly all die if they use the engines twice."

"So, they might go somewhere, and survive, but they could not return." It was not a question.

Volk laughed out loud. "What a shame that would be."

"It is a shame," the vice president said, "that such an expensive mistake was made. At least it won't be a complete waste. In fact, this is an opportune way to ensure the security of the New Federation."

His audience gravely nodded in agreement, and Higgs warily nodded with them, suspecting he was about to witness one of Batastia's brilliant moments.

"How's our list coming along?" Batastia looked to Volk. The blacklist didn't officially exist, of course. It never officially exists, but every respectable bureaucracy had to have one.

All eyes turned to Alexei Volk. The Attorney General shrugged and leaned on the wall.

"Our list is too long—and growing." He spoke with a slight accent. All of Batastia's oldest friends seemed to be from Europe. "But this new starship can reduce it by at least three thousand. The Hanno requires at least two thousand crewmen for optimal function, but can hold another thousand. There are more than enough of these on the list. I suggest that we pretend to compromise with Captain Poluka. He will request people of his own choosing, and we will agree to give him anyone who's already on our list, provided he accepts others who are also on our list. If we lose a few that aren't on the list…well…they probably should have been anyway, if Poluka wants them."

Batastia slapped the top of his desk with an open palm. "Perfect. He will think that his influence has triumphed, and we will get exactly what we want. Thousands whose loyalty is questionable will be smoothly eliminated."

The Exploration Corps had personnel spread across the galaxy when the old Federation fell, and those on the blacklist were not reassigned outside the Solar System after returning from deep space. Batastia kept them close until a way could be found to deal with them, and kept them from joining the renegades who refused to return.

Higgs's idol turned loss into gain but, again, it required killing people who hadn't actually done anything—they just might do something. He sneaked a quick glance at Fisher, wondering if the man felt any disapproval of such cold-blooded maneuvers.

Fisher was gazing at Batastia with glassy-eyed worship, a half-sneer on his pale face.

"Admiral," Batastia instructed Fisher, "I will send files to your office tomorrow, our list and Captain Poluka's list. Find reasons to reject those who don't appear on both."

"Yes, sir."

"By the way, Admiral, who else knows the Starship Hanno is so…unsafe?"

"Um…I believe…an ensign in my department knows, but no one else."

"That ensign is now on the blacklist."

CHAPTER 6

What can I find for Julie to do that will keep her away from the son of a bitch? Elisa was asking herself when the son of a bitch showed up even earlier than usual.

Fisher stood in the center of the room, ran his fingers through his limp blond hair and cleared his throat. "Is everyone here? Good. I have an announcement to make."

Elisa's co-workers gathered around like obedient dogs. She sat on the corner of her desk behind the others.

"Yesterday, I met with Vice President Batastia and other top officials. They're very pleased with how I've managed the Department of Design Review and feel that I'm ready for greater responsibilities."

It didn't escape anyone that he said nothing about them doing a good job. Apparently, his reason for making the announcement was to let everyone know he'd met the vice president.

"Some of our new work," Fisher continued, "will be…uh…evaluating certain manufacturers' financial status, which we've already touched on with the Hanno report, but we'll be going far beyond that in the future.

"Another thing we're going to become involved in is the staffing of starships. This is new to us, but it's not that complicated. I will personally start the effort by taking a good look at the crew requirements of the Starship Hanno."

Something weird was going on. Elisa expected the Hanno report to put the whole construction effort on hold, which would give Stokes a chance to get more funding to fix the problems, but there was no mention of it.

"That's all I have to say for now." Fisher turned to go to his office. "Julie, I want you to help me with some files. You can use the computer in my office."

Elisa didn't see Julie again until lunchtime, when the young woman hurried out of the Admiral's office. Elisa followed her to the ladies washroom.

"Are you okay?"

"Hi, Elisa. Yeah, I'm just going to wait in here until he goes to lunch. You know, he wanted to take me out to a restaurant, but I said I had other plans. Then he asked me if my other plans were more important than he is."

"You didn't tell him what other plans you have, did you?"

"No. I didn't have any plans for lunch."

"Good. If you told him something, he would've checked to see if you were lying."

"My God. Why is he like that? I've got to get a new job. I can't stand this."

"Good for you. Say, I'll go see if he's gone, and then we can have lunch together. I know a little place where no one will bother us."

During lunch Julie mentioned that she was setting up some kind of personnel file, but she didn't know what it was for.

Near the end of the day, Elisa managed to tap into the admiral's computer and copy everything onto a button disc. As she put on her coat, she slipped the tiny disc between the buttons of her uniform and tucked it into her bra where only a determined search would discover it.

A steady stream of government employees emptied out of the building. The shops and services in downtown Wichita were ready for the after-work crowd. The 13th Street station had additional trains standing by, and that's where Elisa was when she saw Julie and Admiral Fisher get into a taxi.

"Oh, great!" Elisa spat. "He got to her. Damn."

Elisa felt sorry for Julie—and more than sorry—worried, too, but there was nothing to do about it until tomorrow, when she would see the young woman again.

Tomorrow came and Julie didn't show up for work. Elisa tried calling her, but there was no answer.

Admiral Fisher didn't come in until after nine and didn't do his usual walk-through. A half-hour later he loudly asked Elisa if Julie had called in.

"No, Admiral. Perhaps I should call her."

"Uh-huh." He seemed like he wasn't listening.

Still no answer at Julie's apartment, Elisa suspected her friend was out looking for another job. She was wrong.

Just before noon a man showed up. He flashed an I.D. that said he was a cop. He asked Admiral Fisher to come down to the city coroner's office and identify a body.

"The next of kin is unavailable," the man said, "and we wanna wrap this up."

"No!" Fisher snapped, and then pointed to Elisa. "I'm very busy. Ensign Santino can identify her."

Her? Elisa's spine became ice. She glanced at Julie's vacant desk.

Everyone was quiet as she left with the cop. She turned to look back at Fisher, and instantly regretted making eye contact. The anxiety in his face confirmed that he'd done something awful, and he saw something, too. He saw that she knew.

She said nothing on the way to the morgue.

It seemed unreal, walking into the coroner's office to identify a friend. Maybe it wasn't her. Elisa couldn't know for sure. She followed the policeman to the elevator, crossed her fingers and tried to believe it might not be Julie.

The morgue was in the basement of the building, just like in the movies, and it was cold, or maybe it just seemed cold. More and more unreal it felt, until they stopped at a wall lined with big drawers.

When the cop pulled open one long, narrow drawer that rumbled on its rollers like far-away thunder, everything became unbearably real. Her dread grew huge. Her mouth became a desert. A trickle of sweat rolled down her spine. The white sheet was thrown back to reveal the still form. Someone said something. Maybe it was a question.

"Julie." She moaned as tears began to flow. "It's Julie Klein."

Julie's naked body had bruises and welts that stood out on her snow-white skin. Her wrists had marks like rope burns, but on her face was the peace that only the dead know.

Elisa was led back to the elevator and up to an office, where she signed a paper that was just a formality. Identifying a body in the twenty-eighth century didn't require a person who knew the deceased. Current technology was far more accurate. It was just a cruel tradition as far as Elisa was concerned.

Now they'd start asking questions, and she'd make sure the

son of a bitch got what he deserved.

"We'll inform the next of kin," the cop told her.

"She has a brother."

"Thank you, Miss Santino." He had a practiced but insincere tone. "I know this hasn't been easy for you. You can go now."

"Don't you want to ask me any questions?"

The cop's eyes left the form she'd signed to look at her. "Like what?"

"Well, aren't you going to try to find out who did this to her?"

"Did what? Julie Klein died of a drug overdose. Happens all the time."

What the hell? A dull pounding filled her head. She tried to maintain control, not knowing if she wanted to scream, or just cry.

"What about all those bruises?"

The cop had no problem with self-control. He leaned back in his chair and faced her with less emotion than a snake.

"There were no bruises. This was just a suicide. Now I think you should go back to work, Miss Santino, and don't let your imagination get carried away."

Tears streamed down her cheeks on her way back to the office. At the 13th street station, she looked out of the train at the building she worked in.

She couldn't go back in there. Not yet.

She stayed on the train until it went all the way through town, through Spaceport, and back into town. It was a forty-minute look at New Wichita, and it gave her time to realize something.

Fisher knew that she knew. If he could make the police cover up one murder, he could get away with another.

When the train returned to downtown, she got out and walked back to the office, pretending she didn't see Admiral Fisher looking down at her from his office window.

None of her friends said anything when she came into the office, told the admiral that Julie had died of a drug overdose, and then asked for the rest of the day off.

"The rest of the day? Aren't you feeling well?"

He was nervous. Otherwise, even he wouldn't ask such a stupid question. She could hear it in his voice. He was scared; scared that his sins will be laid bare for public inspection; scared that the tiny woman in front of him might destroy him.

And she would, she swore silently, but not today. Today she had to save her own life.

"I'm very upset, Admiral. I'll be in tomorrow."

"Of course, Ensign Santino."

By the time she got home, she had the creepy feeling that someone was following her. She locked her door and peeked through the blinds covering the kitchen window.

Help. She needed help.

CHAPTER 7

Christmas decorations, eh? Paul smiled as he watched Aguire drive away. Just the thing to persuade Lynda to reconsider: defiance of the new rules, and as a matter of principle.

Perfect. Well, maybe. Lynda can be stubborn.

He considered calling her right then to arrange a meeting, but then thought better of it. It mustn't seem like it had anything to do with his chat with Aguire. He'd already discovered, quite by accident, where three of the micro-cameras were hidden in his little cottage. God only knows where they hid the microphones.

He got out his paint set and some fine-tipped brushes to spend the afternoon looking innocent and painting his model ship, one tiny brush stroke at a time.

Hours passed and the smell of paint filled the house. He imagined what it must have been like a millennium ago, sailing a wooden ship in search of strange new lands, contending with the forces of sea and wind. The deck and two masts were done before the winter sun touched the snowy horizon. The lights in the house were too dim for mixing more colors.

"Damn. I'll have to call the power company and have a new battery delivered tomorrow."

Centuries ago, buildings didn't run on battery power, but had electricity delivered through wires from a central power plant that could be far away. That ended with the Great Disaster.

By the twenty-second century, most of the world had come to rely on China to supply energy via a worldwide electric power grid.

No one knew for sure how a million square kilometers of Asia was suddenly blasted out of existence, but everyone knew what followed. The earth shook, cities fell, and a terrible shock of wind circled the world, like a hurricane.

Ruin. Plague. Anarchy.

For centuries mankind lived by barbaric standards. Nations ceased to exist. The strong ruled the weak. Only now had mankind recovered to where it had been before the Great Disaster. Some specialties, like medicine and chemistry, still strived for what they were in the twenty-second century.

One technology that became superior to anything in the past was battery power. For the last 600 years people relied on batteries for electricity, and they'd come a long way. Today, every building was powered by fusion batteries that last for years of constant use.

Paul tapped the five-foot-tall cube in its little closet with the toe of his shoe and tried to read the faded date stamped on the side. "I wonder how long you've been here. You get replaced tomorrow."

He called the power company first, then Lynda to have her meet him at Valentines, an upscale restaurant with a reputation for being safe—that is, safe to talk freely. Experts checked daily for eavesdropping devices, and spies of all stripes considered the restaurant neutral territory because it's a gray and fuzzy line that separates gangsters from statesmen.

Valentines was Italian, a steak and seafood place with an excellent wine selection. There was a piano, but tonight it was only recorded music. The best theaters and music venues were nearby, and people came to Valentines before and after performances. It was an elegant place.

Lynda arrived moments after Paul. She wore a white ruffled blouse with black pants and boots. She wore no makeup or jewelry, which was unusual for a woman in a place like this, but Paul could not remember her ever wearing makeup, and jewelry only occasionally. Her trim, athletic figure reminded him of his vow to lose weight.

"Hi, Paul."

"Hello, Lynda. Are you settled into your new apartment?"

"Yes, but I had to go shopping for winter clothes today. I've been so busy setting up schedules at the Academy; this is really my first day off in weeks. Oh, I forgot, the new calendar doesn't use weeks anymore."

Paul laughed, "But everyone else still does."

The tuxedoed waiter appeared and took their order.

"Um, I'll have the prime rib," Lynda said, "with baked potato and sour cream. Blue cheese on the salad."

She looked at Paul with an innocent expression.

Prime rib was his favorite. Thanks a lot, Lynda.

"I'll have the low-cal chicken plate," he whispered to the waiter.

"So, what's up?" Lynda asked when the waiter left.

"Aguire was arrested, or at least cited, for insisting that a store sell him Christmas decorations."

"Oh? I didn't know he was religious, but it's still not enough to change my mind, Paul." Her lips formed that pouting expression: her stubborn face. "I know this means a lot to you."

"It does. Listen, he said he wanted it on his record because it was a matter of principle, and that he wasn't going to let the government dictate what he can believe in." He saw no reason to tell her the purpose of Aguire's holiday party was more carnal than spiritual.

"I'll tell you what, Paul. I'll find a way to meet him and spend some time with him. I'm not making any promises, but I'll give him a chance, for your sake. But you know that's not the whole problem."

"What do you mean?"

"The New Fed will have something to say about it, and you can bet they'll only let you have people that they want to get rid of. Is Aguire on their blacklist?"

"Who can say?" He doubted it. Aguire's record was exemplary, and he never had any political ties.

"Not knowing who's on the blacklist is my biggest problem right now." Lynda frowned. "Bart knows Commander Aguire, doesn't he? Maybe I should talk to him."

"Hanson?" Paul wasn't sure what Bart Hanson would say about Aguire. Hanson was a loose cannon, but a priceless asset to the conspiracy, given his abilities. "He doesn't know him as well as I do."

The waiter brought their food. Lynda slathered butter and sour cream onto her potato. Paul was quiet as they ate, only half listening to Lynda's comments about the instability of the new regime and its rampant paranoia about renegade military forces refusing to return to Earth.

"Are you listening to me?"

"Hm? Oh, yes. They're afraid of General Hebert."

Paul finished the low-cal plate and began eyeing Lynda's beef.

"Right. They think he's putting together an armada to resist the New Fed."

The waiter returned with a small envelope. "A gentleman at the door asked me to bring this to you, sir."

Paul opened the envelope and scanned the note within.

"Thank you," he told the waiter. "There will be no reply."

"Yes, sir." The waiter went about his business.

Lynda swallowed a mouthful of potato and sour cream, and he marveled at how she stayed so lean.

"What is it?" she asked.

"Someone wants to see me outside."

Lynda speared the last of the juicy marbled beef with her fork. He could almost taste it.

"Who is it?" she asked, with good reason. Anyone waiting until Paul was here to contact him instead of just calling him at home was someone with some kind of trouble, government trouble.

"My chief engineer from the Livingston. He wants to meet me outside when I'm alone."

"Hm. Chief Braun. He's not going to be part of the new crew either. Well, you go ahead. I'll take the train home."

"Okay. Are you ready to go?"

"No. I'm going to stay for dessert."

CHAPTER 8

That was it; Fisher had to go—not today, but eventually—before the disgusting bastard could get into any bigger trouble, Admiral Higgs decided after getting a message from the idiot about *accidentally* killing some tart that he fancied, and needing help to cover it up.

It was noon in the Rocky Mountains, but Higgs justified a glass of scotch based on just arriving from two time zones away and getting Fisher's mess dropped on him without any warning. The worst, however, was how the vice president was taking control of his project with the primitives.

Batastia had two thousand adult primitives taken away to god-knows-where in four Navy cargo spacecrafts, all without consulting Higgs. On top of that, Batastia unilaterally expanded the program and was having the Governor of Western Europe start a similar effort there—without any of Higgs's careful oversight. He'd spent years working out how to do it just right. It shouldn't be tried at all without considering thousands of details.

He tugged his uniform straight and looked down from the office window at stony children pacing aimlessly around the yard like little broken robots. These kids were supposed to be the first generation to rise from a barbaric society into Utopia—and he wanted them to appreciate his genius in their old age, not curse him for destroying their families.

The administrator of the camp returned to the office and confirmed Higgs's fear.

"The Navy transports are returning to Earth, Admiral," the man said with a strange tightness in his voice. "They made a fast loop, close to the sun, and dumped their…cargo."

Higgs did not turn to face the man. He finished the scotch in one swallow, and fought to keep it down as he watched the kids below.

CHAPTER 9

It was not yet noon in the city of Desin-Arcturus, but the Queen of the planet wished the sermon would end so she could leave the temple.

Something awful had just happened. She could feel it.

Far away, Earthmen—many terrified Earthmen—had just been murdered.

There were not many at the temple today. The priest was reading the prophecy about an Earthman who would come someday to save their world. It was hard to imagine.

CHAPTER 10

"I knew he could do it." Aguire almost cheered. Poluka left a message: Aguire should attend the classes and he still had a shot at getting aboard the new starship. "It's back to school for this spaceman."

He checked the date and time when the first class would begin. He had about thirty minutes to get there, and made it with one minute to spare before the roll call.

"Thanks for the wake-up call, Donno," Aguire whispered as he slid into his chair.

Donno whispered back. "Where's your notebook...and your computer?"

"It's just a lecture, right? I've got this." Aguire displayed a micro-recorder pinned to the lapel of his uniform. "I'll catch every word and transcribe it later."

"Damn, Aguire. You need a keeper," Donno snorted testily, tearing some pages from his notebook to give to Aguire.

"Thanks, Donno. I owe you. You got an extra pen?"

The class began when an aging man with a mop of snow-white hair that looked as if it had been combed with boxing gloves came into the room.

"Good morning. I am your professor, and you may address me as Professor."

"Professor?" Aguire whispered to Donno, "Is he too old to remember his own name?"

The professor glanced up in Aguire's general direction.

"I remember my name and a great many other things. I am Gentry Stokes Junior. You may have heard of me. I just hope your memory is as good as my hearing."

Aguire did recognize the name, and he remembered those green eyes from the call he made to California—a friend of the

41

skipper's.

Stokes switched on a hologram. Displayed in three dimensions at the front of the class was the image of a starship like no other.

"This is my baby," Stokes said. "The Starship Hanno, named after the ancient mariner who first circumnavigated Africa. I've spent my life to produce this result, and I'll teach you everything you need to know about it.

"The Hanno is a little more than eleven kilometers in length and almost a kilometer and a half wide, not counting the antenna towers." He used a laser-pointer to indicate various parts of the image. "The absolute minimum crew requirement is 375, though the Hanno could easily be home to ten times that number."

The image shifted to a cut-away view, showing the interior of the ship.

The ship was a mobile city, and every part was an improvement over older designs. Like all faster-than-light ships, the propulsion section accounted for over half of the ship's mass. The engines were a new design, something Aguire had never seen before. The professor said the engines would be studied in detail later.

The size of the ship and crew allowed for discrete departments which, on smaller ships, would be shared multipurpose facilities. There were also things that smaller ships could not spare the room for, such as entertainment and recreation areas.

During the lunch break, Aguire went to the commissary to buy another notebook on his way to the cafeteria.

There were some familiar faces going to school with Aguire, but not some that he had expected. There were also some that surprised him.

There were also a fair number of green-uniforms: barnies getting trained for assignment on the Hanno. Only the biggest ships got a permanent attachment of Army personnel. Captain Poluka was a getting a mixed bunch for this crew.

Aguire pondered this as he ordered a club sandwich while looking over his class schedule. The food dispenser at the end of the table opened. A plate of eggs, bacon and hash-browns slid out.

"What the hell is this?"

"It looks like breakfast," said the captain's voice.

Aguire looked up to see Poluka sliding into the seat across the table.

"I didn't order eggs. Good morning, Captain."

Poluka looked around the cafeteria. "So, Commander, what do you think of your classmates?"

Classmates? Not shipmates? Aguire stopped fiddling with the menu. Maybe his assignment wasn't certain yet. "I don't know most of them, but I hope that will change."

Captain Poluka slid the plate of bacon and eggs away from the dispenser and picked up a fork. "If you're not going to eat this, I had to skip breakfast this morning and —"

"It's all yours, sir." Aguire punched in another order for a club sandwich.

"If you have any trouble with the lessons, let me know. You need to do well, Commander, so I can justify your assignment."

A moment later, the dispenser opened and a plate of ham and eggs slid out. Damn.

CHAPTER 11

The introduction to main engine theory turned out to be more complicated than Aguire expected.

"Space travel," the professor began, "started in the twentieth century."

Oh, please, Aguire groaned, not an ancient history lesson.

Professor Stokes continued, "But by the twenty-second century, man had not even gone further than the Solar System with his primitive rocket ships. Modern space travel started with near-light speed, NLS drive, which is the principle still used in standard thrusters. This allowed us to colonize our own system, but not much else.

"Once mankind could travel at NLS, it gave us new knowledge of quantum-space that led to permittivity-drive, which uses the same technology that gives us artificial gravity, which in turn led to tachyon field physics and distortion drive. Now, we have reached the next step in technology. My engine design is like nothing that has been done before. Observe."

The professor displayed formulas and charts and reviewed what every school child knows about transdimensional physics. After that, Aguire became lost in an explanation of higher physics involving two hypothetical spheres, each the size of the universe. Each formula served as a stepping-stone to more complex formulae until becoming a jumbled trail of mathematical proofs.

"So, you can see," Professor Stokes pointed excitedly from one equation to another, "the spheres are side by side, pressing against each other, while at the same time they are one within the other. And if you consider the final equation it becomes obvious that they are not only the same sphere, but those are not spheres at all, but an infinite plane. And that, in a nutshell, is how two places in the universe can actually be the same place."

Looking around, Aguire could see no one else knew what the

Professor was talking about either.

In a week, thirty percent of the crew candidates dropped out. This was expected. Two weeks later, another ten percent were gone.

The last three weeks of training were just for the senior officers, including the Captain, with cross-training on operations that were not their usual duties so each officer would understand the function of every crewman. Commander Aguire was sweating it. The new engines had some quirky timing considerations, and programming was not his strength.

"Damn, Donno," Aguire grumbled when he got back to the apartment they shared. "I just spent four hours in court just to plead guilty and pay the goddamned fine. I'm never going to pass tomorrow's test."

Donno looked up from the small desk where his notes were laid out in neat groups. He'd learned to be organized from watching Aguire run a starship. For some elusive reason, his old friend always seems to loose IQ points when his feet were on terra firma.

"What's the charge this time?" Donno asked.

"I paid some kids to wash my car."

"That's illegal?"

"The Vehicle Services Union turned me in for exploiting minors. Exploiting! Can you believe that crap?"

"You'll be lucky if the Union doesn't file a civil suit."

"It was the kids' idea in the first place."

"Sounds like you'd better pass this test, because you won't like staying on Earth with all these new rules. No, sir. Not one bit." Donno sounded serenely unsympathetic.

"Donno, what can I do? I'm falling behind on this subsystem coding lesson."

Donno scratched his ear. "The New Federation calendar doesn't use weeks anymore."

"Well, I still do."

"Don't worry, buddy. I've been looking out for you, even though it's a thankless and never ending chore. Here." Donno handed him a slip of paper. It had a time and a room number on it.

"What's this?"

"Poluka was looking for you. He thinks this tutor could help you."

"A tutor? Not the professor?"

"No. Her name is Lynda, and you'd better hurry if you don't want to be late."

* * *

"Lynda, huh?" Aguire thought aloud as he searched for the room in the Academy. "Probably an old bookworm."

The room was a large office set up for training small groups, and Lynda, though not old, certainly looked like a bookworm with her honey-blond hair pinned behind her neck and her plain ankle-length dress.

She looked up from the table where she was arranging some diagrams. Her eyes were vivid green, and bright in a way that made her seem more like a doll than a real person.

"Commander Aguire?"

"Yes, ma'am."

"Hi. I'm Lynda. I understand you need some help on subsystem programming."

Except for the eyes, her face was commonplace, pretty perhaps, but not beautiful, and her dress hid her figure completely, buttoned at the collar and reaching almost to the floor. It was the kind of dress some women wear to cover fat. Though she seemed fairly trim, it was hard to tell.

They kept at it until Aguire was able to answer all of Lynda's questions on the subject.

The next morning he returned to the Academy and took the test. A wave of relief washed away his tension when Professor Stokes told him his score. "One hundred percent. Well done, Commander. It seems you were paying attention to the lessons."

It was the first time Stokes ever addressed him personally. The business tycoon invented most of the propulsion technology used in spaceships today, and his father invented what most spacemen were using thirty years ago. His legacy made him an almost mythic figure with a reputation for intolerance that was intimidating for even a seasoned officer like Aguire.

"Thank you, sir." Aguire answered. "I have to admit it was challenging, and I wouldn't have done so well without the help of your assistant."

"Assistant? Oh, you mean Lynda."

"Yes, sir." Aguire suddenly realized that he might not know—or approve—of Lynda's tutoring. "She just helped me on the course work, sir."

"Yes, I know. By the way, she's more than my assistant. She's my daughter. Now if you will excuse me, I've got a meeting to go to. Good day, Commander."

His daughter? Aguire mentally kicked himself. Any fool should have guessed, considering how Lynda and G.J. Stokes both have unusually bright green eyes. He'd been tutored by one of the richest women in the galaxy and hadn't realized it.

He went to the officer's lounge and found a com console to call Captain Poluka.

Poluka's pudgy face appeared. "Hello, Commander."

"Captain, I passed the course. I was just wondering how the officer selection process is going."

Poluka grimaced. "It seems Fisher has more influence than I realized. He's gotten the list of candidates and is making recommendations. I can't say more yet. Give me some time."

"Yes, sir. I'll hope for the best."

Despite the news, Aguire felt a strange confidence that he would be back in space soon.

He got Lynda on the com screen.

"Commander." She smiled. "How'd the test go?"

"Perfect. I wanted to thank you for your help."

"Don't mention it. Good luck with your next assignment." She was in an office somewhere and looked sort of sad. He was sure she had no friends around here and no time to enjoy the city.

"I'll have to wait and see how that goes. In the meantime, I'll enjoy a break from duties and blow off a little steam. There's a nightclub I want to check out tonight with some friends. Maybe you'd like to join us?"

Her eyes brightened at the invitation and she blushed slightly. "Thank you, but I can't tonight. Maybe another time."

She's nice, Aguire decided. Maybe he'd see her again someday.

CHAPTER 12

The rhythm of crunching snow under Lynda's boots echoed between the silent Academy buildings. The moonlit snow was a gray emptiness surrounding her.

She congratulated Commander Aguire this morning, admitting to herself he wasn't what she'd expected. Oh, he was the over-achiever, certainly driven to excel, absorbing new information easily, and capable of extraordinary concentration.

But he wasn't the cold toy soldier she had expected. In fact, the way he would compare complicated theories to ordinary, even comical situations, made him quite likable.

Sure, Lynda admitted, I like him, but that doesn't change his record.

His life is a pattern of conforming to the requirements of a hierarchy, of never breaking away from rules, procedures, and regulations. Aguire never does anything on impulse as far as she could tell. Training, regulations, and official policy are what guide him through life.

The image of his lean face, with his black hair combed back from his chiseled features, returned to her as she waited for the train to take her back to the city.

And his body.

"What a body," she whispered aloud. The sound of her own voice startled her. "What am I thinking?"

She shivered and pulled the hood of her jacket around her ears as the train pulled to a stop in front of her. It was half-full of chatting groups, glad the week was over so that, as Commander Aguire had put it, they could blow off some steam.

Lynda wished she could blow off some steam, but she didn't know how except by exercising. That was her way.

Aguire's invitation for a night out surprised her.

"I should have gone with him." Her lips moved soundlessly. After all, she did promise Paul she'd get to know him.

Last December—her first night in town—she got dressed up and went to a club a few blocks from her apartment. She found herself sitting alone, wishing someone would talk to her, and never felt more out of place when she realized that everyone else there were couples. She never went back.

Her apartment was silent when she dumped her satchel on the sofa before heading for the shower. The hot water helped ease the tension that was growing inside her.

This whole scheme now seemed far more daring than it did three years ago when they first plotted against the old Federation. The fall of the old rule didn't end their plans, but only urged them forward, because the New Fed was far worse.

Officially, it was a change from an evil fascist rule to a benevolent socialist rule. In reality, it was new evil bastards wresting power away from old evil bastards. People got arrested every day. Many were never heard from again. Basic freedoms the old Federation had guaranteed as rights were now privileges. Taxes were up.

When the New Fed amended the Bill of Human Rights last month, Mrs. Shepherd, who'd once been Lynda's music teacher and one of her few friends, sent Lynda a message saying she wanted to organize a public protest. Such an idea would never occur to Lynda, who learned about influence from watching her father wield his corporate resources whenever policies were disagreeable. She'd read the message but forgot about replying until tonight.

She finished her shower, then typed a quick inquiry into the com-console, and was surprised to see that com database couldn't find Mrs. Shepherd. She made a mental note to ask Bart about her.

While drying her hair, Lynda punched up her calendar and saw the local University had added something to the winter break schedule: public lecture. Interplanetary Law under the New Federation. Nine o'clock Saturday morning.

"Hm, that's tomorrow. Sounds pretty vague. Doesn't tell who'll be speaking."

She didn't feel inclined to waste a Saturday morning at a lecture. After all, she'd just graduated at the top of her class. The lecture would be by a graduate student or a teaching assistant, and attended by people with no sort of social life, like Lynda Stokes.

Maybe those are the sort of people I should meet. Hello, I'm Lynda and I don't have a life either. What the hell, I've got to get out and do something—anything.

As exhaustion urged her toward the bed, she found the small zippered bag with her cosmetics and examined every item.

There was lipstick she bought last September and used once; two colors of nail polish she no longer liked; the mascara she bought for her first date, years ago, which had long since dried out.

She never had many dates. Most were the sons of executives her father approved of. The few she liked didn't like her, and never asked for a second date, but she didn't care.

She remembered the girls from college, not close friends, but girls she studied with. They always got excited about dates, and made a huge project of choosing clothes, make-up, and shoes. Oh, my god, how they could spend hours looking for the perfect shoes.

Lynda tried to pretend she understood the priorities, but she was just pretending.

"No perfume," she yawned. "I don't have any perfume."

Lynda woke to sunlight glowing through the window, and remembered nothing about perfume, but she did put on some lipstick before heading out to the University. She dressed like a student in snug jeans and a v-neck pullover that was popular with women her age who like to show their figure, but not every detail.

The lecture hall was sparsely attended by people with careers and businesses who were worried about the New Federation. She found a seat and chatted with a wrinkled old gentleman named Mister Benjamin and his son Sam, both of whom were in the hotel business.

Mister Benjamin was considering moving his whole family: children, grandchildren, nieces and nephews—everybody—to another star system, out of the New Federation's reach.

"I wonder who'll be speaking today." Lynda looked around at the empty seats, and asked Sam, "Do you know?"

"No one," Sam Benjamin answered. "That is, not a real person, a hologram."

Of course. The New Federation was too paranoid to let a

living, breathing person expound on the subtleties of the new laws. An astute speaker might point out that the New Federation's dogma was almost identical to doctrines of the Corporate State, which led to concentration of wealth for the few, and loss of freedom for the many. On the other hand, a truly zealous supporter of the reforms wouldn't be intelligent enough for public speaking.

A hologram appeared at the podium promptly at nine o'clock with the usual wavy lines and streaks of color. It was the image of a man in a casual suit.

The audience near the front stirred. Lynda heard some sniggers and a few outright laughs. The image was a composite of a trim, athletic body but the head on top looked like President Arnold Garane, only younger. Lynda rolled her eyes and shook her head at the vanity of her imperious leaders.

The hologram was oblivious to the crowd's reaction and talked for thirty minutes about things in which Lynda was already well versed. She almost got up to leave, as a number of people already had, when the lecture turned to the subject of worlds that defy the New Federation.

"Worlds that were part of the old Federation are part of the New Federation," the hologram droned. "Any defiance, either by individuals or by local governments will be viewed as an act of treason.

"A small number of worlds that were not already member states have claimed independence. However, it is only a matter of time before these worlds see the light and join the mainstream of the New Federation. In fact, diplomatic efforts are already underway to that end.

"Independent worlds have governments which simply cannot survive. Though some are smaller copies of the old Federation, most are fragmented confederacies, dictatorships, communist states. A few are even monarchies with kings and queens. Quite barbaric, actually."

When the lecture turned to the subject of taxes, Lynda bade Mister Benjamin and Sam farewell and good luck with their hotel business.

She returned to her apartment, which felt like a cage for an animal that could neither be domesticated nor allowed to run free.

"Exercise, that's what I need." She nodded her blond head

decisively, grabbed her gym bag and fled back to the transit stop. The train wound purposefully through New Wichita's business district, stopping at nearly every corner.

Paul was right, Lynda thought, remembering something Captain Poluka had once said. I do use exercise as a substitute for a social life, and for men. Sometimes, she wished she'd gone to school instead of having tutors, and learned to be more social, but Papa wouldn't allow it.

A sense of loss clouded her heart as she recalled how her brother, Gentry, had trouble with his social life, too, only worse. He was too smart even for private schools. He had tutors and computerized courses when the tutors could not keep up with him.

The train left the business district and the hordes of weekend shoppers making a loop at the north end before passing back into town. The wide Kansas prairie glistened white onward to the horizon before the view was cut off by buildings on either side.

Gentry used to exercise too. He had a body that should have brought him admiration, but instead it got him classified as potentially dangerous when he was taken into custody. They said he was crazy because he claimed he was an alien, and dangerous because he was strong. Gentry wasn't dangerous, just confused because he was different.

We're both different. We're strong and fast learners, but we're not aliens.

Lynda glared at the street. Where did he get such an idea?

She was only eleven when they took her big brother away and never understood why Papa couldn't use his influence to get him out. It wasn't until Gentry somehow got himself released, and then disappeared along with Paul's older brother Cliff, that she began to forgive her father.

It was Paul Poluka's patient kindness that finally softened her heart. His brother, Clifford, had been the captain of the Himilco, and Gentry was the navigator. Paul and Lynda shared the loss of their brothers, and now shared a conspiracy that could get them executed.

She stepped out of the train into the slushy street at the west gate of Spaceport, and her dread of the future softened into tentative commitment.

CHAPTER 13

"Come on, Donno." Aguire urged his friend to get out of the small suite they shared. "We haven't had a good workout in weeks."

The longer he stayed on Earth the more alone he felt. Life on a spaceship gave him the constant contact that he missed on this planet filled with billions of people.

"You haven't." Donno snickered without looking up from the book he was reading. "Try dragging yourself out of bed at a decent hour you'll realize that I go for a run every morning."

"You and your running. I'm off to the gym to get a manly workout."

Aguire left for the spaceport gym.

He pushed himself through his routine of weights and gymnastics that felt a bit tougher than it had a few years ago, finishing with the parallel bars.

Heading to the showers he spotted Luther Braun. The elderly Chief Engineer was swapping stories at the poolside with a group of gray-haired buddies.

"Commander," Braun looked up at him, "get your assignment yet?"

"Um, no. Not yet. You?"

"Yeah. I'll be on the Hanno. Hey, there's some of our barnies." He gestured with his chin at the green uniforms: fifteen big men with no necks heading for the men's locker room.

"The Hanno already got barnies assigned to her?" Aguire wondered.

A cool soprano spoke behind him, "Not just any barnies, Aguire, my barnies."

It was Major Melanie Rivers: an imposing figure in her Army uniform, taller and beefier than most men. They'd been comrades-in-arms during the Jupiter War, where she'd shown Aguire that the Army was good for more than just parades and guard duty.

"Major Rivers." He almost saluted, but shook her hand instead. "You're on the Hanno?"

"Got my orders last night. You?"

"I'm expecting mine any time now."

"I'll see you later, Commander. I'm getting my people into shape. They're getting as flabby as you shuttle bugs." She winked and went to the women's locker room.

* * *

Lynda found the women's locker room deserted except for the echoes of her every movement that whispered along the rows of lockers. The air was cool and dry compared to when cadets ran the showers all day.

She entered the gym wearing baggy shorts, tee shirt, and sneakers. A dozen or so men were already there. There were no other women except a tall Army officer just arriving at the locker room.

Oh, great. I'll be really inconspicuous. You'd think at least a few female cadets would keep exercising through the holidays.

She walked toward the weight training area, studying each man's face, hoping they would all be unfamiliar.

The two guys playing one-on-one basketball were young, with cadet haircuts. Cute, too. Probably Navy. Nine older men lounging by the pool and chatting could be businessmen, or possibly spacemen.

Her heart skipped a beat when she recognized Commander Aguire in only gym shorts and sneakers, heading towards the men's locker room.

The commander looked lean and able, reminding her that he was a gymnast, and had even won some awards. She saw scars on his back: his reward as a Jupiter War veteran.

He hadn't seen her. Unconsciously, she moved her right hand to her left forearm and up, into the baggy sleeve of her tee shirt, to feel her biceps.

She's fit, that's all. She shouldn't be embarrassed just because she's in better shape than most women, or men for that matter.

There were twenty weight-lifting machines lined up in two rows. At a machine near the middle sat a large man in a dirty gray sweat suit with cut-off sleeves. He straddled the bench as if he'd just finished bench-pressing or was about to begin.

Lynda went to a machine at the end of the row, and pressed the button labeled curl, selecting the exercise she would start with. The low bench folded into the machine and out of the way. The lifting-bar automatically adjusted its height.

She'd better start light. Say, twenty kilograms. She set the dial, wrapped her hands under the bar and lifted slowly, savoring the strain in her biceps.

She concentrated on her work-out and tried to ignore the distraction when somebody came to the next machine and set it to do curls, but it was impossible to ignore when it became obvious the person was mimicking Lynda, lifting when she lifted, like a shadow.

She glanced sideways, and caught the man in the sweat suit leering at her chest. He seemed at the same time both strong and flabby, as if he drank a beer for each time he lifted a weight.

Just ignore him.

"I'm Frazya," the man said as if she should be impressed. "Captain Frazya. I run a cargo service out of Mars and I'll be on Earth for a few days."

Go away.

Captain Frazya didn't go away. "You're pretty strong for a woman. I like to start with twenty kilos myself just to warm up, then I bump it up to thirty-five. What's your name, babe?"

Babe? Lynda lowered the bar and let it go, turning to face the man. "It's not babe. It's Stokes. Miss Stokes to you."

The man was rather stupid looking and uniquely repulsive. His unshaven face took on a startled expression when he saw her eyes. People never expect such a vivid green.

Lynda twisted the dial on her machine up to fifty kilos. "I'm warmed up."

Captain Frazya's jaw dropped as she pulled the bar up to her shoulders, lowered it, and then lifted again. "Shit, I thought you were a woman when you came in. I guess you wouldn't know what to do with a man."

"I might, if there was one here."

She let go the bar, and walked over to the bag. The

unfortunate fool followed.

The punching bag weighed a bit less than most men, and Lynda enjoyed seeing it move when she tapped it.

Bam! The impact came back through the bones of her right wrist. It felt good. Bam! It was good with the left, too.

"Hey." He didn't shut up when he should've. "I heard of you Stokes people. One of you Stokes got locked up for being a nut."

Gentry. She stopped, her concentration broken.

His large hand grabbed her butt. "Well, that got your attention, didn't it, babe?"

* * *

It was time to start looking like a Corps officer. Aguire had the spaceport laundry service deliver his dress-grays to the locker room, and pick up his civilian clothes.

Everyone had their assignments. Even Chief Braun, whom he thought was staying on the Livingston, got a spot on the new ship.

What if he didn't get a spot of his own, and ended up stuck at a desk somewhere? The thought of starting over, of making new friends, churned in his gut. He'd hang out in HQ today and find out about duty assignments.

He left the gym, began walking toward the Corps annex section, and glanced back through the glass wall in the spaceport concourse into the gym. Major Rivers was jogging with her people around the track. Braun was still at the pool.

Lynda Stokes was walking away from the weight lifting area. It was the first time he'd seen her not wearing a full length dress. She looked good, athletic, like she took good care of herself. A big man with an unpleasant, mean expression on his face followed her, obviously leering at her body and talking incessantly.

Aguire stopped. It was Brian Frazya, a commercial skipper well known as a petty criminal, a trafficker of drugs and prostitutes.

Frazya was strong, thirty centimeters taller than Aguire, and mean as hell when he could get away with it. He used his bulk to intimidate people and take what he wanted from those he could bully, but for all that, he was a coward who never stood up to anyone his own size.

Aguire could well imagine the foul-mouthed suggestions Frazya was inflicting upon the shy, tender young lady. Aguire's Spanish blood demanded chivalry. He turned back towards entrance of the gym keeping his eyes on Frazya, and almost shouted when the bastard grabbed the helpless young woman.

Lynda whirled about to face Frazya. Her hands moved faster than sight, striking the man many times in a blur of violence that made his flesh ripple under each impact and his limbs bend into unnatural angles before he fell to the floor. Then, it was over.

And Lynda was again the wallflower, harmless. Those present who had not been looking directly at Lynda now looked down at a man broken and asked, how did he become this way?

Whoa! Aguire halted in mid-step, squeezed his eyes shut and gave his head a quick shake, certain that his eyes lied to him.

Mike Sullivan appeared almost instantly and had an ambulance at the scene within minutes. Captain Frazya was expected to live, though it was uncertain if he would ever regain the full use of his limbs. Aguire paused by the entrance and considered how embarrassed Lynda might feel if she knew he was watching.

Sullivan's a good cop. He'll handle it professionally and keep it quiet. He'll understand. Hell, he has five daughters of his own.

But where did Lynda learn to fight like that?

Sullivan asked questions. Someone pointed to Lynda. He turned to her keeping his right hand on his pistol while questioning the young woman. Aguire unconsciously moved closer. Lynda just stood there with her arms folded tight against her chest, not moving, not answering.

"You did this, Miss?" Sullivan was skeptical. "Just you? Alone?"

Lynda nodded sharply and bit her lip, trembling slightly while Frazya was carried out on a stretcher. People stared at her. Her lips moved in an effort to speak, but a large tear rolled down her face instead.

"Are you hurt, Miss?" Sullivan's tone became sympathetic. "Can you tell me what happened?"

Aguire's Spanish blood prompted him again. "Sullivan. I saw the whole thing."

Lynda looked up and saw Aguire.

Sullivan let go of his weapon and visibly relaxed. "I should have known. Wherever there's a disturbance, José Aguire is close at hand. What did you see?"

"The man was being offensive to the lady. She tried to walk away, but he wouldn't leave her alone."

"Uh-huh. And where were you while this was happening?"

"In the concourse." Aguire gestured with his thumb. "I just changed into my dress grays for a meeting I have to go to, and I saw this guy bothering the young lady. I was about to do something about it when he suddenly grabbed her ass. Actually, he attacked her. She must have been terrified. You saw how big he was."

"Sure. I saw how big he was while the medics were finding out if he would live or die."

"Adrenaline. Mike, she was defending herself."

"She still has to go to the security office for a few questions."

"Of course, but you can at least let her change clothes first."

"I'm not supposed to let her out of my sight. You know that, Aguire. Is she a friend of yours?"

Aguire raised his eyebrows. "You're going to make her walk through the spaceport in her gym shorts? I sure hope G.J. doesn't hear about this."

"G.J.?" Sullivan blinked. "You mean, G.J. Stokes?"

"Yeah. Lynda Stokes's father." Aguire nodded toward Lynda.

Sullivan's barrel-shaped head swiveled around to look at the richest woman in the galaxy whom, he could now see, was traumatized and obviously a victim in this whole ugly business.

"Miss Stokes, I'm sorry to have troubled you. I was just doing my job. You understand. I'll send a form for you to fill out at your convenience. In fact, you don't have to fill it out at all, if you prefer. We've had complaints about Captain Frazya before."

"Thank you," Lynda managed to whisper.

Sullivan touched the brim of his cap and walked away.

Lynda stood still, wishing she was somewhere—anywhere—else.

I did it again: anger; rage; vision goes gray; and someone gets hurt.

"Lynda?" Aguire was still there. "Go change, and then leave by the door to the concourse. Go before reporters show up."

She found herself back in the locker room. It was still deserted, but the echoes that were so obvious before were missing now, and all she heard was the rustle of her clothes as she pulled them onto her body.

Before she knew it, she was dressed and standing at the mirror. She looked the same as she did an hour ago; blond hair pinned back; blue and white sweater; gym bag hanging on her shoulder.

She was not the same. She'd almost killed a man. Almost a murderer.

And Aguire saw her lose control.

She went to the gym door and peeked out the little square window. People were hanging around, occasionally glancing at the locker room.

"Oh. I can't leave that way."

She found the concourse door, wishing Aguire wouldn't be there.

He waited with his feet apart and his hands clasped behind his back, like a sentry guarding the women's locker room.

"I don't want to make you late," Lynda told him.

"Late?"

"You told the policeman you were going to a meeting."

"Oh, that. I was exaggerating."

Travelers scurried in both directions with baggage and briefcases. A small crowd jammed the gymnasium entrance. A woman with an expensive hairdo and suit showed up with a microphone in her hand, followed by a news-service cameraman.

Aguire took Lynda's arm and led her away.

"Where are we going?"

"Out of Spaceport. Sullivan won't spread any gossip, but people will want to know your name, and they will if you stick around. I'll show you how to keep things like this off the record."

They made a beeline to the Academy section.

"We'll go through the physics department." Aguire steered her. "People are used to seeing us there, so if anyone asks later they won't remember exactly what time we were here."

She got her wits back, walking familiar halls. They came out near the west gate.

"It sounds like you've done this before."

"You'd be surprised what I've managed to keep off my record," Aguire confided.

Off his record? She tried to show no reaction while feeling like she'd just been slapped. She relied on records, made judgments about who would go and who would be left behind based on personnel records; school records; financial records; and yes, police records.

Aguire drove her downtown to her apartment where her by-the-book commander parked his car in a no-parking zone.

"Would you like to come up for a cup of coffee?" she offered, not wanting to let him go just yet.

Aguire didn't want to just drop her off now that she'd revealed that she was more to than a dowdy, intellectual heiress. He replayed in his mind how she'd taken down Frazya like a trained commando, and then instantly changed back to the shy young woman.

"Oh, no." Lynda said as they went to her apartment building.

"What?"

"You parked in a tow-away zone."

"It's a soft rule."

"A soft rule?" She waved her ID card at the lobby door and it opened.

"Yeah. There are solid rules like 'don't rob banks,' which are always enforced. Then there are soft rules, like parking in a tow-away. If you don't do it too often or for too long, it's not enforced."

"I thought rules were rules."

Her place was on the fifth floor. It wasn't big, but it seemed elegant with the dozens of Persian rugs that covered every inch of floor.

"Nice," he said, looking down.

"Oh, the rugs." She smiled. "Papa gives them to me. Every time he hears about a carpet store having a going-out-of-business sale, he has to buy four or five. He's been doing that since before I was born. I think he must have thousands by now."

She went into the kitchen while Aguire looked around at the

rugs that were thrown randomly here and there, at odd angles and overlapping. From the floor up, her place was precisely arranged as if by a decorator: drapes with perfectly straight pleats, and evenly spaced pictures on the walls that were all of desert landscapes. Except for the floor, all the colors were bland and cold, like the waiting room of a doctor's office. Beside the com console was a framed photograph of two men and young girl with green eyes. He guessed the girl was Lynda, but it took a moment to recognize that the Navy officer was a young, thin Paul Poluka.

The other man looked so much like Poluka that he could only be his captain's late brother, Clifford, who'd disappeared in the Zone.

"So where did you learn to keep things off your record?" Lynda called from the kitchen.

"I guess it was in Spain, where I was born," he answered. "I was in an orphanage when I was nine. A couple years later I joined a street gang. You could say it was the Madrid police who taught me the importance of official records."

She returned with two cups of coffee and sat beside him on the couch. "You mean you were a...a hoodlum?"

"Hoodlum? I guess you could say that. I was an ignorant kid, poor and hungry. Actually, the gang was just five of us, all from the orphanage. We swore oaths to each other that were supposed to be binding forever."

Lynda looked closely at him, her eyes more doll-like than ever. "But those oaths don't bind you now?"

"No. We decided to look for a better life, to live like normal people. We left Spain in a cargo vessel bound for Mexico, all except Atzo, who was caught by the police. He's still in Spain—at least I think he is. I can't seem to find any of my old friends with this new com system."

"What did you do in Mexico? Did you find a normal life?"

"At first we went to a public school. Mexico has great schools, and the Mexican girls loved our accents. But when we were old enough, my friends—Milián, Meder, and Jorge—joined the Army.

"For me, the Navy was the right move. Before the war, they offered good deals to get recruits, especially in education. The Navy put me through college.

"After the war, the military downsized and I joined the

Exploration Corps. It was for the best. I'll take exploration over combat any day."

He sipped the coffee. His childhood wasn't something he spoke of often, but he wanted to know something, and sometimes it's better to give a little first, before asking for something.

"Tell me," he asked. "Who taught you to fight?"

Lynda stirred some sugar into her coffee before answering. "When I was fourteen a boy asked me out on a date, so my father insisted that I learn self-defense. I liked it, and have been working at it ever since. I've always been strong. I'm stronger than I look."

She's not going to tell me, Aguire understood, but he was already certain. There are all kinds of fighting styles, but only one other person Aguire knew of could move the way she did.

"You look pretty strong."

She seemed hesitant, unsure. "Is that good or bad?"

"It's good. People always look better when they're in good shape. I wouldn't lose any sleep over what happened today."

"I lost control." She face was serious, pouting. "And I hurt a man very badly."

"Listen, Frazya's done things, bad things that he never had to account for. It's about time somebody taught him some manners. I'm just surprised it was you."

She glanced sharply at him, as if he had accused her of something. "Why?"

"I don't know many physics teachers who can take on someone twice their size."

She lowered her eyes. "I'm very embarrassed."

"You must spend a lot of time exercising."

"I like exercise. I need it. But for the last few years, most of my time has been helping Papa design the starship, and going to school."

"What have you been learning? Physics? Engineering?"

She shook her head and grinned shyly. "Would you believe law?"

"Law? You mean, like, to be a lawyer?"

"Don't look so surprised. Law can be very interesting."

"I'm sure."

"Well, what do you think of the judicial system?"

"It's sort of like a bullfight."

"I've never seen bulls fight."

"No, not that kind of bullfight. Centuries ago, in Spain, a man called a matador would go into an arena to fight an enraged bull. It was a traditional contest."

"Really? You're making this up."

"It's true. You can look it up."

"Okay. How is that like the law?"

"The bullfight is the system. It doesn't know anything about the man. Whether he's a good man or a bad man, if he has a family, or if he is there by his own choice. The bull doesn't care."

"What happens?"

"Sometimes the man lives. Sometimes the bull lives. Sometimes they both make it out alive, then, of course, the crowd is disappointed. They came to see death."

"Sounds barbaric. How can a man win against a bull? Is he armed?"

"He has a cape that he uses to confuse the bull into a vulnerable position, and a sword to drive through the heart of the beast. The matador's chances are determined by how good he is with the cape, the sword, and himself."

"Himself?"

"Yes. It takes something special, a sort of inner greatness."

"You don't give the judicial system much credit for justice."

"Lawyers don't care about justice. Neither the prosecutor, nor the advocate cares which side is right. They only care about winning. Like the bull."

"We have a jury system. There's a hole in your analogy."

"It was unrehearsed." Aguire laughed. "Colorful though, wasn't it?"

Lynda laughed with him. "Well, I'm glad I wasn't arrested today."

"Oh, Officer Sullivan wouldn't have arrested you."

"No?" She tilted her head toward him and raised her eyebrows, expecting an explanation.

"No. Frazya was at fault, and if what happened to him was, um . . . a bit severe, it just makes up for all the times he got away with a lot worse. Sullivan was just going to do a background check—see if you were dangerous or something."

"Dangerous?" Lynda's green eyes opened wide. She folded her arms and appeared indignant. "Why would anyone think that?"

Be careful, José. Don't set her off. "Nobody, but cops can't take anything for granted, you know? You're very strong, and there's a lot of crazy people out —"

"Crazy? Being strong doesn't mean I'm crazy. I'm just different."

Aguire thought she was going to hit him, until he saw the tears in her eyes.

"I'm sorry." He fished a handkerchief from his pocket and gave it to her. "I think you've had enough excitement for one day, and I'm not helping. I should go."

She dabbed her eyes, and sniffed once or twice. "No, no. You've helped me a lot. More than you know. It's just catching up with me, that's all."

"You should rest. I'll go."

"Maybe you're right. I'll see you at the ceremony, won't I?"

"Ceremony?"

"When the starship is commissioned into the Exploration Corps."

He hadn't realized she would be there. He hadn't expected to ever see her again, but he hoped that he would.

"Actually, I never got any official word that I'm assigned to the new ship."

"No? Well, I did. You are definitely assigned to the Starship Hanno."

CHAPTER 14

Donno checked the creases on his dress-gray pants before stepping into them and pulling them up his long, wiry legs. Aguire was at the mirror, fussing with his medals, some from the Corps, most from the Navy.

"You gonna wear all those?" Donno asked.

"Of course."

"You think I should wear mine?"

"Absolutely. This is a formal affair. You're supposed to show off your decorations."

Donno, thirteen centimeters taller than Aguire, looked over his friend's shoulder at the mirror to fix his tie. "So, our little Lynda kicked the shit out of Frazya, eh?"

Aguire glanced up at Donno's reflection. "She did more than kick the shit out of him. She wouldn't tell me, but I figured out who trained her to fight."

"Is that important?"

"Donno, I saw her knock him into the air and then break a dozen bones before he came back down. Does that remind you of anybody?"

It did. "Not our little Viking buddy, Bart Hanson?"

Aguire scowled at Donno's choice of adjective, because he was the same height as Bart Hanson.

"And that's not all," Aguire added. "Captain Poluka is a close friend of the Stokes family. If Hanson taught Lynda how to fight, how come neither Hanson nor the Captain ever mentioned that he knows them?"

"The plot thickens, but there's lots o' things Hanson doesn't talk about. How do I look?" Donno stood straight and tall in front of the mirror.

"So far, so good." Aguire nodded his approval. "Get your

medals."

Aguire insisted they take his car to the banquet hall. After blowing a year's pay on it, he wasn't about to pass up a chance to show off.

Inside was a sea of gray: starched, creased and sprinkled with colorful decorations. An occasional civilian stood out in a formal suit or evening gown.

Army personnel lent contrast to the gray in their dress-green uniforms.

To the annoyance of most, the powers that be scheduled the ceremony during the World Cup playoffs (in Australia this year, France favored to win).

Aguire chatted with Technician First-Class Hilda Harris, privately wondering what the ebony-skinned beauty would look like without clothes.

Lieutenant Maria Rodriguez was trying to hold Aguire's attention and privately wondering what he would look like without clothes.

Donno surveyed the crowd until he spotted Captain Poluka heading for the dining room. He nudged Aguire. "Looks like things are get'n started."

And so they were. The spaceport director got on a microphone and asked everyone to be seated. The crowd of two thousand or so noisily found their places at hundreds of circular tables. On a platform one step higher than the rest, a long table accommodated the spaceport's director, Admiral Fisher, with Captain Poluka.

Admiral Lucile Montague and Chief Braun chatted together, and seemed awfully chummy until Aguire noticed the ten hash marks on Braun's dress-grays, one stripe for every four years in the Corps. Braun probably knew the admiral before Aguire was born.

Admiral Montague left Braun and took a seat by Lynda and G.J. Stokes.

Lynda looked more feminine than usual, wearing an elegant evening gown, necklace and earrings. Aguire guessed her hair and make-up were professionally done. She really made an effort tonight.

* * *

Admiral Fisher sneered at the crowd from his position at the VIP table.

Peacocks. That's all they were, a bunch of strutting peacocks in gray, with no idea they'd been selected for slaughter. It made him want to laugh.

The glittering light on Aguire's decorations annoyed Fisher. He unconsciously toyed with his own medal that he got for valiantly betraying the position of key government leaders so they could be assassinated during the coup.

It wasn't his fault he didn't have more medals. During the war, no one ever let him lead the missions that were sure to bring glory. They never let him lead any missions at all. Others always got the lucky breaks and were sent into combat. Well, the shoe's on the other foot now. They take orders and he gives them. This will be their last hurrah.

It was sheer genius for Batastia to schedule the ceremony during the playoffs. There'd be virtually no news coverage. The Starship Hanno will disappear in a fizzle of anonymity, clearing the way for a more orderly society.

The commissioning began with a few words from Admiral Montague. Fisher found it irritating that the C.O. of the Corps was an old woman. He wondered if his favored position with the new government might put him on the fast track to replace the old bitch. He'd talk to Admiral Higgs about it.

Montague introduced Fisher, who was conscious of the eyes on him, and the one most important eye, the camera hanging from the ceiling which reported the event to the vice president. It suddenly occurred to him that his own neck was sticking way out. If there was any public outcry, it would not be the vice president's fault, it would be Fisher's.

He read the prepared speech. "It is with great pleasure that I stand here in the midst of so many who carry on our proud tradition of galactic exploration, a tradition born in the turbulent years of corporate rule, surviving not only that rule, but the repression of the old Federation as well. Today we usher in a new era of exploration starships with the biggest and most advanced ever built, the Starship Hanno."

Applause.

"The Hanno has the capacity for ten times the crewmen than

our older ships, with greater speed and superior instrumentation. She shall no doubt prove equal to any challenge."

Scattered applause.

"Now, for the big news. Where will the Hanno go on her maiden voyage? What part of unexplored space is long overdue for a visit from mankind? We have gone ever outward along the Orion Arm of the galaxy to the Eridanus Systems and beyond, to places that do not yet have names. After much discussion, debate, and consideration of many possibilities, the Corps has concluded that it is time to open the path to the galactic center. Ladies and Gentlemen, the Starship Hanno will be the first ship in the history of space travel to go to Arcturus."

Stunned silence.

He wanted to shrink from their staring eyes, yet savor their shock and dismay. He stood above them, their superior, telling them they were screwed. It was a moment he would treasure forever. It was a fragile moment, however. He mustn't stray from the script.

"It is with great pleasure that I introduce the man behind this endeavor, Doctor Gentry Stokes."

Admiral Fisher returned to his seat while the old fool addressed the mob. Stokes approached the podium with a big, child-like grin on his weathered face.

"Thank you, Admiral Fisher. This is indeed an historic moment, only possible due to the efforts of many who have gone before us since the beginning of space travel. Thanks to them, we may journey among the stars in greater safety and comfort than ever before. And it is largely due to people like Admiral Fisher," he pointed right at Fisher, drawing every eye to him, "who constantly and thoroughly verify the integrity of the vessels that your lives depend upon."

Fisher groaned as quietly as possible. It was out of character for Doctor Stokes to give credit to anyone but himself. Maybe the old man knew the Hanno was a death ship, and was putting all responsibility onto Fisher.

"I only wish," Stokes went on, "that I was a younger man, that I might be among the gallant explorers on this maiden voyage. Since wishing does not make it so, I will settle for the next best thing. My daughter, Lynda, will go in my place as an observer and I will rendezvous with the Hanno when the mission is completed at Alpha Virginus some 200 light years from Arcturus."

This was news to Fisher. Either Stokes was really just an old fool or he was willing to sacrifice his daughter to come out of this looking clean. Such a cold-blooded gambit was awe inspiring.

* * *

Two thousand kilometers to the east in a palatial residence, three men sipped fine whiskey and watched the ceremony on a huge screen.

Vincent Batastia was convinced that G.J. Stokes was insane. "Can you believe that? His own child. In the old days we understood: family is everything."

Admiral Higgs nodded sagely. "When he hears that she died along with the others, the news will probably kill him."

"Good," Capitol Chief of Staff Crush Skor grunted. "It's time for the Stokes empire to be taken apart and redistributed. He has no other heirs, correct?"

"He had a son once," Higgs told the Chief of Staff, "who was committed to a mental hospital and later died. I'm trying to get confirmation on that, but we've been having problems with the records."

"I'd hoped to get the girl as one of the perks," Batastia mumbled as he poured himself another drink, "but this will do nicely."

Higgs fought to show no reaction. When he'd first heard about the perks, he accepted it as a fact of human nature that, even among the intellectual elite, basic animal passions need an outlet. He expected the perks to be something like an exclusive harem staffed by willing prostitutes. He was quietly distressed when he learned that it was something much uglier.

There was no reason—no good reason—to take Stokes's daughter, except for the fact that Batastia hated G.J. Stokes as he hated everyone who benefited from the fall of the Corporate State forty years ago. Some were arrested or just disappeared, and ended up as perks. They tended to be the loved ones of people Batastia hated. It was Batastia's preferred punishment: harm the family.

A subtle vise squeezed Wolfgang Higgs, testing how much

hypocrisy he could tolerate. The perks appalled him, but he had his own incentive for continuing to follow Batastia. He still dreamed of building the perfect empire.

But was his dream just a dangling carrot meant to keep him loyal?

He peered sideways at Batastia, who was now so drunk he could hardly speak.

Of course it was.

"The speeches are done," Crush said. He clicked off the video. The show was over.

* * *

The commissioning of the Starship Hanno was completed with the signing of papers and a symbolic key being given by G.J. Stokes to Admiral Montague, who then passed it to Captain Poluka.

Amid the creased gray, watching everything, was a petite young woman with the Silver Star of Courage on her chest who had just been demoted again. Nothing was how it seemed.

CHAPTER 15

The snow was melting around New Wichita, and Commander José Aguire felt the call: Space. The great wide universe. It got into the blood.

Perhaps that's how ancient sailors felt about the sea. These days, space travel was not much different than sea travel had been in the seventeenth century. It took weeks or months to go to distant colonies, not to mention a hefty sum of money for the average traveler, and exploration was still hazardous.

Donno muttered, "Look, isn't that Bart Hanson? And he's wearing an officer's uniform."

Across the crowded terminal, Aguire saw the stout, Nordic features of the most dangerous man he'd ever known.

"Yeah. Poluka promoted him to ensign when the Corps approved his transfer. I guess they thought it wouldn't matter much if he was going on a suicide mission."

Donno was surprised. "You think this is a suicide mission?"

"I suspect some do."

The first transport was ready for boarding.

Aguire was first in line. Hanson was 46th and last to board before they left the Earth far below.

The shuttle achieved orbit and the Hanno came into view. Everyone crowded around the glass on the starboard side to ogle the biggest and best exploration ship ever.

"Damn, she's a big 'un," Donno said, "and prettier than the Livingston, too."

The engine section in the back was a cylinder nearly five kilometers long and about two and half wide, tapering down like a cone to 800 meters wide where it joined the midship.

The triangular forward section was at the other end, with the massive antennae and sensory arrays necessary for exploring the

71

galaxy.

The Hanno looked somewhat like an arrow, the forward section being the arrowhead, the long midship the shaft, and the engine section was like the feathered end of the arrow.

The shuttle maneuvered to a docking port. Moments later the side hatch opened into the Starship Hanno.

Captain Poluka waited on the loading gantry with his no-nonsense expression.

"Welcome aboard the Starship Hanno, ladies and gentlemen. The maintenance crew will be leaving on the shuttle you just arrived in. The next shuttle will bring more officers in about twenty minutes. Find your quarters and stow any belongings you've brought with you now. We've got to keep this passageway clear. Onloading of supplies begins in two hours. Be ready. That's all for now."

Poluka stayed in the gantry while his officers moved deeper into the giant ship.

Aguire and Donno headed for the central deck to check out the bridge, while most others lugged baggage up to the accommodation decks. Ensign Hanson wandered off toward the cafeteria.

Some decks were numbered, while others had names reflecting function. Deck number one was in the center.

"This is it," Donno said when they found the central passageway which was called Main Street.

Main Street went the whole six kilometers down the center of the midship in one straight line. Looking back toward the engines, visual perspective made the lines where the walls met the floor and the ceiling converge to a point in the distance. Looking forward, Aguire could just make out the end of the corridor, about one kilometer away.

"Incredible," Aguire breathed with a hushed reverence. "And I thought this ship looked big on the outside."

Main Street was nineteen meters wide to accommodate pedestrian traffic as well as small electric trucks and had two speedwalks down the center, one going each way, so someone in a hurry could get onto the moving walkway and move eleven kilometers per hour faster than if they were just walking on the deck.

"Let's race," Aguire suggested, and leapt onto the speedwalk.

Donno sprang forward with a curse. His long legs pumped hard against the deck, and then pushed sideways to land on the speedwalk. He chased Aguire down Main Street to the forward section, where the plastic strip flowed continuously over a roller and under the deck at the end of the speedwalk.

"You got a head start," Donno complained.

"Of course," Aguire laughed. "Cheating is the only way I can outrun you."

"I could beat you in a fair race."

"Exactly."

"Oh, hell. Let's see the bridge."

There was a guard's station at the entrance to the forward section, which was not yet manned. A corridor beyond led to the foyer of the executive offices.

"Commander Washington's office." Donno pointed to a sign: SHIP'S BUSINESS.

"Support Systems." Aguire indicated a sign on the right. "That one must be Martensen's."

They passed their own offices and resisted the temptation to look inside since an office is, after all, just an office.

The last office on the left had a plaque on the door: CAPTAIN PAUL POLUKA.

"Ah, at last, the bridge," said Aguire when reached the end. He'd seen holograms of the ship's command center, but never truly appreciated how spacious it was until he stood in the center of it.

The command desk dominated the center of the room with small computer monitors rising from the surface on metal stems, like flowers in a raised flower bed. In the front of the bridge were the pilot, navigator, weapons, and probe launch stations, all facing forward where the main viewport and auxiliary screens were.

On the Starship Livingston, the main viewport was three leaded windows side by side, each about a 120 centimeters square. The Hanno's main viewport was a single window of real Radglass, ten and a half meters wide by four meters high, offering a spectacular view.

"Good morning, gentlemen."

Aguire jumped at the cheerful but unexpected voice from the Instrumentation Bay.

"Chief Braun," Aguire said when he spotted the plump, gray-haired engineer sitting at one of the consoles in the triangular bay. "Did you come up with the captain?"

"With him and Miss Stokes. I wanted to check a few things before the maintenance crew cleared out."

"Lynda's already onboard?"

"She was. I think she went back down in the shuttle you came up in. She's meeting her father in West Point."

The Instrumentation Bay, or I-Bay, was a small side room, with the walls angled so everything happening inside would be visible from the command desk, and for as many as ten people to work in at the same time.

Donno went into the Systems Bay, where all operations inside the Hanno would be monitored and controlled. The S-Bay was on the starboard side directly opposite the I-Bay but curving to the right, away from the bridge and back toward the office section, making it more like a separate room.

Aguire found Donno around the corner, glaring at a monitor.

"Donno, what is it?"

"This is a completely different set up than the one we learned at the Academy. It's like it was designed for a different ship."

Chief Braun ambled into the S-Bay. "Oh, yeah. It was changed to accommodate the latest improvements. Didn't you get the memo?"

"Memo?" Donno whirled around to glare at Braun, causing the Chief to back up a step. "This doesn't need a memo, Chief. This needs another week in a classroom...wait a minute. What improvements?"

"Improvements for safety. Some field limiters were added to the new engines. Stuff like that."

"All right," Aguire interrupted. "We can deal with this, but I want to know about all these improvements, now. When the Hanno starts taking on supplies, there'll be no time for relearning."

Donno wasn't particularly pleased when it turned out almost all of the changes affected the Systems Bay, where he would be in charge. It took a half hour for Chief Braun to review the list of changes with them.

More officers showed up in small groups.

Commander Washington dropped in for a glance around before beginning his duties. Washington was next in command after Aguire, in charge of administrative functions.

Poluka came in at eleven-thirty hours and found Aguire at the pilot's station.

"Well, Commander, how do you like our new starship?"

"It's great, Captain, but there seems to be some discrepancies in the Systems Bay."

"I imagine Mister Donno is looking into it now," Poluka said quietly.

So, it's started. Poluka sighed miserably to himself. He knew this was when it would begin. His people were nobody's fools. They would see things didn't quite add up and begin to speculate.

Poluka left the bridge and felt like shit. This was too much like betrayal. His people had a right to expect the truth from him, but he just couldn't let them have it. Not yet.

In his office he found his bottle of forty-year-old brandy and poured himself a drink.

For three years he plotted quietly with only G.J., Lynda, and Bart Hanson. Everyone else he kept on the outside. To keep a secret, you first limit who's in on it. It was a policy proven time and again throughout history, which was always enough to soothe his conscience, until now. Everything he'd kept from his friends would soon be laid bare.

He settled down at his computer and verified the first supply freighter was lining up on the port side. Six more freighters were behind it and spread out across 800 kilometers. The others would be coming soon.

CHAPTER 16

"I still don't get it," Lieutenant McGee complained after hearing Aguire's plan. "If one officer has four trucks, won't that slow things down? I mean, we'll have to keep reprogramming them and we won't know if they're going where they're supposed to."

"No," Aguire explained. "The trucks are smart machines. The old Fed banned smart machines after the Corporate War—"

"Yeah," Lieutenant Swanson interrupted, "and for good reason."

"Listen." Aguire held up his hand to forestall further interruptions. He wanted to clear up any concerns his lieutenants had before they meet with the ensigns who would do the work of moving supplies under the lieutenant's supervision. "These are just trucks, not robot soldiers, and they've got limited memory, so they're not going to go berserk on us. Each ensign will drive one truck to a stockroom with three unmanned trucks following him. If any truck needs specific instructions, it'll obey voice commands. We won't send any trucks off on their own without an officer leading the way. This way we've got more ensigns for organizing the stockrooms, where things always get bottlenecked."

Andrew Swanson and Luke McGee were the best of friends and worked well together despite the incessant jabs at each other over their Ireland-versus-Scotland rivalry, or their mismatched appearance—Swanson was short and wiry, while McGee looked like a mountain of muscle and bone.

"Well, sure." McGee scratched his chin through his bristly beard. "I guess we can try it."

"Let's get started, then." Swanson dropped all hesitation. "If smart machines are going to be used again, we may as well find out early if they're going to have any trouble with McGee's accent."

"Nothing wrong wi' my accent, laddie." McGee amplified his Scottish brogue. "But the way you Irish talk sometimes...."

Aguire ignored the banter. He'd learned not to admit that both their accents sounded exactly the same to him.

The latest philosophy for the initial onloading of a new starship was to have no crew aboard except officers. Otherwise, the officers would just tell crewmen where to put things, never the wiser when things end up somewhere else. Until five years ago, each Exploration Corps ship was unique in its operation and configuration, and supplies were loaded by the crew who would be using them.

It was never a problem when ships were smaller, but the Corps suddenly grew after the Jupiter War, and so did the size of the ships. The larger ships had specialists with their own departments increasing the complexity of supplies exponentially. The first time a ship got stocked with supplies generally determined where things would be from then on.

Finding whatever is needed at a moment's notice means the difference between life and death. It has to be done right the first time, because it becomes an organizational nightmare to start rearranging.

With no way of knowing what they might need, they brought everything. They'd have enough spare parts to rebuild most of the ship several times over, as well as millions of tons of tools, consumable goods, and raw materials.

The electric trucks had open cabs with no roofs or doors. The flat cargo space behind the driver was enclosed with retractable rails on the sides and back.

They lined up with one ensign in charge of each group of four trucks as freight ships began attaching to the Hanno and poured streams of cargo through the loading docks.

Automated conveyors passed from the freighters to the trucks, and the ensigns began delivering tons of supplies to hundreds of stockrooms.

After a couple of hours, Donno called from the S-Bay and asked how things were going.

"Great." Aguire nodded to Donno's image on the screen. "Deliveries are ahead of schedule, and I've got more hands for organizing the stockrooms."

"No trouble with the trucks?" Donno asked.

Aguire waved a hand in a gesture of dismissal. "None. All this worry about smart machines was for nothing. People are just spooked by stories about robot soldiers from forty years ago. These are just computerized trucks. There's nothing to worry about."

"Ah," Donno smiled, "That's terrific. So, you're not missing one of your trucks, then?"

"Huh?"

"It's just that I'm getting complains from the fabrication shops about a truck that's trying to kill everybody." Donno read something on another screen. "It was last seen near textile storage."

Aguire cut the connection without bothering to say goodbye and had a link to textiles open a moment later. On the screen behind Swanson, ensigns scurried among rows of storage bins and shelves looking for something.

"Aye, sir." Swanson admitted. "It got away from us somehow. We'll find it."

"Is it," Aguire swallowed hard, "behaving dangerously?"

"Dangerously? No sir, except for driving too fast. It's keeps running away from us."

There was a shout and Aguire saw an ensign dash across the room behind Swanson. Close behind him was an unmanned truck which turned sharply when it got out into the open, and then accelerated for the open door of the stockroom. Once outside, it turned again and disappeared down the corridor.

"Ah, crap." Swanson said. "I'll get back to you later, Commander."

Altogether, three unmanned trucks got separated from the others somehow and ran amok all over the ship. Two were quickly found and stopped, but the third was still at large long after the onloading was complete. It would turn up occasionally, charging out of an elevator or down a corridor, scaring the hell out of whoever was in its path, only to turn a corner and not be seen again for days.

Aguire called the other ensigns and had them disable the smart machine capability of the remaining trucks. The rest of the onloading went more slowly, but without trouble.

Bart Hanson volunteered to help track down the missing

machine, but had no success.

"It's behaving like a squirrel," Hanson told Aguire later when they ran into each other on Main Street. "It makes a run for it whenever it doesn't understand something."

"Well," Aguire sighed, "it can't recharge itself. We'll get it when it runs out of power."

Just then the errant truck came around a corner onto Main Street, shot across a pass-thru on the speedwalk, and then disappeared down a corridor towards the gymnasium. McGee came huffing and puffing behind it with a massive crowbar in his hands, and dripping sweat. He saw Aguire and tried to speak but could only wheeze.

A passing lieutenant who'd witnessed the chase stopped and laughed, "What are you gonna do McGee, beat it to death?"

McGee nodded savagely and glared murder in the direction the truck disappeared.

"It'll run out of power soon, Lieutenant." Aguire said to the sweating giant.

"Looks like McGee will first," the other lieutenant laughed.

McGee's eyes narrowed as he whirled about to deliver a colorful retort to the man. He flung his arms wide, forgetting that he had a one-meter crowbar in his right hand. The tip of the crowbar swung fast straight at Aguire's startled face, but suddenly stopped inches from his nose with a dull thud in Hanson's palm.

McGee looked back when he felt an immovable resistance through the steel. When he saw Hanson gripping the tool, a flicker of recognition displaced the wrath in his eyes.

"Maybe you should take a break, lieutenant," Hanson said and let go of the bar.

McGee once saw Hanson mop up a nightclub with half a dozen Navy commandos who wanted to find out just how tough he was. He looked into Hanson's icy blue eyes and decided it was indeed time for a break. "Aye, it'll run out o' juice, an' then I'll beat the shit out o' the fookin' thing."

McGee left in the direction he'd come from. Aguire remained silent, contemplating what his head would look like if Hanson hadn't been there, and wondering why the bones in Hanson's hand weren't broken.

"Thanks, Bart," he finally said. "Maybe I'll take a break, too."

On the eighth day, thousands of expendable probes were

loaded, all the latest equipment: sniffer probes for analyzing the atmosphere of gas-worlds like Jupiter and Saturn; cronkite probes for getting optical data and mapping planets; pixies and pingers for radar and laser experiments.

The onloading continued with Hanson acting as Aguire's assistant. It was just a myth that Bart Hanson was a loner. He, Aguire, and Donno were good friends since the war. What did surprise Aguire was that the legendary warrior seemed to enjoy keeping track of the ship's inventory.

"We've got one last freighter, Commander," Hanson said, checking his list. "The doctors arrive today with the medical stores. According to policy, Doctor Payne's staff will handle that themselves."

"Great." Aguire smiled. "Right on schedule. What's our last load?"

"Athletic equipment."

"Oh? What does that include?"

Hanson scrolled through the list. "Baseball; soccer; gymnastics — that's your sport if I remember correctly — American football; tennis; badminton — that's my favorite — fencing; wrestling; horse racing…"

"Horse racing? On a Starship?"

"Just kidding, sir."

Hanson's sense of humor always took Aguire by surprise. "Okay. Let's go finish up this job."

The Hanno had a fine gymnasium in the aft section of the midship just opposite the Med Center where the artificial gravity was most stable and nearly as consistent as natural gravity.

Both delicate surgery and active sports benefited from thousands of gravity simulation rods built into the midship. Each GSR was installed vertically inside the walls of the ship, actually pulling quantum space down and out through the floor to simulate gravity. The forward section got by with a few dozen GSRs. The engine section had none.

After weeks of loading supplies around the clock, the officers gathered in the gym, stowed the last load, and occasionally paused to try out the basketball court or toss a football around. For a few hours at least, they could relax.

"Hey." Hanson indicated an open area of soft mats where a dozen Army officers were practicing martial arts. "Looks like we're infested with barnies."

With true Army machismo, they were using real — and sharp — combat knives to practice disarming a knife-wielding opponent.

Larger ships of the Corps, the Navy, and even commercial outfits were assigned detachments of soldiers in case some remote outpost needed them. The Navy had commandos for boarding parties and rescue missions, but colonies often needed a force that could be left for an extended stay.

Starship crews referred to their Army passengers as barnacles, or barnies, because, like the ocean critters, the soldiers got attached to a vessel without providing much benefit along the way. They generally kept to themselves, with their own activities and procedures.

A slender woman, a Corps lieutenant, watched them. She made some comment to the barnies, which stopped the practice as the soldiers crowded around her to argue about whatever she'd said. She was barely a 160 centimeters tall, making the soldiers seem all the bigger.

"You think she's getting herself into trouble?" Aguire wondered.

Hanson scowled at the group. "I wouldn't want them to think they can intimidate a Corps officer."

Aguire and Hanson moved closer while the barnies stacked some packing boxes against a bulkhead and scratched a small circle onto the front of one box, then set more knives on another box about ten meters away.

It became clear what was happening when a tough-as-nails barnie picked up a knife and faced the stack of boxes. He hurled the knife at the box with the circle. It pierced the cardboard with a solid *whump!* just below the circle. He threw one knife after another, embedding two inside the circle, a couple others near the circle. One hit sideways and didn't stick. His comrades cheered encouragement. Aguire gave up pretending that he wasn't watching.

"Hey, Commander." Major Rivers grinned and waved him over. The tall, athletic woman gestured with her thumb to indicate the Corps lieutenant who stood watching the knife throwing demonstration. "Your Lieutenant Tully doesn't think much of our skill with knives. We're just showing off a bit."

Aguire nodded. The barnies offered Lieutenant Tully a turn at throwing. The woman asked, "What do I get if I can make one stick?"

A barnie laughed. "What do you want?"

Tully looked at the box, which had five knives lying on it. "If I get one to stick in the circle, can I keep one of the knives?"

"Sure." He grinned. "Just stick one in the circle."

She picked up two knives, one in each hand, threw first with the right and then with the left, snatched up two more and hurled them as well. In rapid succession all four knives buried themselves into the circle. She picked up the fifth knife and said, "I like this one. Thanks."

Hanson whispered to Aguire, "I don't think she's intimidated."

"Where'd you learn that?" Major Rivers asked Tully.

"Brazil, in the jungle," Tully answered, "when I was a kid."

Aguire left the officers to their games, and returned to Main Street with Hanson, where they saw the missing electric truck whisk by at full speed. Surprised shouts and warnings echoed along the passage.

"Sooner or later that truck should crash or run into McGee," Aguire sighed, "and I hope it's sooner. This is getting embarrassing. Well, I should report to the Captain. You can take a break if you like, or return to the gym and challenge someone to a badminton match."

"Captain Poluka is working the first shift." Hanson said. "He'll be sleeping now."

Aguire glanced at his watch. "Right you are, Ensign. I'll make an entry in the log, and talk to Poluka at 0600."

After supper Aguire went to his quarters. A quick glance around would tell the casual observer two things about José Aguire: he had more space than he was used to, and he didn't own much. His personal belongings, except for a mound of dirty laundry on the floor, were still packed into a few boxes. Aguire prodded the pile of clothes with his foot. He'd be glad when the laundry got operating.

"I should review the personnel files, but not just now." Aguire yawned. The pace of the last few weeks had him exhausted. "A little nap first, then I'll check the files. Maybe tomorrow."

He lay down on the bed and looked up at the bare wall above

his head. Back aboard the Livingston, he'd displayed on the wall above his bed an antique compass card that Poluka gave him the day they transferred from the Navy into the Corps. It was festooned with gold-leaf, scrolling, and hand-painted colors that were once brilliant before centuries faded them to dull pastels. Poluka told him it was used to navigate a sailing ship in the nineteenth century. Aguire thought it looked tacky but accepted the gift graciously.

"It's still packed away somewhere." He yawned again, and drifted into a dream of a wooden sailing ship, its white sails billowing in violent winds. He rushed from hold to hold looking for something, but the crew kept rearranging and hiding the stores.

"I need that compass card," he shouted, "or we'll be lost."

He heard Poluka laugh. "Where's your faith, Mister Aguire?"

The captain was at the wheel, steering the ship to the edge of the world, where the oceans spilled perpetually over. The wooden ship reached the edge and plunged over into space, among the stars.

CHAPTER 17

"Sorry, Aguire." Donno shook his head. "I've got to set up automated services before the crew comes aboard."

"That's okay." Aguire hid his disappointment and turned to Martensen. "What about you, Commander, care to do a quick walkthrough with me?"

"I'd be happy to, Commander," said Martensen, a tall, blond man who had on occasion been mistaken for Gary Fisher back when Fisher still wore a commander's uniform. The resemblance was only skin deep, however, and Martensen seemed decent enough.

They left Donno in the S-Bay and headed aft on the upper decks to take a peek at the accommodation decks, which housed private quarters for each crew member and comfortable common areas for socializing when off duty. Further aft they passed the infrastructure support department responsible for keeping the ship livable.

Throughout the Hanno the decks were marked with numbers indicating how far from the forward section a point was, with major marks every 100 meters. Halfway down the midship, Aguire and Martensen returned to Main Street and used the speedwalk to rest their feet on the way to the coherent emission fusion reactor at the far end of the midship. Such facilities sometimes powered large space stations or small cities on Earth.

From there, below the central deck, they viewed the bulk air and water storage: steel tanks as big as city buildings in a low gravity zone. Except for occasional inspections, the area would be mostly unmanned.

Fabrication shops were forward from there, and too compartmented to tour now. They opted instead to see the much-talked-about "downtown" area, a recreational facility made to simulate an Earth environment. Such luxuries were found on cruise ships and the bigger space stations.

"I'm not sure this facility's such a good idea," Martensen said. "It'll be a distraction."

"We'll have to develop a policy for it." Aguire rubbed his chin as he considered how different things would be with such a large crew. "If it becomes a problem, we can close it down."

This was the one common area where alcohol was allowed. It had lounges and gaming rooms, a cinema and holographic theater. There was an old-fashioned barbershop with a red and white striped pole, and shops where luxury items could be purchased. It simulated a quaint downtown, with city décor that included lampposts and tacky facades of individual buildings. Most of "downtown" was automated. In the middle was a small park with live trees and grass, where one could sit on a bench, hear recorded bird songs and feel a slight breeze.

The whole thing took up about four thousand square meters and had a brightly illuminated sky-blue ceiling twenty meters overhead. The gravity was close to Earth-normal and the acoustics were tuned to render an outdoor feel. The illusion was disorienting.

"We're not the first ones here." Martensen pointed down the street, where others were exploring.

"Let's not set a bad example," Aguire said.

"Right. I'd like a peek at the missile magazine."

The Hanno's complex passageways forced them to go back up to Main Street to a lift further forward, and then down again to the maintenance shops.

"This won't do," Aguire said. "We can't get anywhere fast on the Hanno."

"Let's put it on a list of issues for the next staff meeting."

Aguire felt gloriously free of burdens since completing the onloading, but there were still plenty of things needing his attention. They moved quickly through the cavernous maintenance shops and on to the missile magazine.

The Corps wasn't a military force, but sometimes assisted law enforcement on the frontier, and missiles were standard equipment. They were also handy for dealing with space junk or asteroids which were a hazard to navigation.

Missiles were an ancient technology that, being simple, had

little that could go wrong, but if something did go wrong, it could go in a big way.

The dim, cold missile section at the front of the midship didn't share any structural support with the rest of the ship in case there was a malfunction. It was silent and entirely automated; thousands of missiles; row upon row of destruction loaded neatly in racks, waiting with unholy patience.

"There's too many," Aguire realized. "There should only be about 400 hummingbirds, 200 scorpions, and 60 hawks."

"Yeah, there's a shitload of stuff that doesn't add up on this ship," Martensen added, pointing at a missile the size of a space bus. "That's an eagle 'city-killer'."

Aguire remembered the war, the sight of missiles streaking toward him, and feeling an alien moon shake beneath his boots from explosions that were aimed at him. They say missiles are impersonal, but it's hard to agree when you are the target.

He nearly jumped out of his skin when two tones, high and low, indicating a ship-wide announcement, crackled from the intercom.

"Now hear this." Poluka's voice came booming through. "This is your captain. The first transports are bringing our crew aboard. Section leaders will receive crewmen within the hour. The senior staff will report to the captain's office immediately."

The crew came up with mountains of baggage. The corridors bustled with confusion as people found their quarters, looked in on work areas, and generally snooped around their new home.

Commander Washington had his SPs —ship's police — stationed at major intersections to handle questions. By 1900 hours things settled down. Poluka welcomed the crew aboard via the info-screens located all over the ship.

The ship's clock was synchronized with the capitol on Earth and as evening shift began, Aguire told the captain, "I still haven't given the roster a good going-over. I'd better do that tonight."

"Oh, I should have warned you earlier," Poluka responded, "we've ended up with more people than I planned. It took a lot of negotiating to get the people I wanted, and the powers-that-be wanted to find a home for all the people who've been waiting for an assignment since the new government took over. I suppose I could have said *no*, but," Poluka shrugged, "this *is* a big ship. Anyway, some will change their minds about going to the Zone, and ask for a transfer. You'll see."

Aguire opened the ship's roster back in his own office and found that the captain had understated the situation. There were almost four thousand entries, double what had been originally planned. It would take hours to get a rough idea of the skill sets aboard the ship.

He decided to get away from distractions and continue the review in his quarters before calling it a night. He found a stack of folded uniforms on his bed, delivered from the ship's laundry.

The sight of his clean clothes brought a lump to his throat, and made his heart swell with appreciation of a well-managed organization. In the military he'd learned the marvel of teamwork, where each had their own duties that meshed like gears with the duties of one's comrades to form something that, as individuals acting separately, they could not rise to. Several teams working together formed a bigger, more efficient unit, and so on, until you had a complete organization of teams, each serving all.

For Aguire, the clean laundry represented civilization in all its splendor.

He picked up a shirt. It was damp and wrinkled. "Son of a bitch."

He called the laundry and testily complained to the attractive women whose face appeared on the screen. She was distinctly Latina with black hair and very dark eyes.

"Damp, Commander?" the slender woman responded with a squeaky, cartoon-character voice that he recognized instantly: Elisa Santino. Two years ago, she'd been a lieutenant in charge of a deep-space rescue team on the edge of the frontier.

"I'm sorry, sir," she said. "I'll send someone for your uniform, and have it back within the hour."

She was the hero who'd saved the lives of three of Aguire's shipmates — and now she was washing his clothes.

"Uh, no. I just thought I'd mention it to you. I'm sure you'll straighten things out."

"Yes, sir. Thank you, sir."

The screen went blank, and Aguire hung his uniform in the closet. The uniform smelled faintly of soap, and had a crease on one sleeve that wasn't supposed to be there. He pulled it back out of the closet, and tried to rub the crease away with his fingers.

He almost got Santino back on the com, but recalled how the

tiny young woman working at the *Last Stop* hub station had disconnected the air supply from her space suit to plug it into the suit of Aguire's shipmate — Luke McGee — who was dying for lack of oxygen, and almost died herself.

"Oh, hell." He shoved the uniform into the closet. "The laundry crew needs some time to sort things out, I suppose."

He sat down at his computer with a cup of hot tea and checked if any more familiar names were aboard. Bart Hanson's listing stood out because it had his name and rank, but nothing else. Apparently Poluka signed him on but didn't quite know what to do with him.

"Can't say that I blame him," Aguire mused aloud, referring to the captain. There was a special request from Hanson for extra storage space. That was odd.

He clicked on the request to see more detail and found Captain Poluka gave him the extra space — *in the missile section?* It didn't say how much space, or what would be stored there. Apparently, the extra missiles were Hanson's baggage.

He clicked through about a hundred entries before sensing a pattern. One name in six had a recent demotion — a rare thing, normally — and many more than expected had no next-of-kin listed.

He went back to Elisa Santino's file. She was demoted twice in two years by Admiral Fisher, from lieutenant to ensign shortly after being assigned to the DDR, and again to CPO when she was assigned to the Hanno. The reasons were conspicuously vague, but there was a note from Fisher recommending her for duty aboard the Hanno. Most people would resign after just one demotion. Aguire couldn't remember anyone getting two.

He rubbed his chin and scowled at the data. He filtered for entries with demotions. There weren't so many among those who'd never been in the Navy, but another pattern emerged: police records showing "undesirable behavior" within the last year.

It was late and Aguire didn't feel like being a detective. He instructed the computer to look for patterns — any kind of patterns. Instantly, all kinds of statistics appeared. He refined and sorted a bit more until he suddenly got a creepy feeling that made the hair on his neck stand up.

"Son of a bitch."

He opened his own file, and read a magistrate's opinion about his "unrepentant defiance of the New Federation policies" over the Christmas decorations thing. There was another note from Admiral Gary Fisher that specifically recommended him for duty aboard the Hanno.

"Computer," Aguire instructed, "filter out entries with the following criteria that occurred since year one of the new calendar: arrests, arrests of relatives, death of relatives, negative comments regarding new rules or laws."

The next screen to pop up had only 68 entries. Of those, Aguire found some clues to suggest loyalty to the old Federation. A few didn't seem to fit into any category but, out of four thousand who did, it hardly mattered.

He was looking at a blacklist: people the New Federation would like see disappear forever, and José Aguire was one of them.

CHAPTER 18

Paul Poluka grunted at the bulkhead he stared at for the last hour and finally gave up trying to sleep. He rolled out of bed and cringed when his bare feet hit the cold floor.

He had a damn good crew and it gave him an icy, dead feeling deep inside, because he got them by lying to them—all of them. He had to. He needed them. The plan needed them. Everything was approaching a critical moment but something was still not right.

Could it be the plan? Maybe the plan itself had a problem. Clifford was always better than Paul at plans. His brother could always predict the outcome.

He scowled at the locked safe in his storage space. Cliff's notebook was there, the one he passed on to Paul that morning ten years ago when the Starship Himilco launched from the Oklahoma spaceport. Cliff's notes gave Paul an edge in his career and made him seem brilliant for the last decade.

He makes his own plans now.

The Radglass window in his office allowed a crystal-clear view of the clamshell antennas while blocking the cosmic radiation. The 200 meter dishes outside gently opened from their storage spaces and obscured his view of Earth.

"Hm," Paul mumbled, "someone's testing the system again." He stretched his back, feeling pops and creaks from joints that weren't active enough. He reached for his boots. "I gotta get out of here."

He found the foyer empty except for a crewman leaving Commander Washington's office. The man turned away, quickly returning to the midship. The shame on the man's face said that he had just asked for a transfer off the Hanno. Washington handled all such requests, and denied none.

Paul felt shame, too, for putting these people through such a test, but it was a necessary test. Once the mission began, there'd be no turning back. If anyone didn't already believe the New Federation wanted them dead, they shouldn't have to wait until they were in the Zone to decide which was worse.

Washington came out of the office with a steaming coffee cup in his hand. Snowy white whiskers and hair framed his coal-black face and made him seem old. He was born near the Navy pilot school in Angola and grew up watching soldiers train. "Starting early today, Captain?"

"Couldn't sleep. How are things, Alex?"

"Coming along. Can we talk about personnel, Captain?" Washington's warm brown eyes reflected conflicting trust and suspicion. He'd surely discovered the pattern in the ship's roster, the common denominator. They'd been friends a long time and, in some ways, he was closer to Poluka than Aguire was.

"We'll talk later, Alex."

"Aye, Captain."

Poluka walked softly through the silent foyer, wondering how his friends would react when they learned the truth. Most would go along with it, he was sure. Aguire was the exception, the most important member of his team, and Poluka couldn't be sure.

Now, when he was exhausted and alone, he finally admitted to himself that he chose Aguire over G.J.'s objections because he needed him. He never could have kept the Livingston going without him. The Hanno will be even harder.

Poluka entered the bridge and found the viewport filled with the planet Earth. Someone had the ship turned to aim all the sensors at the coast of Brazil. In the I-bay Donno and Braun were playing with the cameras and had a crisp, 3-D image of topless women sunbathing on a tropical beach.

Donno spotted the Captain, and prodded the engineer. "The cameras are working, Chief. Let's check the radar."

"Uh-huh," Braun kept his eyes on the screen. "I've almost got the color adjusted."

"Ahem." Poluka made his presence known.

Chief Braun jabbed a button, and the screen went dark. "Right. Let's check the radar. Oh, Captain. Good morning. I didn't realize it was 0600 already."

"It's not, Chief. I couldn't sleep."

Poluka rather enjoyed Braun's discomfort, considering his role in this business with Elisa Santino. Braun had given his captain what amounted to an ultimatum to save a blackmailer, and probably didn't realize how close to death he'd come himself. The deciding factor had been what Santino could contribute to the conspiracy. The annoying little woman somehow hacked into the new government's blacklist, as well as secret files from the Attorney General's office, and the information proved invaluable.

"We'll have a meeting at 0800 hours," Poluka told Donno. "In the meantime, I will be in the gymnasium."

It was a long hike for a middle-aged, overweight skipper. He kept up a brisk pace with his gut sucked in the whole way. He'd already lost a couple of kilos thanks to some pills he was taking. His pants were getting loose around the middle but he was having trouble sleeping.

He didn't relish exercising with an audience and was thankful to find no one in the gym.

"Guess I'll start with the old biceps." He fiddled with the dial on a weight machine, setting it for thirty-five kilos, then wrapped his hands around the bar and lifted.

"Ooh! Better start lighter."

Resetting it to thirty kilos, he tried again. Then he reset it to twenty-five. Then twenty.

"Ah, that's better. I'll make it heavier tomorrow. One, uh, two, uh, three, uh...."

The gym door whooshed open and Aguire walked in. Poluka twisted the dial back up to thirty-five kilos and resumed lifting.

"Twenty-nine...thirty. Ah, Commander. This gym is great. I wish we'd had this on the Livingston. I'm so out of shape, I had to start with thirty-five kilos."

Aguire's expression was troubled.

"Something wrong, Commander?" Poluka asked.

"I went through the ship's roster last night."

He suspects. "Yes? Any problems?"

"It looks like the New Federation manned its newest and best starship with people they won't miss much if we don't survive the Zone."

Aguire was nothing if not direct, but this conversation was expected, sooner or later.

"Do you mean our imperious leaders think this will be a

suicide mission? Well, yes, they do. It was the only way I could get this ship and pick my own crew. Now, don't look so surprised. Think about it." He wiped the sweat from his face, and pointed at Aguire. "The New Federation doesn't want people like you, or me, or any of the other four thousand people on this ship. This New Federation loves people like Gary Fisher. We're all on the blacklist, and people, good people who have done nothing wrong, are being persecuted. You've seen it! You're not blind! People are being arrested. Some are executed—more than we hear about. I decided to let the government, with Admiral Fisher's unwitting help, reach their own conclusion about the Hanno, that this is a death ship, that the new engines will kill anyone who uses them. To make our deaths even more certain, I insisted our first mission be to the Zone."

"You tricked them into sending us to our deaths?"

"Precisely. Pretty clever, eh? You've discovered that the ship's design doesn't match the documents you saw at the Academy, which was an oversight that was not my job to correct. Don't worry, my old friend. This ship will take good care of us. She's as safe as any.

"What you've got to realize it that all of us are marked for death. They would kill us some other way if this wasn't so convenient and politically safe. We will simply disappear and there will be no one to blame."

Aguire's face was the very picture of amazement. "You couldn't let your friends in on it a little sooner? And what happens when we come back alive?"

Poluka would leave those questions for another time. Aguire wasn't denouncing his argument, but he wasn't applauding it either. For the first time Poluka truly feared that G.J. might be right about Aguire.

No, he could control Aguire until it was too late and the commander will have no choice but to go along with the plan. It was for the best.

"Our mission will take some time." Poluka told him. "A lot of things can happen before we see Earth again. Space is dangerous, so we might die anyway, somehow. Or, Batastia could die while we're gone—he's old, you know. Or, some other fate may await us.

"The point is we will not die at the hands of our own

government." He held up his palm in a gesture of denial. "Trust me. Your captain works in mysterious ways. As for the design discrepancies, we'll all get revised and *accurate* documents at today's meeting."

CHAPTER 19

Aguire first met Poluka during the Jupiter War in 2788. He'd always trusted him and always felt trusted. The Captain might manipulate the system with vague and misleading information, but never withhold anything from Aguire. It stung now to find that things were different.

He brought his list of design issues to the meeting but couldn't muster much enthusiasm for making suggestions. The New Fed's real expectations for this mission had him flustered, as did his captain's response to it.

Most of all, he couldn't get over Poluka keeping him in the dark.

As it turned out, G.J. Stokes was tied up with some business on Earth and had Lynda sit in for him at the meeting. She handled the minor issues by approving small changes to both equipment and procedures. When they got to bigger problems, G.J. joined the meeting through a video link from West Point, his grumpy face peering around the room from a screen on the wall.

Fifteen other officers attended the meeting but were mostly ignored while Poluka, Lynda, and G.J. Stokes ran through the list and came up with remedies, or temporary cures for what would later need some major reengineering.

One of the most vexing problems was transportation within the ship. One may go from deck to deck by elevator, but it was six and a half kilometers to get from the forward section to the engine section. G.J. said he'd put the issue on his hot list.

The old man seemed distracted and mentioned having some legal problems with his business empire, which meant nothing to Aguire who didn't know a stock from a bond and had no desire to learn. His attention began to drift.

The Captain asked Stokes, "Will this affect your plans to meet us at Alpha Virginus?"

"Perhaps. I could use someone with Lynda's training, but of course you need her there."

"Understood." Poluka's tone implied he'd just agreed to do something.

Aguire's attention returned to the conversation, and he wondered if he'd missed something.

Chapter 20

Elisa Santino landed at a small skyport in Upper Manhattan with Chief Braun and Bart Hanson. The skyport accepted the shuttle's fake transponder code as identification, and Braun used an I.D. card he'd picked up in the black market to rent a car.

They'd changed into civilian clothes to leave behind the beacon transmitters in their uniforms, and to blend in with the population of West Point. Hanson looked like a common laborer in khaki pants and a work shirt. Chief Braun wore baggy trousers and an old cowboy shirt. Elisa was in a peach-colored jumpsuit, and tied pigtails in her hair with pink ribbons. Standing next to Braun, she looked like a child with her grandfather.

It was a cool mid-afternoon. They drove to a small office near West Point, which was rented to someone who didn't exist. From there, Elisa Santino hacked into the government's most secret files.

The Attorney General was an idiot when it came to protecting computer files, but he was also an idiot at organizing them. It took some digging to figure out what Volk was doing.

Her pocket computer doubled as a com console to send an encrypted warning to G.J. Stokes that the Attorney General was suspicious about inconsistencies in the records concerning the starship construction. Volk also received reports that General Hebert, the rebel leader, was contacting dissidents on Earth. Just to be safe, Volk was going to have Stokes picked up and "dealt with" in case there was a connection. Captain Poluka would also be ordered to return to West Point for questioning in case he had any plans to join General Hebert.

Hanson waited quietly until Elisa finished before asking her to search for information on anyone named *Shepherd* who'd been arrested by the New Fed.

The blue-eye soldier didn't usually accompany her and Braun

down to the surface, but Poluka had wanted him there today.

"There's nothing," she said after checking.

"See if there's anything about a music teacher," Hanson suggested.

She punched in the search, quietly curious whether her muscular escort was a central figure in Poluka's conspiracy to topple the government, or just a pawn.

"Here's a note about a *piano* teacher," she told him. "A woman was picked up at the McConnell Spaceport last November. They found her when she used a public com to call her son. It doesn't say what her name was. I've noticed Volk avoids names in files that could become evidence."

"What happened to her?" Hanson asked. Elisa detected something in his voice, concern perhaps.

She scanned the file and did some cross-referencing.

"There's not much else. She was picked up for questioning," Elisa told him. She saw a hint of worry in his blue eyes as he looked at the report.

"What's this?" He pointed at a name.

"That's Volk's thug who made the report."

"He picked up Mrs. Shepherd?"

"Yeah, I guess so."

"See if you can find out more about him."

She'd only been guessing when she called him a thug. What she found convinced her she'd used too polite a term.

"It's not very explicit. Volk has people he refers to as 'security boys' who do a lot of traveling. Wherever they go, people disappear. This particular 'boy' has been with Volk for a long time, long before the coup. There's no employment code to show which department he works for. He has an apartment in West Point." She pointed at an address on the screen.

"Let's go." Hanson turned toward the door.

"Where?" Braun wondered. "You don't mean you're going to see this man? Look, Hanson, we're already in a dangerous spot. If they even find out we're on Earth, they'll drag us off and question us—literally—to death."

"You can wait in the car," Hanson sighed. "I just need one quick word with him. If anything goes wrong, you can go back to the ship, and I'll say that I came alone, okay?"

The address was a long building of narrow, two-story

apartments with doors on the street. Hanson parked on a side street and got out.

Elisa wasn't a soldier. In the Navy she was a medical tech, and had never even been in a war zone but she understood shipmate loyalty. She wasn't surprised when Braun spat, "Damn Hanson. He's being an asshole, but he's *our* asshole, and I've got to stick with him. You stay here, and run for it if anything goes wrong."

He pulled up the leg of his trousers to get out a pistol concealed in his boot, and stuck it in his pants pocket before stepping out of the car.

"I'm not waiting here." She got out on the other side, "He's my shipmate, too, and so are you."

This was clearly a stupid idea. The security man was a professional, a trained gun-for-hire. To even let him know they were interested in him could have catastrophic consequences.

They hurried around the corner and caught up with Hanson, who didn't say anything when they joined him. He knocked loudly on the door, which was jerked open almost immediately by a man who stood a head taller than Hanson and had a sadistic, twisted grin, as if his mouth couldn't decide if it should smile or frown. He pointed a plasma pistol at Hanson's face and ordered all three of them to get down on their knees.

Elisa knew she was about to die and if she had a moment longer she would try to run, but she didn't have that moment.

Hanson exploded forward into the apartment. Faster than her eyes could follow, his hands did a blurred dance across the man's body. The pistol disappeared from the man's hand and reappeared in Hanson's waistband as if by magic. The snapping sound of Hanson's sleeves whipping back and forth and the little ripples on the thug's clothes where Hanson's hands made contact.

For a couple of seconds Elisa didn't comprehend that the man was injured, and neither did he until he tried to punch Hanson but only got a slight movement from his right shoulder. His arms didn't work because they were broken in many places.

"Get in here," Hanson growled at Elisa and Braun. He closed the door after they stepped inside.

This security boy looked inhumanly tough and mean, but all that melted away as soon as he realized he was helpless. The blood drained from his face and he sagged against the wall.

Hanson grabbed him and set him on a sofa in the front room.

"What did you do to me?" He made a half-hearted attempt to sound angry before breaking down into sniffling sobs. "Don't kill me…please…don't kill me."

Braun drew his pistol and scurried off to search the apartment in case there was anyone else there. Elisa stayed near a window to keep an eye on the entrance. Hanson stood in front of the man and crossed his arms.

"Answer my questions," Hanson finally said to the whimpering thug.

The man had a sheen of sweat on his face and looked like he might pass out, but he nodded.

No further pain or threats were necessary to get everything the man knew. The whole episode was managed by Hanson while Elisa and Braun stood by like spectators.

"You arrested a woman named Shepherd last November?"

"Did I? I mean…yeah…I remember…at McConnell Spaceport."

"And her husband?" Hanson asked.

"Tried to…he killed one of my men…he was fast…stronger than we expected…had to shoot him."

Hanson uncrossed his arms. "Did he die?"

"Not right away. We took him to an interrogation cell where we had the woman."

"You didn't try to save him?"

The man grimaced and clenched his teeth. His breathing came in shallow gasps now.

"Answer me," Hanson said a bit louder.

"I called Volk…I guess you know he's my boss…and he said to put him with the woman so she could watch him die…said it would break her spirit and make her talk."

"He died?" Hanson asked in almost a whisper.

"Yeah, after a while. Then we questioned the woman, but she didn't have nothin' to say. It was another dead end. Oh, god, my arms hurt. Please…I need a doctor."

"What did you want her to say?"

"We're always lookin' for people, people that are against him."

"Him?

"Batastia. He's the one."

"What happened to the woman?"

"She's dead. We worked on her for two days, but she didn't know nothin'. We wanted to know if she was working for someone...someone who was trying to get rid of Batastia...like, maybe one of the Governors."

"What about the boy, the Shepherds' son?"

The man had a blank look for a moment before saying, "Oh, him. Couldn't find him. Maybe someone else got him, but I didn't. The house was empty. I watched for a couple of days. The kid never showed up."

"If someone else got him, where would he be now?"

"They got some place they take kids. I don't know nothin' about it. I swear, I don't."

"Who would know if they got him?"

"Uh...Volk, I guess. All of us who work for Volk ain't allowed to talk to each other about anything. I don't even know most of the other ones."

"What else can you tell me about the Shepherds?"

"Troublemakers...organizing a protest against the government. I dunno what else. I handle lots of cases. I hardly remember them. Please...it hurts real bad."

The man was glassy-eyed now. There was blood in his mouth and Elisa realized that he had other injuries besides his arms.

Hanson turned to Braun and Elisa. "Go to the car. I'll be there in a minute."

"What are you going to do?" Elisa's voice cracked. She was trembling.

"I'll do something for his pain," he answered quietly.

Braun put his arm around Elisa and led her out to the street. It was quiet and sunny. She felt like she might throw up. They got to the car and she saw Hanson was already coming.

"This was not part of the plan," Braun finally protested as they drove away. "Look, Hanson, I'm not going to grieve for that bastard, but you're exposing us to risk. Who are these Shepherd people you're looking for?"

"My aunt and uncle," he answered, and Elisa picked up an unexpected cry in his voice. He wasn't made of stone. "And there's still one more I need to find out about."

Just then her pocket computer chimed with a com link. It was Stokes. The old man asked Hanson to "take care of" the Attorney

General.

"I was just about to go see him anyway," Hanson replied. "It seems he's the only one who might know what happened to Michael."

A flicker of dread appeared in Stokes's green eyes. In a softer, more human tone, he asked, "Michael Shepherd?"

Elisa saw it in the old man's face. He wasn't stone either. Maybe Hanson was closer to Stokes than he was to Poluka. They both seemed concerned about these Shepherd people.

"Now we're going to question the Attorney General?" Braun asked after the com link to Stokes closed. "*The* Attorney General? At the Capitol? You can't just stroll in there for a chat with the evil son of a bitch."

"I'll bet you're wrong, but you should go back to the ship. I've got to pick up another spacecraft anyway that I want to take with us."

"I'm surprised you got away with stashing all those missiles on the Hanno," Braun said, accepting the change of subject. "What kind of spacecraft do you have laying around, a heavy-cruiser, maybe?"

"No, a light-cruiser. Poluka said I should knock out the orbital tracking system if things get ugly. Things are ugly, so I'll be shooting some satellites on the way back."

* * *

"I'll tell you," Braun admitted after dropping Hanson off near the Capitol, "this Hanson scares the shit out of me. We've got enough trouble without him going on some kind of personal rampage."

"I've been terrified for months," Elisa told him. "First it was Fisher, then the government goons, then Poluka and Stokes. You're the only one I could trust, because you're the only one who isn't convinced you've got a mandate from heaven. But this Hanson, I haven't figured him out yet."

Braun peered at her from under his bushy, gray eyebrows and asked, "If Poluka tells him to kill us, d'you think he'll refuse?"

She had a gift for reading people. Hanson wasn't going to kill them. He doesn't even enjoy killing. He just does it exceptionally well. She'd heard of him years ago but never believed the stories, until today.

"I think he chooses for himself."

"I hope you're right." Braun muttered. They drove into Manhattan.

For an instant, she felt guilty about using her sexual charms to involve Chief Braun in her problems, but quickly dismissed the guilt with the knowledge that her alternative was death.

Besides, it wasn't like the Chief wasn't getting something in return. He's a nice old guy, with the usual weaknesses and a slow, gentle way in bed. She'd been with worse. Without Braun, she never could have negotiated with Poluka to get assigned to the Hanno. If only he were rich.

She hacked into Alexei Volk's computer daily while still at the DDR, watching the blacklist grow as more people were added, and shrink when people were killed. The day her own name appeared, she knew there was nowhere else to go.

Assuming they survive the Zone, she'd say good-bye to Chief Braun at Alpha Virginus, catch a ride to Tau Ceti and find some rich man to use.

Chapter 21

"General Hebert doesn't stand a chance," Admiral Fisher repeated for the benefit of Prudence Rival, the most vocal and troublesome senator. He hated the old woman with every fiber of his being, but wore a mask of professionalism when he continued saying, "Every starship rumored to be under the general's command is inferior, obsolete, or just plain worn out. Our planetary defenses can detect any threat and deal with it instantly."

Senator Rival was interviewing Fisher today in the Capitol Building. It was another of her "fact finding" missions, which constantly annoyed the Batastia regime. The vice president would have ordered her assassination a long time ago if not for her overwhelming popularity among the masses who remembered Prudence Rival's heroic defiance of not only the old Fed, but even the Corporate State, some forty years ago when she was the "grenade girl" with the underground resistance.

"But, Admiral Fisher," Senator Rival asked, "if General Hebert's forces are so inadequate, why is he massing them as if for an attack?"

"Madam, the general is showboating. He hopes to attract funding, which is why we…the government… offer rewards for turning in any such supporters. If the risk is sufficient, no one will back him."

Senator Rival placed a hand on the thick document in front of her. "The general's record demonstrates that he is a brilliant strategist, Admiral. During the Jupiter War, he won battles with resources so small that no one considered him a threat."

"He was not fighting against the New Federation, ma'am. The only reason *I* am here, instead of a Navy specialist, is because I am the most qualified expert when it comes to starship capabilities, and it is my opinion that General Hebert's little fleet is not a threat against our military."

Prudence Rival raised her eyebrows, and glanced down at General Hebert's service record, her short gray hair clinging to her head like a helmet. She tilted her head slightly like a dog that was having trouble thinking, and opened her mouth to speak.

Woof! Fisher imagined with a straight face. The door flew open, startling Fisher. A brown-uniformed capitol guard rushed in holding a plasma rifle. From somewhere else in the capitol building the near-hysterical voice of Admiral Higgs was shouting, "Up here! Up here!"

"Sergeant, what's happening?" Fisher demanded.

The man answered, "Admiral Higgs wants you upstairs."

Senator Rival was escorted somewhere else while Fisher raced up the stairs to where the corridor was brimming with guards, weapons ready. A man in a silk suit with a pistol in his hand and miniature radio in his ear waved Admiral Fisher into the Attorney General's office.

Inside, Higgs and Crush Skor stood with their backs toward the door, facing Vice President Batastia, who was shifting his weight from foot to foot and gesticulating wildly with his hands. The murderous, unabated rage on Batastia's face chilled Fisher to the bone.

Higgs was babbling, "The killer must still be close at hand. I wasn't out of the office for more than five minutes. We must all take refuge immediately, sir."

"Here. Right here. How *dare* they!" Batastia snarled through clenched teeth. "There must be a traitor in our midst."

Higgs froze. Fisher was ready to fall to his knees and worship Batastia, if required. Behind Batastia, on Alexei Volk's beautiful mahogany desk was an object that was so out of place it took several seconds for Fisher to comprehend it.

It was a human head, not separated from its body by a blade, but rather torn off with some of the spine still attached. Fisher's lunch rose in his throat, and he swallowed it back down. It was Volk's head. The rest of the Attorney General was absent.

"Mister Vice President," Higgs pleaded. "Shouldn't you go to the bunker until the building is searched?"

"Traitors!" Batastia seethed. His eyes bulged unnaturally wide, but saw nothing. Saliva dribbled down his chin. "Traitors are everywhere."

Crush Score stepped forward, and gently found Batastia's elbow to guide him through the door and down the hall.

"Fisher!" Higgs barked when the vice president was gone. "It's about time you got here. There's a killer loose in the building, or at least there was."

Higgs glanced at the head, and quickly turned away from it. "You got a break after killing that strumpet you hired. Now it's payback time. Keep this quiet, and find out who's behind this assassination. I know you can do it. You know how all that computer shit works. Use our network to find out who's behind this...this horrible crime."

Fisher kept his eyes off the gory head. "Yes, Admiral. I will do anything for the vice president."

Higgs studied him for a moment. "Fisher, the vice president is very upset. You understand that, don't you?"

"Of course, sir."

"No, you don't. He's in one of his rages. If we don't find whoever did this, he will, and it could be anybody. Get it?"

Suddenly, he did. "Yes, sir."

Admiral Fisher begged the chief of capitol security for an armed escort to his waiting transport and fled back to New Wichita. He sat in the back with a pistol on his lap and kept an eye on his pilot. He stifled a whimper and reminded himself that Volk probably had lots of enemies. Fisher didn't have enemies—except perhaps Julie Klein's brother, who'd been demanding to see him, or some relatives of the other women he'd tortured, or the people who worked for him, or....

The whimper finally escaped his lips as he imagined any number of people who might want to kill him. The scariest by far was Vincent Batastia. He'd have to come up with a name—or several names—of suspects. But who?

Could it be? No! Not that monster? Fisher's fingers stabbed at the keys of his computer, tying in to the personnel computer on the Starship Hanno to verify that Bartholomew Hanson was still hundreds of thousands of kilometers away.

Yes, Hanson's personal beacon transmitter indicated he's still up there.

It must be General Hebert, then. Perhaps the threat of attack was real.

Or it could be the labor unions. They're always causing

trouble. Then again, it might be one of the continental governors. Some of them were capable of this sort of thing. Or it could be some corporate power. It might even be a group of primitives. They're getting screwed as much as anyone, and who knows what they're capable of.

He had a long list of suspects, and that was good for appeasing Batastia, but it was also bad because it would have to be a guess, and Fisher desperately wanted the real killer stopped before becoming a target himself.

He would begin his investigation right after visiting the Galactic Bank to set up his escape in case things didn't work out.

Better to be rich and alive in exile, than a dead patriot.

Chapter 22

Captain Poluka read the text message that G.J. Stokes sent from Earth: "I am looking into design issues and will have some answers within the next few hours."

It was a completely unnecessary statement that G.J. wouldn't have sent, unless it meant something else. The part that jumped out at Poluka was *within the next few hours*: a warning. Something was about to happen.

Poluka rushed down to the shuttle docks and asked the supervisor, "Any sign of our shuttle, Mister Townsend?"

"She's approaching now, Captain," Townsend answered, "and another vessel's heading our way, a light-cruiser with Mister Hanson at the controls. I wasn't aware that Hanson was a pilot."

"He's certified as a civilian pilot, Lieutenant, and that vessel is his personal property," Poluka said, hoping it was true. "I've given him permission to bring it aboard."

"Captain, when you asked me to let a shuttle go without any log entries, I went along with it because sometimes rules need to be bent, but I'm going to need some official paperwork if we're going to be carrying private spacecrafts for anyone who feels like—"

"Nonsense, Lieutenant," Poluka interrupted. "The Corps routinely allows officers to bring personal spacecrafts on starships."

"That was a long time ago, Captain." Townsend bristled with as much disapproval as he could squeeze into his British accent. "I'll need the safety inspection report and registration documents."

An alert flashed in Townsend's office as the shuttle approached. Townsend got on his controls, opened a dock for the shuttle, and then signaled Chief Braun to park it close to the bulkhead so the cruiser could share the same dock.

The dock closed and flooded with breathable air when both

vessels were parked inside.

G.J. emerged from the cruiser with Bart Hanson and spoke with Poluka while Braun, Santino, and Hanson changed back into their uniforms. Curiously, Hanson's hair was wet, as if he'd just showered, and Poluka noticed that he had changed into different civilian clothes. Even his shoes were not the ones he wore when he left the Hanno a few hours ago.

"Paul," G.J. asked, "how soon can we leave orbit?"

"Without causing a complete breakdown of discipline, in a couple of hours. What the hell's going on?"

"The government is panicking. I expect the Navy to go on alert within the next four or five hours. At the very least they'll have orders to detain us. They may even be ordered to destroy the Hanno."

"Shit," Poluka hissed. "Get to my quarters. Stay out of sight. I'll come as soon as I can."

He rushed back to the dock control center and set things in motion.

* * *

All along Main Street, Aguire saw hundreds of people who the government expected to die right on schedule.

He felt nauseous. *Relax, José.* He took a deep breath and entered the bridge.

Red lights were flashing. A young ensign was in the pilot's chair. An even less experienced ensign manned the navigator's station. Donno sat at the command desk, barking orders.

"Roll us to starboard. Acceleration to thirty gees."

"Donno, what are you doing?" Aguire sprang forward to check the status screen, and the two ensigns looked over their shoulders at him.

Donno shouted, "Eyes on your instruments! If you're distracted in a real emergency we could be killed."

The ensigns swiveled back to their duties. The status screen was yellow. It was just a drill.

"Donno, what's happening?"

"Captain's orders. We understaffed the bridge with newbies to practice an emergency bug-out."

"That's a military exercise."

"I guess the skipper's feeling kind of military today."

Aguire felt suddenly better. "Maybe that's all there is to it."

"What?"

Aguire lowered his voice. "Poluka's been, well, acting strange. I mean, he's been keeping things from us, which was normal back in the Navy. I think with all the changes he sort of misses the Navy. Past glories and all that."

"Middle-age syndrome or whatever it's called?"

Aguire nodded and sat in an observer chair by the back wall to watch the exercise.

Of course, Aguire had been upset over Poluka keeping him in the dark, but what the captain was trying to do was essentially a good thing. The current government wanted them all dead, and Poluka probably worked out some delightfully devious way to change their minds about it. That made sense. Aguire had just been too upset to see it. Poluka probably had a good reason for keeping the plan to himself. It had to be something like that.

The intercom at Aguire's elbow blinked and Poluka's round face appeared. "Captain to Commander Aguire."

"Aguire here."

"Commander, your report indicated that all secondary vessels were flight tested."

"Aye, sir. I supervised the tests myself."

"So the report stated. However, you seem to have overlooked one vessel. Please report to dock number one. Captain, out."

The screen went blank.

"Aye, sir." *What the hell?* Poluka was mistaken. All forty shuttles and the pinnace were flight tested.

The shuttles were Aguire's favorite part of the job. They represented the true purpose of the Exploration Corps, the hands-on exploration of alien worlds. If they only explore worlds through instruments and computers from a discreet distance, it would be knowledge without experience, trying to appreciate something without intimate contact, like seeing a beautiful woman but never approaching her. Aguire needed more. There are few thrills equal to setting foot on a virgin world. Maybe none.

He went to the upper entrance of shuttle dock. From the steel catwalk above the dock, Aguire saw Poluka and Lieutenant Townsend talking just outside the supervisor's office. The lights were on in the office, casting long shadows of the two men across shuttle number one.

"Sir," he announced his presence.

They looked up at him. Townsend was as cool and unflappable an Englishman as ever there was, but seemed relieved to see Aguire. No doubt Poluka was grilling him.

"Mister Aguire," Poluka said, "come down and get into a jumpsuit."

As Aguire approached, Poluka nodded to Townsend, who reached into the office, and flicked on the dock lights.

Out of the shadows a behemoth materialized, a 61 meter long vessel parked behind the shuttle.

Poluka beamed at Aguire's astonishment. "Behold our light-cruiser."

Across the bow of the near-light-speed vessel were big black letters: EL TORO.

It looked more like a *cucaracha* and was, in fact, based on the Navy NLS cruiser whose profile resembled the notorious insect. Like the Navy version, this model was sixteen meters tall and eighteen wide. It included the weapons systems that the Hanno's pinnace lacked.

Aguire liked the name. The bull had special significance in his culture.

"Captain?"

"She just arrived. I know how much you like a turn at the controls, and you had to watch everyone else have all the fun while the shuttles were tested."

"You saved this for me?" Aguire beamed back, "But what's it doing here?"

"It is a gift from the manufacturer. I didn't know about it myself until today. I guess they figure it will boost sales once it becomes known that we have one."

"Fantastic." Aguire's eyes swept the sleek monster. He slipped into the jumpsuit that Townsend handed him.

Aguire climbed through the bottom hatch and raced up the stairway to settle into the pilot's seat. He wouldn't mind sharing the privilege. Donno came to mind, but he was busy on the bridge. On the top right-hand corner of the instrument panel was the logo of the Quebec Spaceshuttle Corporation: a hawk drawn in the North American Indian style, reminding Aguire that Hanson grew up among the Indians who owned and operated the

Canadian company. Maybe Hanson would like to join him.

Out the window, he saw Poluka still harassing Townsend. Aguire switched on the two-way audio, and Townsend's voice filled the cockpit, "...not even your Mister Hanson can go for a joyride without authorization."

Poluka must have heard the audio click on. He held his hand up to interrupt Townsend, and looked up at Aguire.

"Captain," Aguire asked, "would it be all right if Ensign Hanson joined me?"

Townsend opened his mouth to say something, but Poluka cut him off. "Mister Hanson has other duties. You're wasting time, Commander. Prepare to launch."

The Captain hustled Townsend into the office and the launch procedure started, draining the dock of air before the outer doors opened. The green "go" light flashed on, and Aguire took El Toro out of the Hanno. The blue disc of the planet Earth filled his view.

His right forefinger found the thrust-interrupt button on the stick, and his forward acceleration ceased. Pulling back on the stick rolled the nose up and over until he was facing the Hanno. The craft was beautifully responsive. The Hanno looked like a steel wall with a row of shuttle doors stretching off to his left.

By the time he checked out the basic maneuvering capabilities such as turning and rolling, Aguire had drifted far enough from the Hanno to test the speed of the cruiser.

Within a minute he had El Toro up to twenty-seven kilometers per second. The inertia-compensator needed a slight adjustment, but that could wait.

"Let's see, orbiting at 56,000 kilometers from Earth." Aguire glanced at the instruments and estimated. "That should bring me back to the Hanno in just about two hours. Dinner time."

He switched on the artificial gravity, and made a quick scurry down through the lookout pit and back to the center body to check the air locks for fault lights. On the way, he turned the air circulators all the way up. On the way back, he turned them down again, and noted that they operated properly. Back in the instrument pit he clicked through all the diagnostics and had the results in about a minute.

The only glitch was a failure to link with the orbital tracking network, but the trouble was with the satellite system, not the cruiser.

* * *

Elisa Santino hurried to the captain's quarters, her short legs pumping hard to keep up with Chief Braun. She was numb from months of constant fear and stayed close to Luther Braun, who was her only comfort these days and sometimes seemed like the only decent man left. Hanson joined them on the way. Poluka came in right behind them.

G.J. Stokes was already there with his psycho-bitch daughter who looked like a green-eyed, plastic doll. Elisa figured out early that Lynda Stokes lived in a world of her own: daddy's little puppet. This should be interesting.

"Bart." The psycho-queen nodded a welcome to Hanson. He nodded back. His face was a mask.

Elisa never heard anyone call Hanson by his first name. *There's something between these two*, Elisa mused, too exhausted to care. She wanted to go back to the ship's laundry and do her job until they get to Alpha Virginus where she could finally go her own way.

"I got Aguire off the ship for a while," Poluka said to Stokes, then turned to Elisa. "You were still able to break into the network?"

"Yes, sir," she answered. "I copied everything. We took a quick look at what the attorney general was up to, and found that he planned to arrest Mister Stokes."

"Arrest Papa?" Lynda's eyes widened with indignation, ruining the doll illusion.

Elisa ignored Lynda. "Volk watched Stokes for years and knew something was going on, but he never figured out the truth. He suspected Stokes was supporting rebel groups ever since the New Fed took over. Yesterday, intelligence came in from the Capella System that General Hebert has ships gathering, possibly to attack Earth. Volk was worried that the Hanno might become one of those ships."

Poluka gritted his teeth. "Volk will have us executed just to be on the safe side."

"He intended to," Hanson finally spoke up, "but he's dead."

This was news to Elisa, but she wasn't surprised.

"Dead?" Poluka asked. "How?"

"My idea," G.J. Stokes admitted. "It'll slow them down on acting against us, and he was going to have to die sooner or later anyway."

Poluka suddenly threw his hands up. "Damn it! This could have been handled some other way."

Lynda looked at him reproachfully. "Paul, I'm sure that if my father thought it had to be done—"

"Someone has been killed," Poluka snapped at her. "It had *better* be the right thing, because even your father can't undo it if it isn't."

"It is the right thing," Hanson said. "I wouldn't have done it if I didn't believe that."

Poluka's eyes flicked to Hanson before returning his attention to Elisa. "You got into everything?"

"Like I said, Captain, I copied all the secrets I could find. You can study it in detail."

"Was there anything else of interest?"

"Julie Klein's brother is looking for Admiral Fisher. He's a big man with a quick temper, and he's already torn up a couple of government offices. When he finally catches up to him, I think he'll kill Fisher."

"I suppose that might be to our advantage, a sort of wild card. Is there any other significance?"

"Only if you care about what happened to Julie," Elisa sighed. "She was my friend."

"Yes, of course," Poluka said, not unkindly. "Well, I don't have time to explain our motives to you."

Lynda Stokes frowned at her, as if Elisa was something to be stepped on.

* * *

An orbital test for a shuttle usually takes longer, but El Toro had the advantage in acceleration. He was already half-way around the planet when Aguire finished the required tests, and was enjoying the view.

In space, the stars are always spectacular. Planets look better as you get closer and can see more detail. He rolled the spaceship over so he could look up at Indonesia. The dawn terminator was creeping across Asia. The sea was almost black on the night side, while the sunlit side was a cheery bright blue with wispy gray clouds splashed across the planet. Alaska would soon be in view near the pole, and the Americas.

His car was down there, in storage. He'd spent a year's pay on it.

Money…Hm. His whole mission advance was in the bank, just sitting there earning interest at a minuscule rate. Back on the Livingston, he had no cash and needed to borrow money every time they hit a friendly port. This time he'll take it with him. After all, it was looking like he may never be paid again.

The spaceport said that traffic was light and authorized a straight approach from the west with no delays. He found a landing pad conveniently close to the terminal. A quick jog through the building brought him to the spaceport's branch of the Galactic Bank.

The bank manager was suspicious when he wanted to close his account and take it all in cash, but complied after Aguire explained that he was shipping out on the Starship Hanno.

"Oh!" The manager shook her head sadly. "The ship that's going into the Zone."

He tried not to be annoyed about how people expected the Hanno to be a death ship.

On the way out, Aguire ran into Admiral Fisher who was even more pale than usual.

Fisher's eyes narrowed. "You're here. Why?"

"Good afternoon, Admiral. I came down to get some cash."

"Are you alone?" Fisher cast about nervously. "Hanson's on the Hanno, isn't he?"

"Yes, sir."

"Are you sure?"

"Yes, sir. Is something wrong?"

Fisher held his breath for a moment. "Yes, something is wrong. Something is very wrong. There's been a murder."

"A murder? Who?"

"The attorney general," Fisher whispered reverently. "Volk's head was found on his desk. I just got a message saying that the rest of his body was found in the drawers of the desk. If a killer can get in there, no one is safe."

"That's terrible, Admiral." Aguire suddenly remembered Townsend's strange remark about Hanson going for a joyride. "I should be going, sir."

Fisher nodded, and went into the bank. Aguire took off down the speedwalk.

It would take someone like Hanson to kill someone in the Capitol. Who else could move like the wrath of God?

Aguire climbed into the cruiser. Ten minutes later he was in orbit over the Atlantic Ocean.

Who else?

Aguire remembered seeing Brian Frazya's bones being snapped like twigs, and G.J. Stokes's comment came back to him: *"I could use someone with Lynda's training...."*

Maybe it wasn't her legal training he was referring to, but her fighting skill. Maybe Stokes was asking Captain Poluka to send Bart Hanson.

No, it couldn't be. Aguire shook his head, and smiled at his wild imagination.

The Hanno filled his view like a steel wall, and he parked El Toro where he started two hours earlier.

Chapter 23

Captain Poluka watched from the back of the bridge. Ensign Trimble navigated, and Ensign Hill was the pilot. Aguire came in quietly and sat with Poluka.

"How are they doing?" whispered Aguire.

"These are our youngest officers," Poluka said softly. "A couple more practice runs and I'd trust them to do it for real."

Aguire looked at Poluka's profile. The skipper looked good, leaner, and more energetic than he's been in years. Poluka wasn't behaving strangely by saving the lives of thousands of people who were condemned to death by paranoid politicians. That's just what Aguire expected from his mentor. He never should have doubted it.

Aguire signaled to Poluka that he wanted to talk to him outside. They slipped out to the foyer, where Aguire told him about meeting Admiral Fisher, and about Alexei Volk being murdered.

"Murdered?" Poluka asked. "How?"

"They only found Volk's head. The body was missing. Fisher seemed to think Bart Hanson was connected to it, somehow."

"They're already scared of us, scared of our loyalties, our potential. They'll assume that I sent Hanson if they can't find another suspect soon. They're already willing to send four thousand of us to our deaths just for being a possible risk. Now, I wouldn't be surprised if they simply order the Navy to destroy the Hanno with all hands." Poluka bowed his head, and cupped his hands over his face in a gesture of despair. "Maybe if I go down to Earth immediately for questioning, they'll spare everyone else."

"Captain, we can think of something." Aguire expected Poluka to snap out of it and make a decision, but the moment never came. Poluka just sighed and looked out the window at Earth.

"Captain?"

"Hm?"

"What should we do, sir?"

Poluka kept his face turned away. "Do? I'll go to my quarters, pack a bag, and return to Earth. You have command of the Hanno, my last ship." He waved a hand in a gesture of dismissal. "Go. See how my fine ensigns are doing on the bridge."

Aguire crossed the hushed foyer to the bridge. Helpless anticipation crept up his spine like a swarm of bugs. Poluka always found an idea to cheat death, but Poluka was out of ideas.

Henry Tran was in the I-Bay, producing simulated obstacles for the navigator. The pilot adjusted to every change without hesitation. Everyone performed perfectly this time.

"Mister Donno," Aguire said.

"Commander?"

"I'll take over now."

"Yes, sir."

"Take your position in the systems bay, and verify the Hanno is ready for departure."

"Aye, sir."

"Mister Tran, stand down the simulation and scan for real obstacles."

Ensigns Hill and Trimble sat up a bit straighter.

Looking at her tense back, Aguire recalled that Blossom Hill was a prodigy, excelling in all she attempted, and that her family was killed during the coup.

"Commander," Donno said. "We've got a maintenance team reentering from the aft OAC airlock."

"When will they be inside?"

"The supervisor says they'll be secure in one minute."

"One minute. Fine. Navigator, set a course for the Zone, except the start time will be in one minute."

"Aye, sir." The Navigator's fingers began a frenzied dance across his controls.

Donno said the maintenance crew was safely inside.

"Very good, Commander. Seal the ship. This is not a drill."

"Aye, sir," Donno responded after a barely perceptible hesitation. "Ship's sealed."

"Pilot, stand down the simulation. We are leaving orbit. This is not a drill."

Ensign Hill, the youngest officer on the ship, all but screamed,

"Aye, sir."

The status screen changed to red, and Aguire silently said *adiós* to the planet Earth.

Chapter 24

Lynda rearranged the clutter on Poluka's bookshelf in the captain's suite, frustrated that there was no logical order for the stuff he collected. Her father slouched at the computer, scrolling through sketchy news reports about a crisis in the Capitol.

"Papa," she finally asked, "will we have trouble getting through the Zone?"

"No," he said without hesitation. "The old permittivity drive starships were affected by the Orion cosmic dust cloud, making them go off course in random directions. The Himilco was the last ship to try it since the year 2760, and the robot probes sent later weren't very reliable. There's nothing eating ships out there. They just get lost."

"But the Himilco had tachyon engines, not permittivity drive," Lynda said, referring to the ship her brother was on ten years ago. "Why do you suppose they disappeared?"

Papa turned and looked closely at her. "Lynda, a million things could have happened. The Himilco was designed by amateurs and built from surplus junk. Paul's brother was a fine man, but Clifford wasn't really a spaceman. He was a diplomat, and he chose the wrong people to man his ship, criminals and mental cases."

"Like Gentry?" Lynda snapped at him with more venom than intended. "Cliff Poluka didn't pick people because they had problems. He picked people with exceptional qualifications. Papa, the crew wasn't a liability."

"Okay, Lynda," her father sighed. "But the ship was tiny and not well designed. We can't know what happened until we go and see if there are any clues."

Lynda left it at that. At least Papa stopped short of insisting that Gentry had to be dead.

For years she worked towards this moment, always certain she would one day find her brother Gentry. She was always certain about everything, but not anymore. Inside her, a cold fear and frustration was growing.

The door whooshed open, startling Lynda. Poluka entered with the other conspirators: Hanson, Braun, and Santino.

"We just left orbit." Poluka said.

"It's starting now?" Lynda asked.

"Aguire knows Volk was killed, and it worked to our advantage to convince him we had to go at once. He even thinks it was his idea."

"It's now or never," her father said. "They'll arrest us by this time tomorrow. They'd have seen through the deception months ago if it hadn't been for, uh, unplanned interference."

He meant Elisa Santino. Lynda looked at the tiny, mysterious woman with coal-black hair and large dark eyes. Elisa seemed tired, but steady and alert.

Before the crew was selected Chief Braun confronted them about the conspiracy and demanded protection for Elisa Santino. Lynda scrutinized the woman's records and found she had been a mediocre student until joining the Navy in '91, when she suddenly took off with academic success.

Last January when Lynda asked Poluka about Elisa Santino he said, "That slut screws her way to the top wherever she goes," which shocked Lynda, partly because Poluka put it so bluntly, but also because Lynda never before knew anyone described as a slut.

When asked about the Silver Star that Santino got three years ago, Poluka thought about it before saying, "Well, yes, there was that one time. The Livingston collided with debris from a wrecked freighter and no one else was small enough to squeeze through the damage. She risked her life to save my people. I recommended her for promotion."

The com console chimed repeatedly. Poluka looked at the screen. "Everyone knows we're moving. There'll be some low-level panic. I'll go to the bridge."

"I'll make the rounds," said Chief Braun. "Put out any fires before they spread."

"Good man. G.J., stay out of sight."

Lynda's father muttered irritably and continued perusing the news reports. Hanson stayed with him.

Lynda followed the others into the corridor, not sure what her function was. The Captain strode off without looking back. Braun and Santino hurried aft. Lynda followed them.

No, not *them*. Her.

Lynda needed to understand Elisa Santino. She waited until they left in the elevator, then took the next one down to the central deck and followed them at a distance, not sure what she was looking for, or why it was important.

There are other things I should be doing, she told herself, but refused to listen.

Everywhere they went, people scurried blindly until they saw Chief Braun. A smile and a word from him instantly restored order. He had a surprising effect even on seasoned officers, washing confusion away wherever he went.

The Chief went up to Infrastructure Control. Santino continued on to ship's laundry. Lynda crept in quietly behind her, and then to the side where she could observe unnoticed from behind a vertical air duct.

The laundry was the responsibility of a skinny, pale ensign with freckled skin and curly red hair, Ensign Braque. His record was unremarkable. He was on the blacklist because the Batastia regime feared revenge almost as much as political competition. Braque's father had been executed.

He stood atop a thousand-liter vat with his hands upraised, trying to calm a dozen babbling youths. Hammock-like bags of laundry swung impatiently behind him, halted in their automated motion.

"There's no cause for alarm," Braque shouted. "I spoke with Commander Donno, and there is no emergency."

His effect on the group was negligible. Elisa Santino came to him. The youths stopped talking, and looked to her expectantly.

Lynda frowned. Santino was no longer an officer, and the crew was ignoring the ensign.

The laundry staff was young, and harder to evaluate than officers who accumulated reams of records. This bunch of juvenile delinquents would not have even been considered, but the Hanno required more people than most space stations, and some jobs were simply too menial for seasoned spacemen. Working the laundry was one of them.

These kids ended up on the Hanno when Lynda used Santino's access to the New Fed's blacklist and found hundreds of eighteen and nineteen year olds who were marked for death because they were connected, by birth or association, to enemies of the state.

After that, their only qualification was wanting to be in the Corps, even if it meant working the laundry. Lots of people want a hitch in the Corps. Some just want to be explorers no matter what their rank. A few hoped that by demonstrating good service they would one day be recognized as officer material, and sometimes they were.

"What's going on, Santino?" someone asked.

Her smile brought out dimples beside her straight white teeth, making her look like a happy little girl.

An image of smiling girls wafted up from Lynda's memory, bringing with it a sense of loneliness. She pushed the memory away.

"We've been hijacked," Santino said.

It was an absurd statement, but what really annoyed Lynda was the cheering that erupted from the laundry staff. Ensign Braque gaped down at Santino with wide eyes and open mouth.

"Who's hijacking us?" someone called out.

"Commander Aguire."

A roar of laughter and clapping made the air duct vibrate merrily under Lynda's fingertips.

They really like her, Lynda thought.

Braque lost his footing, and landed butt-first on top of the vat, cracking the plastic housing. Water streamed out, soaking his pants.

"Lieutenant Braque," Santino cried out, "are you all right?"

"Santino," Braque gasped, "you can't be serious. Hijacked?"

"No, sir. I'm not." She helped him stand on the wet floor. "The mission has started, that's all. I just spoke with Poluka and everything's fine."

"You talked to the Captain?" A gruff Scottish accent bellowed from the entrance of the laundry. Lynda jumped slightly in surprise, but stayed where she was.

It was Luke McGee, an enormous, bristly-bearded lieutenant. He said, "I just tried to talk to Commander Aguire and he bit my head off for not going through the chain of command."

Santino turned her head sharply at the new voice, making her gleaming black hair fan out and drape elegantly over her shoulder.

"Hi, McGee. That just proves charm works better than size."

The crew fidgeted, not daring such familiarity with a lieutenant, but admiring Santino for it.

She's way out of line, Lynda thought. *She's not an officer anymore and probably should never have been one. Except for that one time out at the frontier, her records show nothing exceptional. She's just popular. Everyone likes her. They love her.*

Lynda's fingers tightened on an aluminum flange as that image of little girls flew by again, little girls who didn't want to play with her because she was different. The flange bent in her grip, groaning loudly. Suddenly, everybody was looking at her. She pulled her fingers out of the matching dents and stepped out into the gathering.

"Hi. I just came down to see if the, uh...if the manual shut-offs were still a problem."

Elisa nudged Braque in Lynda's direction and waved everyone back to work. "Come on people, we have work to do. The skipper's favorite golf shirt is here somewhere and he's made me personally responsible for it."

The underachievers broke up to perform their duties. Elisa pressed the large white button that started the hanging bags of laundry moving.

Braque showed Lynda the row of iron wheels, ten centimeters in diameter. "They're just too stiff, ma'am. If we get a leak, we won't be able to shut the water off."

Lynda reached out, impatiently gripping one of the wheels in the middle by the crossbars, twisted it closed, and then back open. "It seems fine to me."

Braque stammered something about not understanding, and tried the wheel himself while Lynda watched Elisa Santino checking the automated system separating uniforms from the bed sheets.

She fits right in. Wherever she goes, she fits in. It's not fair. Somehow, it's just not fair.

Lieutenant McGee tried turning the wheel with both hands, getting it to move slightly. Lynda hardly noticed.

Envy smoldered in Lynda's soul whenever a face lit up at Elisa's approach.

How does she do it? I have to know.

She didn't even realize she was walking towards Elisa until

McGee stepped in front of her and quietly said, "Miss Stokes, I heard what you did to Frazya back at McConnell. Let's not have any trouble here."

Behind McGee, Elisa stared wide-eyed at Lynda, like a small animal in the path of a train, too frightened to get off the tracks.

They think I'm crazy—like Gentry, Lynda thought, and an icy fury swelled within her.

"Get out of my way, Lieutenant."

"No, ma'am." He held up a hand, denying her passage.

Faster than sight, she slapped McGee's hand aside and her palm hit his chest, low enough to avoid damaging his heart, forcing air in his lungs to explode from his mouth.

He was surprised but recovered faster than most men would. McGee tried to speak, but gasped for breath instead. He still blocked her way.

Damn him!

Without any conscious decision she focused higher, where his heart was. Her hand flew out, too fast for McGee to stop or even see.

Another hand shot out from somewhere to her right, palm open, faster than sight, meeting her hand centimeters from McGee's chest and saving him from a ruptured pulmonary artery.

The impact of the two open palms was like a crack of thunder, making the laundry staff jump and cover their ears.

It was Bart Hanson. His fingers closed around her hand like a glove of steel. Even with her tremendous strength, she could not pull out of his grip, and they stood holding hands like a pair of sweethearts. McGee stared at the hands that appeared in front of him, becoming aware of how narrowly fate had spared him.

"Sorry to interrupt, Lieutenant," Hanson said to McGee. "Mind if I borrow Miss Stokes for a while?"

It was an ensign's request of a superior officer, intended to leave everyone with an impression of normalcy. Everything happened so fast, it might do some good.

He didn't wait to see McGee gratefully nod his assent, but pulled Lynda along, out the door and down the corridor to the elevator.

"Bart," she finally gasped, then sobbed, "Oh, Bart. I tried to kill him. I am so sorry."

"I know. You should be sorry. That's a good beginning. Come

with me."

She followed him into the elevator. "Where are we going?"

"To Arcturus." He deliberately misunderstood her question. "We're following your brother."

"Everyone thinks he's dead," she said miserably.

"You don't."

"Do you?"

"I think it's just as likely that he just can't get back here, or maybe once they found whatever is out there, they didn't want to come back. There're all kinds of possibilities."

"Not want to come back? And just leave us wondering? I can't believe that." She winced her head from side to side. "Why am I different, Bart? You know, don't you?"

"It's hereditary. Our families have The Gifts: strength, intelligence, speed. It happens. Your father isn't the only brilliant scientist. Others are born to be intellectual, too, or athletic. Your family got both, plus a mean streak a mile wide. Your father is mean in a non-violent way, but he is mean. You've seen it. Gentry was rebellious, a different kind of mean. You break bones, a rather basic kind of mean."

"No, I don't believe you. Why am I stronger than any man, except you and Gentry?"

"Gentry thought his grandfather was an alien."

"I know what Gentry thought, or said he thought. There has to be an explanation that at least makes sense."

Hanson glanced sharply at her, started to say something, but changed his mind.

She was six years old when they first met. He had been twenty-one, the age she was now. Her brother was thirteen back then and just beginning to develop The Gifts, so Papa invited Bart to help Gentry adjust to the change, by teaching special exercises, including martial arts for physical control, and dietary patterns to regulate mood, and how to hide it from the world.

Bart had also come five years later, to comfort her when Gentry disappeared in the Zone.

Lynda started getting The Gifts when she turned thirteen and Bart came again to California to help her adjust, too.

Lynda was quiet for a moment, then, "I'm not mean."

The elevator opened onto accommodation deck three. Lynda's VIP suite could be a comfortable home for a small family. Diagrams and schematics of the Hanno were tacked up over most of the walls with handwritten notes in red ink indicating design changes or things to look into. In a strangely artistic contrast, she had layers of rare, woven carpets covering the floors.

"Wow," Hanson whispered as they entered.

"What?"

"Nothing. If it's not meanness, what makes you violent?" Bart Hanson asked.

"I don't know. I just sort of lose control. I guess I feel persecuted for being different."

"Do you feel superior to other people?"

"Superior? I'm stronger and generally smarter in many fields. I guess I do feel superior sometimes. Is that wrong?"

"Yes."

Such a simple answer startled her. "I shouldn't take pride in my advantages?"

Hanson scowled. "No. Should a prince take pride in being royal? He did nothing to earn it."

Princes were of the fabled past, but Lynda was familiar with the analogy from the story-lessons Hanson used to tell her when she was a child. Parables, he called them.

"Well, I'm not a prince, or a princess either."

"Close enough. You were born into wealth and privilege. You've lived most of your life in seclusion. You care about your father—and your brother—but what about ordinary people? What about the person who sits next to you on a train?

"Does your feeling of superiority prevent you from respecting people, and caring about them? Does it keep you from loving them?"

"Loving?"

She sat down on the sofa, her eyes downcast. He was right.

Chapter 25

"Pilot, make the corrections, and increase velocity to point-five-cee," Aguire said when he was satisfied with the navigator's calculations. He wanted a straight-out trajectory for the quickest route out of the Solar System, and away from the New Federation.

"Aye, sir," Ensign Hill responded now with a dazed smile as she savored the experience of her first real maneuver with the giant ship.

Aguire scrolled through her personnel file and saw that Blossom Hill's mother had been a captain in the Army's Old Guard, which was mostly ceremonial, except on the day of the coup. Blossom Hill was her family's only survivor, and if those bloody bastards on Earth got their way she wouldn't even be that.

Donno appeared at Aguire's elbow. "Sir, all systems are up and running, except for laundry."

"Laundry's non-essential—strike that—everything's essential. What's the problem?"

"They've got a water spill. McGee's down there, and says he'll put things in order." Donno leaned closer and whispered, "Can I have a word with you, in private?"

Aguire glanced up at Donno's hazel-green eyes, and saw the concern, the questions. "Of course. Let's step into the Systems Bay."

Once around the bend in the S-Bay, Donno stopped and faced Aguire. He didn't have to ask, the question was obvious.

"I didn't exactly have orders," Aguire told him.

"No orders? Are you out of your mind?"

Aguire suppressed a grin. "Maybe. I'm sure that's how it'll look if we get caught."

"Caught doing what? What are we doing?"

Aguire was grateful that Donno said we instead of you. "If we don't go now, the Captain will be arrested, and probably killed, along with Hanson."

"Arrested for what?"

"Murder. Somebody killed Attorney General Volk, and Poluka will likely get blamed."

Donno whistled softly. "What does that make us?"

"Out of our minds, I think. I kind of like it."

"Eh? How's that?"

"You know how I keep getting rated as unimaginative every time my performance is reviewed. Well, I just broke through the creative thinking barrier."

"I don't follow you."

"Poluka set me up to do this. I was sitting here thinking 'oh my god, what have I done?' but knowing that it was the best decision I could make. Then I figured out that Poluka wanted this all along. He's a sneaky bastard sometimes, and he got me to think it was my own idea."

Captain Poluka's gruff bark interrupted the discussion. "Commander Aguire."

"Aye, sir." Aguire emerged from the S-Bay. Poluka was at the command desk. Everyone else sat rigid at their stations, feigning attention on their stations while focused on their superiors.

"Commander, this chair is to be occupied whenever the status screen is red."

"Aye, sir. The error is mine, sir."

Poluka was silent. The bridge began to relax.

Trimble's fingers were dancing again, sending new corrections to the pilot. He'd become distracted, and was trying to make up for it.

Aguire quietly suggested, "Don't overcorrect. We've a long way to go."

Trimble nodded and punched in corrections to his corrections, garbling the data completely. By the time Ensign Hill had the correct course, the Hanno was forty degrees off course, and trying to avoid traffic around the king-giant of the system, Jupiter.

"The Hanno is transiting a gravity well," Trimble called out. "Reducing velocity to 23.6 cee to prevent creating a space-ripple."

"Very well, Ensign." Poluka betrayed no satisfaction. He never gave praise for doing a job correctly; it would be like saying that less was acceptable.

Aguire glanced around the bridge. Lynda was there at the back wall with her father.

Poluka swiveled his chair around. "G.J., it seems you'll be coming with us after all."

The old scientist must have come aboard for a last look at his creation. Lynda had an odd look in her eyes, as if she'd been crying.

From Ganymede, Jupiter's principal moon and colony, traffic controllers sent their compliments to Captain Poluka. He gave a short reply.

"There's our destination," Poluka whispered hoarsely when the Hanno paused at the edge of the solar system, where the cosmic radiation stalemates the solar wind. He pointed at the shepherd constellation, Böotes.

Arcturus was an orange dot, slightly obscured by the cosmic dust which has troubled astronomers for the last 500 years. Ancient records suggest the cosmic cloud appeared at about the same time as the Great Disaster of the Twenty-Second century, fueling theories that a celestial collision may have caused both, or that the gigantic generators that supplied the entire planet Earth with electricity in the twenty-second century had somehow sent a beam of energy into this sector and blasted a planet into dust, while at the same time causing the fall of civilization on Earth. A few even theorized that an alien device had come from the galactic center at near-light-speed, creating the dust cloud before slamming into the Earth. There was no shortage of theories about the dust.

Aguire glanced at a status screen, the continuous, scrolling information that the master computer collected, sorted, screened and finally condensed into summary form. He asked the Captain, "When can we try new engines?"

"From the reports I've been getting, I assumed we were ready. Anything new?"

"There's a water spill down in laundry," Aguire said, and noticed Lynda hug herself and turn away with her head bowed. No doubt she was exhausted from dealing with all the minor malfunctions. "I'll handle it personally."

"Try to have everything in order by the time Donno finishes a ship-wide diagnostic. In the meantime, I'm going to the barbershop. I intend to be presentable when we get to Arcturus."

Aguire hustled down to deck four and found some water techs replacing the cracked housing of a bleaching vat. It looked like Ensign Braque had mopped up the mess with his ass, and his uniform was already losing color in places.

Aguire hurried back to the bridge, and met Poluka returning from the barbershop with a buzz-job that made his ears look big and his face like a chubby baby's.

The first-shift navigator and pilot were standing by. Chief Braun was in the I-Bay.

Donno announced, "All systems are error-free. No reports of trouble."

"Excellent." Poluka smiled. "Ensigns Trimble and Hill, you may take a break. Mister Burke, take the navigator's station. Miss Rodriguez, the pilot's station, please.

Trimble and Hill relinquished their posts, satisfied with today's work.

"Mister Donno." The Captain looked over his right shoulder at the S-Bay. "Close the windows."

Two massive armor plates outside the viewport slid from right and left to protect the Radglass with hundreds of tons of alloy. Donno reported that all ports to the outside were covered.

"Captain," Chief Braun said. "I'm picking up a group of small craft, about 200 class-three vessels, inbound from Centauri. They'll pass within a million klicks of the Hanno in about thirty seconds. Could be a caravan that's off course."

"Any distress beacon or other sign of trouble?"

"No, sir. Just commercial transponder codes."

"Good. G.J., will your engines endanger that caravan if we go now?"

"Possibly. I'd wait until they were four or five million kilometers away."

"Chief, how long before they're five million klicks away?"

"Um, ninety-two seconds from now."

"Navigator, enter a destination point just this side of the Zone, thirty-two light-years in the direction of Arcturus. Pilot, we go in two minutes."

Poluka got on the intercom. "Ladies and gentlemen, this is your captain. We will leave the Solar System in just under two minutes. Stand by for further announcements."

Time crawled by. When ten seconds were left, the pilot started counting backward. Aguire unconsciously braced himself. Even the most comfortable, slowpoke spaceliners experienced a noticeable jolt when crossing light speed, and these new engines were supposed to be impossibly more powerful than any other.

Aguire still harbored a splinter of fear about the new design. Stokes's equations employed symbols that Aguire had never seen before: degrees of infinity. Perhaps only Stokes really understood the math. Aguire didn't.

"...three...two...one...mark."

There was a slight sensation, a tickle in the gut. Nothing else. He exchanged glances with Donno, who shrugged and began checking his readouts.

"Should we try it again?" Aguire asked.

"Try what again?" Stokes whispered, and glided with smooth, fox-trot steps to the center of the bridge. "What is our position, navigator?"

John Burke swiveled around to face the captain. "This can't be right. The computer says we've moved thirty-two light years."

"Check the numbers, Ensign," Poluka ordered.

Stokes slapped his hands together in almost a gesture of prayer. "At last! I've done it."

"This can't be," Aguire insisted. Nothing Stokes had taught in the classroom even hinted that this was possible. "It takes weeks to go thirty-two light years."

"Not for the Hanno," Stokes's green eyes twinkled with delight.

"Position confirmed," the navigator gulped. "We're in the Zone."

The bridge crew turned in unison to look at Captain Poluka for leadership, for assurance, for anything.

"We're there? Already? In the Zone?" Captain Poluka looked back and forth between the navigator and G.J. Stokes.

"Of course," Stokes snapped impatiently. "I thought you, of all people, would have expected this. We've been over it a thousand times." He took a pen from his pocket and held it up in his right hand for everyone to see. "This pen is the Hanno, and my hand is the Solar System where we started."

He raised his other hand. "This hand is the Zone, our destination. When the engines were activated, our starting position and our destination became the same place, so far as the Hanno was concerned."

He brought his hands together, transferred the pen to his left hand, and then separated them again. "When the engines deactivated, the two places became distinctly different locations again, with the Hanno remaining at our destination. We are here," he held the pen higher, "in the Zone."

Poluka looked at the armor shield outside the viewport.

"Chief." He cleared his throat. "Chief Braun, what is outside?"

Braun didn't answer. He was hunched over his controls with his neck craning forward to study a monitor screen, his fingers sliding over the controls, making subtle adjustments.

"Braun!" Poluka roared.

The Chief's face snapped to the right, and he saw that people were waiting.

"Sorry. We're not exactly in the Zone, but it is just ahead, almost three light years away. It's safe to open the shields to look at it."

Poluka nodded to Donno, and the armor slid open. The stars of the constellation Böotes were closer but still recognizable as the shepherd. The red giant, Arcturus, was a rosy marble four light years away. Chief Braun pointed at a dot of grayness below and to the left of the star. "There's our hobgoblin."

Chapter 26

Lynda saw a gray smudge painted on a background of stars.

"What is it?" someone asked.

In response, Braun punched up a magnified image to the main screen of what looked like tangled ball of yarn, but was actually curved lines of individual specks, objects of various sizes in meandering trails forming a spherical shape. Lynda's brother Gentry must have had the same view ten years ago.

"An asteroid field," said Braun. "It's big, over 215 million kilometers wide."

Henry Tran, the I-bay supervisor, read the sensor analysis. "The spectrum says it's mostly iron. The largest are jagged, planet-size bodies. Most are smaller, trillions of rocks lined up in loops, probably aligned with magnetic flux lines. Everything's moving, slow at the edges, faster in the center."

Motion at the perimeter of the spherical region was too slow to be perceived but, closer to the center, trails of rocks slowly crisscrossed each other, snaking around a central point that was obscured by the density of the field.

"That explains it," Lynda heard herself say.

"Eh?" Papa turned to her. "Explains what?"

Everyone looked at her expectantly.

"Oh, I mean the Zone is actually a volume much larger than this asteroid field. For ships moving at faster than light speed, the gravity gradient of the field would be like a black hole, inescapable. Even if their original course would miss the field at sublight speed, the peculiarities of faster than light physics would cause any FTL vessel within, say, ten light-years to be pulled off course."

"Well, yes." Papa thought about it. "This thing is what...twelve light minutes wide? It must have the mass of a star."

"Ah." Braun got it. "So a ship can go from Earth to Alpha Virginus and never notice the gravity, but a ship that passes a little closer to this field, like from Earth to Arcturus, would be sucked right into it."

Lynda nodded but was thinking about Luther Braun now, the old man who stuck his neck out to save Elisa Santino even at the risk of his own life. She'd never really appreciated how magnanimous his gesture was.

Her own motives in this plot against the government were never so selfless. She only pretended to care about people who suffered under the new regime, and that she was doing it for them.

Since the first day Paul and Papa talked about uniting the colonies against the New Federation and replacing it with a true republic, Lynda's sole reason had nothing to do with anyone but herself. For her, it was always about finding Gentry.

She looked at Braun's aged face and, for once, admired someone not for what they could do, but for who they were.

She shrank back against the bulkhead, wishing she could melt into it. She'd almost murdered Lieutenant McGee with no more regard for the sanctity of his life than the government had for it.

I'm no better than anyone else, Lynda realized for the first time in her life, and began edging toward the exit, wanting only to hide.

"Lynda," Papa called. "Come and look at this data."

She dragged herself obediently into the I-bay. Papa moved aside, making Chief Braun back up out of his way.

"We need an *expert* opinion." His emphasis of the word 'expert' was an obvious attempt to denigrate the chief engineer's abilities.

Lynda scanned columns of numbers that accompanied the image. The Zone was nearly spherical. Obviously, there was something at work besides gravity and electromagnetic fields, otherwise the asteroids would have formed a disc, or simply collapsed together. In any case, it was a damn big field that was behaving strangely.

Sensors picked up random magnetic fluctuations characteristic of a space ripple, except these just kept coming without end. That must be what her father wanted her to see, so she could warn against moving closer at FTL, Papa's young daughter will figure it out before Braun, to embarrass the man.

"Nothing to say?" Papa smiled. "Mister Braun seems to think the instruments won't work because of a little magnetic noise." He smirked at Braun, and told Paul, "Captain, I think we can get under way using standard tachyon drive."

What? Lynda had it backwards. Braun spotted it, but her father had not.

"Papa, wait."

"What is it, Lynda?"

"He's right. The asteroids form a sphere, so there must be—"

"Pshaw! I thought you would know better. You disappoint me."

"G.J.," Paul asked. "Can we go, or not?"

"Yes, go." Papa insisted.

Paul gave the order and the stars ahead elongated into streaks of light as the Hanno accelerated, becoming infinitely long and winking out when the Hanno attained light-speed.

An alarm sounded.

The pilot called out, "Instruments are blind. Emergency shut-down."

The streaks reappeared and abruptly shrank back to points of light.

"What happened?" Poluka demanded.

Donno spoke up from the I-bay. "The Stokes Tubes aren't working."

Papa glared first at Braun, and then at Lynda before stomping into the I-bay to see for himself.

"Chief Braun," Paul spoke with renewed mastery of the situation, "when you've completed an investigation, we will examine the facts in my conference room. *Miss* Stokes will assist you."

"Aye, sir." Braun betrayed no passion. If her father had offended him, he absorbed it completely, and had no offense to return.

She assisted Chief Braun with deference, really meaning it when she called him *Chief,* hoping to make up for Papa's behavior.

Her father became an immobile obstacle. People work around him while he fumed in silence. Finally, he snorted and stamped out of the bridge. Even his absence was intimidating. Paul fidgeted for a while, and then followed him out. It was easier to work after that.

* * *

Captain Poluka joined the old tyrant in the captain's office, fully expecting G.J. to rant and carry on, demanding that Chief Braun be disciplined for knowing his business better than G.J. Stokes did.

"This is intolerable." G.J. shook his head. "Unthinkable."

"Now, see here, G.J.,—"

"She let me down."

"What?"

"Lynda saw it, and said nothing. She made me appear foolish."

The direction was unexpected but the attitude was consistent. He was still delegating blame. Small wonder his own son accepted a suicide mission rather than return to G.J.'s house.

"How can you blame anyone but yourself?" Poluka cried in exasperation.

"Me?" G.J. gaped at Poluka with genuine amazement.

"That's right. You just wanted Lynda to help you embarrass a fine engineer, and you can't handle it when it turns out Braun knows the instruments better than you do.

"You can't talk to me this way," G.J. growled back at him.

"This isn't one of your corporations. You can't fire me if I don't treat you like a god. You're not a god."

"I…I…" G.J.'s face burned crimson.

"I, I," Paul mimicked, "me, me, me. That's all that matters to you. Vincent Batastia may think he's the center of the universe, but at least he knows he's not the only one in it."

G.J. glared open-mouthed at Poluka, then dropped into a chair facing the window and stared out at the stars. His pouting face was reflected in the glass.

Poluka had said enough, maybe too much, but at least G.J. wasn't arguing.

A minute later, they joined the senior staff to review the data.

Chief Braun reported, "We launched some pixie probes to map the energies surrounding the ship. The magnetic environment acts like there are space ripples everywhere, and whatever's causing the phenomenon seems to be coming from the asteroid field."

"There's no visual distortion," G.J. pointed out.

"Right. There are no real space ripples, but the free hydrogen atoms floating out there, about one atom per three cubic meters of space, are in a state of random precession. When we scoop them up into the Stokes Tubes their vibrations still carry information about what's out there, but not the direction."

"Why not?" Aguire asked.

Lynda answered, "At FTL speed each tube captures about 100 million hydrogen atoms per second, and detects the vibrations left over from starlight photons brushing by them. Our instruments can usually average the ringing from the atoms and correct for any fields that have affected all the atoms. Then it's simple to put the vibrations in order and reconstruct the light that got the vibrations started, but here in the Zone each atom has been affected separately. The averaged data cancels itself out. All we get is noise."

"So we can't extrapolate an image of the star patterns," Chief Braun continued, "not at FTL speed."

"What if we do it the old-fashioned way?" Poluka asked. "Just point the Hanno in the right direction and calculate how long it will take to get there."

G.J. Stokes shook head. "We don't know yet what kind of forces we're up against, and I'm afraid any motion at faster than light speed could be catastrophic. We could go a long way, no telling how far, in an instant. It's a new thing that's never been thought of or studied."

Poluka sighed, "We're stuck until we figure out how to move the Hanno."

"We must find out more about the asteroid field, perhaps even go into it."

"At near-light-speed," Poluka said. "It will take years just to get there."

G.J. pouted. "Well, it's a risk, but we might try several short jumps, checking our position and course between each one. We would have to go very slow, no faster than five times light speed. It'll take over 200 days to reach the asteroid field."

Poluka checked the faces around the table. Everyone was nodding, except Aguire who was looking down with his eyebrows knit together as if reading some fascinating message on the table.

"Mister Aguire, are you with us?"

Aguire leaned back and lifted his eyes from the table. "I'm wondering about another possibility."

"Yes?"

"A message pod can travel at 750 times light speed."

"If pushed to the limit, perhaps." Poluka wondered where this was leading. "So?"

"If we launch a pod towards the asteroid field, it will be drawn to it, right? And not go off course?"

G.J. nodded but said nothing.

"And if we follow close enough we can detect the frame-dragging of space, right?"

Poluka cocked an eyebrow at Stokes. "Well?"

G.J. stared at the ceiling, snapping his fingers and visualizing the idea. "The pod would produce a wake, like a long, narrow funnel that we would be following in. Inside the funnel, space will be distorted. We would still detect nothing, unless we get too close to the sides of the funnel, but that could be our guide. Yes, it should work."

"But how will we know when to stop?" Lynda wondered.

Aguire smiled. "Pods are cheap in light of the alternative. When the pod crashes into the field, we'll know it."

"And then we will crash, too," Poluka added, "if we don't stop immediately. Let's try it."

Chapter 27

Bartholomew Hanson scrolled through the report on his info-screen which included some nonsense about following the wake of a message pod. Just more technocrap.

Hanson didn't know, or want to know, about such things. He did however note the use of phrases like *best estimate*, *in all likelihood*, and the ever fearful *probably*. All indicators that whoever was in charge didn't know much more than Hanson did.

No sense in worrying though. He could do nothing to improve the situation outside of his quarters, so he set about the task of improving the inside of his quarters.

Before leaving Earth, Lynda Stokes let him choose from all her exotic carpets one for his quarters on the Hanno: a gift from his one-time student. He'd been practical about it, ignoring the patterns and selecting one that matched his floor-space perfectly. It was made in Afghanistan, hand woven in some forgotten village before the Great Disaster. The colors were dark, giving his quarters a more homey, less institutional atmosphere.

Junior officer's accommodations on the Hanno consisted of two fairly large rooms, totaling twenty-five square meters— over eight times the size of his prison cell on Callisto, He always seemed to judge the size of a room based on that cell. Couldn't help it, really.

The occasional visitors he entertained over the years thought it perfectly expected to find ancient pistols, swords, and bits of armor decorating his walls. What did surprise them were the religious artifacts like icons, ceremonial objects, and literature. Some were mildly surprised that he could read.

Why shouldn't he have such interests? He was an executioner, and sometimes soldier, not some mindless, brutal murderer!

His adopted father would understand. Hanson pulled a small, framed photograph from a packing box and ran his fingers over the weathered face in the picture, brushing away imaginary dust.

His dad looked serious—always looked serious—until you saw his eyes; humorous, mischievous eyes; eyes full of joy. He was a North American Indian named Peter Angry-Cloud. After becoming a priest, everyone called him Father Peter, except his wife, Anastasia, who had a treasury of nicknames for him that varied depending on her mood.

Hanson unpacked another picture that showed the three of them together; Father Peter dressed in the black cloth of priesthood; his young Russian bride wearing a flowery print dress; and a sad looking, thirteen-year-old boy of alien ancestry. He arranged the pictures on his desk and softly chuckled, "No wonder I'm so screwed up."

Peter and Anastasia had been neighbors and close friends of his birth parents. Peter was attending seminary and got Bart interested in this religion of Earthmen. Everyone had been surprised when eight-year-old Bart asked if he could be baptized. His natural parents wrestled with the idea of letting their son join the Orthodox Church which seemed so alien to them. Eventually they realized that they liked their neighbors, and their neighbors all went to church—so, how bad could it be?

Peter and Anastasia consented to be Bart's godparents, which was why they ended up getting custody of Bart after his own parents were killed. With a name like Bartholomew Hanson, even his adopted parents assumed his lineage was from northern Europe.

He found his photo album and leafed through it, pausing at a picture of his birth parents. Their eyes were as blue as his own. One day he would frame it, too.

Next to come out of the box was a bundle of cloth. "Oh, yeah. I know where I want this."

Just then the pinging of his doorbell announced his first visitor, Captain Poluka.

"Hello, Bart." Poluka twitched a brief smile. "I hope I'm not disturbing you."

"Not at all, sir." He noted that Poluka addressed him informally; something was bothering the captain. He held up the limp cloth to show the woven picture. "In fact, I need a second opinion on where to hang this."

"Very nice. Needs good lighting. Oh, you'll be delighted to

learn that G.J.'s new engines are a success. Any outpost in the Federation can now be reached in minutes instead of months. I think this completely justifies keeping the Hanno out of the wrong hands."

"And in the right hands?"

Poluka's breathing changed rhythm slightly. "It *is* a lot of power, having exclusive control of the technology to gather news from worlds hundreds of light years distant, and then implement immediate reaction anywhere in the galaxy while everyone else has to wait months or years. We must stand by our principles. Temptation to misuse power is always great, but in the hands of someone like Vincent Batastia, temptation is mistaken for a mandate." He took a corner of the tapestry, and held it up to the wall. "What is this picture?"

"It's a scene from the twenty-fifth century, Saint Douglas the Peacemaker."

"I remember. He persuaded the European states to join Russia in building railroads when the dark years were ending."

"A turning point in history," said Hanson.

"Yes. People don't think much about history. Did I ever tell you how my family got the name Poluka?"

"Remind me." With gentle tugs on the cloth, Hanson maneuvered his captain to the wall where he'd already decided to hang the tapestry.

"It was in the dark years after the Great Disaster," Poluka recalled. "People gathered at a place called…what was it, Fort Lauderdale? I think that was it. Well, it doesn't matter—just a place where there used to be a city.

"The people selected a leader and dubbed him the Big Poluka, after some sort of local slang word. Nobody remembers what it originally meant. For hundreds of years the office was held by mostly members of one family until Florida joined the South-East Confederacy in the year 2506. By that time, my family went by the name Poluka."

"A family of leaders." Hanson nodded while holding up his end of the tapestry to the wall. "No wonder your brother was such a good diplomat."

"Yes. Did I mention that we may actually find him alive? His ship, the Himilco, had a Stokes Tube. So, they must have known something was affecting their course and had time enough to figure out the danger."

"Oh? Then Lynda may find her brother, too. You must be very happy."

Poluka held his end of the tapestry. "Yes, indeed. It'll be the most wonderful moment of my life if we ever meet again. You know, Clifford predicted the coup. He was always good at foreseeing political events. He even gave me a notebook full of his predictions and, um, suggestions on what to do about them."

Hanson looked closely at the captain. "A notebook telling you the future?"

"Predictions. Some never happened, but...."

"But some did. Next best thing to time travel. So, that's your secret. You knew the future."

"I wouldn't go so far. There were always things he couldn't anticipate, like this ship, or meeting you on Callisto."

"But he foresaw the overthrow of the government."

"Yes."

Here was the trouble, Poluka's sore spot. Bart asked, "Did he have any suggestions about what you should do now, after the coup?"

"How are you going to fasten this to the wall?"

Hanson overlooked Poluka's evasion, and pulled two bulkhead hooks from his pocket, the small magnetic kind intended for hanging temporary bulletin boards, but more commonly used for pictures and mirrors.

He snapped one hook onto the wall, hung his end of the tapestry on it and handed the other hook to Poluka, who gently pulled the cloth flat against the wall before selecting the spot for the other hook. "Clifford wrote that one military leader would defy the overthrow and eventually have enough support to challenge the new rule, and win. He gave lots of reasons why it had to work out this way, and why the next overthrow would be the most important."

"He wanted you to support this leader? Would that be General Hebert?"

"It seems so." Poluka said, and hung the other corner of the tapestry on the hook.

"And now you're here, instead of with General Hebert."

Poluka pressed his lips together and nodded. "Cliff didn't know about the Hanno. Surely, he would have seen that our plan can also bring about the next overthrow."

"It's been ten years. His notes were supposed to be a tool for you to use with you own judgment, not strings controlling your every action."

"No, certainly not. Well, this tapestry looks fine here. I should be going."

Captain Poluka went to the door.

Hanson asked, "What was your family called before the Great Disaster?"

Poluka froze, thinking. "I don't think I ever heard."

Then he was gone.

Hanson opened another box and found the carved stone he'd picked up in South America. It weighed thirty-seven kilos and was supposed to be a genuine Inca artifact, but one could never be sure. He carefully set the massive relic on the floor.

The *ping-ping-ping* of the doorbell broke his thoughts. It was G.J. Stokes. At first G.J. said nothing, but strolled about from wall to wall looking at everything, with his hands clasped behind his back. An inspection. After all these years, Hanson still felt like he needed approval from the pitiful old man.

And he did pity him, now that he understood the half-alien scientist, but the perpetually suspicious scrutiny still made Hanson feel as though he'd overlooked some damning evidence of imperfection that G.J. would spot immediately.

"Lynda fits right in with the hired help," G.J. said.

"It's always been difficult for her. We should be happy."

G.J. gave him a baleful glare. "Oh, yes. I'm thrilled that she'll turn into another Chief Braun, instead of following in my footsteps. She'll have a fine career following the orders of dolts like Paul Poluka, instead of wasting her time unraveling the secrets of the universe like her father."

G.J. stooped down to pluck the Inca stone from the floor, held it in one hand and turned it this way and that, to see all sides. He rarely displayed the super-human strength which, to the best of Hanson's knowledge, only eighteen people on Earth ever had.

Lynda was never told that she was part alien except by her brother Gentry, but he was labeled insane, labeled by their father to destroy his son's credibility.

"What is this thing?" G.J. asked.

"It's a relic of another civilization." Hanson took hold of the stone with one hand and felt a moment of resistance before the pitiful one decided to release it. "Natives of South America carved these holes over a thousand years ago, and used it to map the stars."

"Oh, yes. Primitive fortune telling. I've heard of it."

G.J. Stokes was the master of several schools of knowledge. This was not one of them.

"Actually, their studies were very scientific."

The old man wasn't listening. He gazed at the twenty-fifth century tapestry with the embroidered Greek letters. "Here's more of the same. This fellow was probably one of their fortune tellers."

"Right."

"Lynda isn't speaking to me."

"How's that?"

"Hasn't said a word to me since that business with Chief Braun yesterday."

"Maybe she's waiting for *you* to say something."

"Has she said anything to *you?*"

"Not since we left Earth." Hanson stretched the truth a bit and laid the stone in a corner.

G.J. continued browsing about the room. "She's mad at me, like Gentry was. If my son alive, he'll probably still blame me for that business with the mental hospital. He never could see things my way. He would have ruined all of us, including you, too. Our advantages won't help if there's nowhere to go. Now, with the Hanno, we have a chance."

"A chance to be with people like us?"

"Exactly."

"People with the same advantages as us."

"Yes."

"Then our advantages won't be advantages any more. We will be the same as them."

G.J. made no sign that he was listening. Hanson abhorred the way he could refuse to hear.

"You should have told Gentry about us," Hanson said.

"I saw no need, and later I didn't want to confirm his belief."

The old man began pacing, waving clenched fists to emphasize each word. "He would have told everyone that an Erosian spaceship was lying under the mud at the bottom of the

Pacific Ocean, and then none of us would ever know freedom again. Oh, he imagined other outcomes, but I knew. We would be studied and questioned and tested for the rest of our lives. But would he ever see it? No! He always thought only of himself, his little personal problems. He thought his strength and intelligence was a curse instead of a great gift. I used mine like my father before me did. Why couldn't Gentry? Because he was a selfish child."

G.J.'s face turned red, and the veins in his temples were visibly throbbing.

Hanson started to be concerned. "G.J., calm down."

"Calm down? He probably hates me. After all these years…he…he probably….oh, I don't feel well." His hand reached out, searching for something to lean on.

"You don't look so good, either." Hanson shoved a chair under the old man, whose breath came in shallow gasps now. "Here, sit down. I'll call for a medic."

The young crewman whose face appeared on the com-screen asked if this was a medical emergency, then glanced down to see where the call was coming from.

"Yes," Hanson answered. "Send a medic immediately."

The young man stared out of the screen, "You're Hanson?"

"That's right. Send a medic."

"Did you kill someone?"

"No, damn it. Doctor Stokes is sick. Send a medic."

G.J. rasped, "Bart."

Hanson hit the mute button. "Yes, I'm here."

"I'm getting old, Bart. I don't know what our life span normally is. I don't even know how old my father was when he died."

"Do you think you're dying?"

"Everyone dies. Listen, will you watch out for Lynda—if I die?"

"If she'll let me."

"If you don't find Gentry alive, and you don't find our people, take her back to Earth." Stokes coughed twice. "And don't let her marry an idiot."

"If you're going to die, there's something you should tell me first."

Hanson knew more about Erosian health than G.J. did. The

old man wasn't dying, but it was a once in a lifetime chance to get some information. G.J. always had control, and Hanson's parents didn't explain their relationship to the Stokes family before they died.

"Tell me about our families."

"I told you before. Your grandparents were subordinates to my father, on the Erosian ship."

"But who were they? Why did they go to Earth?"

"So!" G.J. tried to laugh, but coughed up phlegm instead, "You're just like Gentry after all. Obsessed with your ancestry."

"You're the one who spent a fortune to get back to our people. I'm not being unreasonable."

"You are!"

"I'll persuade Lynda to marry Chief Braun. You'll have a litter of Chief Brauns as grandchildren."

"Bastard!"

"Tell me."

G.J. muttered profanities and pouted before saying, "All right, I'll tell you. I don't know. My father never told me about why they were on the ship. Your people didn't take orders from him. I think they didn't like him. I know *he* didn't like *them*. He resented them for not wanting to go back. They wouldn't help him build the starship he wanted. That's all I know."

"All this time you've treated me like my family owed you something, just to control me?"

"You're one of us. I couldn't have you just fade away, and become too…too…"

"Too comfortable? Too human for you to use the way you use everybody else?"

Hanson regretted that last remark when he noticed G.J.'s veins throbbing again, but two medics arrived a moment later with a stretcher. They did a quick once-over exam, put G.J. on the stretcher, and rushed him to the medical flatbed truck in the corridor.

Hanson thought they were a bit rough with the old man, and said so. They became instantly gentler, and he realized they were hurrying because they were afraid to be near him.

He watched the flatbed crawl down the corridor. It would need to go half a kilometer to find an elevator big enough to take the vehicle down to Main Street. The driver honked the horn, flashed the lights, and shouted to get the pedestrians to press against the walls and let them pass.

He retreated into his quarters and shut the door. Perhaps he should have gone with Doctor Stokes.

No, the old man would rest easier without him and, despite the alien advantages of strength, speed, and intelligence, Earth medicine worked for them just as it did for Earthmen.

Lynda and her brother were born on Earth, and no doctor ever suspected that they were one-quarter alien. G.J. was half-alien, and Hanson was one-hundred-percent, born on Earth, examined by Earth doctors, and no clue ever appeared that they were anything but human.

G.J. would be fine in the Med Center.

It was curious though. Perhaps the biological differences were too subtle to make anyone suspicious, or maybe Earth medicine wasn't advanced enough. It is said that the art of medicine was very advanced before the Great Disaster, more than it is today. Knowledge of that sort almost disappeared completely, until about 200 years ago when a war provided doctors an opportunity to learn about human physiology and scientific methods advanced enough to do something with their observations. Even so, what was lost in the Great Disaster was lost forever. They may have had capabilities in the twenty-second century that the twenty-eighth century can't even imagine.

Chapter 28

By 0800 hours the whole senior staff jammed into the bridge to watch the unprecedented maneuver. If it worked, they'd be making history—not *too* unusual for an Exploration Corps starship—but if it didn't, they'd just be another spacecraft that disappeared in the Zone.

Commander Aguire piloted the Hanno on this occasion. The computer could handle the steering more precisely, but could not make the split-second decisions about ambiguous data streaming in from the detectors. The message pod, just a speck on the radar, accelerated towards light speed. The Hanno matched its speed automatically until crossing over to FTL speed, and then Aguire took manual control and kept the ship within the long narrow funnel of distorted space trailing the pod, matching the pod's velocity.

Aguire's awareness of the bridge faded as he focused on the front screen. A blinking orange dot in the center indicated the pod was still there. Flowing spider webs represented the changing space curves that were so critical at faster-than-light. Information came through his eyes to some primal part of his brain where reactions were born of hunter-warrior instinct rather than educated thought.

It seemed an hour, but in reality the whole operation took about a minute and a half. He slammed the ship back into normal space-time a quarter-second after the pod's signal vanished. He took a shuddering breath. His hand wiped his brow and felt dampness. Then, the other officers began breathing again.

The plan worked. The Hanno followed a simple message pod until it collided with the first asteroid it encountered. Actually, that's not how FTL physics works; there is never a collision with objects at FTL, but rather with the change in the space-curve gradient when the object ahead is massive enough. Same result though, the pod made a catastrophic return to normal space, saving the Hanno by its sacrifice.

"Well done, José!" Poluka cried, gripping Aguire's shoulders from behind with out-of-character familiarity. Aguire grinned until his face hurt as the rest of staff joined in a chorus of congratulations.

He felt like he was glowing from his victory over the Zone as he slipped out of the pilot's chair and Maria Rodriguez took the job of holding position relative to the asteroid field.

Lynda hugged him and G.J. Stokes gave him a sincere "Good work, Commander."

There were some ooh's and ahh's when the asteroid field appeared in the view port. They had seen the Zone using the ship's telescopes, which could do an excellent survey of dust particles from a million kilometers away, so an asteroid field the size of a small star system gave them no trouble, but there was nothing like seeing it with the naked eye.

Henry Tran announced, "The nearest object is 290 million klicks ahead and there's nothing coming our way."

The field filled about fifty degrees of view and was sparsely populated except in the middle where rocks were concentrated and the serpentine trails were more obvious. The center of the maelstrom was completely obscured by smaller rocks and dust.

Braun and Tran started a new survey but Aguire couldn't sit still and was glad when Lynda announced she had an idea that required them to go to the engine section.

He took a brisk walk down Main Street with Lynda who, like himself, was excited and tireless. The combined speed of the moving walkway and their own energetic pace made the midship fly by like surreal scenery. They reached the engine section in half an hour with congratulations and thumbs-up signs from his shipmates all along the way. It was one of those rare days when everything was just perfect.

Even Lynda seemed different, warmer, more animated. She was smiling. That in itself was an improvement. She explained her idea about the field limiters as they walked.

"The curve of space," she told him, "varies depending on local gravity sources, and is usually dealt with by the navigation instruments. But in the Zone the instruments are blind, so why not let the engines' own gradient compensators figure out how to keep from being sucked into the asteroid field? The problem is that the field limiters, which protect the crew from the effects of the engines, also shield the compensators. We'll find a new place to mount the compensators, and with a minor software change, we can use standard tachyon drive inside the Zone for FTL speed."

By the time they were into pressure suits and through the airlock he had a pretty good idea of what she had in mind. It sounded simple enough. After floating around the engines for a half hour they came up with a workable plan, got approval from the Captain and Lynda's father, then coordinated with Donno to have some techs do the work.

The techs, five experienced noncoms who knew their business, got the point of the refit and started working without any further direction. Lynda felt nauseous from the zero-G environment and left for her quarters while Aguire went to the nearest cafeteria to get a quick bite.

The lunch crowd was mostly from infrastructure groups and medical personnel, both of which Aguire hadn't interacted with much lately. He made a mental note to eat at the aft cafeteria more often. A glance at the info-screen told him a standard perimeter survey was already underway; they would make three orthogonal circles around the asteroid field to see what they could find.

He joined Doctor Jayne Payne at a table, and chatted with her while waiting for his sandwich. They had a steamy fling together after the war which neither regretted, but each had moved on and put it behind them. She was a few years older than he, and had taught him a lot about how to physically please a woman. She had a face like a Greek goddess, silky brown hair, and boobs a little too big for her slender body. Her sexual appetite was endless but, like Aguire, she didn't allow it to affect her career.

"Been a long time, José," her deep, sultry voice purred. "I haven't been back to Mars since we got kicked off the planet."

"Martians don't appreciate a good party, I guess," Aguire answered quietly.

"Did you come down here just to have lunch with me, or are you hiding from Maria?"

"Maria?"

"Lieutenant Rodriguez," Jayne did a little body-twist that jiggled her boobs slightly to imitate the lieutenant's habit of making her chest noticed by the men she was interested in.

Aguire smiled. "I have nothing against her, but I'm not interested otherwise. She needs to find someone else."

"She will. I've known her a long time, but what about you? Is there someone you are interested in?"

He almost shook his head, but had to think about it. Jayne noted the pensive expression.

There was a change in the ambience of the cafeteria: something subtle about the background chatter. They followed everyone else's eyes to an announcement on the info-screen—something about another ship being close by.

* * *

Lynda arrived on the bridge just when they found it.

"I'll be damned." Braun's voice cracked to a higher octave. It was a gleeful sound, the joy of discovery. "There's a ship out there!"

Then the import of Braun's statement hit her. It must be the Himilco. *Gentry!*

She turned to Poluka, her green eyes shining with triumphal joy but saw only poisonous dread on his face, and the implication sank in. If the Himilco was stranded here for ten years there would be no survivors. Her eyes jerked back to the screen.

It mustn't be the Himilco. It must not be.

"I've never seen anything like it," Donno said. "It's a disk about 300 meters wide."

"I see." Paul's whisper was a blend of relief and wonder. "I've never heard of a disk design, except in old fables. It's not...."

It's not the Himilco, Lynda silently finished the sentence. She clasped her hands together to stop the trembling. *No, we didn't find Gentry, but we didn't find him dead.*

"It's not one of ours." Donno picked up the sentence on a different thought. "It's an alien ship."

Heads snapped around to gape at Donno. Talk of aliens was one way to end a promising career, but Leroy Donno wouldn't make such a claim carelessly. His education was in spacecraft infrastructure, and he had made a study of design history.

"It's damaged," Braun said, and magnified the edge of the vessel, where broken, twisted metal plates were barely hanging on to the rest of the ship at what appeared to be a loading dock or shuttle port.

"Collision damage," Donno noted. "Those broken girders may have been towers for permittivity-drive engines. Hm, the main hull is untouched. Smooth as a baby's—"

"Hey, look at that!" Braun's shout brought all eyes back to the disk, which had rotated enough to reveal a small shape attached to the rim, a box about two by three meters. Braun zoomed the camera in on the box where big white letters spelled out MOOSE JAW.

"What the hell?" Poluka scratched his chin.

"It's a thruster," Donno concluded, "but it's not part of the ship. It was installed after the collision. See how it's bolted to the girder stubs. I still say it's an alien ship."

"Perhaps, Mister Donno, but the thruster's one of ours. It must have been placed there by—" Poluka began but didn't finish. Aguire returned to the bridge just then.

"Ah, Commander Aguire," Poluka said. "We have made a discovery."

"I saw something on the info-screen about it."

"Commander Donno has determined that it's of alien origin."

"Well," Donno gave a wry smile. "Now that I've said it, I certainly hope it proves to be true. Otherwise, the New Fed will have to send me to a re-education camp." His lighthearted remark, probably not far from the truth, inspired a strained silence.

"Chief Braun," Poluka began.

"It's all quiet." Braun anticipated the question. "And it's cold. There's no sign of any activity, power, or life aboard that ship. The trajectory suggests it's been drifting with the rocks for quite some time."

Poluka asked Aguire, "Will your engine modifications prevent us from maneuvering for a closer look?"

"No, sir. The new engine will be down for a couple of hours, but the thrusters can be used now."

"Excellent. Navigator, pick a path through these pebbles to find a nice parking space about ten kilometers from that ship."

For the next two hours the eleven-kilometer-long Hanno danced its way around and between the slowly writhing strings of asteroids to reach its goal. Excited chatter of speculation filled the bridge, but Lynda was quiet, frowning at the shiny object ahead.

This should not be here, Lynda thought. *This should not be anywhere.*

A stopping point was determined at about eleven and half kilometers from the alien ship, and Poluka called his staff to the conference room. Aguire sat bolt upright, grinning like a child on Christmas morning. Even Paul Poluka, whom Lynda never noted as especially lively, could hardly keep still in his chair.

"Okay, here's what we've learned," Chief Braun began. "The vessel has a thin layer of dust on its surface. Judging from the dust density around here, I'd guess it's about ten years' worth. So, it's likely the Starship Himilco is responsible for attaching the thruster to it."

"You know about the Himilco?" Lynda asked with a glance at Poluka, who gave a small headshake to indicate that Braun didn't hear it from him.

"That's why I wanted this mission," Braun answered. "My best friend Ivan Tershensky was the Himilco's mission scientist."

It never occurred to Lynda that anyone else lost loved ones when the Himilco disappeared, which confirmed and underlined her habit of indifference. Shame kept her from asking more.

Braun continued, "The damaged section is aluminum, bronze and glass, but the hull is the big surprise. It defies spectroscopic analysis. It's either an exotic alloy or," Braun cleared his throat, "an unknown element."

There were some amused smirks from those who thought Braun was trying to be funny for saying something that was patently absurd, but Lynda wrestled with a deeper impossibility: *This cannot be an alien ship, because aliens do not exist.*

"This is too weird," Tran said. "We need samples of materials from the wreck, and some asteroid samples, too."

"Of course." Aguire nodded repeatedly, never losing the ridiculous grin that reminded Lynda of a puppet she had as a child. "We're going out there."

"Are we sure it's an alien ship?" Lynda asked quietly.

"I'm sure," Donno affirmed.

"Of course," her father said, "there's never been any credible evidence, except for ancient legends from the twentieth century, but there's never been any reason to say it's impossible, either. Did the thruster come from the Himilco?"

Donno answered, "I would say yes. The model is called the

Moose Jaw, after the Canadian city where it was manufactured. I found it written up in trade journals. It has a built-in fusion battery, inertial guidance sensors, and a computer which, for the last decade, has kept this alien ship from colliding with asteroids or drifting away. It may also contain information left by the Himilco."

Poluka leaned forward in his chair. "Oh? Can we download it from here?"

"We can try some standard radio queries but, unfortunately, we have no detailed documentation for this thruster. We may have to go over there and plug a computer into it."

"Well, of course we're going," Aguire rubbed his hands together in eager anticipation. "We should decide how to do it, and choose the team."

"This is a three-man job," Poluka decided, "and Lieutenant Commander Donno will lead the mission."

Aguire gave Donno a congratulatory nudge.

"I should be the leader," Lynda's Papa abruptly corrected Paul.

"As I said," Poluka eyes narrowed, "this will be a team of three. An alien vessel may have unexpected dangers as well as unfamiliar technology. I am choosing Donno because he is not only an expert in spacecraft design, he's also an experienced officer who can represent the Corps if we encounter an alien presence. The other two will have to be knowledgeable in diverse sciences, experienced in boarding damaged spacecraft, and physically fit for such duty."

Lynda's father rose from his chair to lean on the table with clenched fists, his face suddenly crimson. "Are you saying I can't go *at all*? Nobody is better qualified than me. You people have no idea—no idea—."

His lips moved but the rest didn't come out. He collapsed onto the table.

* * *

Whenever she saw other people's troubles, like when someone had a parent who was sick or hurt, Lynda never felt much, never had much empathy. She could act like she felt something, but she didn't really.

155

Seeing her own father collapse should have been different, but it wasn't. It was a theatrical melodrama, understood to be serious but somehow distant, impersonal. Only a faint discomfort just below Lynda's conscious awareness kept her from being completely clinical about it.

She knew it was wrong to feel so little. People get scared at times like this, even to the point of hysteria. She should be clinging to him as the medics carried him out, crying "Papa! Oh Papa!", and he would plead for her to stay by his side, calling out her name.

"Poluka, damn you!" Papa's gravelly voice dissolved her fantasy and startled the medics. Lynda and Poluka stepped up to the medical flatbed.

"What is it, G.J.?" Paul asked.

"You know someone like me needs to be on this team, damn it! If I can't go, send Lynda. She knows as much about starships as Donno, and she's strong. You know she's strong."

Paul hesitated for the merest instant before agreeing. The medics took Papa away and she returned to the conference room with the others.

Papa was wrong about her knowing so much about spaceships; she only knew about the Hanno, but she didn't question her new assignment—she never questioned her father—but this time she at least noticed her automatic obedience.

Her discomfort became a stone in her stomach, distracting her while Chief Braun made his argument for including Elisa Santino on the team. Lynda voiced some concern about entrusting so much responsibility to Santino but, even as she spoke, she realized she was speaking for her father, quickly lost conviction and trailed off into vagueness.

Everything happened so fast, too fast, she realized after it was too late. There was something wrong that she couldn't quite identify.

Aguire hustled her down to the Outside Access Center. A tall, beautiful, black woman named Hilda Harris with an exotic accent and a lean, athletic body found a hardsuit in Lynda's size, and stuck a motion sickness patch onto her wrist.

The OAC was an entire department located just forward of the shuttle docks with everything that might be needed for working outside the ship in a spacesuit, including a way out with a whole series of airlocks of different sizes complete with decontamination and quarantine facilities. They had pressure suits, hardsuits, scudder pods, tool vests with tether lines and tools that snap onto the lines. They had six kinds of gophers.

The gopher that Harris recommended was about seven and half meters long and a meter thick with contoured saddle positions for three riders. Fire Hawk Inc. supplied it; a Toronto-based company that Stokes Enterprises sometimes did business with.

Aguire left Lynda there and went to get El Toro ready just in case they needed to pull out fast.

All around her, the OAC crew bustled with an air of professionalism, doing everything right because they were trained right. This stood out now because it showed the problem Lynda had been trying to identify; the meeting she had just come from was not quite as professional. The officers of the Hanno were reacting with emotion instead of discipline. Perhaps she should tell Aguire that they were moving too fast, but he was already gone.

Chapter 29

Braun found Elisa Santino waiting inside his quarters. She was a beautiful young thing. Other men might be jealous of what he was getting from her, but he took what was given and was glad for it. What he never told her was that he would still help her even if she treated him as a father instead of a lover. He would still care about her even if she were not so beautiful.

"I heard Stokes was taken to the Med Center again. Is he okay?" she asked.

She cared about a man who hated her. Braun liked that about her. What she lacked in morals, she made up for in compassion.

"I think he's okay. Doctor Payne is looking at him now. Do you want to hear about the meeting?"

"Of course." Elisa sat on the edge of the bed and leaned over on one elbow, making her curves more obvious. Her subtly tailored uniform was snug in just the right places. Her hair was pinned in a bun behind her head to accentuate the lines of her face and neck. Braun found the pose especially pleasing. He sat down next to her.

"Commander Donno will lead a team to board the alien ship. That's what started the trouble with Stokes. He wanted the lead, but Poluka told him he couldn't go at all. After they took him to Med Center, I convinced everyone that we need someone with proven experience boarding damaged vessels, someone like a deep-space rescue officer."

"Someone like me." Elisa showed that beautiful smile.

"And after it was agreed, and they were wondering who on this ship might have such a background, I suggested that you were a perfect fit. Poluka would have killed me if there were no witnesses." Braun chuckled at the memory. "Your record proved your qualifications, and I pointed out that you were demoted by Admiral Fisher through no fault of your own. Poluka knew where this was going, and gave up. You've got your rank back, Lieutenant."

"Oh, thank you!" Elisa gave him a sincere hug and kissed his lips, then looked into his eyes. "I hope I am not getting you in deeper trouble with the captain. What about Commander Aguire? Did he have any objections?"

"On the contrary." He returned the kiss. "The commander remembers you from the Eridani sector and thinks very highly of you. By the way, Lynda Stokes is the third member of the team."

He felt her stiffen. Her eyes popped wide open, and her squeaky voice cried, "*She's* going?"

"Well...yes. What's wrong?"

"What's wrong? She's insane—and dangerous—and she hates me! She'll probably get me killed!"

Elisa told him what happened in the laundry, and he remembered seeing Miss Stokes beat the shit out of Captain Frazya while Braun was chatting with friends by the pool at the McConnell gymnasium. He knew of similar stories about her brother, stories of rage and violence.

Boarding a derelict ship is always dangerous, even with friends. Boarding an alien wreck with an enemy who has a history of violence is just asking for trouble.

"You say Hanson got her out of there? And kept her under control? Go back to work. I'm going to visit Bart Hanson."

* * *

Elisa didn't make it back to the laundry before Poluka found her.

"Santino, you're relieved of your laundry duties. You will join Commander Donno immediately in the forward OAC. Follow me."

"Yes, sir."

Damn! She thought it would take longer, and Braun would have time to talk to Hanson. Besides, it was too soon to board an unfamiliar vessel. Research should be done first. Any captain should know that. She followed Poluka to the nearest lift. As soon as they were in and the door closed, he glared down at her.

"I suppose you and Braun had this all worked out since you first plotted to interfere with my plans. You got away from

159

Admiral Fisher, and now you get your rank restored. This better be the end of your scheming, Lieutenant. You may not realize this, but you probably would have been on this ship anyway if you had done nothing—without going to the trouble of pissing me off.

"Braun, on the other hand, should still be on Earth. That old fart's long overdue for retirement."

His anger toward her stung, but her face flushed and burned when he spoke against Braun.

"Chief Braun is the only one who can save you from Stokes' bullshit assumptions, Captain, and you're lucky to have him! And your plans? Your plans are to drag the entire crew into committing treason without giving them a choice, so don't bother throwing that at me, sir. You've been playing god for so long, you're almost as bad as Stokes."

She suddenly ran out of breath and expected a fresh onslaught from Captain Poluka, but he stood facing the door of the lift as if he were deaf.

* * *

Lynda was struggling into the hardsuit when Poluka showed up with Elisa, who eyed Lynda cryptically. When she was almost into it, she looked back and saw that Elisa was already in hers, fastening the final buckles on her tool vest.

Chief Braun and Bart Hanson appeared. Hanson came to her. Braun watched her for a moment before going to Elisa.

"So," Hanson quietly said to Lynda, "now you get the chance."

"To walk in space? Or to see an alien ship?"

"To make up with Elisa."

Lynda froze. Make up? She never considered it, never imagined it.

"Oh, Bart, I—." The stone in her stomach blossomed into genuine panic. "I don't know—I don't think—."

"Good. Don't think. Don't know. Just do. You're human enough."

Human enough? She searched Bart's face for something more.

"Be human," he said. "You've shown her your inhuman side. Now show her that you're just a scared young woman, like she is.

She's been living in fear for a long time. Braun's over there right now telling her that she doesn't need to be afraid of you. Now you've got to tell her, too."

Crewman Harris reappeared with a helmet, slipped it over Lynda's head and snapped it airtight onto the hardsuit, then clicked on the power. "Have you worn a hardsuit before? No? Hardsuits give more protection than a simple pressure suit. Can you hear me?" Harris' voice came through the circuit.

"Yes."

"Good. Let's go introduce you to your gopher."

She led Lynda into an airlock the size of a house. The Fire Hawk gopher, a long, silvery cylinder, was moved to the center and held to the deck with its own grapples—steel claws—at the end of mechanical arms.

Donno and Elisa put on their helmets. Lynda heard a tiny click in her helmet, and they were connected by radio.

Harris quickly recited a list of safety procedures and instructions for operating the gopher.

Suddenly it was time. Harris was gone. The inner door was sealed. The air was quickly pumped out while pulsed artificial gravity swept stray air molecules into a vent and tickled Lynda's body like massaging fingers. A voice announced that the gravity was being turned off. She felt a disorienting sensation like being in an elevator that was dropping downward, faster and faster, until she was simply falling freely.

"Lynda," Donno cautioned. "Hold onto the bar."

She gripped the metal bar that ran the length of the gopher, and tensed her body to keep her feet from drifting. Without a word, Elisa took the end of Lynda's tether, reeled it out of Lynda's hardsuit and plugged it into a socket on the gopher. She heard another soft click as the gopher began supplementing power and air to her hardsuit.

"Thank you," Lynda whispered. Elisa glanced into Lynda's eyes and nodded. Elisa's eyes were not so mysterious now, and had a complicated expression of excitement, fear, and confidence.

In a flash, Lynda understood why Elisa's career took off when she became a rescue officer. This is what she loves doing. This is Elisa's territory: outside duty—floating in space. The suit was her ship, and she was her own captain.

"Releasing the grapples," Donno announced. "It'll begin

drifting. Just pull yourself into the saddle, and clip your suit onto it."

It was a bit like sitting on bicycle seats equally spaced around the nose of the machine. It gave Lynda a false sense of up and down. Looking 'downward' past her right knee, Lynda saw Donno; to the left, Elisa. Both of them seemed to be hanging nearly upside down, about to fall off the gopher. Then she intensely felt herself falling, and clung desperately to the machine. There was no up or down, just a sensation of falling. She fought the panic and nausea of weightlessness. The chemical patch on her wrist helped a bit.

Donno signaled Harris. The outer door opened. A slight thrust sent them gliding into space.

The asteroid field filled everything ahead with a synchronized dance following loops of magnetic flux. Left and right was the outer hull of the Hanno, also looking huge. Everything was gigantic. Lynda felt like a speck of dust floating in a sea.

The alien ship was eleven kilometers away and not much bigger than a space-bus, appearing about six times as wide as the Earth's moon as seen from Earth. When they were on target, Donno cut the thrust and they drifted to save power.

"Lieutenant," Donno spoke. Lynda saw he was looking at Elisa. "I didn't get a chance to welcome you to the Systems Group."

"I'm proud to serve under your command, sir." There was caution in her voice.

"Glad to have you. That was brilliant of Braun to suggest it, and you got your rank back. You deserve it, Lieutenant."

"Thank you, sir. It means a lot to hear you say it." The timbre of her voice changed from caution to relief.

"I'm glad too, Lieutenant," Lynda offered. "I'm glad you're on the Hanno, and that you got your rank back."

Elisa looked into Lynda's eyes, and hesitated for only an instant. "Thank you, ma'am."

"Call me Lynda."

Donno interrupted, "Time to check in with the Hanno."

He did something on his control panel and text popped up in Lynda's helmet that appeared to be floating in front of her: AUDIO LINK>>HANNO.

At the same time there was a burst of clicking and whining.

"Hanno, this is Donno. I'm getting a lot of interference—kind of unexpected. Are you hearing me okay?"

"Poluka here. Yes, we hear you fine. We're getting the noise, too. Chief Braun is nodding. Chief?"

Braun's voice came through. "It's just echoes. We'd probably do better with low-tech radio. Every pebble out there is reflecting your signal and screwing with the digital timing. If we lose voice, switch to text."

"That's fine, Chief. How's our progress?" Donno said.

Poluka again: "Looks good. You're on course. Start decelerating in 47 minutes. Watch out for static charge when you get close."

"Will do. Donno out."

HANNO LINK END flashed in their helmets for a moment.

Donno busied himself with the radar, watching for hazards as the asteroids slowly curled through invisible loops of magnetism hundreds of kilometers away, but big enough to seem like Lynda could touch them with an outstretched hand.

Elisa and Lynda worked together with the cameras, studying the Zone and the alien vessel. About halfway there, Lynda looked back at the Hanno. A minute later, she looked again. When she looked one more time Elisa laughed softly.

"What is it?" Lynda asked.

"You're wondering if we're really moving."

"Actually, I was thinking the Hanno must be moving with us."

"It's an illusion. Out here, distance and scale are hard to judge."

"Okay." She looked ahead and saw that the alien ship was definitely closer.

Elisa had a nice laugh. She wasn't laughing at Lynda. She was just laughing. Bart said that Lynda was human enough. Well....

"Elisa, you were getting along well in the laundry—I mean with the crewmen there."

"Hold on." Elisa glanced quickly at Lynda, then to Donno. "Commander, mind if I cut you out of the conversation for a minute?"

"Go ahead," Donno responded. "I'll break in if anything happens."

"Thanks."

Elisa pressed a button on the gopher, and a message popped up in Lynda's view: PRIVATE LINK>>SANTINO.

"It's just you and me now," Elisa said.

"I'm sorry about what happened," Lynda blurted out the first thing she thought to say. "I just couldn't understand how you fit in with everybody. They all like you. I wanted to learn how you do it. When McGee stopped me, it was like everyone assumed something was wrong with me. I guess I didn't prove them wrong, but—I'm sorry. And I'm ashamed. I just wanted you to know that. There are a lot of things I've been ashamed of lately."

Lynda looked for some indication that Elisa heard her. Finally, Elisa spoke. "It's true; McGee and I did assume there was something wrong with you."

Lynda felt the stab of confirmation, but Elisa continued, "When I approached your father with my knowledge of your scheme and asked for protection, you both took it for granted that there was something wrong with *me*. All I did was join your conspiracy. I didn't change it or stop it. And I had to, or Fisher would have had me killed to keep me quiet. There's no reason I should have to worry about what you or your father think of me. But, I did have to worry, because you could get me killed, too. You may not realize this, but you have a reputation for violence. So, do I need to keep worrying?"

A drop of water appeared on the glass of Lynda's helmet and she knew it was a tear when a miserable sob surprised her by escaping her lips.

"Stop! Lynda, stop crying! You'll get your helmet wet. Listen, I'm not trying to hurt you, or accuse you. I just want to fix this problem we have. Okay?"

Lynda reined in the outburst and tried to keep her voice from shaking. "Okay. Can we start over? Like we just met? And I promise you don't have to be afraid of me."

A deep breath came through, then, "That's all I want. I just wish we worked this out earlier. We have to rely on each other to survive this mission. It's scary enough and we're doing it all wrong."

"What do you mean?" Lynda asked.

"If we're going to discuss the mission, let's get Donno back into the conversation."

"Okay."

Click!

"Commander?" Elisa got Donno's attention.

"Here," Donno answered.

"We were just thinking that this is all happening kind of suddenly. Isn't there a protocol for the possibility of finding aliens? We didn't take time to review it."

"I know." Donno sounded embarrassed. "That's been bothering me, too. We rushed this. Everyone got caught up in the excitement. When I was picked to lead the team, I should have pointed it out, but…with Poluka and Aguire pushing full steam ahead, I just didn't. Now it's a bit too late."

"Agreed. But do we even have a clear objective?"

"Recon. We just go look around and try to figure out what we have."

The alien ship was much closer now, seeming cold and haunted. The details were clear now, even in the darkness. Dust on the surface spoke of years without any witness to its slow orbit, and the dangling bits of metal at the damaged section told of some catastrophe that kept this ship from leaving the Zone, a catastrophe that may not be over, but just waiting for one misstep to start again.

And it was all alien. Nothing could be taken for granted.

Lynda asked, "What about this protocol? Do you remember what it says?"

"I don't." Donno sighed. "I think I skimmed through it when I joined the Corps. Lieutenant?"

"Vaguely. Maybe we could call the Hanno and get it downloaded to us."

Lynda asked, "Is there anyone on the Hanno who's already expert with the protocol?"

"Braun would be the one," Elisa said. "I think he must have been involved in writing the thing."

"Braun?" Donno was surprised. "That was ages ago."

"Yeah, but he's been in the Corps since it began. He was part of the Meduza affair."

"Ah, that was it. He mentioned knowing someone named Tershensky. Now I remember where I heard that name. Tershensky was the pilot who killed the Meduza swarm."

"That's a true story?" Lynda looked at the alien object ahead, dark and eerie. This is not the moment she would have chosen to be reminded of the Meduza story.

Every schoolchild knew the story of the space monsters that lived near Earth, mutant cell colonies, like jellyfish. Cosmic radiation caused them to rapidly evolve in the abandoned sewage tanks of ancient space stations in the centuries following the Great Disaster. The founding fathers of the Corps destroyed the Meduza when they started eating the early spaceships, forty or fifty years ago when mankind returned to space. She'd always thought it was just another space myth.

"Okay." Donno sounded reassured. "Let's just ask to be reminded of the proper procedures from time to time. I'll bet Poluka and Aguire are having this same conversation right now, and they'll get input from Braun as needed."

Donno mentioned it to Poluka when it was time to begin decelerating, and dropped some hints that Braun might be familiar with the Alien Encounter Protocol. As it turned out, they were already reviewing the document. That Braun was familiar with it was news to Poluka, however.

About 100 meters from the wreck, Donno increased the deceleration.

"Ready, ladies?"

Chapter 30

A pinging alarm from the I-bay jolted Aguire's attention to the computer graphic that mapped the zone around the ship and showed the position of the alien vessel and the nearby asteroids.

Braun spun his chair around to shout, "Radical change. The magnetic field is growing fast in the local loops. There's a lot of rocks coming our way at about six kilometers per second."

He transferred the graphic to the main screen. A cluster of concentric loops of asteroids was expanding outward. Rocks were colliding with each other and breaking formation to form another loop further outside the others. From a thousand kilometers away it all seemed very slow, but the motion could be seen. Some rocks would reach them in a matter of minutes.

"Warn Donno," Poluka yelled at the com tech, then to Aguire, "Get down to the cruiser and stand by."

Aguire ran for the door and through the foyer to the midsection. A stab of anxiety went through him when he saw the red lights flashing all the way down Main Street: general quarters.

Of course, he should have realized the rocks were coming at the Hanno, too.

His mad rush to the shuttle dock was just a blur until he snapped into his harness in the pilot's seat of El Toro.

Ensigns O'Riley and Burke were suited up and in their seats. They had the foresight to keep the engines powered up and the flight checks completed. Townsend drained the air out of the dock and stood by in the control room to punch open the outer door.

Then they waited. Aguire tried getting information through the net, but it didn't tell him much. He signaled Townsend to find out what was happening.

Townsend's voice came back. "The alien ship got hit hard. There's no sign of Donno and the others."

Aguire's heart pounded. "Damn it. Townsend! What are we doing?"

"The Hanno's moving, Commander. Scorpion missiles launched. We're trying like hell to avoid—hold on—we're hit!"

A vibration shivered all the way through El Toro from the deck of the shuttle dock. Lights flickered. Aguire gripped his harness release, unsure if he should return to duty aboard the Hanno, or continue waiting. Burke watched him from the copilot chair. O'Riley was fidgeting down in the lookout pit.

"Commander Aguire, prepare to launch," Townsend signaled almost calmly. The outer door slid open.

Dark flecks of rock peppered the edge of the hatchway, some moving like bullets, glancing off the deck and showering the walls. Others drifted in like leaves on a gentle breeze. The port side of the Hanno was no longer facing the Zone, but a dozen or so asteroids perhaps as big as El Toro were visible, racing past the ship.

Poluka's raw, scratchy voice shouted through the com, "Aguire, you're getting coordinates now. We moved away from them—didn't have a choice. The rocks have passed by but there's more coming. You've got about a half-hour. Go find them."

El Toro shot out of the port side of the Hanno into a storm of jagged iron pebbles and Aguire found the vector to the alien ship's last known position. His lookout officer cursed softly from the pit, but Aguire resisted the temptation to see what O'Riley was witnessing behind them, back at the Hanno.

The Hanno was still moving, but slower now. The alien ship showed up nicely on the passive sensors but radar was almost useless amid the billions of constantly moving iron rocks.

Aguire made good use of the cruiser's power and covered the distance in about half a minute, slowing when he got within fifty kilometers so O'Riley might locate their missing friends.

"Nothing," O'Riley reported, "except the gopher. It's mostly in one piece, but it's trashed—about five klicks from the ship and moving away. No beacons from the suits yet."

"We'll move in closer," Aguire strained his eyes in the direction of the alien vessel. "Burke, switch on the spotlights."

Megawatts of white light lanced through a panorama of debris that appeared like dirty water in a fish bowl stretching out far beyond the alien ship. With all the dust knocked off it, the wreck shined like a jewel in the intense beams coming from El Toro.

As Aguire turned the cruiser towards the other ship he saw a visual phenomenon that he'd heard of, but never saw before. His forward lights were so bright and the dust so evenly dispersed that the beams seemed to bend like flexible cones as he turned the ship, because of the delay of the light returning through clouds of material for millions of kilometers.

A calm southern drawl rose above the radio's popping and crackling. "I don't suppose y'all could give a lift to three tired explorers."

"Donno!" Aguire shouted back, "Hang on, mi amigo—soon as we locate you, we'll pick you up."

"Just head for the ship. We're all safe and sound inside."

"You're inside the alien ship?"

"Just inside the door. We've been takin' pictures while waitin' for a ride."

"We'll be right there, Donno. Is everyone okay? No injuries?"

There was a moment of silence before Donno answered. "A few bumps and bruises. We got knocked around inside the ship, but nothing more serious."

Burke contacted the Hanno while Aguire closed up the last few kilometers.

"I'm not getting the bridge," Burke said. "But Townsend's says there's been heavy damage to the midship at the twenty-six mark, on the top side."

Top side was, of course, the side that is up when the artificial gravity is on. Aguire tried to visualize the design drawings. 2,600 meters down the midship from the forward section would be just…about….

"Oh, my God!" Aguire cried. "It hit the accommodation section?"

O'Riley was half way up the ladder from the pit, also focused on Burke.

"It hit the aft edge of accommodations." Burke quickly read the text message. "A power station is destroyed, and an air reservoir for the shuttle docks is ruptured." He looked at Aguire, then O'Riley. "There are casualties—doesn't say how many."

They dropped into impatient silence and completed the maneuver to line up the top hatch of the cruiser with the hole in the alien ship. Donno signaled again and asked about the Hanno.

Aguire told him the news.

O'Riley switched off the gravity, then scrambled back to the center body of the cruiser and deployed a boarding tube that reached out of the airlock and over to the opening in the alien ship, a span of about ten meters. Aguire watched on his monitor and got a look inside the alien machine. He still saw no dents or scratches on the shiny hull, but the inside was a mess.

Twisted, broken beams and battered machinery were clumped together, some floating free and endlessly tumbling, others caught in the weird dance of bouncing around in springy tangles of cable—slaves to the law of harmonic motion. Finally, he saw his missing people coming through the boarding tube.

They'd taken a beating. Donno's hardsuit had deep gouges across the left arm and chest. Santino's suit actually had a crease across the abdomen, and her tool vest was reduced to a few ribbons on her shoulders. Lynda's suit was in better shape but, for some reason, she'd removed the outer armor from her gloves— not a good idea around so many sharp edges.

As soon as they were aboard and the hatch was sealed, Aguire began easing away from the wreck. By the time Donno, Santino and Lynda crowded into the flight deck he had El Toro charging back to the Hanno.

"Nice of you to drop by, Commander." Donno smiled, and then became serious. "We'll tell you the whole story later. What's happening with the Hanno?"

Donno's could always bounce back to normal after a crisis. Elisa Santino's expression glowed with a wild intensity. She'd need some time to unwind. Lynda looked dazed.

They were well, but worried. Aguire nodded to Burke, who answered the question.

"A group of asteroids hit the Hanno at about five kilometers per second. Most of them were small, a couple of centimeters. A few were bigger. One was several meters wide. It hit the dorsal surface and penetrated the hull at the twenty-six mark. Atmosphere was lost in decks eight through twenty."

Elisa gasped and squeezed her eyes shut. Lynda swallowed hard, and asked, "Did the emergency hatches close?"

"Yes, and there weren't as many trapped as there might have been because they were at general quarters. Most people were at their posts." Burke grimaced before adding, "But there are casualties. Possibly hundreds."

Aguire's grip tightened on the controls. The Corps rarely had fatalities, and the safety of the crew was a top priority in all operations. He couldn't think of another instance where the Corps had lost so many.

"Here she is," Aguire announced when El Toro punched through a cloud of dust and caught the Hanno with the spotlights about ninety kilometers ahead. He reversed acceleration to keep from overshooting the Hanno. In about five seconds, they were within a couple of kilometers.

There was a hole at the 2,600 meter mark on the dorsal of the Hanno. It seemed small, just a pinpoint from this distance, but the shuttles and even the work platform from SERFS seemed small from two klicks out. What looked worse was a split in the outer hull, and some missing plating. A row of life pods was exposed to space, as well as some of the air and water lines that ran between the inner and outer hulls.

SERFS, the Structural Evaluation, Repair, and Fabrication Shop had their biggest platform out there, with maybe a couple dozen people in hardsuits. The platforms were essentially mobile workshops open to space, with air tanks to replenish the worker's suits so they wouldn't have to stop working to refill.

"See if we can get the bridge," Aguire said.

Burke got through to a lieutenant in the S-bay whose eyes were frantically darting from one screen to another. Junior grade officers fill the S-bay with a flurry of activity, but Aguire didn't see any familiar faces.

"It's ugly, Commander," the lieutenant told Aguire. "But we're getting it under control. The Captain and Commander Washington are in the electric power station behind accommodations. Lieutenant McGee has search parties in looking for survivors. Commander Sirenko from SERFS is in one of the shuttles directing repairs."

"Understood. Is there anything we can do from here, or should we return to the dock?"

The question caught the lieutenant unprepared.

"Uh, I...I'm sorry Commander. I forgot to ask if all of you are okay. Poluka left me in charge of the bridge—there wasn't anybody else."

"That's understandable, Lieutenant. We're fine. Everyone got out okay with a few bruises. I think we should come aboard and help out there."

The lieutenant's face showed both embarrassment and relief. "Yes, sir. I'll signal the shuttle dock. Lieutenant Townsend isn't there. He's out with Commander Sirenko. I'm not sure who's running the docks, but I'll make sure someone is there for you."

"We'll wait for a signal."

It turned out a tech was manning the docks alone. Burke coached him through the docking procedure.

O'Riley helped Donno, Santino and Lynda strip off their hardsuits, and asked Lynda what happened with her armored outer gloves. She pulled them out of her sample bag and handed them over.

"Jeez, they look like they got caught between a hammer and an anvil," O'Riley observed. The bismuth-steel armor was made to protect the hands from impact or sharp objects. Hers were bent to hell, and the hinges on the joints were broken. Some pieces were missing, too.

Elisa Santino looked over his shoulder at the gloves and said, "That happened when an asteroid hit the ship, and the wreckage inside shifted. A loop of copper pipe pinned me against some wreckage. Even with the hardsuit it was squeezing me pretty hard. It would have cut me in half if I was in a regular pressure suit." She ran her hand across the crease in her own hardsuit, and then looked up at Lynda. "She bent the pipe away from me until it broke."

O'Riley looked at Santino's hardsuit with the centimeter-deep depression across the middle of the rigid alloy, then at the broken armored gloves. "I don't get it."

Santino reached into her own sample bag and handed him a twenty-centimeter-long piece of pipe. It was copper, about four centimeters in diameter. There were dents in it that looked like finger marks. A piece of bismuth-steel was imbedded in one of the dents.

The accommodation decks were laid out like a passenger ship but used Navy specifications for structural strength.

"I reviewed the design of that section a hundred times,

Commander," Lynda told Aguire. "I know those decks down to the individual rivets. I know the power systems and the emergency systems." She didn't want to be sent off to her quarters, or to the bridge, just to be kept out of the way.

"I can't order you into a dangerous area." Aguire said as they waited for the shuttle dock to fill with air.

"No, but you can allow it. Commander, I can help."

"Well," Aguire's brown eyes searched her face as if measuring her qualifications, "we sent you into an alien wreck. I guess having you help with the Hanno can't be much worse. Go with Santino and O'Riley to the damaged section, but don't do anything without approval of the officer in charge there, which is probably the Captain.

"I'll be in the bridge in case we need to bug out of the Zone. Donno, they need you in the Systems Bay. Burke, you take command of the shuttle docks until you're relieved." Aguire looked around to make sure everyone got it. "Let's go."

Lynda followed Elisa and O'Riley in a two kilometers jog down the speedwalk. Hundreds of voices filled the corridor as people in pressure suits brought the injured out from side corridors, passed them to others, then returned to find other injured people.

Some who were brought out got first aid immediately, others were escorted down the speedwalk to the Med Center. Lynda's stomach knotted when she saw bagged bodies placed along the wall. She saw the tear-streaked faces and heard the sobbing of those who'd lost friends and comrades.

A trail of black, grimy footprints lead to the power station at bulkhead twenty-six. Crew's quarters were on the other side of the split and buckled bulkhead. A ladder was in place to get to the accommodation decks through the breach.

SERFS must have sealed the hole outside. The air was breathable, but a stench from burned power circuits stung Lynda's nose. The walls were blackened from an arc-flash that must have come from the main lines.

Commander Washington was on an upper gantry with a computer and a radio, and every level of the station had people rushing to help.

Captain Poluka came charging down the ladder from the breach in the bulkhead. He grunted as his feet hit the deck, and pulled up short when he saw Lynda. "Thank God, you made it back. I'm glad to see all of you, but I've got to go to Med Center. I'm leaving Washington in charge here."

He rushed off without another word.

Lynda looked up at the buckled section of wall and saw a soot-smeared, scratched and scraped Bart Hanson leaning out of the breach. He motioned with a flashlight for her to climb up. O'Riley went to help carry someone out and didn't see when she hurled herself up the ladder faster than a person should be able to move, like a cat climbing a tree. Elisa saw, but said nothing.

Bart guided her quickly down a carpeted hallway that had dim emergency lights running on batteries. Groups led by Luke McGee were moving bagged bodies toward the still sealed emergency hatches which had slammed shut when the air pressure suddenly dropped.

They stopped at a honeycomb room, an integral part of the inertia compensator system. Hundreds of these rooms were scattered around the ship. Each polished silver honeycomb was sealed inside iron walls to shield them, along with laser equipment that bounced its beam around inside the honeycomb, looking for shifts in the light path that indicate changes in motion.

The door of this one was open a few centimeters, just enough to peek inside. Bart pointed his flashlight at something inside on the floor and stood aside for Lynda to take a look.

"He must've been working inside with the door shut when we got hit. The door won't open all the way. If I try to force it inward, I'll probably hurt him worse."

She saw a young man in a tech jumpsuit lying on the iron floor between the honeycomb and the laser. His head was in a puddle of blood and his eyes were closed, but he was breathing. She pushed on the door with no success and then tried reaching through the opening to find out what was blocking it, also without success.

"Together," Bart said, "if we pull sideways, we'll rip the hinges out."

Just then, Lynda saw someone behind Bart. He followed her gaze with his flashlight. Elisa was there with a medical kit. Her big dark eyes were filled with concern.

"Just get him out," Elisa said, "I won't tell anyone."

Lynda touched Bart's arm. "She's already seen it."

Bart handed Elisa the light, and then reached through the narrow opening to grip the edge of the door. Lynda got both hands on it lower down, with one foot braced on the doorframe, and her muscles strained harder than any exercise she'd ever done. She blinked away tears and pulled harder. The wall creaked for a moment before the hinges snapped with a booming roar that shook the hallway. They leaned the door up against the wall and Elisa rushed into the small room.

Lynda helped get the young technician all the way to the Med Center while Elisa and Bart stayed to help in the damaged area.

She felt something. She never realized how little she always felt, until now. She was connected to these people, to Elisa, and José Aguire, and to this young man.

She cared. She didn't just see the people around her, she cared about them.

Yesterday, Bart said that she was mean. He may have been right, but she didn't have to be mean. She didn't want to be.

* * *

G.J. Stokes didn't design the Hanno alone. Literally thousands of designers, scientists, and engineers contributed to the effort. The team who designed the Medical Center used all of the accepted guidelines and criteria, and went further, to make it better than anyone thought was necessary to serve the needs of up to four thousand.

Unfortunately, the Exploration Corps guidelines assumed that injuries would not happen to a thousand people all at once, nor did the Corps anticipate that hundreds might die, and need to be put somewhere. The Corps never saw such a tragedy, and had simply come to assume that it never would.

Doctor Payne was dealing with it. Ensign Harper from Hydroponics showed up with some manpower and organized triage for her. She commandeered officers from Water Management behind the Med Center to handle admissions, and got them to patch up the minor cuts and scrapes that came in while doctors handled the serious cases.

For some, it was too late. Some died while waiting or, like this boy that Lynda Stokes brought in, didn't get treatment before loss of blood caused permanent damage to the brain.

"We'll just have to wait and see," she told Lynda. "Frankly, it doesn't look hopeful, but we won't know for a while."

It wasn't much to offer, but Lynda nodded in understanding while she stood by the bed, holding the hand of the young tech with tears rimming her green eyes. It wasn't the image Doctor Payne expected after all the talk she'd heard about the young heiress, but there was no time to think about it. She moved on to the next bed where a red haired ensign from the ship's laundry had a broken neck. It was another case that little could be done about.

When all of the wounded were finally brought in and the emergency medics returned to help, the load eased. Doctor Payne made the rounds and found Lynda with her father. Whatever caused his collapse was still a mystery, but Stokes was not young and geriatrics was not a specialty of the Hanno's Medical Center.

In the next room, Doctor Payne found Lieutenant McGee sitting quietly by his friend Andre Swanson. McGee looked up at her. His eyes were red, and tears made tracks down his face and into his beard.

"He's gone," was all he said.

She checked Swanson, and then pulled the sheet up over his face.

"I'm sorry, McGee," she told him.

When she turned around, Lynda Stokes was standing behind McGee with her hands on his shoulders. Lynda was crying, too.

Chapter 31

The next day found the Starship Hanno another ten million kilometers further from the center of the Zone. Captain Poluka told the night crew on the bridge to let the Hanno continue drifting outward while watching for any more magnetic field disruptions.

Around 0400 hours he gave in to fatigue and slept fitfully for a few hours before going to Med Center again. He walked from bed to bed with a word of encouragement for the survivors.

He couldn't shake the feeling that every decision he made was wrong, that he was leading thousands to destruction through his own incompetence. What had he been thinking to pick a path through the Zone for a first mission? There had to be some other way to get this ship and all of these people away from the New Federation. His brother would have found a way.

Cliff was always better at everything. Hell, he probably would have defeated the New Fed without even leaving Earth, somehow.

Paul Poluka, Captain of the Starship Hanno, descended to the lower decks and took a longer route back to the bridge to avoid seeing people along the way.

* * *

Lynda's schedule had her working with Victoriya Sirenko in the early morning, and then with Infrastructure to assure the damage got repaired properly. Victoriya helped Lynda coordinate efforts with Power Distribution and Water Services, which had formidable repairs underway.

She liked the dark complexioned commander of the Structural Evaluation, Repair, and Fabrication Shop. Victoriya always wore SERFS coveralls and boots, but was still very feminine with her dark, eternally sad eyes and overly large lips. Her long black hair was a tapered single braid down her back, customary for women in the Corps. She had a no-nonsense approach to getting things done, and the absolute devotion of her people.

Sirenko got onto the New Federation's blacklist by being overly religious: a dimension of character that Lynda found difficult to evaluate when she was choosing the crew for the Hanno. The New Fed, on the other hand, had no difficulty evaluating religious beliefs—they were dangerous, and bad for society.

In the late morning, Lynda joined her father at the Med Center, and they went together for a working lunch with the senior officers. She studied him carefully as they took the speedwalk to the forward section. He seemed as strong and steady as ever, but unusually quiet and thoughtful.

"Papa, is something wrong?"

He glanced sharply at her, then looked away.

"You know, Lynda," he said slowly. "I thought the Hanno was perfect, but I suppose I've was wrong to be so confident."

Lynda smiled. "You? Wrong? Now there's something I don't hear every day."

"Lynda! I'm trying to be serious." He grimaced in annoyance. "Actually, there's more to it than that. Ever since we found that ship out there, I've been wondering if, maybe, he really could still be alive."

Lynda's smile faded, and her bright green eyes lost some luster when she admitted, "I know you thought he was dead all this time, and I didn't. But when I was in the alien ship and saw all of the damage," Lynda's voice began to quaver, "I started thinking, maybe, he could be dead."

She wiped her eyes with the back of her hand, then looked intently at her father before asking, "Papa, you told me and Gentry that our ancestors came from some frozen region around Finland that became isolated after the Great Disaster, remember?"

"Ah... the disputed territory around Finland and Estonia," he answered slowly. "Why do you ask now?"

"Well, you said that's why we have special gifts of strength and speed, but when I was on the alien ship, I started to wonder...."

"Wait!" He whispered hoarsely and pointed at the end of the speedwalk. They were just moments away from the bridge. "We're here. We'll talk later."

The memory came clearer to her now. When she was about six years old and her brother was thirteen, Papa told them about The Gifts. They would become strong and fast, just as they were already smarter than other people. Gentry was already getting the strength and speed that Papa said would come, and Papa was teaching him how to handle it, and how to conceal it from others.

He told his children that their ancestors came from the isolated territory encompassed by Latvia, Estonia and Finland, and survived the twenty-second century disaster because they were strong, fast and very smart. He taught them the concept of natural selection and how, after many generations of isolation in the frozen north, these traits became concentrated into their genes. It made perfect sense.

When Papa explained that they—Gentry and Lynda—would become so strong and fast that people will think they are strange, his children accepted that he was quite right about hiding their special gifts from the world.

Papa said that this is also why grandpa had a strange accent, as did Bart Hanson's grandparents who'd immigrated to America together, just about at the turn of the century, and that is why Bart had the same special gifts.

Lynda's brother eventually came to believe that Papa had lied to them, that grandpa was really an alien. Gentry became obsessed with the idea, until he finally decided to go to Bart's grandparents for answers. He never made it there, but ended up in a psychiatric hospital in Los Angeles. Lynda never questioned her father's version of events, but now she had a very uncomfortable feeling about it.

Aguire and Donno were already in the executive conference room when Lynda and her father got there. Commander Washington arrived a moment later with Chief Engineer Braun. A buffet set up on a side table and people were filling up plates before taking their seats.

Commander Redbird, the tall, quiet American Indian who was the night-shift bridge commander, and Lieutenant Davis representing Infrastructure, came in at exactly noon.

Captain Poluka came in a few minutes later and stood at the

doorway looking around as if he had forgotten why he was there before finally getting a cup of coffee and joining the others. There was a distinct lack of spirit in the room, and weariness showed, along with grief.

"Thank you all for coming," Poluka said. "Mister Tran is collecting the results of analysis on the recent behavior of the Zone and will be a bit late. I also invited Lieutenant Santino to join us, but she asked to be excused. She did, however, ask me to pass along her recommendation that we send some tugs out to the alien vessel and bring it into the SERFS main work bay, which is just barely big enough. Lieutenant Santino believes that if we take the alien ship as a prize it will help the morale of the crew, especially now. Unfortunately, Commander Sirenko of SERFS could also not join us. Otherwise, I would ask her to evaluate the possibility."

"Take it with us?" Lynda's father exclaimed, "That's an excellent idea."

"I think so, too," Aguire added. "Besides, if we can figure out how to make a hull like that ship has, we'll never have to worry about asteroids again."

Donno shifted uneasily in his chair. "Before we consider going after a prize, I feel that we need to put together a plan better than we did the last time. We got a little carried away and rushed it, I think."

Captain Poluka seemed to sag into his chair. The loss of life on his ship, which totaled 207, not to mention about 600 injuries that would have permanent effects, weighed heavy on him. Lynda saw that Commander Aguire was watching the captain, too.

Poluka stared unhappily at Donno, but Aguire spoke up first.

"Well, of course, we all got excited and rushed things, but we can do it right this time. Lieutenant Santino made a good point about morale. We're explorers, and this is the prize that mankind has been waiting thousands of years for. That alien hull will teach us what we need so that no ship will ever be so vulnerable again."

Lynda finally picked up on what Aguire was really concerned about. It was Poluka. Paul was blaming himself for everything, and for more than Aguire knew; Paul Poluka had committed everyone on the ship to deserting the New Federation, which would earn them all a death sentence, and then to lose so many by entering the Zone without careful planning made each death his personal responsibility.

Poluka seemed to perk up a little with Aguire's encouragement, and turned his attention to Chief Braun who'd spent the morning studying the artifacts brought back from the alien ship.

"Chief, what do you say?"

"Captain, this is the holy grail of exploration. The people of the twenty-second century largely believed there were alien civilizations, and many believed that aliens had visited Earth. But this conviction disappeared after the Great Disaster. Today's accepted wisdom on the subject is that there isn't any intelligent life in the galaxy other than us, which is based on relatively new theories about the age of the universe, the likelihood of life spontaneously appearing, and how long things take to evolve. We now have proof that these theories are wrong, and that the science supporting these theories is flawed. We can, and must, now put scientific thinking back on track. But, most important, we have proof that we are not alone. I absolutely agree that we must take this ship with us."

"What have we learned from the recordings and artifacts?" Poluka asked.

Braun punched up a visual presentation to the two-meter screen on the wall.

"Commander Donno took a wideband event recorder into the alien vessel, which caught everything from infrared up to x-rays. This was running from the moment they started looking at the thruster. The video recorders in the hardsuit helmets were running for the entire trip. We will start by watching all of them on a split screen. They're synchronized, starting at the encounter with the thruster that was bolted onto the alien ship."

Chief Braun stood by the screen, and was uncharacteristically animated, energetically pointing out details in each image, and rapidly telling the significance of each item.

The thruster was indeed from the Starship Himilco, and had that ship's name printed on it. The socket they wanted to plug a portable computer into was completely destroyed from years of abuse in the Zone, so they got no information out of it. Then, there was the warning from the Hanno about the asteroids. The images jumped crazily while they clung to the gopher, and made a run for the opening on the other side of the ship.

"Miss Stokes?" Braun said. "Could you tell us what happened at this point?"

Lynda watched the video change from asteroids to metal walls, and said, "I remember the gopher getting hit and knocked out from under us just as we were reaching out to the ship.

"There was nowhere else to go. We pulled ourselves inside. It was completely dark except for our helmet lights. Lots of things were moving inside. Some big pieces of walls, decks, and machines were floating freely. Others things were connected to cables, but still able to bounce around when touched."

The images showed a jumble of shapes, hardware and broken panels in a confined space. Then the whole scene abruptly shifted sideways. Recorded shouts and groans were heard and the debris tumbled violently around them, smashing together and against the walls.

"I think the ship was hit by a large asteroid here." Lynda continued. "The hull moved suddenly and slammed into everything inside it."

She didn't tell how Elisa got caught between a clump of shattered machinery and curved pipe that was pinching her across the belly like a giant cheese slicer. She wasn't ready to explain how she'd snapped the copper pipe in half like a dry twig. The recording failed to capture the moment, but it was clear that Elisa was in trouble, and somehow came through it all right.

It all came back to life for Lynda, but was much more meaningful now that she could be more objective, and Braun's comments were helpful, especially when the recording got to the point when they were looking around inside the ship. The images were adjusted for lighting, and Braun paused the playback to show things like the huge shaft with a giant gear that went straight through the center of the disk. He speculated that the aliens actually rotated their decks around the shaft to simulate gravity using centrifugal force. It made sense, though the technique was unexpectedly primitive.

When images of a control panel came up, Lynda's father asked for a hard copy that he could study later, and Lieutenant Davis became very interested in a sort of rectangular box that was broken open, revealing a foamy interior in baffled sections. She thought it might be a sort of biological oxygen generator.

What got the most interest was the fabric caught between

collapsed decks. Enhanced images brought out details of a finely woven work of art that had stylized images of people reminiscent of ancient Roman or Egyptian art.

"They look human," said Commander Redbird. "Are we sure this is an alien ship?"

"It definitely is," Braun answered. "The symbols on the control panel don't match anything in our library, and every technology used on this ship is completely different from ours. Oh, the principles are known to us, but the implementation is definitely alien.

"Also, look at the mix of development. They have no artificial gravity, other than centrifugal force, but they have a hull that we can't match. This ship is barely larger than a space-bus, yet it is clearly an interstellar craft. We can't make such a compact starship."

"But they do look human," Donno said. "Could this be a depiction of us? I mean our ancestors, assuming they had some contact with Earth a long time ago?"

Lynda shot a quick glance at Papa, who sat tight-lipped and unusually quiet, before she speculated aloud, "Maybe aliens can look just like us."

Papa looked at her and quietly grunted, but she ignored him.

"Yes, that's entirely possible," Braun went on. "Maybe we'll find the answer when we get the wreck into the SERFS work bay. Now, look at the artifacts that were brought back."

He picked up a box from under the table and began passing items around. Most were ordinary metal fixtures whose use was obvious, such as clamping brackets or air valves. Others were not so obvious, but none were of any exotic or unknown material except on a piece of control panel, which Chief Braun pointed out.

"You will notice that there are no buttons—only knobs and levers. The backside has ordinary electrical contacts, the sort of which we've been using for about a thousand years. The front side, however, is quite interesting. Take a close look at the material. The panel is a very dense-grain wood instead of metal or plastic, and chemical analysis verifies that these knobs are made from carved ivory."

"Ivory?" Aguire looked up from the knob he was examining, "Like, from an elephant?"

"We don't know yet. I'm going to run it down to the pharmacology lab and see what they have to say about it. But the point is, whoever built this ship had very different ideas about starship design."

"I'll go speak to Commander Sirenko after lunch," Captain Poluka said with fresh decisiveness. "We'll see about getting the SERFS bay ready to take on the alien ship. Commander Aguire, perhaps you could talk to the tugboat commander—what the hell's his name?—and have him coordinate with SERFS.

"Commander Donno, you were quite right in observing the need for proper planning. I would like for you to review the protocols, and please tap into anyone else who may help us do the job right. We won't rush into this until we're sure of what we're doing."

Captain Poluka acknowledged Donno, Lynda and Elisa Santino for risking their lives, and expressed sincere relief that they'd returned unharmed. He also mentioned the extraordinary efforts by all hands during the emergency. The meeting ended on that sobering note and people left for their various tasks, which mostly included going to other meetings.

Henry Tran finally showed up. He seemed rushed, and out of breath. The captain spoke with him, and they went together to the Captain's office.

* * *

Tugboat crews refer to their boats as a fleet and somehow get away with calling their commander "skipper"—a term normally reserved for a captain. They even had slightly different uniforms, which contributes to the *breed apart* attitude that often rubs people the wrong way. Aguire liked the Hanno's colorful tugboat personnel, but their overly romanticized image of themselves gets old after a while.

Lieutenant Commander Kern in the Tug Center seemed to think he was making all the decisions about the proposed operation. Commander Aguire managed to keep a straight face when he saw that Kern had his office wall decorated with a saber and a collapsible telescope that he referred to as a spyglass. He was good at what he did though, and in under a half-hour they'd wrapped up the discussion to Aguire's satisfaction.

Next on Aguire's list was a visit to the Med Center. The injured were constantly on his mind, as were the dead. Only in glamorized fiction can spaceships suffer casualties and then bounce back to the old routine as if it were normal. In reality, spacemen are deeply troubled by the loss any shipmate for any reason, and none are immune to the horror of losing so many.

Even with a new crew that hadn't served together more than a few weeks, the mood on the Hanno was so dark that normal operations were affected. Aguire could see it in the grim, unsmiling faces. The ship was traumatized.

The Med Center was quiet considering that nearly a thousand patients, doctors, nurses, and visitors were packed into the facility. It was a quiet of sober reflection. This kind of quiet was never heard in civilian hospitals, where the slightest discomfort or inconvenience would bring unending complaints from some people.

Aguire moved though the wards with a wave and word for each of the injured, stopping to chat for a minute, and trying to convey confidence in the hospital's ability to right all wrongs.

* * *

Captain Poluka listened intently to the Henry Tran's report, and understood immediately the importance of it, that's why he decided to order Lieutenant Tran to keep it a secret.

The I-bay supervisor was shocked, and it showed on his face. Having come up through the ranks in the Corps without any military experience, keeping a secret from his shipmates was an idea more alien than that ship out there.

"It's just for the moment, Lieutenant," Captain Poluka explained to Tran's incredulous expression. "The possibility that some alien intelligence attacked the Hanno will distract our team before we can put some safe distance between us and the Zone."

Tran's expression didn't change. In fact, his face seemed frozen in gaping disbelief.

Poluka tried another approach. "You understand that most of the crew is ex-military?"

This got a nod, so Poluka continued. "So, if we tell them that this event, which killed 207 of us and crippled hundreds more, may be a deliberate attack, how do you think they'll respond? I'll tell you. They will all want to get even. They will want to mount a counter-attack against the center of the Zone."

Tran blinked and looked at the floor, imagining such a scenario. Ever since the end of the war, there had been some us-and-them attitudes between those who were in the Corps during the war, and the ex-Navy types that transferred later. Some veterans had trouble adjusting to an organization which never had an enemy, but was otherwise not much different from the Navy. He could well imagine the worst possible outcome of going public with what he'd uncovered, and yet it seemed so wrong not to.

He nodded again, but promised nothing.

Chapter 32

"Papa," Lynda asked, "do you think aliens ever visited Earth?"

The old man looked up from the computer in his daughter's suite.

"There's no such thing as…" he began automatically, and then gave his head a quick shake. "Well, of course there are aliens. We know that now but, frankly, I don't know what to make of this ship. I would expect an alien starship to be a little more sophisticated. If that ship, or one like it, reached Earth today, it would be spotted by our Navy pretty quickly. So, I suppose it's unlikely that they ever reached Earth."

"Papa, what was it that made Gentry think Grandpa was an alien?"

She hadn't asked him, or even herself, this question for at least ten years. Papa didn't like to talk about it. There were things that never really made sense, but she'd always trusted Papa to know what's best and left it at that.

Papa's eyes flashed to her face, and she saw a flicker of pain in them. He stood and slowly paced while he chose his next words.

"Lynda, your brother was having trouble. It was hard for him to live his life with the special Gifts, the secrecy, and he never made friends the way other boys did. You did quite well, compared to him."

The qualifier "compared to him" stung Lynda with unexpected shame.

"But, Papa, please, tell me something, some real reason that made Gentry think—"

"Stop it, Lynda!" her father snapped at her. "If we find him alive, you can ask him yourself."

He stomped back to the computer and sat down, obviously prepared to ignore any further questions on the subject.

She turned away and stalked out of the suite with clenched

187

fists. She didn't have anywhere to go and just roamed the halls of deck 3.

Her nose got sniffly, but no tears came. All her life she had no one except Papa and Gentry, and her brother was missing for half of it. Papa wasn't enough to fill her universe, and she felt like she didn't really have him either. Maybe she never really had him. He only started spending time with her after Gentry was gone, and now that Papa thought Gentry might still be alive….

"Damn it," she hissed at the vacant hallway. "Did he ever really want a daughter?"

She felt like breaking something: a serious whim for someone with many times the strength of most men. Bart tried to teach her to control such impulses.

Bart was one deck up. She went up to deck 4. A minute later he opened his door to let her in.

"Lynda, I was just thinking about you." His smile faded as he looked into her eyes. "What is it?"

"I needed to get out of my place for a while. I thought we could talk."

He waved her to one of the two soft chairs in the center of his cabin.

His quarters were small. She felt a little embarrassed that she had taken a suite designed for visiting dignitaries, while he got a room the size of her kitchen. He had his collection of ancient weapons and spiritual art nicely displayed. The chairs in the middle made it cozy. He had a couple of books on the coffee table, and a huge photo album.

She sat down while Bart got a couple of beers. He served them in frosty glass steins, with a bowl of roasted nuts to snack on.

Lynda sipped the beer and asked, "Is this how they do it in Finland?"

He choked on his beer and had to set it down while he took a wheezing breath and wiped his chin.

She'd first met Bart when she was six years old. Her brother was thirteen then, and just starting to get The Gifts. Papa invited Bart to come and help Gentry make the adjustment.

Gentry was always suspicious of Bart, who was introduced as a distant relative whose grandparents came to America with Lynda's grandfather in the year 2720. Bart always impressed

Lynda with how nothing seemed to catch him unprepared, until now.

She watched him, strangely amused at his reaction to her question, and vaguely offended in the certainty that Bart and her father kept a very big secret from her.

It took a moment before Bart would even look at her. He paced back and forth with his head down, looking at his hands as if expecting to find something there. Finally, he turned to her. She saw something in his eyes she'd never seen there before: guilt.

"I knew it would come to this," he said so softly that she almost missed it. "I knew it would be me who would finally have to tell you. Damn your father."

At that, Lynda no longer suspected, she knew. The revelation froze her mind and emotions. She could only sit with rapt attention while Bart slid a large photograph from the album on the table and said, "You want to know what aliens, real aliens, look like? I'll show you."

He turned the photo toward her, holding it by the top corners. She dropped her gaze to the picture of fourteen smiling people posing on a patio behind a house. In the center of the group was a young couple holding a baby. There was also a boy about ten years old that Lynda recognized as a very young Bart Hanson.

On the far right was one man who was not smiling. He scowled out of the picture with vivid, green eyes. His hair was not yet gray, but she recognized her father. She looked closely at the other people in the picture. There were no other green eyes, but many as blue as Bart's. The woman standing beside Lynda's father had sea-gray eyes, but otherwise looked so much like Lynda they could have been twins. She felt drawn to the woman whom she hadn't seen since she was a child, and unconsciously reached out to take the photograph from Bart.

"Mama," she whispered. An ache of loneliness stabbed her to the core. She looked up at Bart and said, "Tell me."

"You recognize your father, who is half-alien, and these with blue eyes are also aliens. The younger ones were born on Earth. The children of one alien and one Earth-parent don't always inherit the blue eyes.

"In the year 2720, a spaceship crashed into the Pacific Ocean. The survivors knew a lot about Earth, and assimilated by pretending they came from the corridor of land called Finland, Estonia and Latvia, where most people have fair skin and blue eyes. It worked well, because that region was chaotic during the end of the Corporate State, and there were no reliable census records that could trip up their new identities."

Lynda's heart hammered in her chest. Everything she believed was torn apart, but she could only go forward. She needed the truth. She needed it now.

"Go on," she said.

"It was hard for them. The Corporate War started a few years after they arrived. Earth was unfriendly then, even for people who were born there. For our people, it was hell trying to blend in, learning the culture and the language while the Corporate State was making everyone paranoid. They survived, and eventually made good lives.

"This picture was made when Sam was born." Bart pointed at the baby. "His grandfather is an alien, so he's one quarter alien, like you."

She looked at the brown-eyed baby, and at the young couple holding the baby. Then she noticed another child in the photo, a boy about two years old, crawling at Papa's feet and distracted by Papa's shoelaces, her brother.

"Like me—and like Gentry. He was right." She looked at Bart with tears pooling in her eyes and suddenly sobbed, "Oh, damn, damn! He was right. Why weren't we told? Don't we have a right to know who we are?"

Bart sat down beside her, and took her hands in his own.

"We are Erosian. Our people have traveled the galaxy for thousands of years."

"Erosian?" Lynda sniffled.

"Yes. All four of my grandparents were Blues. They call themselves Blues because they have blue eyes. Your grandfather was a Green. Blues and Greens are both Erosian, but from different genetic stock. My real parents explained some of it to me when I was a kid growing up in Quebec. After they died, I had the other Blue families to help teach me about our people, but I kind of lost interest. I felt no sense of urgency.

"The Blues intended to blend into Earth society and were content with their new adopted world. There were problems in the Erosian nation. They came to Earth fleeing from trouble, and intended to stay. I don't know what kind of trouble they were running from. When we get back to Earth, we can go to the older Blues and ask them."

She studied Bart, seeing him anew. She grew up not knowing the truth about her ancestry. Now, she considered what it must have been like for Bart, who knew, but thought there was plenty of time for answers and had to concern himself more with being an Earthman, or at least appearing to be one.

"Two couples, including my grandparents, eventually settled in Western Canada. Another Blue couple, Sam's grandparents," Bart indicated the baby in the picture, "wound up in New Jersey.

"Your grandfather moved around for a while before ending up in California. He wasn't content to assimilate and become an Earthman. He wanted to return to the Erosians.

"He wouldn't live in the underground economy that existed before the Corporate War, like the Blues did. He established credentials that allowed him to get employment as a chemist in a big corporation. He had knowledge beyond anything known on Earth, so he could easily do the job, and he wanted access to laboratories and industrial equipment, not to mention a decent salary.

"When the war ended, just about everyone on Earth was surprised when the new government was actually pretty good, at least for the first couple of decades. The thing that made a huge difference for your grandfather was that the Federation changed the patent laws. The Corporate State always controlled intellectual property, so there was no incentive for engineers or scientists to come up with new things. After the war, your grandfather was able to patent Erosian technology and claim that he invented it. This is how he started the Stokes business empire.

"He felt it was beneath him to become an Earthman. He dreamed of returning to the Erosian nation among the stars. He spent his life developing space technology to do just that, and he resented the Blues for not helping him."

"How many of us are there?" Lynda asked. She squeezed Bart's hands with a grip that would have crushed the bones of another man, and then relaxed her hands as she struggled to control her emotions. Bart smiled kindly and answered.

"I know of thirteen who are still alive." Bart sighed and looked away for a moment. "I know of four who have died, and there is one missing whom I hope is still alive. You know him, too."

Lynda's mind raced. Who did she know that could be an alien—an Erosian?

"Who is it?"

"You remember Mrs. Shepherd?"

"My music teacher?" She couldn't imagine how Mrs. Shepherd fit into this. Lynda hadn't thought about the cheerful, patient woman she liked so much, since one night in New Wichita. Her music tutor had wanted to protest against the new government, and Lynda couldn't locate her.

"You never met her husband, or you would have remembered his blue eyes."

"Mrs. Shepherd married an alien?" Lynda's eyebrows flew up in surprise.

"My uncle. My mother's brother."

"He's missing?"

"No. He's dead. So is she."

Lynda jerked back, releasing his hands. There were few people she ever became really attached to; few whom she wanted to have as friends forever, too few like Mrs. Shepherd. *She used to come to the house to give Lynda piano lessons. They tried singing lessons too, but Lynda was hopeless. She was never much good with the piano, but at least she could go through the motions and bang out a melody. Over the years since then, Mrs. Shepherd would visit occasionally, and write letters to her. Lynda always looked forward to her visits. One time, Mrs. Shepherd brought her boy....*

"Little Michael?" Lynda groaned. "It's Michael who's missing?"

"Uh-huh." Bart nodded. Worry for the young boy showed on his face. "His parents were killed by the Attorney General's security troops. That's why I went along with your father's insistence that Alexei Volk should die. Sooner or later I was going to kill Volk anyway, for murdering my uncle and my aunt.

"Volk didn't know where Michael was. He told me everything he knew before he died, and so did the man who did the actual killing. I...questioned them both the day we left Earth. The Feds don't have Michael. I think he's hiding, out on his own somewhere. I know the other Blues are looking for him, otherwise I would still be there, beating information out of people."

Lynda was dazed. Yesterday, she thought she knew who she was. Today, everything turned out to be different. It was too much too fast. She picked up her beer and drained the glass, then held it out toward Bart.

"Got any more of this?"

He did, and somehow that made it easier.

Bart didn't know much about the Erosian nation, or his grandparents' position in it. He'd been taught some cultural things, and a few historical anecdotes, which he promised to tell Lynda later. He didn't even know for sure how many survivors had come off the crashed ship, 75 years ago.

"My parents taught me the things a child should learn," Bart explained. "They would have gotten around to telling me the rest, if they had lived."

He sipped his beer and flipped to another photo in his album. Lynda looked at his fair-skinned, bright-blue-eyed parents with the baby Bart on his mother's lap. They were good-looking people, but had a haunted expression. She imagined what it must have been like for them, to hide in plain sight on a strange new world, always worried their secret would affect their child someday.

"Anyway," Bart set his beer down and pushed it away, "your grandfather chose the name Gentry Stokes when he created his new identity on Earth, because the name Stokes was similar to his Erosian name, and the English word *gentry* means someone who was not quite, but almost, nobility. That's how he saw himself."

"But why did he name my father Gentry? And for that matter, why did Papa name my brother Gentry? Why three generations of Gentrys?" Lynda wondered aloud, not really expecting an answer. She looked up when Bart laughed.

"What?"

"I'm sorry. I just have to tell you. Greens are known for not being too creative."

Lynda sat up a little straighter, wondering if she'd just been insulted. Bart raised a placating hand before she could speak.

"I'm talking about artistic creativity, not engineering. Your grandfather was too proud to just pick an Earthman's name for his son. He actually told some of the Blues that if the name Gentry worked for him, it would be fine for his son, but they thought he just couldn't decide on a new name.

"When your father named your brother Gentry, it was because he inherited a sense of superiority from your grandpa, and felt if two Erosian men could be named Gentry then, by God, it must be better than some common Earthman name, and he passed it on to your brother. The Blues used to make jokes about it."

"I don't think it's funny," Lynda said seriously. "Anyway, how else are Greens and Blues different?"

"You know, I'm not sure. I mean, there are some small differences, like Greens focusing on a goal more than Blues do, and Blues being more socially adaptable, but I'm getting all this from a small group of Blues who may be biased. To be honest, I never gave it much thought.

"After my parents died, I really concentrated on living in Earth society. I visited the others sometimes, but my life was with my adopted family and the community of Sainte-Agnes-de-Bellecombe in Canada.

"Except for the Gifts, I think we aren't much different from the people of Earth. Since we can interbreed, I suppose we could even be considered the same species."

"Bart, my brother thought Grandpa came from Arcturus. Was he right?"

"No. I asked my uncle," Bart pointed to a man in the group photo, Mrs. Shepherd's husband, "but he had no idea where Gentry got the idea, unless it was from your mother."

"Mama? Did she know about Grandpa?"

"I'm sure she did. I think she figured it out somehow. I'm sorry that I don't have all the answers, Lynda. There are some answers I would like myself. I've tried to get your father to tell me things, but he won't. He doesn't tell anything that he doesn't have to."

Lynda studied the group in the photograph. Mama looked like she was in her twenties when the picture was taken, maybe the same age Lynda is now. Her eyes were gray and kind. Her smile was coy, as if she had a secret that she wanted you to guess. When she looked at the other faces, one other seemed familiar somehow—the father of the baby Sam.

"Who is this?" Lynda asked, and indicated the thin, brown-eyed man.

"Sam's dad, Jeremiah Benjamin."

"Benjamin?" She'd heard that name recently. "Does he own a hotel?"

Bart looked curiously at her. "That's right. In Texas."

"I think I met him, and Sam, too, in New Wichita."

"Oh, I know he was there for a few days last March. I spoke with him but he didn't mention meeting you. They're a terrific family, but your father doesn't like them and they know it."

"Well, I'm not my father. I'm going to visit all of the Blues the next chance I get. Bart, you said the Erosians have been in space for thousands of years. They're far more technically advanced than us, I mean, than Earth, right?"

"Yeah, much more advanced."

"Then who built this alien ship? It can't be Erosian."

"That's been puzzling me. Will there be another attempt to explore it?"

"We'll try to get it into the SERFS work bay. We can study it in detail then."

"Hm, good idea, I suppose. When will this happen?"

"I would guess in another week or so. We're not going to rush it this time."

She stood and walked slowly around Bart's cabin, sipping coffee and looking at his icons and ancient weapons. She wondered what Erosians, living in their own world, would have on their walls.

"Bart, if Erosians don't come from Arcturus, where do they come from?"

"Many worlds, all over the galaxy. Wherever their original home world was has been forgotten by most of them. At least, the ones that came to Earth 75 years ago don't know. They have old stories about their origins, but it's like asking someone from Earth to explain where the Garden of Eden was.

"My uncle thought the Erosian culture simply reached the end of its lifespan, and those who survive will do so by joining other, younger civilizations the way we did."

Lynda was sorting out her father's behavior. "That's what building the Hanno was all about? Grandpa wanted to return, and now that's Papa's plan, right?"

"Yes, your father has always wanted to rejoin the Erosians."

"But Papa chose not to tell me and Gentry. Do you know

why?"

"I know your grandfather was nervous about keeping the secret, and worried one of the Blues might let the secret out. In fact," Bart pointed at the group photo, "three of these people are not at all alien. Sam's father here, and Sam's grandmother here." Bart pointed them out. "And of course, your mom. She was the only one who didn't know before she got married. The Blues have never kept the secret from a spouse."

"Or a child, I'm sure," Lynda responded bitterly.

"Lynda, I'm sorry I didn't tell you a long time ago."

She wanted to be angry at somebody, but not at Bart. In fact, as much as she was sure that she had a right to be angry, she wasn't. She was numb, still digesting information. It was like some kind of fantasy, completely unreal.

CHAPTER 33

Lynda almost skipped the meeting, but her father expected her there, and old habits die hard. Besides, the need to discover the fate of her brother burned brighter than ever and that alien ship might be the key to finding him.

She surveyed the scene through the smoke-tinted glass before entering the conference room. About thirty officers were already there. Her father was sitting beside Paul Poluka at the horseshoe ring of tables. Lynda chose a seat next to Donno so she could watch her father across from her.

"Are we all here?" Poluka asked Aguire.

"Everyone except Elisa Santino," said Aguire. "She's filling in for an injured officer elsewhere. And Henry Tran is missing."

Lynda saw the aching guilt in the captain's eyes, and something else: determination perhaps. She didn't find out until later that the guilt wasn't about the injured people on board.

"Ah," Poluka addressed the group. "Mister Braun is in the engine section looking at the modifications. If I knew he'd take so long I would have asked him to do it some other time. We'll get started. Commander Aguire will give us a general outline of our plan to bring the derelict vessel into our SERFS main work bay. Commander?"

"Yes, sir." Aguire punched up a graphic to show the relative position of the alien ship and the asteroid field, then explained how the tugboats could maneuver the wreck back to the Hanno and into position while the SERFS crew attaches a scaffolding frame around it before pulling it into the SERFS bay.

The tugboat commander, Kern, gave a long-winded speech that was light on operational details and heavy on the indispensable excellence of the tugboat fleet. Lynda found the colorful discourse charming, but Captain Poluka was fidgeting and obviously annoyed. Since learning that she was part alien,

Lynda kept analyzing her every reaction, wondering how her perceptions might be different from those around her. She'd always taken the role of managing situations, not trusting others to make decisions, but now she felt detached and content to be a spectator.

"That's fine, Commander Kern," Poluka said at last. "We understand that this is well within your team's capability. How does SERFS feel about this operation?"

Commander Victoriya Sirenko nodded and said, "Yes, we can do this provided the damaged vessel is stable enough to be moved by the tugboats."

Lynda liked Victoriya's melodious alto and slight Russian accent. The commander continued to describe her part of the operation, which would include keeping the work bay in vacuum and without artificial gravity until the wreck was examined for hazards.

Poluka then called upon Commander Donno. Lynda clasped her hands in her lap and tried to not laugh while Donno explained that aliens may be so different from humans that communication may not be possible, hence, the procedure called for patience and caution.

"After all," Donno said, "aliens may see our most friendly gesture as threatening, and respond in a way completely unexpected."

Lynda looked at her father, who wore his usual scowl of disinterest, and Lynda thought, *"Should we promise not to bite them, Papa?"* which almost made her laugh.

"Yes, of course, Commander," said Poluka, "but we've already been inside the ship and we know now there are no aliens here. So, the part about observing the wreck for up to several weeks before approaching it doesn't apply in this case, does it?"

Poluka looked at faces around the table. Heads nodded, and he continued. "And the part about not touching alien hardware because we may inadvertently activate some unknown function is not applicable since everything is already smashed to bits, true?"

"I guess so," Donno reluctantly agreed.

Lynda's father was quiet for most of the meeting, but now seemed puzzled, not by anything Donno said, but by Poluka, who timed his comments carefully to seem not prejudiced against the Protocol.

"I understand you've worked hard to become our resident expert on the Alien Encounter Protocol, Commander, and we don't want to discount whole sections of it, but we must use it as it applies to the current situation."

It went on like that, with Poluka disallowing every reason Donno could think of for being cautious.

"It's true," Braun said, "the Protocol was written for a more complex scenario but, in this case, we see no sign that there's even anyone out here with us—just broken hardware to salvage."

Poluka nodded, his lips pressed tightly together as if forcing himself to keep silent. Lynda understood that her father routinely misled people, but she never doubted Paul Poluka, until now.

"What I'm most concerned about," her father said, "is the asteroids. That fluctuation came out of nowhere. Mister Tran was studying how that happened, and we haven't seen his report yet. Will he be joining us, Captain?"

Poluka shrugged with his hands spread out in a *'what difference does it make?'* gesture. "Tran's findings are inconclusive, so he will refine the data, and perhaps take additional measurements. In the meantime, we should still work out a plan, even if we need to revise it as new information becomes available."

The meeting concluded without any surprises. Lynda got a call from Bart asking her to join him and Elisa Santino for dinner.

* * *

Lynda would never underestimate Elisa again.

"Bart?" Lynda looked at him for guidance. He'd told her about their alien ancestry, but not what to do if someone else guessed it.

"I don't feel like denying it," Bart said without taking his eyes off Elisa. "But I'd like to know how you reached this conclusion." He sipped his coffee and glanced around the nearly vacant cafeteria. No one was nearby. Aguire and Donno had a table far away by the windows.

Elisa looked back and forth between Lynda and Bart with a half-smile on her face.

"Now we know that aliens exist," she explained, "and that let me see previous clues in a whole new light. Both of you are stronger and faster than people are supposed to be, and the

Stokes family has higher than normal intelligence, not to mention unusually bright green eyes, just as you," she said to Bart, "have unusually blue eyes. To top it off, I know that Lynda's brother believed their grandfather was an alien. I read his file before deleting it from the government database.

"After seeing Lynda's strength and speed firsthand, I started wondering if maybe Gentry Stokes the Third had been right all along. When I saw how you two saved that tech's life, I was convinced. I was also convinced that it's safe to tell you I figured it out. You let me see your secret rather than let him die. I don't think you'll kill me to keep the secret."

Lynda didn't know what to say, but Bart did.

"You're in the club now and, you're right, we're not going to kill you."

Elisa repeated what she'd said last night just before Lynda and Bart ripped a 400-kilogram door out of a wall. "I won't tell anyone."

"I know." Bart smiled at her.

Lynda found unexpected comfort that Elisa, a normal human being, could so easily accept Lynda for what she was.

"I'm curious about how aliens came to be living..." Elisa began, but stopped when she saw that Bart was staring at the window. She and Lynda turned and saw a dozen tugboats off the port side of the Hanno, heading away.

* * *

The Hanno's crew outnumbered the population of some colonies and could easily fill both of the ship's main cafeterias, but at this hour the forward cafeteria was quiet and seemed almost cavernous to Commander Aguire.

Aguire and Donno had a table on the port side with a panoramic view of the stars through a RadGlass window. The alien ship was millions of kilometers away, impossible to pick out among the asteroids. Bart Hanson, Elisa Santino, and Lynda Stokes were at another table across the room.

"Here comes Chief Braun," said Donno and waved for Braun to join them.

"Hi, fellas," Braun said. "I found out that Henry worked all morning on the analysis, and was ordered to inspect the engines just before the meeting. They say he was upset when Poluka sent him to inspect the engines."

"Sounds like Poluka didn't want him there," said Donno. "The way Poluka's findin' reasons to hurry this operation just ain't right."

Aguire had an uneasy feeling, too. The captain was up to something. Poluka was a good actor, but not good enough to fool Aguire.

He noticed Hanson, Santino and Lynda hurrying towards him, but looking past him at the window. He glanced over his shoulder and saw the formation of tugs already far away.

"Oh, shit," Aguire groaned, and led the others in a jog to the bridge.

Commander Redbird was sitting at the command desk. Poluka was in the I-Bay with Henry Tran and Commander Washington. Tran looked scared.

"Captain," Aguire said. "I see that the tugs are deployed."

"Commander." Poluka turned nonchalantly toward the new arrivals. "I left a message for you and Mister Donno, but decided not to wait. Conditions seem good for making some observations of the situation, and I thought it wise for the tug fleet to make a practice run out to the alien vessel."

"A practice run?" Aguire was unprepared for such a ludicrous statement. A practice run would only expose the tugs to the same dangers twice instead of once.

"Right. They'll have a chance to study the objective, and give recommendations before we go any further. Besides, I think we need more data for Mister Tran's analysis. He seems to think that the magnetic fluctuation could be a result of our near-light-speed motion around the Zone. We need to know if it could happen again when we move at NLS."

Tran started to say something, but Poluka cut him off. "How long before the Fleet is within a thousand kilometers of the vessel, Mister Tran?"

"Eighty-three minutes, sir."

"Excellent." Poluka smiled. "Let's go to my office and hear Mister Tran's report."

They followed him, leaving Redbird in charge of the bridge.

Tran began by punching up a diagram of the asteroid field.

"Here," he said, pointing at the bottom of the picture, "at the six o'clock position is where the message pod was destroyed as we arrived at the field."

Next, Tran added a red dashed line circling the field counter-clockwise. "And this is our course around the field to the one o'clock position, where we found the alien ship, and stopped."

He pressed a button and the line continued—yellow this time—around to the ten o'clock position.

"This is where we would have been at the time of the accident if we hadn't stopped."

He pressed another button and added motion to the shape of the Zone.

"This is what happened when we got hit."

The field convulsed and rippled. A whip-like bulge of matter emerged near the center, to uncurl and gain velocity until the tip swept out and across the point at the ten o'clock position where the yellow line ended. It represented asteroids totaling many hundreds of times the mass of the Earth propelled through a long arc. The velocities of some reached as high as one thousand kps. A minor—much smaller and gentler—ripple went through the point where the Hanno had been yesterday.

The implication was not lost on Aguire. If the Hanno had not stopped, the main force of the phenomenon, at the ten o'clock point of the graphic, would have been unsurvivable.

"Oh, my god," Donno whispered. "We got lucky."

"There's more," Tran continued with a glance at Poluka. "The chemical analysis of the asteroid material suggests that it's unnatural."

Chief Braun groaned and held a hand to his forehead. "Oh, no."

"What?" Aguire asked. "What does that mean, unnatural?"

Tran looked at Poluka again before answering, "The rocks are not asteroids. They are manufactured, a sort of ferrite material. That's why our radar doesn't work, and the magnetic fields are behaving so strangely. The Zone was created by aliens."

Chief Braun spoke. "I should have seen it. The field has a dynamic magnetic field that can't be natural...wait a minute...oh, crap!" Braun stared in horror at the end of the yellow dashed line. "You're saying we were attacked?"

Poluka raised both hands in a placating gesture. "That is one theory. As I said before, I believe the analysis is inconclusive and requires further investigation, but please, let Mister Tran continue. He has some thoughts about how the Hanno's position was tracked, assuming that his theory is correct."

Tran took a deep breath and indicated the point where the Hanno first entered the Zone. "Here, our pod crashed and released a lot of energy, which might seem like we were attacking the Zone. Moving at half light-speed in a circular course caused our engines to radiate anti-tachyons towards the center of the Zone. If something at the center was interested in our location, the anti-tachyons might be enough to track us. When we stopped, we were no longer emitting radiation, but someone could have just assumed we were still on the same course."

Poluka interrupted. "There are several assumptions here, and this is what I consider inconclusive. I agree that it's quite possible the Hanno's movements may have caused a reaction, but I am not convinced we have proof of intelligent behavior. The reaction, if that's what it was, could be natural when something like the Zone has anti-tachyons bombarding it, or it may simply be a coincidence that it happened while we were here."

Aguire detected no obfuscation this time. Poluka believed what he was saying. He was so reasonable and convincing that Aguire wanted, desperately wanted, to believe that Poluka was acting responsibly.

But Poluka had kept this from his people and sent the tug fleet out there without consulting his senior staff, even timing it so the boats would be on their way before anyone could question it.

"Captain, it's highly irregular to order such a mission before notifying your senior officers. I feel that—"

"Commander Aguire." Poluka was angry now. "It is the captain who is ultimately responsible for everything. I have carefully considered what is, or is not, appropriate in this circumstance. I'm calling a meeting with all senior officers, from all three shifts, at 0700 tomorrow. Until then, I have an operation underway and the safety of the tug fleet, as well as the Hanno, is foremost in my mind."

He regained his composure as he spoke, and gave them a fatherly smile.

"The analysis of the Zone does not indicate immediate danger. Even if Mister Tran's highly speculative theory is correct, the Hanno would not become a target again until we start moving at NLS velocity along a curve that would generate synchrotron radiation. I felt it wise to gather more data before bringing all of this to the senior staff in the morning. It didn't occur to me that some officers might get their noses out of joint by having to wait until then."

Braun was scratching his chin, studying Poluka. "So, if you don't see a reason not to, will you order the tugs to go ahead with the salvage? Or is this going to be, as you said, a practice run?"

"I hadn't considered it," Poluka responded as if it were a new idea. "They'll be arriving at the wreck shortly. Let's return to the bridge, and see what they learn."

With that, he shooed them out of his office while Aguire was catching up to Chief Braun's logic; bringing the wreck back now was Poluka's plan. He was just going to wait until everyone agreed that there was no reason not to, before giving the order.

At 2300 hours, he did give the order. Nine tugboats with thirty remote pushers made physical contact and maneuvered the alien ship to the SERFS work bay.

A door the size of a football stadium slid open on the starboard side of the Hanno, and the SERFS crew extended a steel framework of scaffolding out to meet the wreckage.

By 0500 hours the next morning, the giant door closed again with the alien ship safely clamped inside.

When Poluka informed everyone of the night's activities, it all sounded like a logical progression of decisions. There were still plenty of officers who weren't happy about a major change in plans happening while they were sleeping, but there was little they could do about it.

"We will take a straight-out course from the Zone," Poluka told them, "nice and slow, after leaving some automated survey probes to gather more data."

There was some debate about whether the Hanno should wait for the data, or continue on to Arcturus, but the captain artfully steered the thinking around to the latter option.

CHAPTER 34

Elisa leaned on a table by the window overlooking the SERFS work bay to watch the scientists going into the alien ship, while Viktoriya sipped coffee and reclined in her chair with booted feet up on a desk.

Crewman Hilda Harris was in the adjoining control room monitoring the space suits she'd brought up from OAC, and occasionally joined the conversation.

Lynda sat on the corner of a desk, enjoying a cup of mint tea. She felt grungy after two days without sleep or a change of clothes. A nap and a shower were sounding pretty good.

The SERFS bay was immense compared to most other enclosed spaces on the Hanno, spanning the entire half-kilometer width of the Hanno's midsection, and nearly that long from front to back. Various offices, including the one Lynda was in, had windows overlooking the alien spacecraft, which gleamed bright and shiny in the well-lit work bay. They kept it in a space-like environment with no gravity or atmosphere, even chilling the walls of the bay so that it would not absorb radiated heat. A dozen mechanical arms with pneumatic cushions held it in place.

Lieutenant Debra Davis was running the show in the bay, directing space-suited scientists and engineers who were doing the grunt work of swimming around inside the wreck, bringing out everything that was already loose. The artificial gravity in the office spilled over into the edge of the bay, keeping the debris from floating away from where it was stacked. The SERFS control room broadcasted the whole operation to the crew on one of the info-channels.

Debra emerged from the alien ship with a group of mini-gophers and waved to Lynda, who waved back through the glass wall in the office and watched the little robots deposit bins of broken alien junk on the floor eight meters below the window.

Lynda couldn't think of another time when she felt so at ease with a group of women.

The Hanno was on its way. Survey probes were deployed in the asteroid field after being cleverly programmed to sneak around like spies in hostile territory. Lynda was amazed at the sophistication of the program the Hanno's officers had come up with. She reminded herself—again—to stop underestimating people.

Arcturus was the next stop, about one light year away. Standard tachyon-drive would get them there in eighteen hours.

"Well," Viktoriya speculated, "just because we're close to Arcturus doesn't mean that's where this thing came from."

"Then it would have to be from closer to the galactic center," Elisa added. "We'd have seen some sign of them already if they were from another direction."

"Maybe we have," said Lynda.

"What do you mean?" Viktoriya asked.

"People have been in space for a couple of centuries now. There's always been a huge reluctance to even suggest that aliens might be behind some mysteries. I'll bet if we look again, knowing that aliens do exist, we might find we already had some clues."

"Well, I can tell you one thing." Viktoriya took her feet off the desk, and rocked forward in her chair. "I never believed the doctrine about Earth being the only source of intelligent life. Most people can accept this." She gestured at the alien ship. "What people will have trouble with is the Zone. If that was made by aliens, then they not only exist, they're also superior to us."

"Maybe 'superior' isn't the right word," Lynda said.

Debra's voice cut in over the radio. "Hey, look at this." She dangled by one hand from a cable that was lifting her past the other side of the window. Her space suit was followed by a hoisting spreader attached to two corners of the mysterious fabric from the alien ship. The bottom edge of the fabric was held down to the floor by elastic straps. It slowly spread out and opened to reveal a finely woven work of art. Fully opened, it was a square fifteen meters on each side, completely dominating the view from the window, and it was spectacular.

Debra appeared again, slowly free-falling down to the window, where she grabbed onto a rail and looked in at them with a grin.

"Ta-dah!" she laughed. "This thing's pretty tough, so I thought it could handle the reduced gravity well enough to hang here for now."

It was a tapestry of intricate scenes in rich reds, blues, yellows, and browns of alien symbols and images. There were man-shaped figures wearing robes and sandals. Animals like horses, birds, and perhaps bears and other, stranger creatures, all depicting action and emotion. The scenes were arranged in curved rows circling the center of the fabric. Each man-figure was about ten centimeters tall, and there were few places without some picture woven into it. It was too much to take in all at once.

"God, I love my job," Debra whispered over the intercom.

Her team scurried up the rails on the bay walls and clung there in their space suits to marvel at the alien masterpiece. The video broadcast alerted the entire ship that something extraordinary had come out into the light and people began showing up in the windows around the cavernous bay.

A technological wonder could not have matched the effect of this woven material. Alien though it was, it showed something understandable; feeling and passion; reverence of beauty and art; a soul that longed for something.

Donno arrived with Lynda's father.

They stood staring for a minute before Donno informed them that Captain Poluka was searching the personnel database for crew members who have any kind of education in art to study this artifact.

Lynda saw a sort of hungry eagerness on Papa's face. She hadn't told him about her talk with Bart yet, and didn't know what to say to him.

Donno said to Viktoriya, "The metallurgy people will start examining the hull immediately."

"Thanks, Leroy. I'll be here all day. I wouldn't miss any of this. Will the captain be coming?"

"I don't think so."

Something about the way Donno said it got Lynda's attention.

"Is something wrong, Commander?" she asked.

"The captain's down in Med Center right now—visiting. He's been pacing back and forth in the bridge all morning."

Lynda first met Paul Poluka when his brother Clifford recruited Gentry to be the navigator of the Himilco, and Papa invited Paul to their home in California. Lynda was beginning to understand that, even then, Papa was looking for someone like Paul to be the captain of the Hanno.

After all these years of knowing Paul, Lynda had a pretty good idea why he was getting flakey; Lynda's hopes were higher than ever that her brother was alive, but she had the sickening suspicion that Paul was hoping his brother was dead.

Jealousy of his big brother's accomplishments was always masked by poignant grief that slowly faded into nostalgic admiration. Now, after losing hundreds of lives with a reckless decision, he finds that his brother may yet turn up to outshine him again.

"Viktoriya," Lynda said, "I'm going to Med Center for a moment, and then turn in for a nap."

Elisa went with her. "I'll go too. I need to see someone there."

They walked silently to the elevator. When they were alone, Elisa looked sidelong at Lynda and said, "You had me worried there for a moment."

"What? Why?"

"When you said something about us already having clues that aliens exist, I thought you were going to tell Viktoriya about…your secret."

"Yeah, sure." Lynda's lips curled into a playful half-smile. "Someday, everything about me will be common knowledge, but I just learned the truth yesterday. I want to figure out who I am before everyone else takes a turn at it."

"Yesterday? You mean you didn't know?"

Lynda shook her head. "Papa never told us—me or Gentry. When Papa wasn't shocked, or even surprised, to find out that aliens exist, I started to suspect. So, yesterday I got Bart to spill the beans. He's always known. His grandparents are alien, too, though he and his parents were born on Earth."

Elisa's dark eyes grew big and round. "You've lived your whole life being different, and didn't know?"

Lynda shook her head. "We'll talk later. Here's the Med Center."

They moved quickly through the disinfected aisles, passing row after row of silent forms, some sleeping, some comatose. Many were awake but glassy-eyed, expressionless, and eerily quiet:

hundreds who went too long without oxygen. There was little the doctors could do for them.

Lynda stopped when Elisa fell behind. She went back to find her friend standing by a bed like a sad statue, head bowed and hugging herself.

It was Braque's bed. The red-haired young man from the ship's laundry lay awake, looking up at the ceiling, but not moving. He could never move again.

Lynda hugged Elisa and felt the invisible trembling of her weeping. There was nothing to say. Lynda lost the will to search for Paul Poluka, and it was time for Elisa to report for duty.

Lynda went alone to her quarters. She felt grubby. A shower would be good, but exercise and then a shower would be even better. She got hold of Bart on the com-net and invited him join her.

During FTL transits spacemen could squeeze in a few hours a day of exercise or entertainment and still keep up with the work load, so there were about 200 people in the gym now.

"No privacy." Lynda frowned. "I'd hoped we could practice fighting, like we used to."

"Out of the question," Bart half smirked as he looked at the dozens of crewmen congregating at the boxing ring, "People are already scared of me. Believe me; you don't want that kind of fame."

Lynda glanced sharply at him. "I thought you liked having a reputation. I mean—you're a soldier—don't you want people to know you're dangerous?"

"No." Bart frowned. "*You* have trouble making friends. Imagine how it is for *me*."

"I'm sorry, Bart. Of course, I should have realized."

He shrugged and pointed across the gym where a net was set up.

"I find badminton beneficial. Come try it with me."

She'd played it as a child, but thought it strange Bart would enjoy a game that didn't challenge the limits of his great speed and strength.

She found herself lost in concentration as she focused on the shuttlecock and her body got into the rhythm of matching her footwork to the changing position of her target. At first she was clumsy, but soon got her movements synchronized to the returning path of the shuttlecock.

It was like a strangely hypnotic dance that made her attain complete control of her body. She lost track of time until she suddenly realized people were watching them. It wasn't like a crowd of gawking spectators, but, here and there around the gym, people were observing the back-and-forth of the game.

She caught the shuttlecock in her left hand and approached the net. Bart joined her quizzically.

"They're watching us," she whispered.

He shook his head. "Don't worry about it. They're just watching the game. We weren't playing to win, so the birdie hasn't hit the floor for about ten minutes. They're wondering how long we can keep it up."

"If we're not playing to win, what are we playing for?"

"How does it make you feel?"

She considered the question. "Good, or...better...it's like I feel sort of rested, I guess."

"Me too. I think it's different for us. It gets us balanced somehow. You see? We both benefit with no one losing. It's a concept more people should think about."

CHAPTER 35

Commander Alexander Washington's department was Ship's Business, which put him at the head of personnel, finance, public relations, and law enforcement aboard the Hanno, though he had subordinates heading each individual department.

He could also hold his liquor better than Poluka which, at the moment, was fortunate because they now had half a liter less whiskey than they did an hour ago. Technically, they shouldn't be drinking, but an FTL transit was the best time to bend the rules, and it would be two more shift changes before returning to normal space. They were alone in the skipper's quarters and Poluka was starting to say things he might otherwise keep to himself.

They'd served together on a heavy-cruiser before the war, and had their hell-raising days long before these younger officers came along. It was pretty obvious that Poluka deliberately managed to get a crew that the New Fed wanted to get rid of. Washington had been privately working out possible explanations.

"Things were different before the war," Poluka grumbled. "These new kids just don't get it."

"Get what?" Washington's slouching figure on the sofa belied his razor-sharp attention.

"The way a ship is supposed to be. In the Navy there weren't any fast promotions. We worked the same job for years, and never questioned the captain's decisions—never."

"You wouldn't be referring to Aguire?" Washington inquired carefully.

"Aguire's good. I mean he probably should be in the Corps." Poluka tilted his glass to scowl at the contents before draining it. "But I don't think he was ever really Navy material."

"Eh? How's that?" Washington heaved himself up a little straighter on the sofa.

"There's trouble brewing back home." Poluka rambled on, oblivious to Washington's consternation. "The new government's starting forced relocations of millions of people, and mandatory reeducation programs to make people politically acceptable. There's bound to be resistance. They don't tell us, but there's been some killing. It's time for old soldiers to choose sides."

"What are you talking about, Paul?"

"I'm talking about another coup. I know you hate what's going on as much as I do. Batastia's a lunatic. He's gotta be stopped."

"He will be, Paul. I know the military's gonna turn on him, and there's General Hebert. He's gathering his forces, I've heard."

"Gathering? They're gathered. Hebert is attacking Earth right now."

"How do you know that?" Washington kept his voice even. Poluka was either imagining things, or was involved in Hebert's counter-coup. He'd prefer it to be the latter and might welcome the opportunity to get involved himself. Still, if that's what his captain was into, he'd prefer to have been told a long time ago, instead of it slipping out after a couple of drinks.

"When Lieutenant Tran ran the recorded sensor data through an analysis, he ran all of it—all the way back to when we left Earth orbit. Do you remember there was an inbound convoy at the jump point? We had to wait until they passed before switching on the new engines."

"I remember. Was that General Hebert?"

"The data strongly suggests it was."

"That sounds better." Washington smiled grimly. "So, Hebert's going to take down Batastia."

"He'll try. He may succeed, too, but we could do it faster. We've got the Hanno. We're faster than anyone else, and we're armed too. Have you been to the missile section? You should see the shit we've got."

"Paul, the Hanno's not a warship. Sure, we've got capabilities, but…"

"You know," Poluka stared blindly at the wall, "my dear brother predicted this new government. He also predicted that a great military leader would rise to the occasion and overthrow the New Fed."

"General Hebert?"

Paul Poluka slammed his glass down on the desk, and shouted, "Why not *me*? Why can't *I* be the one?"

Washington jerked upright at the sudden outburst and spilled his whiskey.

Poluka lurched to his feet, and flung his arms in exasperation. "He said when this leader shows up, I should support him—be his fucking follower for Christ's sake! He never considered that I might be the leader and Hebert can do the goddamn following!"

Commander Washington quietly put the cap back on the whiskey bottle.

* * *

Aguire finally got the time to go see the alien ship when he was relieved by Commander Sheffield. Chief Braun and Tran went with him to the SERFS admin office where they got space suits from Hilda Harris. She'd just finished with a group of engineers coming out of the bay, and was busy refilling the air supplies, sanitizing the interiors, downloading the data recorders, and the dozen or so other things required for proper suit maintenance.

She gave a quiet grunt while pulling the suit up his legs.

"Aren't you due for a break?" he asked her.

Harris smiled, and wiped a hand across her sweating ebony complexion. "I'll take a break when you get back, Commander." She pulled the suit up to his chin.

"Then I'll try not to take too long."

He snapped his helmet on and could hear the overlapping conversations of workers in the alien ship. The radio automatically adjusted the volume coming from each of them depending on how far away they were, simulating the normal acoustics of an air environment.

He cycled through the airlock with Braun and Tran. They were giving each other meaningful looks as if they were up to something. He figured it was just an engineer thing. The lock opened and they pushed off, leaving the fringe of artificial gravity and gliding into the cavernous bay.

Chief Braun spoke up with a clear, relaxed voice that held no hint of concern, "I'm glad we could join you, Commander. Of course, we're not scheduled to be here now, so we should try not to interfere with the current operation. Maybe we should do a three-way link."

He pointed to the communication controls on Aguire's suit.

"Harris," Aguire called the control room. "We're going to a private link so we won't interfere with the work going on."

When the link was confirmed, Braun spoke quickly, "Let's go down to the alien ship, and look around while we talk, shall we?"

Micro-thrusters built into their boots propelled them to the hatch of the alien vessel. From there, they pulled themselves hand-over-hand on a cargo net that was spread out inside for the convenience of the people working inside. The alien ship completely captured Aguire's attention.

The interior of the vessel was mostly clear of debris now, and the net was anchored to the few intact structural supports that remained. There were still some original walls and decks that survived years of impacts against the little ship, but much of it was empty now.

There were perhaps twenty others in small groups exploring the nooks, and studying the overall structure. Aguire tried to imagine aliens living here, caught by the Zone and unable to escape.

"I wonder what happened to them," he said. "There weren't any bodies, so they must have been rescued. Maybe they had other ships close enough to help them."

"Chief!" Tran gave a raspy whisper. "Tell him!" Aguire turned so his helmet light shined on the man's face. Tran had a sheen of perspiration on his forehead despite the cool air inside his suit.

"What is it?"

Braun answered. "We got some information out of the thruster that was left by the Himilco. Apparently, ten years ago, the Himilco met the crew of this ship. They all left together. They went to Arcturus."

"When did you get the information?"

"Before we left the Zone." Braun raised a hand to stop Aguire's protest. "I know, I know, there should have been a ship-wide announcement, and a big damn celebration, but we were...concerned.

"Poluka ordered Tran to keep quiet about the Zone. He's got us worried. Elisa Santino discovered that Poluka and Stokes were hiding things from the Admiralty, and from the New Federation."

"I know," Aguire said. "I saw the pattern in the personnel files and talked to Poluka about it. He said he was taking as many as possible who've been blacklisted, to protect them."

"Oh? Did he tell you what all the missiles are for? Did he tell you that he wants to turn the colonies against the Federation, and make them independent?"

A sour, sinking feeling overcame Aguire. A few more pieces of the puzzle fell into place, and it was not looking good. "Stokes is part of this?" He was thinking more of Lynda than her father.

"From what I understand, he's been encouraging Poluka in that direction. They've been planning it at least since the war—maybe they started during the war. But, what I know may be wrong. Like I said, Elisa discovered it while working in the DDR. She was doing the design review, and started seeing how Stokes was hiding some of the engine fabrication so not everyone would see the complete design. He funneled work though contractors and back to his competitors in Canada. Some of the work went through Firehawk—did you know Mister Hanson is a major stockholder in Firehawk? Apparently Hanson has been in on this for quite some time, too.

"Elisa was going to blackmail Stokes to get herself an early retirement—she felt she was cornered by the new bureaucracy, and couldn't stay in the Corps any longer—but then something terrible happened. Admiral Fisher murdered Elisa's friend, Julie Klein, and was going to have Elisa killed, too, because she knew he did it. She came to me for help, and together we put the pieces together about what Poluka was really up to.

"We confronted Poluka and demanded that he take us with him. He had no choice but to agree, but now that we're out here, and they are committed to their plan, they could just kill us, like they did the Attorney General.

"Elisa and I've been trying to just fit into this crazy plan that Poluka and Stokes came up with, but now Stokes keeps collapsing, and Poluka is becoming a loose cannon with his unilateral decisions, withholding information, and these unpredictable mood swings. Am I leaving anything out?"

Aguire stared dumbfounded at Braun's round cherub face, absorbing the flood of information as best he could.

"You forgot the part about the data we got from the thruster," Henry Tran put in.

"Right. When the captain told Henry to keep his mouth shut about the Zone, he said it was because of how the ex-Navy types like you would react. Now, we have a video of aliens hobnobbing with the captain's brother. By the way, did you know that Clifford Poluka was always better than our captain at everything he does? It's true, I knew Cliff Poluka. I think that's why the skipper's getting weird on us—he lost a lot of lives in the Zone, and can't stand the idea that his brother got in and got out without losing anybody. Now, if we tell him that his brother not only got in and out, but actually rescued another ship's crew, he may go completely off the deep end. We've been debating whether or not to tell him."

Aguire wrestled with the two images he had of his captain: the Poluka he knew for years, who is steady as a rock and totally trustworthy, and this new Poluka who commits treason and is dangerously unpredictable. He believed what Braun was telling him, but it was a lot to grasp all of a sudden.

"I…I think I'd like to see the information myself, before Poluka does."

"I thought that's what you'd say." Braun looked at Tran. "Give it to him, Henry."

Tran handed Aguire a button disc. He took the disc and plugged it into his own suit's data logger, and hit the replay button. A virtual video screen popped up in his field of view. The recording began with the face of a man who looked a bit like Captain Paul Poluka.

The man began speaking. "My name is Captain Clifford Poluka of the Starship Himilco…"

A half-hour of video flew by, showing Commander Aguire what the interior of the alien ship looked like when it was operational, and what the aliens looked like while they were operating it. He saw their faces, heard their voices speaking a strange language, and got the impression they were as human as he was. Their uniforms were light-green tunics with huge pockets on the sides, and brown pants tucked into knee-high boots. The alien captain wore a finely braided cord around his neck with a crystal hanging on it that may have been a diamond about two centimeters wide. He had a calm, tough-looking face, with brown eyes that gave an impression of knowledge and courage.

Clifford Poluka reported that four of his crew had died from an asteroid collision, and that the ship's surgeon had also died, though he didn't say how that happened. He explained how they'd found the damaged alien ship in the Zone, and had established communications through Ensign Emerson, the Himilco's linguist, and an alien woman named Ella Dann, whose role on the alien ship was not completely clear. Clifford Poluka thought she might be the first officer.

The alien ship could not be repaired, and it was mutually agreed that the Himilco would transport them back to their home world, in the Arcturus System.

At the end of the video there was a text portion of the recording listing all the Himilco's crewmen by name.

Following that, there was another list of the alien's names—thirty-eight in all. Beside some names were titles to show their rank, or role, on the alien ship. The first line read: Aga Ayab—Captain of the Starship Fledik.

The recording ended. Aguire drew a deep breath before refocusing his eyes to look for Braun and Tran, who'd moved off to look around while he watched the video.

"Fledik?" Aguire reached out and touched the alien ship. "That's the most amazing thing I've ever seen."

"That's exactly what I said when I saw it," Tran said as he and Braun emerged from a side passage they had been exploring. They were hesitant to share the news of an important discovery—and now, so was he—because of doubts about the captain. It was as if Poluka's problem was contagious.

They left the Fledik. The alien fabric had been moved. It was now suspended further to the port side of the bay and away from the walls where there was no artificial gravity at all. A mini-gopher hovered in front of it with an event recorder, taking pictures in microscopic detail.

The temptation to go look at the artwork tugged at Aguire, but duty called and there was still the question about his captain.

"Listen, guys." Aguire explained his position. "The recording indicates the Himilco lost at least five of its own personnel. That's what—twenty percent? I hate to treat fatalities like statistics, but if the captain—our captain—is rating himself against his brother's mission, he's doing okay. I don't like how he's been making decisions lately, either, but he's still just one officer on this ship, even if he is the captain. The rest of us will keep him from straying too far.

"I say, let him see the recording. You can tell him it was coded in some obsolete format and you just now figured it out, but I would suggest that you bring it to the meeting before we get to Arcturus, so everyone can see it together. Let's not tempt our captain to keep any more secrets. Does that sound okay to you?"

The two engineers agreed.

G.J. Stokes was still a big unknown in all this. He was a businessman, and didn't seem terribly interested in the fate of common people. If the colonies tried to break away from the New Fed, it would probably destroy him financially. So, what was he up to by rocking the boat?

They pushed off from the alien ship at an angle that sent them into the wide, open volume of the bay, and then used their thrusters to fly towards the airlock. When they got close, they flipped over to connect with the wall feet-first. As he did his flip, Aguire glanced at Commander Sirenko's office window, and saw Lynda Stokes watching him.

He liked Lynda, and wondered how much she knew about all this.

* * *

After showering, Lynda asked another woman in the locker room to show her how to braid her hair the way women in the Corps do. Her honey-blond locks were just long enough to make it work.

When she returned to the SERFS office after a nap, she enjoyed the comments her new hairstyle got from ladies there.

Three space suits came out of the alien ship and angled towards the airlock. Harris went down to let them in. They glided headfirst, waiting until they were close before flipping around to connect feet-first with the wall. The one in the lead made a graceful half-summersault, instead of the easier, backward half-flip.

"Pretty slick." Viktoriya was watching the maneuver. "You know, I used to be a gymnast, too."

"Is that Aguire?" Lynda asked.

"Uh-huh."

The three men cycled through the lock and stripped out of

the suits while frost was forming on the suits from moisture in the air. They were in the office a moment later.

Lynda wondered why Aguire gave her an odd look before realizing he was looking at her hair. It was the first time in years that her face suddenly warmed with a blush. She pretended to watch the activity in the bay, hoping the pink glow would fade quickly.

"…absolutely priceless," Chief Braun was saying when they entered. "We've got the find of a lifetime. That section of crew quarters is almost intact with personal possessions. I can almost picture them living there."

"The technology differences are puzzling though," Tran added. "They have things that operate on principals we're familiar with, but they've used primitive materials for a lot of it."

Unable to pretend anymore that she was more interested in the activity in the bay than in the conversation, Lynda turned around and asked, "Will we have enough information for a review before we get to Arcturus? If we run into some live aliens we're going to want to know what to expect."

"I'm sure we can at least get a summary of the contents and materials." Aguire glanced at the info-screen. "We've got about nine hours. I need to get some rest before we arrive. I'll ask to have a presentation ready in about six hours. That'll be around 0500 hours."

"Great. Maybe I should take a nap, too, and be rested when we enter the system."

Aguire stepped closer to Lynda and lowered his voice. "Have you talked with Poluka lately?"

"No." She couldn't keep the worry out of her expression. "I tried to find him earlier, but…."

"I haven't seen him since we crossed over to FTL. Do you think he's…going to be alright? He's been keeping things from me lately. You know more than I do about what he's doing with the politicos back home. Is there anything I should know—something that could affect the safety of the ship?"

Lynda thought that was a remarkably diplomatic way to ask.

"I don't think he's going nuts. He made a mistake that cost a lot of lives. We all did. We got caught up in the excitement, and rushed things. He's feeling the responsibility for those deaths, and for those still in Med Center who probably won't recover."

She paused. The memory of quiet beds haunted her.

"Of course," Aguire sighed. "I want to feel that Poluka is up to it."

She searched his eyes and found sincerity there.

"I'm sorry. I just don't know the answer."

CHAPTER 36

At 0530 hours the senior staff was spellbound by the ten-year-old recording of earthmen encountering aliens for the first time in human history. Having seen it before, Aguire could spare some attention to the reaction of his peers, especially his captain.

Poluka sat in goggle-eyed fascination, the same as everyone else, with perhaps a bit more intensity whenever his brother appeared on the screen, but that was to be expected.

It left the room breathless, but more subdued than Aguire had expected.

Poluka invited comments and discussion. Joseph Redbird asked if there was anything in the protocols about technological imbalance.

"What do you mean, Commander?" Poluka asked.

"I mean, so far it looks like these aliens aren't as advanced as us. What will be our relationship to them?"

"I still don't follow you, Commander."

Redbird seemed annoyed. "In our own ancient history, when Europeans first came to America, the explorers had big ships and superior weapons, not to mention a culture of conquest. For centuries, the Native Americans were treated horribly. So, this seems like a similar situation here."

Poluka finally got the point. "That was long before the Great Disaster and, even by the time of the Disaster, the people of old Earth learned to behave better. However, you've brought up a valid point, Commander. We'll review the protocol with that in mind."

After the meeting Poluka had the historic recording broadcast to the crew, which Aguire took as good sign that the Captain was finished with keeping secrets.

It was the consensus of the senior staff that they should translate back to normal space earlier than originally planned, well outside the Arcturus System. Knowing that an alien civilization lay ahead, it seemed prudent. After all, they'd be appearing unannounced and unexpected.

All bridge commanders were on hand. Captain Poluka was at the command desk. Aguire was in the copilot's chair. Maria Rodriguez was piloting, and John Burke was navigating. The I-bay was crammed with engineers. Officers that didn't really need to be there were hanging around by the emergency lockers against the back wall.

"Coming up on six light hours from the star, Captain," Burke announced. "In five minutes."

The ship was sealed, and armored shields were closed on every window, not because of anything that could happen at faster-than-light speed, but because when they translate back to normal space, there was no telling what they might find themselves in the middle of.

The long-range survey done before leaving the Zone was encouraging. The ship's telescopes had six-meter mirrors that could see anything brighter than a candle from one light-year away, provided there was nothing in the way. Still, it pays to be careful.

At Aguire's suggestion, Poluka authorized some hummingbird missiles staged for launch, just in case there was a misunderstanding with some aliens.

At faster than light speed they had only the Stokes Tubes to tell them what was beyond the tachyon envelope surrounding the Hanno and, at best, it gave them a fuzzy picture of the stars that wasn't much good for anything except navigation.

"Begin the translation at the six light-hour point, Mister Burke." Poluka ordered.

Aguire slipped into the S-bay where Donno was monitoring everything on the ship. The small work area had a curved floor plan that kept most of it out of sight from the rest of the bridge, making it easier for Donno's people to concentrate.

"This ship couldn't be more ready for anything that may happen," Donno told him. "I think the cafeteria even polished the silverware. All hands are taking this seriously."

"So am I," Aguire said. "Do we have any weak spots?"

"Sure." Donno's good humor faded a bit. "Some of our best are gone. That accident forced us to shuffle personnel to fill in key positions. Not everyone has experience in their new assignments, but they're all good people. We'll manage. By the way, Lieutenant Santino asked me if she could temporarily return to laundry duty."

"Really? Why?"

"The whole laundry crew is a bunch of kids. Have you seen them? When Ensign Braque ended up with a broken neck, they took it pretty hard. Santino knows this bunch, and wanted to spend some time with them."

Elisa Santino's skills were wasted in the laundry, but Aguire could tell from the way Donno mentioned it that he'd already agreed to her request. He was strict, but not a hard-ass.

The Hanno began the translation. There was the expected tremor that ran down the eleven-kilometer length of the ship as the tachyon envelope disappeared, and then they were in normal space again.

The near light speed engines wound up to full power as they began decelerating to a reasonable speed. NLS technology was developed nearly 300 years ago to defy time dilation and the other relativity problems, but there was no way around Doppler shift and other observational difficulties. They needed to slow down to look at the Arcturus System on the way in.

Ensign Burke watched the 3-D graphic on the main screen. The long-range survey forewarned them of at least six planets. Four would be on a plane almost parallel to their entry vector. Two objects were far off that plane, and nowhere near where the Hanno was entering the system.

"I see it, Mister Burke, right where we expected it," Captain Poluka said, just as the navigator pointed to a dot on the screen representing a gas giant about 73,000 kilometers wide and right in their way. "Take us a little further off the ecliptic, toward galactic zenith, at your discretion."

"Aye, sir." Burke fed the course change to Rodriguez and the Hanno made a slight shift in direction, which brought some grumbles from the I-bay. Apparently, the engineers had some measurement going that had to be started over, now that the course was changed.

The new projected course showed they would intersect the ecliptic plane halfway between the gas giant and the star itself in about four hours as they decelerated down to fifteen thousand kps relative to the star.

"Mister Tran," Poluka called to the I-bay. "We await your analysis. There are people here somewhere. Tell us where to find them."

"Yes, sir. We're working on it."

The Hanno held course with a constant deceleration. The sensor towers extending to port and starboard from the forward section scanned every rock bigger than a peanut within nine light hours of the star. Here, within the gravitational and solar wind influence of the red giant, the interstellar dust of sub-micron size particles was swept away and the view was clear.

Thousands of antennae, cameras, spectrometers and biosensors flooded the I-bay computers with data that was sorted, analyzed and reconfirmed with blazing speed. The graphic on the main screen quickly filled in with new information.

The gas giant they had avoided was seven-point-two light hours from the star, and the furthest from Arcturus, with one moon, half the diameter of Earth.

The planet that was next closest to its sun, about three light hours from the star, was a bigger gas giant, mostly hydrogen, about the size of Jupiter, and had twenty-seven small moons as well as some spectacular rings. It was on the far side of the star, but they had a good view since the Hanno was above the orbital ecliptic.

The next was about one light-hour from Arcturus, and would be getting just about the right amount of energy from its sun for supporting an Earth-like planet but, it too, appeared to be a gas planet, not a giant, but still half again the diameter of the Earth. Its atmosphere was a soup of gasses and dust blowing around the planet at hurricane velocity.

There was a very small planetoid scorchingly close to its sun at only 156 million kilometers. The red giant Arcturus was a 180 times brighter than Sol, including infrared energy, and this poor little world was molten metal with a metal vapor atmosphere. It gave plenty of data that was exciting for the scientists, but didn't bring them any closer to finding the life they were looking for.

The last two objects orbited on a sharply inclined plane in a long narrow ellipse. They were irregularly shaped rocks that were also orbiting each other. By conventional definitions they were the second and third planets of the system, having an orbit that would pass between the molten planet and the small gas world at their closest approach, though, at the moment, their long elliptic course had them almost as far from the star as the fifth planet.

The next step was to release passive buoys near the star, and near each planet, to see how fast they accelerate from the gravity. This would get the numbers needed to calculate mass for each object. Arcturus had been observed by astronomers since the beginning of history but, sometime after the Great Disaster of the twenty-second century, the galactic dust cloud which now plagues astronomy had appeared to obscure the star from modern observations. They had some pretty good estimates about its mass, but no one had ever been close enough for direct measurements.

"All right," Poluka said after patiently hearing Tran's report. "We can't pass up an opportunity like this. Prep a buoy for stellar mass measurement. Tell our navigator where you want us to park the Hanno. Damn," he sighed wearily. "There should be a habitable planet here."

"Mister Donno, you're our expert on the Alien Encounter Protocols."

"I suppose so, sir."

"I'd like for you to take some time today, and consult with whomever you think might have good advice on the subject. I would like to know how wise it would be in our current circumstances—knowing that aliens were on their way here aboard the Himilco ten years ago—to send a signal to attract their attention, assuming they are somewhere nearby."

"Attract their attention, sir?"

"We're having trouble finding them, Commander. Maybe *they* can find *us* if we encourage them to look."

CHAPTER 37

"I've found them," whispered Lapastra, the Queen of Arcturus. She opened her eyes and the flickering candle on her prayer table replaced her vision of the mighty, arrow-shaped spaceship. "They are passing the outer planets."

She rose from a kneeling position and rushed to the door of the balcony. The red aurora of dawn was just finished and the land was gathering light for a new day. Her dark eyes searched the garden as the chilled morning breeze toyed with her curly black locks. She saw the King walking with their friend and advisor, Eeja Burr, on the stone-paved path that meandered from the palace through the flowerbeds and onward through the blossoming orchards. They were still far, but heading back to the palace.

She wanted to urge him to hurry, and almost projected a telepathic message to her husband, but the chill wind clawed at her light brown skin, reminding her that the world can be unkind. She noticed now the unnatural ripples in the telepathic fields; spies from the college were probing the royal household again.

Lapastra pulled her white silk gown higher around her neck and shoulders, and pressed her thumbnail into her fingertips just hard enough to be slightly painful: a routine she'd learned as a child to mask her psychic gifts with a distracting physical sensation so that other telepaths would not sense her secret ability.

In a world where thoughts could be probed from a distance, keeping secrets was nearly impossible, but they managed it. No one guessed the royal couple's bold gambit. This time, Elpastre's image as an inconsequential ruler worked to their advantage. The low esteem the Old Rulers afforded Elpastre and his wife made them assume the royal couple was simply incapable of such a devious scheme, and so never devoted much effort to spying on them.

Beyond the citrus and nut trees was the dark, wild forest in the East. She was born on the other side of that forest. Now, as troubled times were beginning, she longed to see her little village again, but that would not happen soon. The Old Rulers will know about the ship from Earth before the day was finished.

By the time her husband returned, the psychic fields had returned to natural patterns. It was breakfast time for the headmistress at the psychic college.

"Mata Buray likes a big meal." Lapastra allowed herself a bitter smile. "She won't be good for anything until midmorning."

The King of Arcturus returned to the palace. Eeja Burr, the royal chronicler and friend of the royal couple, had just relayed an unofficial message from the Matriarch of the Old Rulers, which put the King in a sour mood.

The palace was an old stone building, built a hundred generations ago in a time the Earthmen call the third century, with three levels above ground and a basement below, which was unusual for such an old structure. On Earth, people have been building much taller buildings for thousands of years.

Elpastre, the King, learned much about Earth, and the knowledge made him worry that his enemies might be right about that world.

"I don't like troubling you with this, Elpastre," said Eeja as they entered from the garden, "since I can guess what your answer to the Matriarch must be."

Elpastre slipped his coat off and handed it to a waiting attendant. "Of course you can guess my reaction, and I can guess Lapastra's reaction. You're lucky that I'm the one who will tell her that Aylata Naray wants her son to marry our daughter. A generation ago no one would even consider joining the royal family to the Old Rulers. Now Aylata dares to suggest that it's the only reasonable response to this visit from Earth."

"The matriarch's opinion of Earthmen gets worse with each day," Eeja said. "And yet I believe she still hasn't actually met one. She must know that her 'offer' will be viewed as shocking, but perhaps its purpose is to plant the idea in our minds and then manufacture a situation that will make it seem less repugnant."

227

Elpastre frowned. "When Aylata was young she thought I should marry her, and somehow managed to show up at events where my parents took me to meet young women."

Eeja turned sharply to face Elpastre. "She thought she could marry you? She must have been insane."

Elpastre smiled and led the young chronicler to where a servant was preparing tea for them. "That was before she committed herself to the Clan of the Old Rulers. You're too young to remember, but Aylata's ancestry is mixed, and she could have denied her ties to the Old Rulers. Now, of course, she denies being anything but pureblood aristocracy of the Old Rulers, a true Daughter of the Island, as they say. The bitch started out half mad, now she's gone the rest of the way. I'm terribly worried of what she might do when the Earth ship actually arrives."

"Mm…time is running out." A hint of worry appeared on Eeja's expression. "If the headmistress is correct, the ship will arrive in the Season of the Twins. The Earthmen may be here in as soon as 400 days from now. Of course, Mata Buray is frequently wrong with her predictions. If she wasn't the matriarch's cousin, Teki Ko-ray would be the headmistress, and then I'd be worried."

Elpastre glanced at Eeja, sorry that he couldn't tell the young chronicler that he knew—really knew—that the headmistress was wrong in her prediction, and that the Earthmen might arrive at any moment.

The Queen, Lapastra, was perhaps the greatest seer of modern times, but this secret was all they had, the only advantage over the Old Rulers that the royal couple could use to tip the balance and save their world from extinction.

"Try the tea." Elpastre said, "It's from the Southern wilderness."

"I really must be going." Eeja shrugged, but took a sip. "My wife needs me today, and I will contact the spy we have in the psychic college, who may have some insight to the matriarch's strange offer."

"Ugh." Elpastre glared out the front window towards 'the Island', an ugly building nearly as old as the royal palace, where the matriarch presided. "And I must go up to Lapastra and tell her that Aylata wants her spoiled brat to marry our Princess Miyuree. You'd better hurry if you want to be out of throwing range."

Eeja smiled warmly and bade his King farewell. Elpastre went up the stairs and found his wife in the parlor with their map unrolled upon the desk. It was an ancient scroll that showed long forgotten cities and highways where today there was only wilderness.

"Elpastre, my love, I have some news." Her thick black hair hung in wavy locks, framing her face and reminding him of how she looked the day he first saw her, and fell in love. For the millionth time, he was thankful that she married him.

"Ah, you mean about the message from the matriarch. Just let me say…"

"No, no, about the ship. The ship from Earth has arrived."

"Are you sure?"

"Yes, they will make three landings very soon and the first to land will be on the far side of the planet—a crash landing—on the other continent."

"Which is virtually unreachable." Elpastre grimaced. The other continent, whose name means birth land of the fledik, was an uninhabited wilderness far across the Great Sea.

"It doesn't matter. They will be rescued by the younger Poluka, who will then come to our side of the world." Her finger lightly traced around the north coast on the map. "The important landing will happen right…about…here."

"Just where you foresaw." He nodded. "And in the Season of The Bull, but has any other seer detected it?"

"Not yet. But soon" Lapastra's eyebrows drew together into a worried expression. "I detected the headmistress snooping the palace earlier. But it's safe to talk now."

"You say there will be three landings?" Elpastre asked.

"Yes. This so-called King of Earth will land in the desert, near the pyramid, as the headmistress foresaw. As soon as they learn the ship has arrived, the Old Rulers will send their best psychics there, hoping to gain an advantage over us. Some of the survivors from the Himilco will go as well."

"I see. It's becoming clearer. The headmistress was right about a landing at the pyramid, but it will not be Clifford Poluka's brother."

"That landing will be near, but not at, the pyramid. Mata Buray was wrong about that, too, and everyone waiting at the pyramid will not meet this King of Earth."

Elpastre smiled, too. The HEADMISTRESS, and several other psychics, said the King of Earth was coming to their world. It was only Lapastra who discovered that this was one of those classic mistakes that novice psychics are so often warned about: a mix of signs, words that can have more than one meaning, supporting a false conclusion. The headmistress may lose her position over this, despite being the matriarch's cousin.

"Clifford Poluka tried to tell people that their king—or president, as they call him—would not come. But Aylata couldn't consider it. She wants only a king from Earth."

"We must prepare our daughter for the journey to the desert." Lapastra said. Her voice trembled. "We must have our best guards watching over her."

"Of course." Elpastre took his beautiful wife into his arms and kissed her. "We wouldn't send her at all except that the Old Rulers would become suspicious if no member of the royal family went to meet the King of Earth."

He understood well what it meant to be called a king, and have it mean nothing. They could not waste this opportunity to be the first to meet Clifford Poluka's brother.

"What were you saying about a message from the matriarch?" Lapastra asked.

"Ah...well...you see..."

By then Eeja was indeed out of throwing range, and didn't see the flowerpot hurled out the balcony window. He was even too far down the road to hear the Queen cursing.

CHAPTET 38

A big weary sigh started and Poluka just couldn't stop it. There were no fast answers in sight. He waved his old friend over to him. "Commander Washington, take the watch. I'm going to see how our people are doing with the alien ship."

"The Fledik." Washington said. "A least we have a name for it now. I wonder what it means."

Poluka marched down Main Street at a brisk pace, musing over how this discovery would affect history. Contact with aliens was the premise of countless novels and movies, and yet there were scores of scientific studies 'proving' with statistics and logic that Earth was the only place in the galaxy where intelligent life had ever evolved.

Oh, there may be moss growing on Alpha Virginus, and fish in the Tau Ceti Sea, but nothing more evolved than lizards could possibly be out there. The careers of some prominent scientists had crashed into obscurity after suggesting otherwise.

This discovery will make the crew of the Hanno the most envied in history, and Captain Paul Poluka will be remembered as...

His enthusiastic stride down Main Street slowed almost to a stop.

I will go down in history for turning against the New Federation—that's the plan. Our discovery of aliens will be overshadowed by political upheaval. Even if our rebellion succeeds, it could be years before anything gets done about alien contact. And if it's not successful, maybe nothing will ever be done. The names of the discoverers will be remembered as traitors who caused needless death and misery, and the glory of this historic find will be lost forever.

As he passed the entrance to the Med Center, his mood darkened further. Clifford's ship had lost five, which was a lot for such a small ship, but history would always point at the Hanno and Captain *Paul* Poluka for the highest number.

A way must be found.

He picked up his pace with renewed determination.

One field of knowledge that excelled after the Great Disaster was metallurgy. If anyone could figure out this alien substance, it would be Major Doyle.

"Major." Poluka nodded first to the middle-aged chemist, then to the silvery metal fragment Doyle was holding. "What will it take to produce more of this?"

"We can't do it, Captain," Major Doyle confessed. He had a sad, hound-dog face, making him look terribly serious. Doyle was regular Army on loan to the Hanno, but it was analytical prowess rather than military expertise that elevated him to the rank of major.

He could study and explain just about anything, but never knew when to just shut up, especially about government policy, which was why he was on the government's black list.

"You can't duplicate it?" Poluka asked.

"Duplicate it? We can't even guess what it's made of. This substance is slightly lighter than aluminum. It's got to be some combination of the lighter metals, and maybe some non-metals." The major held up a ten-centimeter shard of silvery metal. "See this? We couldn't get a piece of this off that ship with lasers, saws or torches. Particle beams and high-temp plasma couldn't do it either. Acids have some effect, so we came up with a nasty mixture that managed to weaken the stuff."

He rubbed the edge of the metal with a cloth. What seemed like a razor edge crumbled like sugar, and he dropped the metal crumbs into a beaker of liquid. The solid fragments instantly dissolved. "See, where we hit it with a jet of liquid acid, it lost all its strength. When we analyze this mixture, we find only the acid. There's no trace of the metal. All we've learned so far is that it liberates helium when the acid hits it."

"Chief Braun suggested this may be an unknown element," Poluka said.

The major sheepishly glanced around at the other scientists. "Well, you know, the periodic table is pretty full already. We've done the spectroscopy, of course, but..."

"You mean that you won't even *look* for an unknown element because the textbooks say there aren't any?" Poluka couldn't keep the irritation out of his voice.

"Captain, everyone knows —"

"Everyone knows *aliens* don't exist, Major. If you're afraid of how it will look, just say you're following my orders."

"You're ordering me to see if it's a new element?"

"Yes."

"Yes, sir. Thank you, sir."

Poluka left the fabrication shops and wondered if intelligent life ever really evolved on Earth.

He stopped by some other researchers who were finding odd things about materials from inside the ship, such as natural crystals that were cut and mounted for directing beams of light, possibly for carrying information.

Poluka wanted to visit the ship's library where the alien fabric was being studied, but a call from Washington alerted him to something happening in the bridge. When he got there, G.J. waved him into the I-Bay.

"Paul, we've found something." G.J. pointed to one of the screens that showed a cratered surface. "This is the moon of the fourth planet. When we measured the mass of the planet, it matched the Earth's mass almost exactly even though its diameter is 50 percent bigger. So, I went back to the calculated energy that was reaching this planet from the star. It's almost the same as the Earth's. If there's a habitable world it would have to be this one. We can't see any surface through the stormy atmosphere, so we took a closer look at its moon."

He zoomed in on the surface until an object revealed itself to the camera. It was a life-pod. The faded name *HIMILCO* appeared on it.

Poluka imagined the worst: a crash-landing with one pod making it to the moon, the others probably burning up in the gas-world's hurricane atmosphere. The mystery of his brother's fate was solved, and a dark place in his heart rejoiced.

"We need to retrieve it, find out if there are bodies inside."

"No need, Captain. A standard transponder query got a response. The pod sent back a text message. It was recorded in five languages and repeated a thousand times from different parts of the pod's memory, along with the entire video recording which we downloaded earlier from the thruster's memory."

G.J. pointed to another monitor where a message read:

Message from Captain Clifford Poluka commanding the Starship Himilco.

On this day, 27 March 2786, we are transporting the officers and crew of the alien starship *Fledik* to their home world by landing on the surface of Arcturus-4.

The captain of the Fledik assures me that an Earthlike environment is below the turbulent outer atmosphere. We are unable to confirm this with our instruments, and the probes we launched to study the planet have not survived entry through the atmosphere.

The Himilco is designed for direct landing on Earth-like planets but we may not be able to launch again if we can even survive the landing.

We considered every possibility, including returning to Earth with our new alien friends. Unfortunately, the Himilco suffered damage during the voyage from Earth that will make it impossible to return without repairs that may be possible on the planet surface with the help of the indigenous people. We have nowhere else to go.

We have every reason to believe the people of Arcturus-4 are honorable and may be approached in friendship. It was their hope to reach Earth for the purpose of establishing friendly relations.

If you have come from Earth and cannot contact the crew of the Himilco, it may be that we did not survive the landing, and that the people living on the surface know nothing of our attempt, or the fate of the Fledik.

Within this life-pod are letters written by every member of this ship. If we do not survive, we ask that these letters be retrieved and delivered our loved ones. There is also a package of letters written by our alien guests, the crew of the Fledik. I ask you to deliver it, if possible, to the leader of this planet, who is known as Elpastre. There is a letter of introduction that may be shown to any native of this planet to obtain directions to Elpastre.

I have also included a copy of the ship's log, which is the property of the Exploration Corps of the Planet Earth.

<end of message>

* * *

Arcturus-4 looked like any other gas-world, but smaller. Most are giants, bigger than even Jupiter. The swirls of gasses on this one were moving at 300 kilometers per hour, with hurricane patterns polka-dotting the globe.

Inside the life pod were two packages of letters and a logbook. The letters written by aliens would not be opened at this time, though a visual recording of the strange writing on the envelopes was made.

Of the letters from the crew of the Himilco, five were addressed to people currently aboard the Hanno. The Captain saw no reason not to deliver them.

There was a letter for Poluka from his brother, and another for G.J. and Lynda from Gentry Stokes. Chief Braun got one from his old friend Ivan, who was the mission scientist on the Himilco. Bart Hanson also got one from Gentry, which no one had expected since they were not related, but the one that surprised everyone was addressed to Maria Rodriguez, the senior pilot. It turned out that the Himilco's dentist was her uncle, but she'd never mentioned it because she never really believed they'd find any sign of survivors.

Lynda went with her father to his quarters to receive their letter which had handwritten names on the envelope: *Gentry Stokes Jr. and Lynda Stokes.*

She gazed out the window at the planet. It was beautiful in its slowly swirling patterns of many colors, and hideous for being the end of the fantasy that kept her going for the last decade.

He's here, or he's dead. Either way, this is the last place Gentry ever went.

"Papa," Lynda whispered. "Please, open it."

Before breaking the seal, he said softly, "I don't believe he's dead."

The note said nothing terribly exciting, but it brought back to Lynda the sound of his voice, the smells of California, and the adoration an eleven-year-old girl had for her big brother.

Mostly, her brother praised his captain and shipmates. He mentioned the thrill of meeting aliens, and assured them that they were wonderful people. He said he'd made a friend onboard—Emerson, the linguist. Finally, at the end, he said that he loved them both.

"Well," Papa sighed. "I suppose there wasn't really too much to say."

"We're not very sentimental," Lynda said.

"Eh?"

"Green-eyed Erosians." Lynda's voice was ice. "We're not sentimental."

His own green eyes stared with horror for a moment before becoming angry. "Damn him. Bart told you!"

"Why didn't *you* tell me, Papa?" Lynda asked quietly. She wasn't angry. She only brought it up now because she couldn't see any reason not to.

"You didn't need to know." His pouting expression appeared.

"Ever? Would you ever have told me?"

"How could it help you? Look what it did to your brother."

"How did he get arrested, Papa?"

"Arrested?"

"He was legally an adult when he left for Canada, but you reported him as a runaway child. You told the police he had psychiatric problems, didn't you, and had him committed?

"I had no choice." His brow creased in anguish, remembering that day, the day he had his boy locked up. "Lynda, you have no idea the position I was in. I don't know how much Bart told you, but you must realize that our origin *has* to remain a secret."

"Papa, I understand that, but you lied to me. I just want to know the truth."

"Lynda, I...I did what I thought was best. I..."

"Papa, you're red. Lie down and relax, or you'll end up in the hospital again. We can finish this later. I just want you to know I've learned some of the truth and, when you're up to it, I want you to tell me the rest." She helped him to the sofa.

He collapsed like a fragile sack of twigs. "He loves me."

"What?"

"In the letter, my son said he loves me."

"So do I, Papa."

* * *

Aguire deployed pixie probes into low orbits just over the horizon to shoot lasers through the top layer of gas and back to the Hanno for determining the chemical composition at different altitudes. Then the pixies measured the refractive index, allowing them to estimate the wind velocities and air pressures.

"Look at this." Tran showed Aguire a computer simulation that showed a shell of atmosphere around the planet, and around that atmosphere was a second, outer layer of gas separated from the inner shell by a layer of low pressure.

Tran indicated the inner ring. "This one is at the planet surface. We don't know much about it yet. At high altitude, around a hundred kilometers, it thins out a bit. Then there's a distinct boundary, above which the weather is completely different. That's where the hurricanes are. Wind shear and oddball molecules in this upper atmosphere make it hard to see through. There's a lot of refraction and reflection going on from the barometric pressure differences and water vapor.

"The spectral data would have led us to this planet," Tran explained, "even if we hadn't noticed that the mass was so close to Earth's. The nitrogen-oxygen-cee-oh-two ratio is also a pretty close match. The presence of bromine, chlorine, phosphorus, and other chemicals gave me the run-around at first, but then we found that the atmosphere is in two layers. We don't know how it works yet—it's weird—but this hurricane weather is only at high altitude. The inner shell of atmosphere doesn't have the toxic elements."

"Okay." Aguire rubbed the tip of his nose. "That explains why it's hard to see the planet surface, but why are there two distinct atmospheric shells? Do we know what's separating them?"

"Uh…no," Tran conceded.

"Do we know if we can take a shuttle through the upper shell? Or if the surface is livable?" Aguire asked.

"So far, we can tell that there's a solid planet, and a lot of water. We've detected enough to know that there are mountains, and that the planet's rotation is almost the same as Earth's. There's a weak magnetic field lined up on the poles of rotation. I think it's time to drop some probes. We'll have to modify some sniffers so they can do some cartography."

Cronkite probes, made for mapping a solid surface, would never make it through the stormy upper atmosphere. They got their name from a famous explorer who spent years mapping planets and developed a compact, inexpensive package that could be put into orbit, or dropped straight down as an expendable instrument, getting the most usable data for the least cost. Captain Cronkite's original probe was no longer in use, but his design philosophy and name stuck with the new models.

Sniffers were designed for atmospheric analysis, not imaging, but were more rugged than pixies or cronkites. With some modifications and a little clever programming, a sniffer could do the job of a cronkite.

"Okay." Aguire rubbed his hands together in anticipation. "Let's get it done."

* * *

Paul Poluka didn't quite know what to make of it, except that it felt like a great weight lifted off of him. He folded and unfolded the letter a couple of times, and read it again.

Cliff had been humble when he finally faced death. He'd confessed his mistakes and regrets, even expressing some shame—well, maybe not shame—arrogance was the word he used—at trying to predict the future, and for advising Paul on how to face his choices. At the end, Cliff turned out to be merely human after all.

It may not have been the end, however. He may have survived the landing. He may be alive even now.

A sudden energy filled Poluka. Almost against his will, he propelled himself out of his chair and out through the door of his office. In the bridge he heard from Commander Aguire that survey probes will be modified by tomorrow.

"I see, Commander, but why not launch some *unmodified* sniffers to determine the severity of the outer atmosphere? Then you'll have some idea what it will take to get a probe to the surface. After all, it's still just an assumption that the cronkites won't make it through, isn't it?"

"Yes, sir." Aguire smiled crookedly. "I should have thought of that myself. I can have one launched in five minutes, and then try another after we analyze the data from the first one."

"Negative." Poluka frowned. Aguire still wasn't thinking. "Commander, we have thousands of probes and they're all expendable. Launch 20 of them, all at once."

"Twenty?" Aguire's eyebrows shot up so fast that Poluka struggled to keep a straight face. "But, sir, this is an inhabited planet. What if we hit something?"

"They're small probes, Commander, and whatever's left of them when they hit the ground will be even smaller. Launch them, please."

The captain sat at the command desk and felt pretty damn good. His was the finest ship in the galaxy, and he knew how to make his own decisions. Aguire still had a lot to learn, but at least he does what he's told.

The probes launched in rapid succession, each with a different trajectory, entering the planet's atmosphere at evenly spaced points. A live image of the planet appeared on the main screen with superimposed icons representing the probes.

As each probe plunged through the atmosphere, the scientists in the I-Bay seemed frozen, watching the streams of data flowing back from the probes to report the experience.

While waiting for the results, Poluka browsed the log entries on his screen at his desk, clicking through Hydroponics; Water Systems; Infrastructure; Med Center….

He almost skipped Med Center. His finger lingered on the button to advance to the next item. With a deliberate effort, he opened the log entry and was relieved it wasn't another update on fatalities, but a short note indicating that Doctor Payne had gotten a call from Lynda Stokes that her father was feeling faint.

The I-Bay sprang to life with a burst of activity and chatter. Braun and Tran huddled over the data. Aguire scratched his head and fidgeted.

"Mister Aguire," Poluka finally asked, "what have we learned?"

Aguire came out of the I-Bay frowning. "It's another mystery, Captain. The probes went in as expected, just as if it was a typical gas-world, then they hit something."

"Hit something, like what?"

"*That* we don't know. At the bottom of the upper atmosphere we expected an abrupt transition of air pressure. Instead there was an impact—like an invisible wall. Eight of the sniffers stopped transmitting, but we could see them all on radar. They just hung there for almost a full minute, and then began falling again. The air currents were pretty tame further down, and the composition was about what you'd expect on Earth, too. Then the signals faded out and we lost them."

"So, except for this impact against an invisible wall, everything looks promising for finding a habitable surface."

"Uh…well, yes, but whatever the probes hit isn't showing up on radar."

"But the sniffers got all the way to the bottom of the outer atmosphere without damage, and were still transmitting?"

"Yes, sir, until they hit bottom, then some went dead. The turbulence wasn't as bad as we expected, but that barrier at the bottom—"

"—is reachable," Poluka finished for him. "Theoretically, we could get to it with a shuttle."

"A shuttle?" Aguire seemed alarmed, which annoyed Poluka.

"Something to consider, Commander. In the meantime, try to figure out this *invisible wall* thing using the data we have," Poluka said, his annoyance increasing when he saw the relief on Aguire's face. "But, we won't rule out the possibility of using a shuttle if analysis doesn't take us anywhere. You have the watch, Mister Aguire. I'll be in my office."

Poluka had always been impressed with José Aguire. After the battle at Ganymede back in '88, the Navy sent Aguire, Leroy Donno, and Luke McGee to replace Poluka's officers who died in a rebel ambush. He'd never seen anyone as driven to succeed as the young Spaniard who'd lied about his age to get into the Navy. Poluka had been amazed at the impediments that José overcame to rise from ignorance and poverty to become an officer and a war hero. But now he wondered just how great a Navy officer Aguire had truly been. After all, he'd only followed orders—bravely, to be sure—but not really making the critical decisions.

After the war, when they joined the Corps, Aguire was invaluable for handling the routine operations of managing the Livingston, but, again, not really calling the shots. No, that was always Poluka's role.

Back on Earth, he was so sure that he needed Aguire for the day to day management of the Hanno. Now he wondered why he'd been so sure. Maybe G.J. had been right all along, and it was a mistake bringing Aguire into the picture.

CHAPTER 39

"Ivan was my best friend." Braun passed his letter from Ivan Tershensky around to his friends. "We were in the Corps when the original charter was written, before the end of the Corporate War.

"I was young and naive about everything. Ivan had been a child soldier against the State before fleeing Russia and living underground. We met when I was a student. I got him interested in space, but he was always smarter than me. He'd probably be an admiral by now had it not been for the Meduza incident."

"I thought I heard that name somewhere." Donno handed the letter back to Braun. "He was that pilot who killed the Meduza, wasn't he?"

The engineers stopped to listen. Tershensky was a legend who'd risked his life and thrown away his career. Something was attacking spacecrafts nearly half a century ago. First it was automated navigation beacons, and then a private yacht was found torn to pieces near Saturn with two dozen casualties. When it was discovered to be a new metal-hungry life form that had evolved from bacteria into giant cell colonies like jellyfish, the State ordered that some be captured for study. Tershensky disobeyed the old Corporate State. Yet, despite being condemned at the time, his bold initiative still shaped attitudes in the Corps today.

"Yes," Braun answered, "and I was his copilot. When the creatures started heading towards Earth, we intercepted them and they came after us. The swarm didn't want to get closer to the sun, so every time they started to break off the attack, we let them get closer to us. They were hungry and couldn't resist. When the swarm couldn't escape the sun's gravity, we pulled away. It was almost too late for us, too.

"The State put Ivan in prison for disobeying the order to

capture the creatures. I got off with a few harsh words from the magistrate only because Ivan swore I didn't know what he was planning." Braun sighed. "Ivan was in love with Lucy Landess—another captain in the Corps—but she married someone else by the time he got out of prison. He was still young, but couldn't get work as a spaceman. The old Fed was better than the State, but it was based on a military model, so anyone with a history of disobeying government orders, even orders of the old State, was considered a liability. Cliff Poluka gave him a break."

Just then, the captain returned to the bridge and asked Aguire, "Have we reached a conclusion on the…invisible wall, Commander?"

He emphasized 'invisible wall' with a mocking smile, making Aguire all the more uncomfortable.

"We're unable to detect any physical barrier," Aguire said, "nor do we see any evidence of an energy field that could account for this phenomenon. We do, however, have a plan to investigate it further."

Poluka stood with his hands clasped behind his back, and rocked back and forth on his heels. He was attentive, but his expression was like a schoolteacher who was bored with a child's attempt to grasp the lesson. "And what is your plan, Mister Aguire?"

"We can deploy some pixies probes. Pixies are light and durable. They can also maneuver within the atmosphere instead of just falling. So—"

"Excuse me, Commander Aguire," Poluka interrupted.

"Sir?"

"You cannot confirm that there is any sort of barrier at this point, correct?"

"Well, the sniffers hit *something*. They stopped falling for nearly a minute, and most of them were damaged."

"But, they continued falling afterwards. I think we could try getting a shuttle through this…barrier, and down to where we can see the surface. We can reduce speed at the bottom of the outer atmosphere so that, if there *is* something there, we won't hit it too hard."

"I…" Aguire began, but Poluka had already walked away.

* * *

Poluka didn't actually *order* Aguire to set up a shuttle mission. He wanted to see if he had to make it an order, or if the commander would just do it. Something bothered him about Aguire—he couldn't quite put his finger on it.

He paused at his office door. A shot of brandy tempted him, but he continued down the corridor to the midship instead, past the smoke-tinted glass walls of the conference hall. He did a double-take when he spied his reflection, and turned to assess his profile, sliding his hand down his belly and smiling at the improvement. The pills were working.

Marching down Main Street with his head high and a nod for each crewman, he wondered if he could petition the Admiralty to adopt the Navy rules of saluting. The Corps only saluted for ceremonies and formal meetings. He missed the Navy. Right from the beginning, he'd felt like he'd found his home. Now, he couldn't really say why he'd transferred to the Corps after the war.

He went to his quarters and sent a requisition to stores for a new uniform in a smaller size. Then he called the bridge to see what progress Aguire had made.

When the commander appeared on the screen and explained that he was still investigating that invisible wall instead of organizing a shuttle mission, Poluka's patience finally ran out, which is exactly what he told a very flustered Commander Aguire before ordering a meeting in one hour.

He clicked off the com-link as Aguire opened his mouth to respond. Next he called Doctor Payne and ordered her to prepare antibiotics for 30 people who may be exposed to an alien environment. He had to tell her twice not to interrupt him with questions before he closed the link and stomped off back to the bridge.

* * *

A painful hush flooded the I-Bay and spilled into the bridge. Only the most unprofessional officers would chew out someone over a com-link, with no control over who else might hear it. It was uncharacteristic of Poluka.

Aguire glanced around the bridge. No one looked at him.

Donno appeared almost immediately from the S-Bay to ask

what the hell was going on.

"I don't know, Donno, but the skipper's really pissed at me right now. I don't know what's eating him."

"Well, you're not the only one that's noticed things," Donno said quietly. "Even before we boarded the Hanno, things didn't seem right. And the Captain's behavior since the collision is gettin' people spooked."

When Aguire discovered Poluka's dangerous political game, he should have told his best friend. Donno always stuck by him, even when he screwed up royally.

"Donno, we've got to talk, but not here." Aguire pitched his voice to sound like he was having a routine conversation, but quiet enough that no one could make out what he was saying. "Meet me in my office in five minutes."

Washington took the watch when Aguire left the bridge. Aguire's eyes swept the foyer leading to the midship in case Poluka returned early. He found Donno waiting in the office with his arms crossed, leaning one shoulder against the window frame as he looked out at Arcturus-4.

"So," Donno asked, "what's the old man up to this time?"

"He's rushing things again," Aguire watched Donno stiffen in apprehension. "And he's pissed at me for not following his lead. He's ordering a shuttle mission into the atmosphere—hell, he might even order a landing. But that's not what I wanted to talk to you about."

Donno uncrossed his arms and straightened up.

"Donno, I found a pattern in the personnel data base. Every member of this crew has a problem with the new government."

"Uh-huh, I noticed that, too," Donno said. "And I'm not the only one. Have you figured out what it means?"

"I asked the captain about it. He admitted that the New Fed thinks this is a death ship and that this mission is unsurvivable, and they're counting on us to politely die because we're black-listed."

Donno digested this without expression. "When was this?"

"The day we left orbit." Aguire hastened to add, "He didn't want to tell me and he didn't say much more, except that he and Stokes led them to believe that the ship design was flawed—he made them think they had an easy way to get rid of us—and him, too—without getting blood on their own hands. Poluka said he wanted to get the blacklisted personnel away from Earth in order to save them—us—from arrest and execution. I should have told you right away but, hell, that was just days ago. Usually, we have months in transit with plenty of time to talk."

Donno searched his eyes for a moment, discerning what was troubling his friend. "Okay, but I wonder what the captain has in mind for us to do if we manage to not get killed."

Donno's acceptance of his implied apology was soothing. Aguire hadn't realized until now how heavily it weighed on him.

"He wouldn't tell me. He said I'd just have to trust him."

Now that he repeated it to someone else, he heard how stupid it sounded. They were Poluka's senior officers. It's inconceivable that he'd keep them in the dark about their purpose.

"He can be a real asshole sometimes. So, where's all this takin' us? Can we ever go home?"

"That's what I'm worried about. Henry Tran told me that Poluka specifically ordered him to keep quiet about the Zone reacting to our presence. I don't know what he'll do next, and I wanted to make sure you know as much as I do."

CHAPTER 40

"You're leaving now? Right now?" Lynda watched Hanson on the com screen as he zipped up his jumpsuit and slipped his boots on.

He looked up with a humorless smile. "Poluka's gone completely off his rocker. You should've heard Aguire when he called me. He almost apologized when he gave me my orders."

Something close to panic clenched her. If anything happened to Bart it would be like losing another brother. "I'll go to the bridge and see what's happening."

It took a moment to explain to her father that she had to leave. He was groggy, but understood.

Main Street was nearly deserted between the lift and the Forward Section. Lynda ran the whole way. The captain wasn't there, but Washington confirmed that a shuttle mission was scheduled within the hour. He called it a "double-one-twenty mission", which he had to explain.

"Look at the map." Washington pointed to a screen on the command desk showing a 3-D graphic of the planet divided with latitude and longitude lines. "Shuttles will descend into each hemisphere, three in the north and three in the south, 30 degrees from the equator and spaced every 60 degrees around the globe."

His finger traced out a zigzag pattern showing positions above and below the equator.

"So," she understood, "in each hemisphere they'll be 120 degrees apart."

Washington nodded. "And then each shuttle will fly at high altitude around the planet for a 120 longitudal degrees, taking pictures of the surface before returning to orbit."

"What kind of maneuver is that?"

"A Navy maneuver, Miss Stokes, a quick and dirty recon maneuver."

A strange note in his voice made her look into his warm brown eyes and see a deep unhappiness.

"Commander Washington, is this mission a good idea?"

"No, Ma'am." He returned her gaze without the slightest surprise at her question. "It never did the Navy much good, and the Corps has never used it, but that's the order."

She didn't notice Chief Braun wander over to look at the graphic over her shoulder, and she jumped slightly when he spoke.

"You weren't here when we found the barrier." Braun told her about the probes crashing into something invisible, and then falling again.

She ran again—this time to the shuttle docks.

The captain was in an observation booth where the windows look down into three of the docks. He seemed like a statue with his feet apart and his fists on his hips, as if daring fate to get in his way.

In the docks below, people in pressure suits were boarding the small shuttles. Voices overlapped on the intercom as each group worked with the control office, and reports from the S-Bay trickled in about launch support.

He didn't turn away from the windows when she asked him about his decision.

He saw no reason to worry about the barrier between the atmospheric shells.

He saw no reason to worry about anything.

"But, Paul—"

"*Captain.*"

"What?"

"As long as I'm in uniform, I am addressed as *Captain.*"

What the…? He didn't sound angry but he wouldn't look at her either.

"Captain Poluka, are you feeling all right?"

"Just a moment." He raised a hand, gesturing her to wait. In rapid succession, the voices reported that each shuttle was ready.

Another voice said, "Captain, this is Shuttle Control. All six are ready for launch."

"Launch on my authority," Captain Poluka answered.

The deck trembled and an orange hue spilled through the observation booth as the outer doors opened. The planet, illuminated by the red giant, filled the view outside.

Lynda strode to the nearest window and watched a shuttle glide out.

"Come on," Poluka called over his shoulder as he turned away from the windows. "We'll monitor the mission from the bridge."

She hurried after him. He reminded her of when he was a young captain in the Navy, walking briskly, with his head high and his arms swinging casually. Now, she noticed that he was thinner than just a few months ago.

As they rode the lift up to Main Street, Lynda asked again, "Paul...I mean, Captain Poluka, are you feeling okay?"

"I feel great. Why do you ask?"

"I think you've lost some weight."

He smiled broadly and slid a hand over his belly. "You noticed. I let myself go since leaving the Navy, but I've been dieting, exercising, and...well...I got motivated."

"Paul...Captain, don't you think we're rushing things a bit? We could still learn a lot from orbit."

This brought a scowl to his face. "My officers thought so, too. They've gotten soft. We're experienced spacemen. We can handle this mission. If we wait until every little detail," he held up his thumb and forefinger in front of a squinting eye, as if examining some tiny thing, "is known before we actually *do* anything, we may as well stay home and study the galaxy through telescopes. Besides, Lynda, we have other business. Let's not forget our plans to defeat the New Federation. We never planned on any of this alien stuff. Don't get me wrong—it's fantastic that we've made this discovery, and that we'll finally know what happened to the Himilco."

The lift opened on Main Street, and they walked silently to the bridge. Her mind raced, trying to think of something to say, but she wasn't even sure he was wrong. He was the professional explorer. She wasn't.

But she saw the doubt on the faces of Commander Washington and the engineers in the I-Bay. Maybe he had a point, but surely this was no typical situation, not something even experienced explorers should rush into.

Still, he seemed so confident, so much like he used to be when she'd been a terribly impressed thirteen-year-old and he was a young Navy captain, already with exciting stories to tell about fighting pirates and insurgents on the trade route. He was a rising star in the Navy's hierarchy, born to lead.

Papa liked him immediately, and invited him to visit often. Paul had liked *them*, too, and came to visit nearly as often as he visited his own family.

She'd seen him change when he left the Navy for the Corps, and she thought he was happier exploring rather than fighting. Maybe he wasn't. Maybe she didn't know him as well as she thought.

For all her supposed intelligence, she never could deal with people very well, and doubted she could get him to recall the shuttles, or even whether she should.

The I-Bay was buzzing when they entered the bridge. Commander Washington said the six shuttles would be on their planned vectors in eighteen minutes. Captain Poluka slipped into the chair at the command desk. Lynda stood behind him where she could see everything.

A wireframe graphic of the planet was on main screen with the hurricanes indicated by big green circles. Six red diamond icons were spreading out to circle the planet, each annotated with the name of the officer commanding the shuttle. 25 pixies orbited farther out to relay communications from the shuttles.

Donno's icon was on the near side of the planet, and Aguire's was 120 degrees ahead of him, both in the northern hemisphere. Redbird was between them but in the southern hemisphere. On the far side, Martensen was in the North, Garcia and Sheffield in the South, all on vectors going east, spiraling down toward the atmosphere.

They spread out to evenly cover the planet and drop into the atmosphere between the circles that represented the worst of the weather patterns.

"Captain Poluka, why did you choose this maneuver?" she asked, trying to keep it conversational.

His eyes flicked away from the display for a moment to look at her. "Several reasons, actually. First, shuttles are much more controllable than probes. They can hover if necessary, and they'll have direct human observers on hand to study the situation.

"Second, I believe that this so-called barrier will turn out to be a simple atmospheric phenomenon that our instruments are having trouble observing. And finally, I find it interesting that in the message from Cliff that we picked up on this moon, he indicated that if he can't make it down to the surface, the indigenous people may never know that they were even here. That means not only do *we* have trouble seeing through this atmosphere, so do the aliens on the surface. They don't know we're here, and they're not expecting us. From what we've seen of their technology, they can't match our instrumentation. So, I decided to use a recon plan developed by the Navy to get a quick estimation of what's down there in terms of landing sites and populated areas. You with me so far?"

She wasn't. She understood every word, but didn't see how he justified this operation, especially the assumption about the barrier, or why a military maneuver that would only tell them about a tiny portion of the planet's surface was worth risking so many lives.

As if reading her thoughts, Paul explained. "I don't think this barrier will prove to be a problem, but I'm not discounting the possibility. If it's too hazardous, each shuttle may abort on their own authority. If, however, they get through it, they will get at least some data on likely landing sites and surface conditions. If contact with a shuttle is lost, the commander may return to orbit or even land, as seems prudent at the time."

Data began streaming in from the shuttles. The video from the bow cameras was a chaotic burst of color as the shuttles punched through clouds at around 500 meters per second.

Commander Martensen reported that turbulence was knocking them around pretty hard, and his gyros were dead. He aborted the descent after less than a minute.

Donno called in next to say that he hit a layer of air that was moving faster than expected, and he had to adjust his velocity. Redbird had the opposite situation and was losing speed in a jet stream pulling him off towards the south.

"Don't worry," Poluka told her. "They can handle it."

"Captain," Tran called over his shoulder. "Their signals have dropped 60 dB. If they drop another 60, we'll lose contact. Sheffield will reach the barrier in 15 seconds followed by Aguire, then Donno."

The tension on the bridge swelled. All talking abruptly stopped. Poluka leaned forward and knotted his hands on the desk. Lynda watched the telemetry of Commander Sheffield's shuttle. The altimeter was showing the estimated distance from the barrier—only 400 meters to go—and the rate of descent was slowing.

Sheffield's voice cut through the bridge. "Hanno, I'm having trouble keeping the speed constant. Lot of turbulence…I see it! I see it…"

A crackle of static ended the message just as the altimeter reached zero distance from the barrier. Then the telemetry signal was lost, too. His icon changed from red to blue and stopped moving: last known position.

Poluka stabbed a button on his desk to connect to the communications center down the hall. He opened his mouth to bark an order, but stopped when the com screen showed the engineers frantically keying in commands to the orbiting pixies.

* * *

"This isn't what these shuttles are designed for," Aguire muttered too quietly for his crew to hear. The gyros lost calibration after the first few minutes of buffeting, and inertial navigation wasn't meant for orbital maneuvers. The smell of overheated stabilizers threatened to make him sneeze as they fought the weather.

He dreaded what would happen at the barrier, but Hanson pointed out that if things couldn't fall through, there'd be mountains of meteorites there already, and he suggested simply landing on it, and then wait.

With every muscle in his body tensed and ready to react, Aguire gingerly set the shuttle down on the reddish surface, many kilometers above the actual planet surface. It bore the weight of the small craft, about four tons, without even sagging. The barrier had no friction, and the small craft slid and spun with the rise and fall of the barrier. O'Riley recorded everything he could.

"Aguire, we lost you…" was the last word from the Hanno. With the engines idling and the radio silent, it was eerily peaceful. Everyone was quiet now.

O'Riley hunched over the sensor panel, his face illuminated by the instrument's glow. Hanson was strapped to a seat with a safety harnesses, absently fingering the small gold cross he always wore on chain around his neck. He already had his helmet sealed to his pressure suit.

Newhall and Tully were glued to the back of the pilot's seat, gaping over Aguire's shoulder at the big lazy waves undulating around them. It was shiny and reflected the clouds above them. Aguire found the constant rolling nauseating.

* * *

Aguire's voice came through to the Hanno. "Hanno, I don't know if you can hear me but we've landed on the barrier. It looks like a...red surface, reflection maybe..."

The video cut out randomly, but showed what the shuttle crew was seeing out the front window. It was like a storm over the sea with swirling mists racing across the water.

Through this sheet a hazy surface could be seen, the planet itself, far below.

Another voice said, "Oh, shit. This is gonna hit us." The camera showed a wave rising far above the level of the shuttle. Aguire's signal vanished, and his icon changed from red to blue.

CHAPTER 41

When the surface began swelling in the distance it took a moment to recognize that it was a wave, maybe 300 meters above the rest of the surface and growing. They might not have even seen it except that their entry point was on the dark side of the planet, and the wave started rising ahead of them just as they reached the terminator where dawn was breaking. Red sunlight shone around the bulge like a halo and its contour became more obvious.

"Oh, shit. This is gonna hit us." O'Riley tore his eyes from the spectacle to look at Aguire. "We might be able to out climb it."

"We got more alarms. But we can't stay here." Aguire pointed to the flashing lights on his console, and noticed that, except for Hanson, the others had neglected to wear their helmets. "Seal you suits, everyone."

His best guess about what the wave would do to them was based on what had happened to the probes: they broke.

Without warning the shuttle slipped through the surface and began falling. Lieutenant Carolyn Tully made a small chirping cry as the floor dropped out from under them. The hull creaked and shivered.

The strangest thing was the sudden change in color. Above the barrier, everything had a reddish tint. Looking up, the barrier was just pale gray swirls. The planet below was pastel greens, blues, and grays like you'd see on Earth from high altitude.

There was no time to ponder or speculate. They were falling. The shuttle was sluggish, but Aguire got the nose lowered and established some forward velocity.

"O'Riley, what's outside?" Aguire asked his lookout officer.

"We're high. 60 klicks above uneven terrain—mountains, I guess. No signals, no radar, no nothing."

"Newhall," Aguire looked back at the young ensign whose

haircut made him look like he had blond needles sticking out of his scalp, "check for damage. This vessel isn't military grade. We might have some cracks."

Newhall's face took on a determined and less terrified expression now that he had something to do. Aguire didn't personally know the kid. It ticked him off when Poluka assigned personnel for each shuttle. Team leaders usually had a lot of say in picking their own teams, but Poluka made some insane speech about giving experience to junior officers who show potential for leadership. The captain wouldn't listen to anyone, and he all but threatened to discipline anyone who had any objections. Aguire didn't let his annoyance with Poluka spill over onto Newhall, but he would have preferred bringing a scientist.

Carolyn Tully was another one that Aguire hardly knew. He remembered seeing her cheat some barnies in a knife throwing contest when they first came aboard.

"The gyros—if we can trust them—say we're pointed east," Aguire said, as much for the flight recorder as his crewmates. "Velocity is one-point-five kilometers per second. Air pressure at this altitude is...about one-point-oh kilopascal. The ground is 60 kilometers below."

"Commander," Hanson spoke up, "should we continue?"

"I am considering that question already, Ensign. We weren't counting on the rough ride—or with being cut off from the Hanno." Aguire's brow crinkled with concern. "I'm tempted to try contacting the other shuttles, but we'd be broadcasting to the whole planet. I'm not ready to announce our presence just yet."

"Commander," Tully asked, "can we even get back out? I mean, we landed on that barrier and waited for it to let us drop through. We can't land on the bottom side of it."

A chill went up Aguire's spine and he felt like kicking himself. He had no answer, but tried to project confidence while privately cursing Captain Poluka. "We'll get back out. Now that we're in, we can study the phenomenon directly. Besides, that alien ship— the Fledik—got out."

O'Riley interrupted, "I've got...I think...trees on the camera...and a couple of rivers...and possibly a road."

He punched an image over to the center monitor. When all five of them scrunched in to look at the same time, they banged their helmets together. Aguire found it unexpectedly comical and had to restrain an unprofessional laugh. "Okay, it seems the hull isn't leaking. I think we can take off our helmets for now."

"Here," O'Riley said as he pulled off his helmet. "See this thin line. It follows the mountain contours, but some sections are perfectly straight. I'm sure it's a road. We're still too high to get good images." He raised an eyebrow and looked at Aguire.

"Right," Aguire sighed. "We'll continue the mission…and fly lower. This road, if that's what it is, goes east, so we'll track it until we see something interesting."

They began a sharp descent. After a minute or so, the scantily forested hills were replaced by thick forests that O'Riley said were "giant" trees, some over a hundred meters tall. The mountains became less jagged and lower until they were wide rolling hills. Then the road just ended.

"Damn," Aguire said. "There's always something at the end of a road, or else why have one?"

"There is something there," Tully said. "Go to black-and-white."

O'Riley did it, and the color disappeared from the screen. He tweaked the contrast and a checkerboard pattern appeared.

"Farms!" Aguire tried to keep from shouting. "I'll be damned. It's farms."

"We've got to land," Tully said.

Land? Meet some aliens? Aguire wasn't so sure. On the other hand, another alarm flashed on the control panel—stabilizer fine control was gone. The burning smell was getting worse.

"Absolutely." Aguire tried to sound confident. "Let's find a landing site."

The trees were everywhere except in the checkerboard farms, and Aguire wasn't about to drop unannounced into some alien's crop of who-knows-what.

Two klicks further east was a wide grassy meadow. Their altitude was down to 400 meters. Aguire tried to hover for a look around, but the port stabilizer made a popping sound followed by a puff of smoke from a side panel. The shuttle started listing to the port side.

"This looks like a good spot," Aguire decided. A soft landing was out of the question. He just hoped to keep the craft right side up.

Ensign Newhall was leaning on the hatch frame when the skids met the ground. There was a sudden *Ka-Pow!* as the door frame around the locking mechanism splintered to pieces and the hatch sprang open. Ears popped from the sudden change in air pressure, and Aguire nearly panicked as Newhall fell out of the shuttle.

Hanson cried out, and sprang to the hatch. The others followed in a mad scramble. By the time Aguire got to the hatch and remembered the possible biohazards, everyone else was already outside helping the young ensign to his feet.

They scurried back into the shuttle. Newhall needed help; his ankle was hurting. A quick examination indicated it was at least sprained. Otherwise, he seemed okay.

Aguire just hoped the antibiotics Jayne Payne injected them with would work against alien microbes.

The air actually smelled pretty good with a piney, grassy scent. There was just the slightest breeze, and the temperature was comfortable, like a spring day in New Wichita.

Tully determined that flexing of the chassis had cracked the seam where the hatch frame was embedded in the hull. "We can probably patch it, but it will be permanently closed until we get it back to the Hanno. We still have the other hatches."

"The stabilizers need some work, too," Hanson added. "Maybe Newhall can work on it while the rest of us go looking around."

There was an enthusiasm in his voice that surprised Aguire. The possibility of alien contact was both exciting and scary. They'd already seen on the recorded video from the Himilco that the aliens were friendly, and even looked like humans, but still, it was a monumental event full of uncertain ramifications.

O'Riley tried to contact the Hanno again with no success. Contacting the other shuttles would be down in the megahertz band, and the whole planet would get the signal. Maybe it didn't matter, but at this point there was no rush.

"Um…we'll work on repairs while Ensign Newhall monitors communications." Aguire decided. "I want this shuttle capable of evacuation before we start introducing ourselves to the neighborhood. Mister Hanson, run a particle and toxin analysis of the air."

The door failure rattled Aguire; if the air outside had been poisonous, that would have been the end of them right then. Now that he knew Newhall was okay and there was no immediate danger he was getting his composure back and joined the others in looking at the landscape out the front window.

It could have been Earth except for the unusual size of the trees. They were conifers, or something very similar, and lush green grass carpeted the meadow. Bluish mountains in the distance looked just like they did on Earth.

"It's not red," Tully noted, "but then, they used to call Mars the red planet, which doesn't look red either, when you're there."

"The color changed when we passed through the barrier." Aguire recalled. "I guess the outer atmosphere filters the light."

O'Riley turned from the lookout computer, "I've mapped the area based on video. We managed to set down in almost the exact center of this meadow, so it's about a kilometer in any direction before reaching the forest. The farms we saw are in the west," he gestured with his thumb toward the back of the shuttle, "about three klicks from here, but the terrain may prevent a straight approach. We don't know more than that."

Aguire leaned forward to look up through the window. "I can't see the sun. In fact, I don't think it's possible to see the sun from the planet surface. It's just a glow in the sky. We may have trouble determining how much time we've got before it gets dark. The gyros lost calibration on the way down, but they can still measure how fast the planet is revolving. Set it up, O'Riley, while we start repairing the shuttle." Aguire then turned to Ensign Newhall. "You stay off your feet and watch for signals from the Hanno, or the other shuttles—or from any locals."

Hanson and Tully got busy with some nasty-smelling liquid patch compound to seal the damaged hatch while Aguire replaced circuits for the stabilizer control and ran diagnostics on the rest of the systems.

O'Riley had the gyros feeding data into a program that would check the planet's rotation over a period of a couple of hours to determine how long a day was on this planet. Then he went out the top hatch to sit on the roof with binoculars, and watched the area in case something or someone happened along.

By the time the work got done, the glow in the sky suggested it was almost noon. Back on the Hanno, it was the night shift. Aguire was tired, but he'd had some time to think about their situation, and decided to risk a brief excursion. He'd been pissed off at Poluka's haste in starting this mission but, now that they were here, the thrill of discovery was just too tempting. He'd tramped around in a spacesuit on dead alien worlds and been thrilled then, but this was the first planet ever found to have well-developed indigenous life. It was just too good.

Newhall stayed in the shuttle. The rest of them would walk west for a couple of hours, and could still get back before dark.

They had a bite to eat before donning their field gear. Each had survival supplies, event recorders, radios, and sidearms. The standard issue pistol for the Corps was the Aurora-5, a German-made molecular accelerator, firing packets of silver plasma at ten kilometers per second. The Army barnies called it a sissy gun, but at least it was light and could fire hundreds of times between reloads. Tully brought the combat knife she'd won from the barnies.

Aguire, Tully, O'Riley and Hanson reached the edge of the forest in about ten minutes and checked the radio link to Newhall before picking a path westward under the green canopy.

Every little thing they saw—a flower, another bush, a sprouting sapling—distracted them and burned up memory in their recorders as they took pictures.

The first half-hour was like a walk in a park. The ground sloped gently up from the meadow, and became more uneven and rocky before leveling off and getting a spongy carpet of pine needles. The evenly spaced trees provided cool shade without much undergrowth or fallen branches. They were truly pine trees, despite the great size. The branches were bare where the sunlight didn't reach, but the twiggy ends had a thick growth of needles similar to any fir tree of Earth.

They came upon a narrow, slowly flowing river perhaps seven or eight meters wide and only a few centimeters deep, with the pebbly riverbed clearly visible through crystal-clear water. The spectrographs in their event recorders indicated it was nearly pure water, but they didn't touch it.

A chattering sound in the branches overhead was the first

animal life they encountered: rodents that looked and behaved like squirrels, except that they were twice as big, maybe 40 centimeters including the bushy, flicking tail. The creatures were elusive but watchful. Soon after, they saw a larger four-legged animal stalking the squirrels, about a meter long with a pointed snout and luxurious fur which was pale pink! It, too, stayed well away from them, but did not seem afraid. They got some good pictures of it.

They followed the riverbank with the idea that if they found a way to cross—fine—otherwise they would return to the shuttle.

There was another kind of bushes growing where more sunlight could get through, and the terrain was more level. They saw the end of the forest on the other side of the water, and open fields maybe another 50 meters away.

Aguire was in the lead, but didn't spot the bridge until Carolyn Tully cried out and pointed at the moss-covered structure. The near side was overgrown with vines with broad leaves twice the size of an open hand.

It was made from square-cut wooden beams about ten centimeters wide, and long enough to extend a meter and half onto the land on each side of the river. The beams were laid side-by-side, making a walkway about two meters wide, and anchored with cement into cut-stone blocks embedded in the soil on the banks of the river. There were waist-high walls on the sides made of one-by-three centimeter boards. There were no nails or screws. Everything was cut and fitted with notches and held in place with some kind of glue.

They transmitted images back to Newhall, who was understandably envious of their discovery. Technically, the crew of the Himilco was the first to encounter aliens ten years ago, but this was damn near the same thing. Aguire forgot all about being angry at Captain Poluka.

In fact, everyone's spirits were high until they crossed the bridge and found the far side not firmly anchored, and the beams were splintering from rot. One of the sidewalls broke loose when O'Riley touched it, and now it barely hung onto one end of the bridge, while the other end was actually in the water.

"Oops!" O'Riley looked back at it. "I hope we don't have to pay for that."

Aguire frowned. O'Riley had a point. There's no telling how the owner of the bridge might react to them crossing it, much less breaking it.

"Keep alert." Aguire studied the faces of his team for signs of fatigue. He hadn't slept in about 20 hours, and was feeling the strain. "Let's not let anyone take us by surprise."

Hanson checked the crumbling cement. "This is all old. I don't think anyone's used it in a long time."

They continued west. Hanson split off from the others a short distance to get some pictures of bushes that were like twisted, tangled vines with big circular leaves. Some stood three meters tall with leaves a good 30 centimeters wide and dagger shaped thorns on the edges that were as long as a man's fingers.

Hanson raised his recorder as he got within a couple of meters of one of the bushes, when the whole tangle of vines jerked violently. One branch shot out straight at Hanson. A leaf folded together around his recorder with a powerful snapping motion. He leapt backward with a startled cry. Aguire's right hand moved like a coiled spring to draw his sidearm and aimed at the bush before he had time to think about it.

"Hanson, are you hurt?" Aguire's voice cracked, and his heart pounded like a hammer.

Everyone had their weapons out, covering the area in all directions.

"No, sir," Hanson hissed, and glared at the quivering bush. "It's eating my recorder. It reached right out and grabbed it."

Sure enough, inside the thorny leaf was squeezed a shape that could only be Hanson's recorder. The leaf squirmed and rubbed together in a grotesque chewing motion, and thick juice dripped from it. A corner of the recorder lay on the ground, sheared off by thorns that worked like chisel-hard teeth.

Tully drew the combat knife from her belt and used the point of the fifteen-centimeter blade to slide the fragment of Hanson's recorder away from the plant that was enthusiastically munching on the rest of it.

"Be careful!" Aguire warned as she got her hand on the piece of the recorder, and leapt back from the bush.

The device had a thin aluminum housing, and was crammed with quantum logic boards, all of which were cleanly sheared by the thorny spikes of the leaves.

"Hey, if that thing is digesting the camera," O'Riley said, "what happens when it gets to the battery?"

"Let's move." Aguire waved them into motion and they scurried further west with their weapons held ready. As if on cue, the bush got through the shielding on the tiny nuclear-fusion battery.

NF batteries are pretty safe these days, but the designers never anticipated a carnivorous plant crushing the shielding and mixing digestive fluids with the chemicals inside.

Not all of the potential energy was released, but enough to blow the leaves and part of the branch to smithereens, as well as set fire to some other branches. The bush didn't take it well. It writhed and jerked until the ground gave way and some of the roots flopped loose, with dirt flying in all directions. For an instant, Aguire feared the thing was breaking loose from the ground so it could chase them, but a moment later it stopped moving.

"Keep going, but don't run," Aguire shouted. "And stay clear of these other plants."

They sent pictures to Newhall as soon as possible. The ensign spotted the resemblance to an Earth plant immediately.

"We've a species that has similar leaves, though much smaller, and it can eat flies and other insects. By the way," Newhall added, "we just got a short burst from the Hanno. They turned up the transmission power and punched through a compressed message. Three of the shuttles returned to the Hanno. Commander Donno's shuttle is still flying eastward near the equator. Two are missing—ours and Commander Sheffield's.

"The Hanno advised Donno to try and contact the two missing shuttles. So, if I don't hear from them in the next few minutes, I thought I'd try to get a signal to either Donno or Sheffield myself."

"Sounds good, Newhall." Aguire was relieved. He'd been worried about the other shuttles. He was still worried about Sheffield's team, but he'd just have to wait and see. "By the way Newhall, how's the data looking for the planet rotation?"

"Got it. This rock is spinning a little slower than the Earth. One local day is 24 hours, 58 minutes and 12 seconds—call it about 25 hours."

"Great." Aguire studied the obscured sun in the sky. "I guess we've got around five hours of daylight left. We may not be able to get back across the bridge, and we don't want to get our feet wet just yet. If we can't find another way to cross the river, we might spend the night out here. I hope not, but don't be surprised if you're all alone tonight. In the meantime, set up the sensors to alert you if anything approaches the shuttle."

"Are you kidding? That's the first thing I did after you left. It's all quiet here, except I've seen some birds and insects. Nothing alarming, but I'm keeping the doors shut. Hey…I'm getting something from Donno."

"Good," Aguire sighed, "we'll continue on and check back with you soon. Aguire out."

CHAPTER 42

"Don't lose them," Captain Poluka demanded for the third time in the last five minutes.

"We've got them," Lieutenant Buckmaster patiently replied from a screen on Poluka's command desk for the third time. "But I can't say what will happen when Commander Donno's shuttle meets the dawn terminator."

The Communications Center had the most sophisticated radio and laser equipment in space, and was getting continuous and unwanted attention from the captain.

Commander Sheffield's shuttle vanished for a while, but reappeared moments after crossing over the terminator to the night side of the planet and reported being over an ocean. Donno's shuttle entered the atmosphere on the night side and had not yet seen daylight. Aguire dropped down into the atmosphere almost on top of the terminator, going to the day side, and was immediately lost. It didn't take a detective to figure out that signals had trouble getting through while the local sun was overhead. This theory would be put to the test in about 20 minutes, when the sun rises on Commander Donno's position.

Captain Poluka grunted something about keeping him informed, and then cut the connection to the Com Center. He knew he was being a pain in the ass and tried to get a grip on himself.

He'd done it again. Against all the advice of his best people, he'd screwed up and needlessly risked their lives. He knew it, and worse, they knew it. He could still come out of this okay, but only if nobody gets hurt. He tried to look like he wasn't backpedaling when he agreed to Tran's request to continue launching probes to study the atmosphere, and made it look like it wasn't a last-minute desperation decision to have the cruiser readied for rescue and evacuation. El Toro was a military-grade vessel, and was probably what should have been sent down in the first place.

The shuttles came from a Martian company that had a good reputation, but like any craft made for flying through atmosphere, all bets were off in bad weather. Poluka grimaced as he remembered Aguire pointing out that the shuttles weren't designed for this kind of mission.

"Sheffield's reporting," someone in the I-Bay called out. A moment later the subdued British accent of Commander Nigel Sheffield came across from the planet. In the background there was a babble of conversation from his team.

"We're still over an ocean, but we see mountains ahead. We expect to be over land in ten minutes."

Shuttle telemetry indicated a four-kilometer altitude with one-point-five kps velocity. The bow camera showed a strip of land on the horizon topped with jagged, triangle-pointed mountain peaks.

Donno's team dropped in over an ocean, too, but found a coastline just ahead that was an arid region, became sand dunes further east. Somehow his shuttle ended up south of the equator, but it didn't really matter because the whole double-one-twenty maneuver was blown when three of the six shuttles aborted.

Aguire was still missing, and Poluka resisted the urge to ride his engineers to do more to find them.

"Commander Donno is signaling, sir. He's got the missing shuttle on the radio."

Captain Poluka hadn't realized he'd been staring at the deck until his head jerked up at the announcement. His face flushed with sudden joy.

Leroy Donno's lean face appeared on the front screen. "Hanno, I've got Ensign Newhall on the com. He reports one minor injury, and their shuttle's taken some damage. They landed on the planet. The shuttle's been repaired enough to evacuate if necessary, but Newhall is alone. The others have gone to recon some farms that were spotted before they landed."

"Commander Donno," Poluka cut in, "can you relay Newhall through to us?"

"Aye, sir."

Donno disappeared, and was replaced by a young man with a

boyish face and short blond hair that covered his scalp like prickly fuzz. His eyes widened and he straightened up in the pilot's chair when he realized he was looking at the bridge of the Hanno.

"Ensign Newhall," Poluka smiled, hoping to put the boy at ease. "I understand you are alone. Are you in contact with the rest of your team?"

"Yes, sir," Newhall said. "I spoke with Commander Aguire just a moment ago. They're about three klicks to the west of my position. They've found a bridge across a river."

"I see. You know, Ensign, we hadn't actually planned on making contact with the indigenous people on this excursion. I'd like for you to contact Commander Aguire and...."

A shout from the I-Bay cut off Captain Poluka's instructions.

"We have an emergency! Sheffield is under attack!"

The connection to Newhall was routed back to the Com Center, where an engineer explained to the ensign that he should sit tight and use his own judgment until the captain had time to get back to him.

In the bridge, an audio message came from Sheffield's lookout officer. Through a background of shouts and alarms, he kept a calm and level voice, with just the slightest tinge of fear leaking through.

"—it came out of the water—we're going down—"

That was all. The telemetry was gone except for a locator beacon showing the shuttle at very low altitude, still moving east, though no faster than five meters per second.

"She's in the water," Chief Braun guessed, and advised Tran, "Replay all their telemetry. Find out what happened."

Poluka added through clenched teeth, "And figure out how far they are from that coast."

Then the sun rose on the side of Arcturus-4 where Donno was, and the com link to him was lost.

CHAPTER 43

It used to be a farm. Aguire could see how there were once rows of crops, but now it was mostly weeds. They took some samples of the plants. Wooden poles marked the boundaries between fields, and they found a path that might have been a wide dirt road before grass started encroaching on the edges some time ago.

Farther down the path they found houses. At least, they could have been houses once. They were small buildings made of bundles of straw and wooden poles that blended into the environment so well, they might as well be camouflaged. Fifteen little structures lined both sides of the path, spaced roughly ten meters apart. Each one was about ten by five meters, and three meters high, with a low peaked roof, a door and some windows. Tully said, "It all seems the right size for humans."

Aguire's judgment about their next move teetered on a razor's edge: his little group would be making contact as representatives of Earth, which they were not really qualified to do, but then, who was? Poluka, with his erratic behavior? Anyway, everything here looked deserted.

He advanced cautiously, and called out a "hello" before getting into the middle of the structures. All was quiet.

They checked each structure with infrared before stopping at the last one to look inside. The door, a frame of thin boards covered with woven grass, opened easily into a room that was clearly an abandoned dwelling.

There was dust on everything. They found a bed without sheets, and other simple furniture, but nothing else. A quick sweep of the other buildings got the same result. Aguire told the others, "I'd guess this was for farm labor."

"Why do you suppose they did this?" O'Riley pointed to the

front wall of one of the houses. There was a circular pattern woven into the wall like a decoration.

Aguire hadn't noticed it before, but a quick glance around told him that all the houses had the same pattern: a circle about a meter and a half wide, and no matter what direction the front door faced, the circle was always on the side facing the path, and on the corner furthest west. Aguire checked the time. He was short on sleep and felt a bit punchy. "It's getting late. Let's head back."

A moment later, Newhall called.

"I talked to Commander Donno, sir," Newhall explained, "then I got patched through to the Captain."

"We still don't have direct communication?" Aguire asked and waited for a reply, but none came. He repeated his transmission. This time Newhall came back with a crackling and popping signal, full of distortions.

"You're breaking up, sir. Uh...no. We don't have a link to the Hanno, and I think I smell something burning in the com-console." The ensign sounded nervous. "Sir, Sheffield's shuttle has been attacked."

A jolt of adrenaline hit Aguire, and the rest of his people stared at the radio before looking warily around at the alien world.

Newhall continued, "I was talking to the skipper when they got an emergency call. Then I got cut off. I checked with Donno, but all he knows is that Sheffield was going down, and he said I should avoid using the radio except to call you, sir. As I was talking to him, he lost contact with the Hanno."

"Newhall, we're heading back to you. Stay inside, but watch everything. If you see anything that looks dangerous, send a text burst. Arm yourself, and keep listening for news from Donno. Aguire out."

The pleasantly wooded landscape seemed more sinister now, and the diffused light made directions maddeningly difficult to judge. Now that they had a definite destination—the shuttle in the meadow—they became painfully aware of the progress they were making on the trek back. The path that seemed so clear an hour ago was now an indistinct thinning of grass that twice sent them off in wrong directions.

Under the cover of the forest, the light was noticeably less now. The bushy-tailed rodents they saw earlier were racing through the treetops, making swishing noises overhead.

"We should've marked our path." Aguire managed to sound like he wasn't worried. "If anyone thinks we're going astray, don't be shy in speaking up."

O'Riley kept checking the area with infrared. Hanson took the lead, and stalked silently toward where the light seemed to be getting stronger ahead.

Hanson was a natural in the woods. O'Riley and Aguire moved fairly stealthily, but Tully was amazing. He didn't know much about the Lieutenant, except that she had no military experience, yet she could glide soundlessly through the brush like a ghost.

After an hour, they'd come back fairly close to the same point they'd entered the forest. There were quiet nods and smiles when Hanson pointed through a gap in the forest at the waiting shuttle. It was only another 30 meters to the edge of the grassy clearing.

They closed up their formation and picked their way around the undergrowth. By the edge of the flat grassy field, peering out at the shuttle, were two aliens. Their backs were towards Aguire's team and they seemed unaware that Hanson was five steps away.

Hanson checked to make sure Aguire and the others saw the aliens. All of them froze, unsure of what to do. The aliens were men about the same height as Aguire, dressed like hunters with deep-green jackets and trousers, and high, black leather boots. They carried spears about three meters long, with points like long knife blades of some shiny, black material.

Aguire's hand found his Aurora-5, but didn't draw it. They couldn't back up unnoticed, and anyway, the aliens were watching the shuttle. The ones they'd seen in the video with Clifford Poluka had been friendly, but they'd also needed help. Aguire's team was on their turf now, uninvited and unannounced, and those spears looked awfully sharp.

Hanson quietly moved to one side, clearing the line of fire if any shooting started. Aguire's heart skipped a beat as one of the aliens turned around. He had a very human face. If he was startled he hid it well and looked at them each in turn, then nudged his companion, who also turned to look at them. They both had light tan complexions and brown eyes. Their faces reminded him a bit of Elisa Santino's South American features.

"Buenas tardes," Aguire murmured automatically. This got a raised eyebrow from one alien. The other one made a small, almost apologetic shrug, and pointed to something behind Aguire. He wasn't about to take his eyes off these two, but someone had to look back.

"Tully, what's behind us?"

He sensed her turn and look. She rasped a warning, "We're surrounded."

Aguire turned slowly, keeping his hand on his weapon. There were aliens all around, maybe 40 in all. Some had spears. Others carried crossbows and arrows that had wicked-looking points.

One, the tallest, towering 20 centimeters over Aguire, carried a simple wooden staff perhaps two and a half meters in length. He had longer hair than the others, down to his shoulders, and his complexion was a smooth golden tan. He looked young, perhaps Aguire's age. His oval face had a couple days' growth of beard.

The aliens were all dressed the same, and Aguire discerned that the green outfits were a uniform. The tall one had a cut crystal hanging on a braided cord around his neck. Aguire remembered the captain of the Fledik had worn such a stone.

There were no smiles on the alien faces. Their eyes were deadly serious, flicking from one to another of Aguire's team. The tall one kept his eyes on Aguire and stepped forward.

Again, Aguire felt like he could strangle Captain Poluka the next time they met. Captain Clifford Poluka of the Himilco had left a letter of introduction in the native language for just this sort of situation, and Captain Paul Poluka hadn't thought to give copies of it to the shuttle teams. There was only one alien word that Aguire knew.

"Fledik," he said, and pointed to the stone around the alien's neck.

The tall alien's eyes twitched in recognition and he fingered his crystal. He spoke with a pleasant accent "Fledik? Aga Ayab?"

Aguire nodded, hoping that a nod meant nothing more than he intended, and that invoking the name of the alien starship would get a friendly reaction. At least they understood what he'd said, and knew the name of the captain of the Fledik.

The big alien looked over Aguire's jumpsuit, and his eyes came to rest on the patch that bore the emblem of the Corps. "Dona," he whispered, squaring his shoulders as he suddenly solved the puzzle.

Aguire was at a loss. The word "dona" meant nothing to him. He'd run out of ideas. The next option was to tap into his team for ideas. He turned slightly to ask for opinions, but before he could speak one of the aliens startled everyone by dashing up to the tall one, babbling something in a raspy whisper.

Aguire firmed his grip on his weapon, and took a quick look around. All his people had their hands on their weapons, except Bart Hanson, who stood with his knees slightly bent, like a coiled spring.

At a quiet command from their leader the natives turned and faced the forest. Their spears and crossbows leveled to a ready position. They spread out in two rows with the spears in front. The tension in the aliens swelled and spread to Aguire's people. In a slow smooth motion, he drew his Aurora-5, but kept it pointed at the ground. To his right, he saw Tully had hers out, too.

Everyone's attention, Earthman's and Arcturusian's alike, suddenly jerked to a spot further back in the forest, where a crashing of wood jarred the air like an explosion.

A treetop 50 meters away abruptly swayed and twisted as something disturbed the trunk, out of sight, closer to the ground. A deep rumbling snarl, full of violence and wrath, echoed around the trees. Aguire's blood ran cold: a beast—something huge enough to wobble one of the giant conifers, and scary enough to make 40 armed natives get into defensive positions.

The leader gave a hand signal and his group began moving forward. He didn't check what his people were doing, and each of his followers obeyed the signals without hesitation or discussion.

Aguire signaled his own people to move with the aliens. They crept back into the forest, staying a few steps behind the green-clad locals. The alien leader glanced back once and locked eyes with Aguire. There was approval on the man's face when he saw they were following, and Aguire felt mildly reassured that whatever communication problems they had, right now they understood each other well enough.

For an instant, Aguire's mind flashed back to the Jupiter War, when he'd searched for enemies through a domed city on Ganymede. His men couldn't use their radios for fear of giving away their presence. They'd used hand-signals, with Aguire in the lead. No enemy detected them, but stealth didn't help against booby traps. He lost three of his team that day, and got the scars he carried on his back.

A thunderous growl shook the forest, and brought his attention back to the beast they were, for some reason, walking towards. It sounded farther away now—maybe a hundred meters. The alien men seemed to relax just a fraction. Their leader turned to them, and smiled.

"Sarg-nah schema vo," he said, and pointed at a shape that could barely be seen through the underbrush. It was gray, furry, and many times larger than a man. It was heading away on four legs at a good pace.

Spears and crossbows lowered. The aliens relaxed, broke formation, and returned their attention to the Earthmen. Aguire holstered his weapon, and his people did the same.

Tully whispered to Aguire. "What the hell was that?"

The tall alien guessed the meaning of her question.

"Sarg-nah." He held his arms up, indicating something very big and made a pantomime of gestures to describe a snout with long teeth.

CHAPTER 44

Maria Rodriguez piloted El Toro westward around Arcturus-4, with John Burke as her lookout officer. She kept the cruiser at 65 kilometers above the planet, where the air thinned out enough to keep the velocity at six-point-three kps. She'd have them on top of Aguire's position in about 80 minutes.

It was night on this side of the planet. The barrier above them seemed unthreatening, but there'd already been enough unexpected hazards to keep her from getting too confident. Rodriguez had followed Aguire's example and tried to land on the rippling sheet that shone red in the cruiser's bow lights but, like Donno's shuttle, they slipped through without even feeling any resistance. It seems the scientists aboard the Hanno were right; the barrier was weaker on the night side of the planet: some sort of interaction of the sunlight with the ionosphere but, beyond that, they were stumped as to what the barrier actually was.

Like all scientific mysteries, this one would eventually yield its secrets, but so far, all they knew was that it was a laminar boundary, and impervious to objects with a lot of momentum.

Captain Poluka and medical personnel were down in the midsection of the cruiser, getting more details from Sheffield, whom they picked up a half-hour ago on the western shore of a continent about the size of Africa. Their shuttle was a total loss. The entire frame was bent like a potato chip with a gaping hole on the starboard side.

Half a dozen barnacles were also aboard El Toro, armed to the teeth in case things went sour.

At first, Poluka thought Sheffield was joking when he said a fish attacked his shuttle.

"It jumped out of the water?" Poluka asked.

"Yes, sir," Commander Sheffield said. There were nods all

around from the four other sopping-wet officers, all wrapped in blankets and sipping coffee. "Well, maybe not all the way out. We watched it swimming at a depth of about ten meters for a while, and never would have seen it if it hadn't been so damn big. We dropped down to get a better look. I guess we were 30 meters above the water when it came at us."

"How big was it?" Major Melanie Rivers asked. She was the senior Army officer on the Hanno, and brought her best five soldiers along with some pretty impressive firepower.

"We estimated about 50 meters long, Major," a lieutenant answered. "We've got recordings if you'd like to see for yourself."

"Later, Lieutenant. I'm just thankful that all of you made it through this."

Poluka had seen the tooth marks on the wrecked shuttle, but it was hard to imagine a fish taking down a spacecraft. "I can't blame you for wanting a closer look, but anything that big deserves some distance. We'll count this as a lesson learned."

Sheffield continued. "We hit the water and couldn't get airborne again. So, I gave it all the forward thrust we had and plowed through the water. We were only a couple of klicks from the shore, and the fish didn't bother us again."

"So you waited on the beach for help to arrive," Poluka concluded.

"Well…we did try going inland a bit to see what resources were available in case we needed to stay longer. It turns out there's some unfriendly wildlife there, so we returned to the beach."

"Wildlife?"

"Yes, sir. We didn't get a close look at them. They were…something like wild boar…but bigger…maybe the size of buffalo. They were mean, too…came after us. Chased us across the sand dunes, but they didn't seem to want to get too far from the jungle. We stayed on the beach after that. It was pouring rain and we got soaked, but the shuttle was stuck in the surf, half-full of sea water."

Major Rivers shook her head. "Giant fish, giant boar, and Aguire's team tangled with something like a venus fly trap the size of a tree. Is everything on this planet gigantic?"

Captain Poluka ran a hand across his chin and noticed one of the rescued men, Ensign Harper. The boy was spooked, constantly looking out the window expecting the next calamity to strike. Poluka had picked him because of the initiative he'd shown in organizing emergency medical teams during the crisis a few days ago. Poluka wanted to give Harper some exploration experience as a reward. All Poluka's decisions were turning out to be crap.

Burke shouted down to them from the flight deck, "We'll be at the terminator in two minutes."

Poluka told the rescued people, "We'll reach Aguire's shuttle in a few minutes. In the meantime Doctor Moorpark will check you out."

He left them and settled into a seat on the flight deck. The barrier above was dark gray. Ahead was a bright red horizon. His eyes swept across the instruments and took in the situation.

They were coming around to the dayside of the planet, and the signal from the Hanno was still strong. Lieutenant Rodriguez had dropped the altitude by ten kilometers, but she kept the speed up. The center screen on the panel had a com link open to the bridge of the Hanno. Commanders Washington and Redbird were both on the screen, and G.J. was sitting at the back wall by the emergency lockers.

"Here we go." Burke's quiet observation brought Poluka's attention back to the window. Night was falling on the sea below them, but they were passing from night to day as they outraced the dusk terminator. The redness of the sky was a flickering, whipping aurora above them that circled the planet from north to south in a band maybe 70 or 80 kilometers wide. Ten seconds later they finally saw what Arcturus-4 looked like in the daylight.

The outer atmospheric shell appeared hazy-gray above them, but the sea below was as blue as any sea on Earth. Banks of clouds, rimmed with blazing white, stretched out to mark the weather patterns below. Peeking between the clouds ahead was land, another vast continent. The cruiser's great altitude provided a vista which revealed the curve of the planet, and a land mass that stretched to the horizons north, west, and south.

"It's too bad this cruiser doesn't have the instrument suite the shuttles have," Poluka murmured to himself.

Burke overheard and replied. "We're getting all the data we

can, sir. At least El Toro's tougher than the shuttles."

Poluka grunted. The shuttles were a disappointment. He'd have to see if Tran had some answers about how to get back through the barrier. The night side of the planet was obviously the best route, but Poluka wanted some scientific reason to believe the shuttles will survive the attempt, before he actually commits lives to such an experiment. He looked at the com screen. It was black except for a message indicating that the link was lost. Burke saw it at the same time.

"Oh, crap." The ensign checked the system before announcing, "Communication with the Hanno is gone."

"Try Aguire," Poluka suggested. "We need to let them know we're coming."

Burke pinged the shuttle. A moment later, Ensign Newhall's face appeared. The kid was wild-eyed, and couldn't seem to hold still. He had a pistol in his hand. Poluka's blood turned to ice.

"Newhall, report."

"Captain," the young officer squealed, "...aliens...they've got them...in the forest...."

"Slow down, son. Tell me what's happening."

Newhall squeezed his eyes shut for a moment, taking a quick breath. "The others, sir...Aguire and the others. I saw them coming back. They were almost out of the forest. Then a group of aliens came out of nowhere. The aliens were armed and surrounded our people."

Rodriguez and Burke exchange glances. Newhall stared out of the screen with pleading eyes, desperate for guidance.

"Can you still see them, Ensign?" Poluka gave it his calmest, most reassuring tone.

"No, sir. They've moved back into the woods, and the shuttle's com system is burned. I can't contact Aguire's radio or pick up the jumpsuit beacons. The ship-to-ship com seems okay though."

"Listen, Ensign Newhall, I'm in a cruiser right now, and I'll be at your position in...."

"40 minutes," Maria Rodriguez said instantly.

"40 minutes," Poluka told Newhall. "We'll leave this channel open and stay in constant contact. I want you to power up the shuttle and stay ready to lift off at a moment's notice...but not without my orders. Is that understood?"

"Sir, I'm not a pilot."

"I know, son, but if you have to leave the ground, it will only be to hover out of weapon range," Poluka lied. He had no idea what kind of threat there might be to the shuttle. "You said the aliens were armed. What kind of weapons do they have?"

"I don't know, sir. I didn't have good visibility."

"All right, Ensign." Out of the corner of his eye, Poluka saw that Burke was getting a text message, and hoped it wasn't more bad news. "Hang tight, and we'll let you know when to turn on a beacon signal."

"Yes, sir."

Turning to Burke, he quietly asked, "What is it?"

"Sir, Newhall's signal was weak, but Donno's is almost unreadable. Radio waves don't seem to go far on the day side of this planet. We can only get text bursts from him now. He says he's seeing a pyramid in the desert, and wants to go down for a closer look."

"No! Absolutely not! We've got a team that may be prisoners already. I want Donno's team to meet us at Aguire's shuttle. Send him those orders, and turn up the signal strength to make sure it gets through."

"Aye, sir."

No more. Poluka would make no more on-the-fly decisions. He started with a solid plan before leaving Earth, and every impulsive choice he'd made since resulted in disaster. He'd revert to the original plan: find out what happened to his brother and the crew of the Himilco, then go down the trade route, and bring together the colonies and independent worlds that are willing to stand against the New Federation. The Hanno will be an exploration ship no longer.

Soon, he would know the fate of the Himilco and get on to the next step: bringing the Hanno's officers into the conspiracy. That could be dicey but, done correctly, there would be minimal dissent, and those who couldn't go along with the plan will be left safe and sound on a neutral world, such as Tau Ceti.

He worked it out with G.J. three years ago. It should work out even better than planned since the New Fed was becoming openly brutal.

Ensign Burke interrupted his thoughts, "Sir. No response from Commander Donno. He may have received the message, but can't confirm."

"Damn those shuttles," Poluka sighed. "Alright, maybe we'll get through to him later."

Except for large rivers and lakes, the land below was indistinct. There were no crisp, clean shadows to give the terrain three dimensions. The sun was just a bright region of sky that left everything well lit, but vague at the same time.

CHAPTER 45

Aguire might be dead or a prisoner along with Hanson, O'Riley, and Tully: one more thing on Poluka's conscience.

Major Rivers directed the approach, which was customary when the Army was called upon to fight for Corps personnel. He could have pulled rank on the grounds that this was initial contact with aliens and therefore beyond the scope of Army policies, but he didn't. He couldn't. He no longer trusted his own judgment.

Fortunately, the Major was not one of the ceremonial types used strictly for parades and gate guards. She was the real thing, with front-line experience going back to the insurrection on Eridanus and the Jupiter War. For the last couple of years she'd been training recruits in hand-to-hand fighting. She also had a master's degree in history, which Poluka found strangely intimidating.

The other five soldiers were combat veterans who wore the crossed daggers patch of the First Infantry Advance Recon Group, five men with no necks. When they refer to Navy types as shuttle-bugs, they say it with a sneer, and they never, ever lose a fight.

Major Rivers contacted Ensign Newhall ten minutes ahead of time to get an update, have him turn on a radio beacon, and check the direction where Aguire's team was last seen.

Aguire's group was west of the shuttle when armed men intercepted them. Newhall was sure no one else had crossed through the clearing. So, Rivers thought it likely—but no guarantees—there would be no threat from the east. Just to be cautious, they'd do a quick scan for heat emissions as they flew over.

They would come straight in—low and slow—from the east, fly over the parked shuttle and touch down a kilometer west of it, just a few steps from the forest. They'd do a fast drop of the Army personnel, and then take off again to circle around and try to pinpoint Aguire's location while the six soldiers go in on foot.

"Sounds like the best we can do with the information we have," Poluka said after hearing Rivers explain it to everyone.

"We'll still be taking some big chances," Major Rivers said. "We don't even know if the locals have done anything unfriendly. Newhall's observations are inconclusive. We can't take the chance when our people are unaccounted for, but we don't want to cause an incident that's not warranted. Also, everything about the local situation—technology, politics, culture—everything, is unknown. The messages from the Himilco didn't prepare us for this. I'm inclined to believe that our people are safe since the Himilco's captain said that any native would give us directions to their leader. That indicates a single nation of friendly people...unless I'm being overly optimistic."

Major Rivers's voice was definitely feminine, more so than her muscular physique or her two-centimeter-long, strawberry-blond hair. There was a reasonable calmness in her soothing soprano, giving an impression of all-knowing competence that Poluka found mesmerizing. He gave himself a quick mental shake before reacting to her appraisal.

"I think the situation is quite hopeful." He managed to sound like he'd been concentrating. He couldn't remember how long it'd been since he slept, but it was starting to catch up with him. The next chance he got, he'd take one of his weight-loss pills; they always gave him more energy. "But we must be prepared for anything at this point. As you said, my brother's messages didn't prepare us for this. It's also possible that what he told us is out of date. I'm sure your plan is the best we can manage without knowing more, Major."

"We'll be there in three minutes," Burke called out from the lookout station.

"One more thing we might try," Rivers added, "if you agree that it won't endanger our missing people, Captain."

"What's that, Major?"

"Newhall's low-frequency com system isn't working, but ours is. If we try to contact Aguire, do you think it might alarm the natives, and put our people in worse danger?"

"I should have thought of that." Poluka's face heated with embarrassment. Major Rivers waited for an answer with absolutely no expression on her face. Poluka worried that she guessed he was having trouble. A spasm of suspicion twisted his gut as he wondered who else thought he might not be up to par these days. Did Aguire? Did Redbird? Washington? No, not Washington. He could count on Washington. But the others…he didn't know.

And what about Rivers? She was suggesting contacting Aguire with no expression on her damn face to give a clue what she's thinking. Does that mean she thinks it's a good idea, or is she just covering her ass in case things go wrong?

"We'll monitor the frequency, and wait for Aguire to initiate communications," he decided.

Rivers blinked, and seemed to consider it for a moment. "Very well, Captain."

El Toro was just meters above the treetops when they reached the meadow and silently ghosted over the parked shuttle, angling down to reach the ground on the far side. The cruiser's quantum gravity thrusters were so silent that Ensign Newhall wouldn't even know they were there if he weren't watching for them.

Lieutenant Rodriguez was the best tactical pilot Poluka had ever seen, and when El Toro touched the ground just long enough for six barnies to jump out, she didn't even leave a mark on the soft turf where the skids touched.

El Toro gently gained altitude and snuck around to the north, circling to a point ten klicks to the west, then climbed to a thousand meters before heading back towards the meadow. They would try to pick up Aguire's location, or the aliens, with infrared cameras. Major Rivers's team was already in the woods heading west.

CHAPTER 46

The tiny aircraft was freezing cold, and the constant whining of air rushing past the thin canvas fuselage became brain numbing after nearly 20 hours. Still, the pilot held his course and was overjoyed when he spotted dry land below.

Elpastre, the tall, somber monarch of Arcturus asked him to carry a message to, of all people, Paul Poluka, and chose him for this task not just because he had the aircraft, but because the King trusted Gentry Stokes.

The King and Queen gave Gentry a conflicting impression of both wisdom and naiveté. There was something indefinable about the royal couple, a compelling sincerity that inspired trust, and more, a candid depth of feeling that you could see in their eyes.

They'd waited until the last moment to tell even Gentry for fear that the Old Rulers find out. Not even Clifford Poluka could be informed that his brother would be landing at a place called Himeka-ar-Vod, six thousand klicks across the North Sea, and that he would land today.

Only the Queen, Lapastra, foresaw this location and time. All of the other psychics said the landing would be at the pyramid, and only Lapastra foresaw the date and time.

Gentry shivered and pulled his thick jacket closer. A spacesuit helmet kept his head warm and supplemented his oxygen at high altitude. He had built the aircraft on an ancient Earth design that used wings for lift. The engine was a thruster salvaged from a life pod, and the power source was a bank of fusion batteries, also from a life pod. The frame was incredibly light, porous wood with a lacquered canvas skin stretched tight as a drum to cover it. He designed it with a little coaching from the local glider engineers who supplied unpowered aircraft to the Royal Guard.

Gentry had to land soon. He was just too damn tired, and he wouldn't see the landmarks when night comes.

He wondered about the hasty conversation with Elpastre. Could he be right?

He was reluctant to take part in a political intrigue without really understanding the implications, and was not fully convinced that the Queen's information was correct. All of the psychics on the planet, except for Lapastra, thought Earthmen would land at the pyramid in the desert at some later date. Gentry especially hated that Clifford didn't know about it.

Night was coming, and Gentry needed to find that clearing before it got dark.

* * *

Aguire was in the forest, only 50 meters from the clearing where Newhall waited in the shuttle but, right now, 50 meters seemed like a long way. The daylight was fading already. Aguire hadn't slept for nearly 24 hours and he caught himself yawning while the alien leader was talking.

O'Riley was in the same condition. Hanson and Tully were okay; they'd slept just ten hours ago, but they couldn't just start back now. They had no way of explaining anything to the aliens, and they couldn't just say adiós and walk away.

The tall alien's name was Oppo Gunn. He gave Aguire the impression that Oppo believed Aguire came from Dona, which was apparently their word for Earth and, somehow, the Hanno's arrival was not such a big surprise. Aguire gave his own name, and pointed to the members of his team, saying, "Tully; O'Riley; Hanson."

Oppo Gunn looked closely at Hanson's blue eyes with obvious wonder, and asked, "Bart Hanson?"

Aguire perked up a bit. He, O'Riley, and Tully turned to Hanson. Their blue-eyed companion seemed as surprised as they were.

"I guess I'm famous."

"I guess you are." Aguire turned back to Oppo Gunn with a questioning gesture.

The alien saw their reaction and grinned. He said a few words, out of which Aguire caught the name "Gentry" and it became clear how he'd heard of Bart Hanson.

Hanson's eyes widened and he sucked in a deep breath when he heard the alien words.

One of the aliens hissed a warning and the others surprised Aguire by leaping into defensive positions again, this time enclosing them in a circle with their weapons turned outward. Despite being in the middle of a forest, there was a lot of wide-open space around the giant conifers and there was little undergrowth, yet they saw no threat.

Aguire and his team drew their own weapons, expecting another encounter with some fearsome beast.

"Did you hear anything?" Aguire whispered to his people.

Heads shook. Even the alien leader seemed puzzled.

* * *

"They're here," the hushed voice of Major Rivers informed Poluka over the radio. "They're among armed aliens, 40 of them, but they don't seem to be prisoners. The aliens detected our presence, and are set to defend their position. Your Corps people have their weapons drawn and appear to be supporting the aliens' defense. They don't know it's us yet. Are you getting the video?"

The image on the screen in El Toro's flight deck showed that Aguire and the others were clearly prepared to fight alongside the aliens. Poluka almost cheered with relief that his people weren't dead or prisoners, but he realized that things could still go horribly wrong. El Toro was flying three klicks west of Rivers' position and could be there in seconds, but they mustn't alarm the natives.

"Captain." Burke tried to get Poluka's attention.

"Not now." He waved a dismissive hand at the ensign. "Major, do you think you could…."

"Captain Poluka!"

"Ensign Burke! Just wait…."

"Incoming craft, sir!"

"What the hell?" Poluka gaped at the radar screen. A small object was coming straight at them, maybe ten seconds out. The cruiser's computer analyzed the emissions and suggested it was a stealth weapon.

"Hard to port. Get some speed, and see if it follows us."

Maria Rodriguez didn't need to be told twice. She'd seen it coming as soon as Burke spotted it. The radar showed a tiny target, maybe 20 centimeters wide, but infrared made it to be larger. It had to be built for stealth, with just a few parts that reflect radar, and the speed was just right for sneaking up on someone. The cruiser shot north for a couple of kilometers before she realized the object was not pursuing them.

"It's heading for Aguire's position," she said.

"Oh, shit." Poluka assumed the worst. "Bring us around. Burke, lock a laser onto it."

* * *

Major Rivers overheard the whole drama taking place in the cruiser, and held her breath waiting for it to play out. She couldn't move her people now, not with a bogey bearing down on them, and the already-jumpy aliens surrounding Aguire's team. The bogey, whatever it might be, was heading for the alien group...or it might be aiming for her team of soldiers. Her finger found the selector switch on her weapon, and clicked it to fire rotating gravity pulses, hoping RGP could destroy the threat.

"Get under cover," she hissed into her microphone, and her people did the best they could to find a rock or a log to cozy up to. She found herself with no place to hide from an airborne attack, so she scrunched up next to a tree as small as she could make herself, and waited.

* * *

"I'll be damned." Gentry grinned. "It's a...a...I don't know what it is...but it must be from Earth!"

He watched the vessel move to the north and then circle back towards him. Lapastra was right. Someone from Earth *is* landing here today. Gentry started looking for the clearing which was supposed to be just ahead. He hoped it really was Cliff's younger brother. That would really be something if....

The strangest thing suddenly happened. A flash of intense light filled his tiny aircraft, and there was a puff of smoke. The whistling of the wind sounded different now that two holes, one on each side of the fuselage, appeared as if by magic. The holes were half-centimeter circles, and the edges sparkled as if they were burning.

Burning?

"Oh, you bastards! You friggin' BASTARDS!"

Gentry dove for the trees. Another beam of light flashed just above his head, putting two more smoldering holes through his aircraft. He had to kill some speed, but he got under the canopy of the forest and wove a path through the trees. Branches slapped hard against his fragile vehicle, and the frame creaked as it frantically banked from side to side, but he missed the massive trunks that would have meant instant death.

His mind was blank with panic. His hands reacted on the aircraft controls automatically, trying to avoid hitting anything as the trees whipped by. Then there were no more trees. He was in the clear and utterly relieved that he'd made it through the forest. When he saw the shuttle parked in the middle of the clearing he suddenly remembered why he'd flown into the forest.

"Damn." He gripped the throttle, unsure if he should run for it, or land. The decision was made for him when night suddenly fell.

Night comes on Arcturus-4 with a spectacular flashing of crimson aurora high in the atmosphere. Where the sun's rays are parallel to the barrier surface, the ionization of the phantom mesons begins to break down, and the index of refraction fluctuates wildly. It took years for the Arcturusians to teach Gentry enough of their science for him to understand how the barrier works, and the nightly aurora still seemed more like magic than physics.

Right now, it meant that he must land. His simple aircraft dedicated all its power to the thruster. It had no lights. He got it down on the ground at the same instant the aurora passed, and the only light remaining was a soft glow from the moon of Arcturus. The small craft hit the ground just right, but the ground was uneven and covered with thick tufts of grass. The wheels wouldn't stay straight. He fought the controls to keep from turning too sharp and driving a wingtip into the dirt. As the craft slowed to a stop, he saw that he'd just missed the shuttle, and was a few paces from its starboard hatch. Someone was looking out the pilot's side window.

Gentry popped open the canopy and heaved himself out into the moonlit meadow, intent on talking to whomever was in the shuttle.

"Crap," Gentry muttered at the holes burned through his vehicle. "Someone's got to answer for that."

The shuttle's hatch sighed open, spilling light into the meadow. A kid with a ridiculous haircut and a weapon in each hand sprang out like a friggin' jack-in-the-box and started shooting!

* * *

Oppo Gunn barked an order when a strange, small craft suddenly plummeted down through the trees and screamed past, towards the clearing. The entire group of aliens took off south but stayed in an ordered formation. Aguire and his people rushed to keep up. To the east, camouflaged figures sprang up from the ground and waved weapons wildly around, apparently trying to track the flying object. With a numb realization, Aguire recognized the Army uniforms and knew they were here looking for him.

Aguire stopped running and looked at the barnies, then at the aliens who, with Hanson, O'Riley, and Tully, were still moving south. He'd lost control of the situation. His tired, foggy brain couldn't react fast enough, and his body was all out of adrenaline.

The sky above the treetops suddenly blossomed into crimson sheets of light that flickered violently and threw the whole forest into a crazy jumble of shifting shadows. He heard confused shouts from the barnies and alien commands from Oppo Gunn.

O'Riley's voice was calling Aguire's name.

He ignored all of it. His body suddenly discovered a little more adrenaline as his eyes followed the dim shape of a huge, furry monster running towards him. The beast had returned.

He saw now that it was shaped somewhat like a raccoon. It was coming from the north, and was almost on top of the Army personnel now. They didn't see it because their attention was on him and the aliens. He raised his weapon and took aim at the huge creature. Just as he squeezed off a burst of metal plasma that lanced through the forest and between soldiers, he also saw the wide-eyed alarm on the faces of those soldiers. Part of his brain understood that they would assume he was shooting at them, and they would return fire.

* * *

Sheffield followed the progress of the operation from the com-console in the midsection of the cruiser and guessed what had gone wrong. He scurried up to the flight deck and watched in horror as the camera picked up Commander Aguire standing alone between the giant trees—and the sky around them suddenly repeated the aurora effect they'd seen earlier—just as Aguire fired his weapon at Major Rivers's people.

The needle-thin beam glowed ultraviolet as electrons rejoined the positively charged packets of silver plasma. The red light of the aurora in the sky reflected off the beam as well, producing an eerie effect that drew all eyes to it.

Captain Poluka raged with incoherent obscenities while the Army's return barrage of RGP's made the infrared display blossom into indistinct figures running about among burning branches and smoke.

Sheffield ignored Poluka, who was babbling something about landing in the forest, and leaned forward to rasp into Lieutenant Rodriguez's microphone, "Major Rivers, cease fire!" then, to Burke, "Put a floodlight on the whole area."

Rodriguez got the point and held the cruiser at a hundred meters above the treetops. The whole firefight on the ground was the result of some kind of misunderstanding, and the people down there needed to sort it out. The only thing El Toro could do for them at the moment was light up the area so everyone could stop guessing about what was going on.

* * *

Bart Hanson rushed, faster than any human could move, straight at Aguire. Hanson tried not to hurt him, but he had to slam Aguire hard to move him before the soldiers could squeeze off a burst in his direction.

287

There was almost no way to do it without hurting his friend, but the Army's weapons could vaporize steel, and their marksmanship left no doubt that broken bones was the best choice.

It was all he could do to knock Aguire ten meters to the side while trying like hell to not break his neck or back. He couldn't spare any effort for the other parts of his friend's body and was sure Aguire was going to need a doctor. It helped that Aguire was exhausted and handled like a sack of rags.

A sound like thunder, and flashing beams of sickly-orange light swept the area as Major Rivers's people unleashed rotating gravity pulses in short bursts. Some of the bursts hit branches farther back in the forest and started small fires. Some hit the ground and tore open the turf, launching flaming sod and leaving a smoldering trench.

Aguire was missed completely. Unfortunately, Hanson wasn't.

* * *

The crisis on the ground subsided, and Major Rivers reported that there was one fatality, and that one of Aguire's team needed immediate medical assistance.

Captain Poluka took Commander Sheffield's advice and had Rodriguez put the light cruiser down at the edge of the clearing, 50 meters from the injured people in the forest. The medical group went in on foot. Poluka chewed a fingernail and wondered who the fatality was, but didn't ask Rivers for more information.

Sheffield's original shuttle team armed themselves and walked out to the shuttle where the strange object they'd shot at had apparently crashed, and was now burning. They couldn't reach Newhall, who had been having trouble with the radio and, hopefully, that's all there was to it.

Captain Poluka's memory of how it all happened was jumbled and confused. He'd gone too long without sleep, and probably the pills were affecting him, too. All he knew for certain was that things had gone wrong, but could have been a lot worse. Thank goodness he'd kept a cool head and ordered Rivers to cease fire. He couldn't actually remember giving the order, but there was so much happening at the time.

* * *

One of Major Rivers' people met Doctor Moorpark at the edge of the forest. Figures were moving around a smoky area just ahead.

Moorpark got his experience in the Navy and was no stranger to battlefield injuries, or to battlefields, but this was the most unnerving situation he'd ever faced.

To start with, his captain was completely unpredictable and rapidly losing touch with reality. Now, he was going among aliens—*aliens*, for crying out loud!—with no idea how to communicate with them, and who had, just moments earlier, been fired upon by his army.

He found Major Rivers examining a gigantic, dead, hairy creature that must have weighed a good thousand kilos with fangs at least fifteen centimeters long.

"Oh, yeah," Moorpark muttered. "That's just perfect."

Rivers must have heard him because she turned just then, and directed him to where Commander Aguire was lying.

Aguire's eyes fluttered slightly and his breathing was shallow but regular. Moorpark and two medical techs checked for broken bones. The right tibia was clearly snapped, judging from the extra bend in his leg below the knee. As they splinted the leg for transport, the other techs reported that Ensign Hanson was dead, with flash burns over half of his body. They didn't know the cause of the damage because a direct hit from an RGP wouldn't have left a body. Moorpark took a quick look, and determined that Hanson's water canteen had been hit. The plastic and water became a 10,000 degree plasma that caused his death.

"Poor bastard. What a waste."

CHAPTER 47

Even with her dark complexion, Elpastre could see that his wife had gone pale. She sat like a statue, focusing her awareness on events far away. The last thing she'd reported was that the Earthmen had attacked Gentry, and then they had attacked *each other!*

Dread and doubt stabbed at Elpastre while he waited for his wife to see the outcome of the landing. All the poisonous wisdom the Old Rulers had been offering the nobles for the last ten years was proving to be true: Earthmen were violent and incomprehensible. They would only make things worse.

Elpastre gave his head a small shake and reminded himself of the prophecy. Of course the Earthmen were violent, and so were Arcturusians in their own way. He must have faith, or his world would soon die.

The King and Queen of Arcturus had crossed the inland sea Vodita last night while Gentry flew his machine to meet the younger Poluka brother. They were now at the village of Arvod, which was once a great city before the decline of this world's civilization. Here, they'd hoped Gentry could bring the visitors from Earth.

"Elpastre." His wife stood up. Her eyes were troubled, and possibly angry. "The Earthmen are not only violent, they are stupid, too."

She told him what she'd learned and he began to sweat.

"This can only get worse unless we can do something from here. You say they are with Oppo, even now?"

Lapastra nodded wearily.

"You were always close to him. Can you reach him from such a distance, and make him understand?"

"I will try."

* * *

"Newhall is here, Captain," a voice came from the radio, "but someone knocked him out and left him tied up inside the shuttle. He says he saw a man outside and tried to shoot him, but whoever it was moved too fast for him. All the weapons are accounted for, but there's no sign of anyone else."

Paul Poluka stared at the radio, struggling against the fog in his brain to comprehend. "Sheffield, the craft that went down— was it a manned vehicle?"

"Yes, sir. It's built like an antique airplane, but powered by NF batteries and a mini-thruster—must be parts from the Himilco. The batteries blew up when Newhall shot the craft."

"Understood." Poluka's head cleared a bit. "Stay with the shuttle and check it out. Make sure it's ready to fly and prepare to take it back to the Hanno."

"Yes, sir."

Everyone kept telling Poluka the aliens were friendly, and possibly just a hunting party. Lieutenant Tully was adamant about showing them that Earth-people didn't go around shooting everyone, and she was right. It was one hell of a first impression when you sent camouflaged soldiers to kill people for no reason.

An unexpected sob of misery escaped Paul Poluka's lips, and he held his head in his hands, covering his face. Everything had gone completely wrong from the moment they left Earth, and it was all his fault. He'd back off this time, and try to explain to the "hunting party" that they could go about their business while the nasty Earthmen returned to space for a while. He had to get Aguire up to the Med Center. Tomorrow, he'd figure out how to contact this…what was he called…Elpastre, the leader of the aliens.

"Mister Burke, you have a link to the Hanno?" Poluka asked.

"Aye, sir," Burke croaked hoarsely. He'd gone deathly pale when the doctor reported they were bringing Hanson back in a bag. He punched the connection open without turning toward his captain.

"Hanno, this is Captain Poluka."

Commander Redbird had the watch, and took the news with

an iron expression.

G.J. and Lynda were on the bridge, both shaken. Poluka never saw Lynda cry before, and it filled him with shame. He ended the message by saying they would return to the Hanno shortly, and Commander Sheffield's team would bring up the shuttle.

He heard shouts outside the cruiser. The starboard camera showed Major Rivers' people standing between a group of agitated aliens and the medical people. Paul rushed down the ladder to see what the trouble was.

Finally, he came face to face with real, live aliens. They appeared human. They didn't all look alike; some were fair, others dark-skinned, and their hair varied in shades of brown from black to almost blond.

The leader, Oppo Gunn, was taller than the others. He stood within arms-reach of Major Rivers, staring into her eyes, and growling something in his language through clenched teeth. His tone was urgent, and demanding. Rivers stood defiantly, staring back into his eyes, but unable to respond to demands she couldn't understand.

"Captain," Rivers explained, "they won't let us move Hanson."

My god, he thought, do they think we'd leave him?

The aliens were still holding their weapons. His people were holding theirs, too. He got a sick feeling about how this would play out, but help came in the most unexpected way.

"Oppo!" A voice rang out from the darkness astern of the cruiser. "Oppo Gunn. Ina ehya. Sien okin!"

Major Rivers half-raised her weapon as a figure moved into the light. Poluka could see the tension in her people, just as he saw the relief on Oppo Gunn's face. A man came into the light. The newcomer looked at Poluka with his bright green eyes and said, "Captain Poluka, I presume."

Poluka gaped bug-eyed in sudden comprehension. "Gentry! My God! Gentry!"

* * *

Another message came to the Hanno. Elisa Santino ran all the way to Lynda's quarters to tell her. Lynda and her father couldn't believe it until they saw Gentry on the screen and heard his voice.

She cried again, and for the first time in his life, Gentry saw his father cry, too, and then his own eyes were flowing. They wanted him to come to the ship immediately, and he wished he could.

"Bart isn't dead. They made a mistake. We got a message telling us to check him again. He's in shock from his injuries, but his heart is still beating. It's faint and irregular, but it's beating. He might still be saved, but we have to get him to a doctor immediately."

"Alive!" Lynda's father cried, "That's fantastic! It's wonderful! You must bring him. We have good doctors aboard."

Lynda could only nod vigorously and grin through her tears, but her brother gave them a tight smile and shook his head.

"I'm afraid your doctors won't quite be up to this. The Arcturusian doctors are much better. Medicine is something they excel in. If anyone can save his life, it will have to be them. But you can come down here—I want you to come—I'll have your Mister Burke send the coordinates when we get there. I don't know how to explain where we're going."

They wanted to argue. They wanted to be with him sooner, but they agreed to come as quickly as possible. Gentry told them the cruiser was already on the way, taking them west to where doctors were waiting.

After they'd talked for a while and promised to meet soon, Gentry said good-bye and his image disappeared from the screen. Lynda and her father left for the bridge to arrange a shuttle.

"I wonder who sent them a message," Papa said, "I mean, about Bart still being alive."

* * *

Commander Redbird didn't like any of it.

He'd relieved Washington at 2300 hours, before Poluka did his mad rush in the cruiser to rescue Sheffield's team. Soon after, he'd gotten the report about the disastrous encounter with aliens, and ground his teeth at the thought of Poluka representing all of Earth in the eyes of this alien civilization.

Then there was the encrypted com from Doctor Moorpark to

the Med Center. Doctors had their own encryption privileges because of doctor-patient confidentiality, but it was damn strange to use it for an emergency field-op.

Doctor Payne came up to the bridge right after that, and asked to talk to Redbird in private. She told him that Doctor Moorpark had observed the captain taking a pill. There'd been speculation among medical staff that the captain's recent behavior had all the earmarks of drug use, specifically, zippies. The illicit pills were widely used by people who wanted to lose weight, and the captain had lost maybe 20 kilos in just a few months.

Doctor Payne wanted Redbird's permission to search the captain's quarters.

"That's a law enforcement act," Redbird answered automatically, but his mind was racing. If it was true, it would explain a lot, and it opened up some ugly possibilities. It would have to stop, but a captain is the law on any ship. To hold him accountable—officially accountable—would require extraordinary measures that most of the senior officers would have to agree on, and, even though it was right and necessary, it would be an embarrassment to the Corps, which would also hurt the officers who took such action. Still, it was just speculation so far. Maybe a search would clarify things somewhat.

"Give me a little time to consider what to do," he told Doctor Payne.

In the meantime, Poluka was off to another part of the planet, this time to take members of his crew to alien doctors. His only assurance that they were better than the ship's doctors came from a man who'd been missing for ten years, and had once been committed to a mental hospital.

Poluka had also allowed 40 armed aliens into the cruiser with them, outnumbering Poluka's crew by over three to one.

To top it off, Stokes and his daughter were no doubt on their way to the bridge to demand the use of a shuttle (and pilot) to take them through the barrier, which they still didn't know much about, and down to an alien civilization that they knew even less about.

Commander Redbird didn't like any of it.

* * *

Paul Poluka was reaching the end of his strength. Those damn pills kept him going without feeling the need for sleep, and now he couldn't concentrate. He couldn't make decisions. If he could just close his eyes for a few minutes, he might feel better. El Toro would have them at their destination soon, and he had to hold on. He couldn't commit his people to the care of alien doctors without carefully appraising the situation. Gentry assured him that it was for the best.

Gentry…he found Gentry! Lynda will be so pleased…did she already know? Did he already tell her?…can't remember…

* * *

"He's asleep." Doctor Moorpark covered the captain with a blanket in the small first-aid room aboard the light-cruiser. Aguire and Hanson were on the two cots, both unconscious. Poluka was in a chair.

"What's wrong with him?" Gentry asked.

"He's just tired. He's been pushing himself too hard."

Gentry used to have trouble telling when someone was lying to him, but after living for ten years with people who rarely lie, it was remarkably easy to spot one now. He didn't question the doctor further.

But Moorpark had some questions of his own. "How did this…Oppo Gunn…know that Hanson was still alive? My own people missed it, and they listened for a heartbeat."

"The Arcturusians have abilities that we don't. There are some people here who can get information even from a great distance. Oppo got a message from his sister, who had observed that Bart was still alive."

"They have medical equipment that can diagnose over long distances? I thought they only had primitive technology. How far away is she?"

"Let's call it different, rather than primitive. We're going there now, about six thousand kilometers west. Oppo's sister is the Queen of Arcturus. When you entered this star system, the Queen sensed it, and also determined that there would be three landings today: the first on the far side of the planet—a crash landing. Another would be in the desert near the equator, and the third would be where I could find Paul Poluka. She pinpointed the locations about 25 hours ago, and sent me just in time to meet you."

Moorpark listened carefully, putting aside his skepticism. Gentry Stokes explained that many women of this strange world had psychic abilities that made these things possible.

The doctor might have discounted the story, except for the fact that Gentry had shown up at the right place and the right time to meet them, and that Oppo had been right in insisting that Hanson wasn't dead. It was too much to call a coincidence. He'd keep an open mind, and when Gentry assured him that these were not primitive people, that their doctors were better than Earth's…well, he hoped it was true, because he didn't know how to save Hanson's life.

Gentry looked at Paul Poluka's sleeping form, and remembered how he looked, years ago, when he used to visit them in California. He looked a lot like Clifford.

Gentry said, "I'm surprised he didn't ask about his brother when we met."

"He's just tired," Moorpark repeated.

Gentry went up to the flight deck, where Commander Sheffield was mapping the terrain as they approached their destination. He pointed through the window. "That inland sea is called Vodita. It means the Little Sea. On the eastern coast is the capital city."

Burke zoomed in with the belly camera and got a good shot of a sprawling metropolis with tens of thousands of buildings connected by meandering roadways paved with white bricks.

"Wow. I never thought I'd see something like this," Sheffield said. "Where do we go from here?"

"What the hell is that?" Burke pointed at a screen that showed a wideband optical analysis. Several shafts of ultraviolet light were rising from the city. "Lasers?"

"Yes," Gentry answered. "Don't worry, they're for communication. They encode information on the beams and aim them at the atmospheric barrier. Other cities have telescopes watching the spots of light and decoding the signals. It's how they send messages between cities. Keep the altitude above ten thousand meters. We don't want to spook anyone down there. Cross over this body of water to a village on the far shore. The royal family has a private residence there. We were supposed to meet them there, anyway, and they also have a hospital nearby. I'll show you where to land when we get there."

* * *

Akka Pamm was the latest of eight generations of physicians in his family. He'd seen just about every kind of injury imaginable, but never treated an earthman before for anything more serious than a runny nose. He watched in fascination as the giant flying machine gracefully descended and lightly came to rest on the south lawn of the hospital.

He knew the old prophecies, and he knew they were happening. He didn't actually get nervous until the door opened on the craft, and two huge men who had no necks came out. They looked like grim, violent thugs. Akka was relieved when the next aliens to come out seemed more normal, and he realized the first two were guards of some sort.

Doctor Pamm had his orderlies take the injured aliens into the hospital.

Emerson, the Earthman whom the Queen was so fond of, was with Doctor Pamm and acted as translator for the alien Doctor Moorpark. Emerson had come on the first starship from Earth, the Himilco. He had been the first to communicate with the crew of the Fledik.

The one with broken bones went to a specialist, Doctor Tahl, accompanied by three of Moorpark's medical assistants and one of the alien guards. The one called Hanson went straight to the burn trauma center with Pamm, Moorpark, an alien officer called Sheffield, and another guard.

Hanson was nearly dead, but after an hour of treatment his condition stabilized enough for them to consider what to do about the damage. Half of his skin was dead along with part of his nervous system: tricky, but treatable. The immediate problem was to make his body cooperate with the treatment. So much pain and damage made autonomous responses throughout his body malfunction and shut down. It was bad.

Emerson whispered to Doctor Pamm, "Hanson is Erosian."

Pamm carefully showed no reaction to the information that might help in treating the man's injuries, and he made no note of it in the hospital record.

CHAPTER 48

The ship's time on the Hanno was 0330 hours. The bridge was quiet. A few techs were keeping an eye on the systems. Ensign Hill was sipping tea, and chatting with Jack Trimble, the navigator, neither of whom had much to do as long as they maintained this geosynchronous orbit.

Commander Redbird stood at the Radglass viewport and gazed at Arcturus-4, a globe 43,000 kilometers away, filling as much view as a soccer ball held at arm's length. The thin, sparkling, red line of the terminator was creeping slowly from east to west. The flashing aurora was a constant reminder of the strangeness of this alien world, and the dark side of the planet was slowly shifting around to where Captain Poluka was right now.

Poluka was asleep down there. As long as he slept, he couldn't cause any more trouble, but he wouldn't sleep forever. After Sheffield reported that the captain was exhausted and sleeping, Redbird examined all the daily reports, and determined that Poluka had gone at least 36 hours without a break. This drug Doctor Payne was talking about could keep a man on his feet that long, at the expense of his judgment.

If Redbird followed regulations—as he intended to—he would speak to Commander Washington before authorizing an investigation. The end result would be no investigation. Washington would never let this become official, but talk to the captain himself and try to straighten him out unofficially, which might be for the best.

The other issue Redbird was wrestling with was how the native people were going to be affected by contact with Earth, and how all Poluka's talk about protocols was just hot air. The big ape went charging in and started shooting at the first place he found indigenous people.

A representative of Earth would need to meet the alien monarch. Redbird fervently prayed it would not be Poluka. Sheffield was a much better choice—or Aguire, if he recovered in time.

Two hours remained until the sun sets at Arvod. An hour after that, Commander Washington relieves Redbird of the watch and makes the decisions. Washington always favored a strong military approach, and would certainly feel that more soldiers should be at the captain's side.

Redbird crept over to the com in the S-Bay, and quietly ordered the pinnace ready to launch in two hours. He then poked around the personnel database to choose people whom he thought should be present at a meeting with the local government.

"We've got Commander Donno," someone said. Redbird looked up at the screen. Donno was in the shuttle but not at the pilot's station; he was in the passenger area. The four people with him were wearing strange clothing and Redbird had never seen them before.

"Hanno," the Commander said, "I'm pleased to report that the monarchy of Arcturus officially welcomes us to this star system."

* * *

Gentry was discretely directed to Doctor Pamm's office, where Elpastre and Lapastra were waiting. He could speak their language well enough to confirm what they already knew, and fill in some of the blanks they were not clear about.

"I am sorry, Gentry, about putting you in danger. I didn't realize that they might attack you," Elpastre said with genuine regret. "The ways of Earthmen are so different from ours. I'm terribly concerned that, despite our efforts, the Old Rulers will convince the people that we cannot allow further contact with Earth."

"Well, I don't see how they can prevent it, Elpastre. Besides, you have the prophecies."

There was no honorific address on Arcturus equivalent to the old Earth "Your Majesty" or "Royal Highness". The word

"Elpastre" was both a name and a title, and the only proper way to address the King of this planet.

"When the scientists learned that ours is a dying race," Elpastre told him, "the prophecies concerning visitors from Earth began to make sense, and it became clear, at least to some, what must be done. But the prophecy was, like prophecies tend to be, still unclear. It did not promise salvation, but merely a chance, a last hope, for salvation."

"It was not clear about many things," the Queen sighed. "What was clear to the Old Rulers is that Elpastre will have to become vulnerable, or let his people die. It will be their chance to finally regain their place as the new rulers, and take revenge on all who denied what they consider their birthright. They were the ruling families during the Epoch of the Flood, at the fabled beginning when mankind first appeared on Arcturus. For nearly five thousand Earth years, the Clan of the Old Rulers have neither forgotten nor repented of their claim to supremacy. They have been building a network of power over many generations for this purpose."

An aching sadness touched Gentry as he perceived the relentless ambition and bitterness of the Old Rulers—an evil passed down for hundreds of generations, waiting for this time.

"Elpastre, isn't it time to inform Clifford Poluka that another ship has come from Earth, and that his brother is here?"

Elpastre looked out the window, into the east, where nightfall was moments away, and he could see flickers of red aurora over the inland sea.

"Clifford Poluka is on his way across the sea by now. I sent a message to him when our daughter, Miyuree, met the Earthmen at the pyramid. The truth could not be hidden from the Old Rulers after that, anyway. They, too, will cross the sea."

Gentry understood the basic problem they faced, but it seemed, now that a starship was orbiting Arcturus, there was no way to stop more from coming.

"Gentry," Lapastra guessed his thought, "the Old Rulers would find a way to stop this starship from leaving. If necessary, they would even kill all the Earthmen. They want their own interpretation of the prophecy to be fulfilled."

The Queen smiled despite her gloomy words. She was an

enigma to Gentry: beautiful and wise, and yet childlike and detached from worldly cares. She was wearing a simple sky-blue dress that covered her arms, and reached to the floor, such as any woman might wear to the market, and no jewelry or other sign of high position. Yet, even someone who didn't know her would sense immediately she was not just any woman.

Her husband was a tall, reasonably good-looking man, but was otherwise ordinary. It was only when he spoke that one would suspect he had an inner greatness.

"Kill them?" Gentry asked. "Could they do that?"

"Possibly," Elpastre answered for her. "If they convince the nobles, and most of the people, they might be able to do enough harm to stop the ship from leaving."

"But you wouldn't allow it!"

"For 171 of our years—over two thousand Earth years—they have resented the rule of my family. Now, they have an opportunity to make me the last Elpastre. They want it." Elpastre frowned at the window facing the sea and shook his fist in the direction of the capital city. "They are planning it."

* * *

A dream faded into consciousness, and Aguire opened his eyes. He was in a cozy room with white walls, and nice wood trim around the door and window. The comfortable bed urged him to continue sleeping. Commander Sheffield was there, typing on a pocket computer.

Leaning on the wall, and looking out of the open door was an Army officer. When she turned her head and glanced back at him, he recognized Major Rivers.

She peered at him for a moment, and then said a word to Sheffield who looked up from his computer, and grinned when he locked eyes with Aguire.

"Commander, how good of you to join us. I'm told you'll be right as rain in a few days. Unfortunately, I can't give you a few days. We've got work to do, Mister Aguire."

His head was clear, but he felt unnaturally calm as they helped him get dressed and quickly brought him up to speed. His body was sore but it was hard to believe that, in the space of a few hours, he'd gotten several bones broken, and then unbroken.

They couldn't tell him exactly how he and Hanson got injured. By all rights, Bart Hanson should have been completely out of the line of fire, and Aguire should have been vaporized. Hanson would be staying in the hospital for a while, but Aguire should meet with the monarch of the planet.

Captain Poluka was unavailable at the moment.

They said Lynda's brother Gentry was here, and the pinnace was about to land, bringing Lynda and G.J. Stokes. Donno would be here in few minutes with his team and four crewmen from the Starship Himilco.

"Where's Poluka?" Aguire croaked with a voice that felt rusty.

"Ah…well…he's sleeping," Melanie Rivers said, and exchanged a meaningful glance with Sheffield.

"José," Sheffield said, "we've been talking. Commander Redbird, Doctor Moorpark, the Major here, and I have come to the conclusion that our Captain has…well…a problem."

Aguire listened carefully with a growing unease.

CHAPTER 49

The pinnace brought Lynda and G.J. to the planet surface, and easily held the 52 passengers that Commander Redbird put aboard her as well. Redbird sent a broad mix of skill sets. A few more barnacles came, too, chosen by Redbird for their expertise in things like history and diplomacy, rather than combat skills. All personnel were in formal dress uniforms, and brought the same for those already on the ground. There was also a group from the Med Center that Doctor Moorpark requested for a tour of the Arcturusian hospital.

Lynda hardly noticed. She held Papa's arm and silently resented the slowness of the landing. Night had fallen on their destination. As the pinnace made its gentle descent over the village, she could see streetlights below, tracing out cobblestone avenues. Some buildings were well lit, but this was definitely not a metropolis.

She'd waited ten years for this. She wondered what she would find, and if Gentry would be a stranger to her.

She could see the landing field now, a flat expanse of short grass where El Toro and a shuttle were already parked. There were two Army people on the grass with lights, and another man….

Papa groaned when her grip tightened like a vise on his arm. He looked a question at her, and then followed her shining eyes to the window.

"Gentry," he whispered. His son, Lynda's brother, was standing behind the soldiers, waiting for the pinnace door to open. He was wearing native clothing, and looked older, with experience and tales to tell, but they knew him.

The air was humid, and rich with the scent of grass and trees. Lynda rushed to hold him in her arms. He returned her embrace with a strength that would have hurt another woman. When she stepped back to look at him, he had tears in his eyes, and she found that she was crying, too. Papa's eyes were streaming as well. There was much to say, but for now they just held one another.

Another man, dressed in native clothes, approached and smiled, sharing their joy, and spoke softly in a strange language. Gentry glanced at him before saying to Lynda and Papa, "I want to tell you so much, but we need to go inside. We'll be meeting Elpastre."

Lynda looked at the stranger. He was an alien, but not like her. She wondered what sort of people these were, and if they knew of her people, the Erosians. She looked back at Gentry, and said, "You were right about us, Gentry. I know now."

Then, she remembered Bart, that he was here and terribly wounded.

"How is Bart?" Papa asked before she could speak.

"He'll be fine, but he'll be here for a while. You can see him tomorrow. Paul Poluka is here, too, but something is wrong with him. Doctor Moorpark has him in there." He pointed to the light-cruiser. "He won't let anyone near him."

Inside the hospital, there were more Arcturusians—doctors and nurses mostly—as well as some officials who were counselors to the royal family. They were all different: some tall, some short; light and dark complexions; all different, but remarkably human.

The strangeness that Lynda expected was not to be found. Even the clothing and the furniture would not seem out of place on Earth. Most, but not all, had brown eyes.

The building was much the same as hospitals on Earth, except that wherever corridors intersected, there was an atrium with live trees and a decorative fountain.

Commander Aguire was there in his dress-gray uniform. His eyes had slightly constricted pupils, but he was alert and organized. He called an impromptu meeting to explain that they would be walking through the village to the royal residence for a formal audience with the planetary head-of-state, and that no one was authorized to speak as representatives of Earth, except himself, Sheffield, and Donno.

Donno looked stoic and gorgeous in his dress-grays, with only a slightly tight-lipped expression to betray that this was an extraordinary occasion. Then, Lynda remembered that he had reported that his shuttle team met a member of the royal family. He'd landed near a pyramid in the desert, where a child princess had officially welcomed him to the planet. Lynda wanted to hear more about that, but it would have to wait.

A group of 28 from the Hanno was led by an officer of the Arcturusian Royal Guard through a village that reminded Lynda of some places she'd seen on Earth; the cobblestone streets wound around low hills and had shops and cafes all along the way. The sea breeze made it a pleasantly cool evening, and the softly glowing street lamps kept their feet from stumbling.

Curious but wary people came out to watch them pass. They didn't come too close, but otherwise seemed friendly. Some smiled and nodded a greeting when the people from Earth would look at them. Others just stared.

The royal residence was a three-story building with impressive columns and a well-lit façade carved from white stone. Eight spear-carrying guards in pale green uniforms were at the gate leading to a courtyard. They parted at the officer's command, letting the entire group pass and be ushered into a hall big enough for several hundred to gather comfortably.

The architecture was all columns, arches, and vaulted ceilings, with huge, ornate tapestries on the walls. Dozens of carved and polished wooden pedestals around the perimeter held spherical glass bottles, about 40 centimeters wide, filled with luminescent fluid to light the room. Their number must have been sent ahead because the correct number of cushioned chairs were set out, facing a low dais that had two similar, but more elegant chairs on it.

When they were seated, more guards—unarmed this time— stood on each side of the dais. A man and a woman came from a door behind the dais. The man was dressed in a blue long-coat with many buttons down the front. He tall and thin, fair complexioned, and a high forehead. The woman was slightly taller than Lynda, with wide-set dark eyes, an olive complexion, and wavy black hair that draped down to her shoulders, a beauty in a flowing, lavender dress. They took their places in the raised chairs. The two had crowns of braided gold wire, with hundreds of embedded diamonds all around. When she was a child, Bart used to tell Lynda stories about kings and queens, and these two somehow fit what she'd always imagined. They had kind faces, and seemed to be about 40 years old.

Another man joined them. This one was also thin and about 30 years old with curly brown hair, a big smile, and sparkling, excited eyes. He stood in front of the dais and addressed the group.

"Welcome to the planet Arcturus. My name is William Emerson. Ten years ago, I was a crewman aboard the Starship Himilco. I will be serving as the translator for this meeting. And now, I will introduce the reigning king and queen of this planet." Emerson's voice rose, almost to shouting, as he turned to the two behind him, gesturing in their direction. "Elpastre and Lapastra, may their reign be beneficial to all good people."

All eyes turned to the royal couple, who stood, smiled, and inclined their heads slightly in a sort of bow, and then took their seats again. The King, Elpastre, said something and Emerson translated.

"Elpastre greets the brave travelers from neighboring Earth on behalf of all the people of this world, and he is glad that you have come."

Aguire made similar diplomatic statements, and got the official niceties out of the way. Intellectually, Lynda knew it was a thrilling historic moment, but felt it was a distraction from the really important thing: that Gentry was sitting next to her. She kept looking at him, comparing his face to the memory of a very young and troubled man that she knew ten years ago. He seemed whole and complete now, as if he'd found the answers that he'd longed for.

* * *

It was the sort of thing that explorers dreamed of, and Aguire loved every moment of it, but at the same time, felt he was rushing headlong and out of control into the unknown. Something was coming; Gentry Stokes had dropped enough hints that the King had some urgent matter to discuss with them, but wouldn't just come right out and tell Aguire what it was.

The next hour was a history lesson. Emerson converted the Arcturusian years to Earth years and distances to kilometers, making it easier to follow. Aguire was lost in rapt attention to the translated words that Elpastre poured out for their edification:

"Nearly six thousand years ago, around 3000 B.C. on Earth, there was a terrible catastrophe on Arcturus. We believe the moon moved into a different orbit...or perhaps we did not have a moon until then. We do not know. We know almost nothing of those times, but we are certain it was the gravitational influence of the moon, as it circled the planet in almost a geosynchronous orbit, that caused the Epoch of the Flood.

"As our world turned, the moon, which was always over the equator in those days, would orbit almost exactly once each day, advancing only slightly, west to east. We never saw it because it was always on the side of the planet opposite of where people were. The oceans of our world were pulled to the side of Arcturus where the moon was overhead. The Flood moved slowly from west to east with the moon, and the entire ocean would circle the planet once each year (that would be about fourteen and a half Earth years).

"To survive, man and beast had to walk east continuously, carrying everything around the world ahead of the water. At the equator, the sea advanced about eleven kilometers each day, forcing all living thing to do likewise.

"The constant migration took an immediate toll on the education of the young ones. All of our history and tradition was lost. Whatever our culture was like before The Flood was forgotten in a single generation.

"The advancing coast on the west and the receding coast on the east were regions of perpetual rain storms. There was no barrier in our atmosphere in those days, and we could see the stars at night, but we never saw the moon or guessed its existence until the Epoch of the Flood ended, a thousand years later.

"Any skills that were not essential for survival were replaced by new skills. Fishing, for example, was no longer done on the sea, nor in rivers, nor lakes. We ventured into the rainy areas near the receding eastern coast, and picked up fish that were stranded when the sea flowed out from under them. We learned to make fire, and smoke fish, in pouring rain, but forgot everything about

308

boats. The sea had become too dangerous and frightening for us because it was always coming from the west, and anyone who could not stay ahead of it would perish.

"A man watching the eastern coast move away from him, could make a home on that spot, and stay for seven Earth years before the advancing Flood came from the west.

"A system of migration developed, with planters following the east coast, ahead of the others, to start the farms which were maintained for over six years. In that last year, maintenance dropped off as people moved east abandoning the farm before The Flood came.

"Some people worked their entire lives on farms as they moved ever eastward. Others drove cattle, or hauled harvested crops, or carried the seeds east to the planters for new farms. Fruit trees were potted and moved with the people, and many other arrangements were made to preserve all that we could from The Flood. A few things could be planted on mountains far to the north and south where The Flood did not reach, but these places had other dangers to prevent us from making a permanent home there.

"A great caravan formed as a mobile headquarters for our rulers, and to take care of potted trees that would take too long to grow in the ground.

"We understood after about 20 Earth years (just over one local year) that we had circled the planet, and would continue to do so as long as the flood continued. Our tradition from those times tells of the Eternal Creator of the Universe being angry, and using this hardship to cleanse the people of wickedness.

"It did, in fact, change us. We believe that, before the Epoch of the Flood, we were much the same as the people of Earth. Our essential character was reshaped in the 50 or 60 generations who had to work together, trusting that those ahead would plant farms in the east, and those behind would harvest and bring the crops from the west.

"Little more is known of the earliest times. It is believed that this constant migration to the east lasted for a thousand Earth years. It shaped our culture, and affects us even today.

"Our rulers, traveling in the great caravan, came to think of their survival and comfort as the purpose of all other people.

They were suspicious of each other and did not pay much attention to a religious culture that developed among the common people. There were holy men that walked with the poorest and slowest, with the sick and elderly who could barely stay ahead of advancing flood. They taught compassion, mercy and generosity. When they prophesized about the end of The Flood, the rulers ignored them, but the common people did not. Many fell back to western edge of the land to help the slowest, and when the holy men said it was time to prepare for a new age, the common people prepared for a sudden change. The rulers did not.

"Our moon changed its orbit that day, and the sea stopped circling our world. The eastern coast, which had been moving away, ahead of our migration for a thousand years, reversed its course for a time, flooding low places that non-believers had assumed would be safe.

"Many of the rulers died, but not all. Those rulers who survived were devastated; their caravan was destroyed and their fortunes were lost. By the time they found their way westward to where the common people were flocking to the holy men, they were no longer needed or wanted as rulers.

"The place where people gathered after the Epoch of the Flood was not far from this village where we are now. There were perhaps 200 million people here, though most of the planet remained unpopulated for a very long time.

"The people were content with the rule of the priests for some years, but eventually wanted a king. The priests advised against it, but gave in to the will of the people. A king was chosen, and since then, the form of the government, and the family that rules, has changed a few times, but never did the Clan of the Old Rulers regain the supremacy they enjoyed during the Epoch of the Flood.

"My family became the royal family just over two thousand Earth years ago, in what was about 300 A.D. on Earth. Since then, the King has been called Elpastre, which is both a name and a title, and the Queen has been called Lapastra."

The King paused in his speech when the Queen lightly touched his arm, and spoke softly to him. She had a resonant voice, very feminine and confident.

Elpastre smiled, and nodded to Emerson who translated: "Lapastra suggests that we take a short break from the history of Arcturus, and enjoy some refreshment. There is a banquet prepared in the garden outside. If you will follow me, I will show you the way. Also, we are expecting Clifford Poluka to arrive at any moment."

The garden covered acres of groomed land with carefully placed trees and flower beds, stone statues of people and animals. A fountain in the center was made of huge natural crystals that surrounded the water, and towered up from the center of the water like a jagged monolith. Water gushed from the top of a crystal spire, and all of it was somehow lit from below the ground. The effect was a liquid rainbow, dancing in the midst of the garden.

"What d'ya think?" Donno asked when he and Aguire got out of earshot from the others.

"It's fascinating, but I don't know quite where this is leading. How's this compare to what the Protocol advises?"

"Oh, we're way beyond the Protocol. Most of it deals with how to get up to the point we're at now. As soon as we get recognized as friendly visitors, we're supposed to turn it all over to the State Department. If that's not an option, we're supposed to keep it short, promise nothing except that diplomats will be sent at a later date, and get the hell out as soon as possible."

Chief Braun wandered over and heard the last remark.

"Keep in mind," he said, "that the Protocol was written with the assumption that aliens would be…well…alien. These people are human as far as I can tell."

"Could that be it?" Aguire wondered. "Could they be originally from Earth? I mean, they don't know where they came from before that Epoch of the Flood, and we don't know that much about what was happening on Earth five thousand years ago. Maybe someone had some space travel capability back then."

"Interesting thought," Donno conceded, though he seemed far from convinced. "We should check our own history records when we get back to the Hanno."

"Well," Braun pointed out. "They haven't finished the story yet. Maybe they know the answer already."

Donno made a small look-over-there gesture, and Aguire

turned to see Maria Rodriguez and a man about 50 years old. They both had huge smiles, and were quietly chatting together.

"Her uncle?" Aguire asked.

"Yeah, Hank Rodriguez. He came back from the desert with me in the shuttle."

"You haven't told me about this princess you met."

Donno became pensive as he recalled the occasion that he would forever remember as one the best moments in his life.

"We'd spotted a pyramid in the desert, and there were people there. It seemed like a whole temporary village of tents and strange vehicles, like cars. Poluka told us to not make contact, but then we got a radio signal from Ivan Tershensky. He was in another vehicle about five klicks from the pyramid. I couldn't get another message through to Poluka, so I made the decision to land and meet Tershensky. After all, he's an Earthman, and a member of the Exploration Corps. I figured Poluka's instructions didn't apply.

"There were three vehicles on the road—big, steam-powered cars—with Tershensky and two other Earthmen—Gus Barret and Hank Rodriguez. There were also some locals; a man called Eeja Burr who is a royal chronicler, sent as an observer; and about a dozen guards that look as tough as any barnie. They were there to protect the princess.

"Her name is Miyuree. She's a lovely child, about nine or ten years old, I guess. Ivan Tershensky speaks the local language, and acted as translator.

"They'd gotten some kind of prediction that Earthmen would land at the pyramid, and Princess Miyuree was sent to represent the monarchy, and give us an official greeting.

"She's about yea tall." Donno smiled at the memory, and held his hand out at about waist level. "So, she stood inside the side door of one of their vehicles, so she'd be up off the ground. She didn't seem the slightest bit afraid of us, and was very happy to meet us."

"What did she say?" Aguire asked. His friend's eyes shined as he relived the moment. Aguire knew he wasn't easily impressed by rank or position. This princess had been something special.

"She wore a purple velvet gown," Donno said, "and had a crown of woven silver wire with thousands of tiny diamonds. She looked like a candle shining in the desert. She had a prepared statement, which Tershensky translated. I can't remember the whole thing, but we got it all on an event recorder. I can't remember now if she spoke, or sang the statement. Her voice was like that.

"It was a formal greeting from the monarchy, full of welcoming words. I did my best to respond on behalf of Earth, and tried to give the impression that we're friendly people who don't mean any harm. It's funny but, as I spoke, I got the feeling the princess knew what I was saying, even before Tershensky translated it into her language."

"Maybe she did," Aguire told him. "We've learned that some of the women here are clairvoyant. Do you think we'll get to meet this Princess Miyuree?"

"Mm...not for a while. After speaking with her for a few minutes, she pointed out that hundreds of people were rushing down the road from the pyramid to see us. She had a discussion with her guards and Tershensky, and they thought it was best if we go before the mob arrived. Tershensky got her permission to leave her, and came with us as our navigator so we could find this village. We brought all the Earthmen, and the chronicler, Eeja Burr with us. I offered to give the princess a ride, but when Tershensky translated the offer, the head bodyguard almost had a stroke and insisted there was no way she was getting into the shuttle."

Braun nudged Aguire, and said, "My god, It's Clifford."

An older version of their skipper was walking toward them, slightly taller and trimmer, with a care-worn face and completely gray hair.

CHAPTER 50

Commander Washington paced from the I-Bay to the S-Bay and back again, his boots slapping the deck with angry thumps.

The day-shift bridge crew had missed the shouting when he'd relieved Redbird, but by now they'd all heard what transpired during the night shift, with Redbird sending a pinnace full of people down to the surface, and that the captain was mysteriously unavailable.

Washington couldn't do anything until getting more information from the planet, and they weren't telling him anything. There was a limit though. If he didn't hear directly from the captain in the next six hours, he'd take a security team down there to find out why. He glanced at the clock again—1159 hours—seven hours since he'd found out that asshole Redbird sent the pinnace down without any Corps security people. He'd sent more Army personnel instead, and not ones Washington would've chosen.

Then there was this drug thing. He would've thought Redbird was making up the whole damn thing, except that it was too serious. This idea to search the captain's quarters was way out of line. He'd talk to Poluka about this diet pill thing, but if he mentions Doctor Payne's request, the skipper would probably have her thrown out of the Corps, and maybe he should.

For the moment, the most Washington could do was have four shuttles standing by with 32 heavily armed SP's, and wait.

* * *

The last Poluka remembered was landing to pick up a wounded man at about…what was it…maybe 0200 hours?

He heaved himself out of the cot, and wobbled to the

lavatory. When he came out there was a medical tech waiting with a big cup of water and some vitamins. Poluka didn't even ask—he took the pills and downed the water.

"Doctor Moorpark is on the way, Captain, with Commanders Aguire and Sheffield."

"Aguire? Aguire was wounded. Is he alright?"

The tech nodded but offered no further comment.

Half an hour later, he'd been briefed by Aguire on the meeting with the local head-of-state, and got a rough overview of what was happening. The news that Hanson was alive and recovering came as a soothing balm to his ragged conscience, but hearing how the first official diplomatic contact with the alien government happened without him was troubling; it would look damn peculiar in the history books. He was still hazy about how all these things got decided while he was unconscious, but he stopped wondering about it when Aguire brought up the subject of pills that he'd been taking. Doctor Moorpark produced his pill box, which they'd taken from his pocket while he was sleeping.

"People call these pills zippies," the doctor said. "They're made by TerraPharm for treating side-effects from other drugs. A lot of people have been using this drug for other reasons, but most doctors believe there isn't really any good use for it. What are you using it for, Captain?"

Poluka looked at their stony faces. He felt cornered, but not helpless. He was still the captain.

"I don't have to answer to you. I am—"

"Captain," Aguire interrupted, "this mission's been full of surprises, and with so many casualties there's bound to be a lot of scrutiny about how decisions got made. You're among friends right now. It would be better if we knew everything, and worked this out before anyone else gets involved."

There was a short struggle inside his brain as Aguire's words sank in. It was outrageous that his subordinates would demand an explanation of him, but as his head cleared a bit, all of his recent screw-ups took on an ugly aspect when tied to the use of a drug. The faces he first saw as stony, now seemed more concerned rather than condemning, and the value of keeping this quiet was obvious.

"I was trying to lose weight," he admitted. "It worked, too. I lost something like 20 kilos in a couple of months."

"When did you start taking it?" the doctor asked.

"When I got to New Wichita, in January."

"Well, as of right now, you're off it. You may experience some anxiety for a while, but it will pass. I want you to report to Med Center at the earliest opportunity for a physical."

"Okay, but I'm fine. The pills weren't affecting my decisions—at least, not until the last few days, but that was mostly because I hadn't slept enough."

The doctor knew he was lying to himself, and so did Aguire, but a starship captain couldn't admit more, not to his own subordinates, and they all knew it.

"Well, then." Sheffield looked at Aguire. "If the captain has had enough rest, perhaps we should get him back to work."

"Right." Aguire's face relaxed somewhat, and Poluka felt that a crisis had just passed. "There's an urgent request from Commander Washington for you to contact him. He's been understandably concerned that he hasn't heard from you in nearly ten hours. Also, there's someone waiting outside to see you, Captain. It's your brother."

Commander Aguire left him. Like all good first officers, he juggled tasks to make everything work. He'd had to report the safety and status of the ship's personnel to the skipper as soon as Poluka woke up, then resolve the diet pill issue to Doctor Moorpark's satisfaction.

The next thing would have been to tell his captain about how the meeting with Elpastre ended, but he didn't. Aguire decided to leave that for Cliff Poluka to explain and, of course, that meant the captain had first to be informed that they'd found his brother. He couldn't very well jump his skipper straight from a long awaited reunion with the brother, right into an interstellar crisis without giving him a few minutes.

He'd asked Clifford to hold off talking to the skipper about it until morning, when they could do it all together.

In juggling all the immediate concerns, he only let one slip away: he forgot to make sure Poluka called Washington after meeting his brother, and he'd later kick himself for that.

* * *

It was midnight on this side of the planet, cool and damp, but the cruiser's floodlights kept the area illuminated.

Paul marched up to Clifford and gripped his big brother's shoulders. He looked at his face, hardly daring to believe his own eyes. Clifford smiled with misty eyes, and pulled Paul close for a big hug. Paul hugged him back, and then pulled away to look at his face again.

It was really Cliff, but he seemed much older than his ten-year absence would account for. His hair was longer, and completely gray. Fine wrinkles that deepened when he smiled were around his eyes, and a furrowed crease lay across his brow. His face was more tanned than Paul remembered.

"Paul." His brother grinned. "I didn't know it would be you coming here. I'm so glad to see you. They tell me you exhausted yourself with a rescue operation."

"Yeah, it's been like that. Damn, Cliff, I can't believe it's you!"

They started with Paul catching Cliff up concerning their father and sister on the farm in California, then talked about the Jupiter War which happened after Cliff had disappeared, and how Paul had transferred to the Exploration Corps afterwards.

Finally, Cliff told about arriving at Arcturus a decade ago, and the crash landing near the capitol.

"The captain of the Fledik managed to warn us of the hazards of the atmospheric barrier by drawing diagrams of the planet."

"So, if you knew about the barrier," Paul asked, "what happened with your landing?"

"It was the design of the Himilco." Cliff grimaced. "We didn't fully test everything before the mission, and some systems just didn't perform well. We'd already had some damage from the Zone, but the killer was that we couldn't see our landing site from orbit. We wanted to come down close to the capitol city, but we had no way of knowing when to drop through the barrier to be right over it. As it happened, we came down on the wrong side of the planet and had to fly a long way through the atmosphere. The Himilco wasn't designed for that.

"It's my fault. I controlled the design of the Himilco. I took 33 people into unexplored space with a ship that should have been a short-haul passenger ship."

"Don't blame yourself." Paul said. "Your crewmen were all spacemen. They could evaluate the risks even better than you could, and they still chose to do it."

A secret corner of Paul's heart was glad to hear the admission of imperfection and got some satisfaction from hearing his brother confess to being merely human.

"I understand you had a rough trip yourself, back in the Zone. Commander Aguire told me about it."

"Uh, yes." Paul silently cursed Aguire, but was relieved that he didn't have to tell the tale himself. "We lost a good many. We left some probes behind to study the Zone while we continued on to Arcturus."

"You've got a lot of injured up there."

"Yes."

"Well, you have an opportunity to help them here. The Arcturusian doctors are fantastic. Their medical knowledge is far beyond ours. I suggest you let your doctors take Doctor Pamm to the Hanno to see what can be done."

"Doctor Pamm?"

"He's the senior physician at this hospital. He's having your Mister Hanson grow new nerve endings right now, along with new skin. He should be as good as new in a few days. They repaired three broken bones for Commander Aguire, completely healing him in a few hours. These people could do a lot for Earth medicine. They could do a lot for your crewmen right now."

Paul nodded warily. He wanted—desperately wanted—to do something for the people in Med Center, but he felt like his choices were being made for him. Cliff was watching his reaction until finally he said, "I'll authorize a study."

"I guess Aguire told you about the meeting with Elpastre." Cliff changed the subject.

"The head-of-state? Yes, I… regret not being able to attend. I'm hoping to meet with him later, perhaps tomorrow."

"Well, let me give you a little more information, something I don't think your Mister Aguire quite understands yet."

They had been strolling about the lawn beside the hospital, and had come to a place with a park bench where one could look out over the small town, and to the inland sea beyond. They sat in almost complete darkness while Cliff told Paul about the political problems facing the monarchy.

"There is a group numbering in the tens of thousands called the Clan of the Old Rulers. Most are harmless. They're a fixture in the culture, dating back to the earliest times, and their aristocrats are constantly at odds with the King.

"Because the people spent 60 or 70 generations in the Epoch of the Flood, their culture was forced to become one of peaceful cooperation. Also, they've always been one people with one language and one leader. They never had a culture of war as Earth did. This gave them the stability needed for unbroken progress but, without the adversity that comes from war and competition, their early progress was very slow. They lived as hunter-gatherers for another thousand years after The Flood, with only simple farms to make life easier. To this day, many of the tools they use are made from stone, as Earth men used in the most ancient times.

"The stability of the civilization made conditions ideal for keeping the King in power. For thousands of years there's been just a few times when the form of government or the monarchy significantly changed. Never before did the Old Rulers have a real chance of toppling the government and taking over, but now they do. With the arrival of Earthmen, everything becomes uncertain.

"Paul, I came across the sea yesterday to get here from Desin-Arcturus, the capitol city." Cliff pointed at the glimmering water in the distance. "Close behind me were boats carrying agents of the Old Rulers. They will want to talk to you, to convince you not to listen to Elpastre. These Old Rulers are vicious people, Paul. Don't trust them."

"Wouldn't the King prevent them from talking to me?" Paul asked. "I mean, if aliens came to Earth to open a diplomatic dialog, the Federation wouldn't let just anybody talk to them."

"This is a different culture…a different kind of politics." Cliff smiled as if remembering something. "If Elpastre denied anyone access to you, it would be like saying they're a credible power that must be defended against. It would weaken his position considerably."

"And what is his position…concerning us? How is it different from the Old Ruler's position?"

"The monarchy of Arcturus wants to have relations with

Earth that would be mutually beneficial. The Old Rulers don't want any relations with Earth. They've spent the last ten years trying to convince everyone here that the people and government of Earth are too violent and devious to coexist with Arcturus. Basically, they're saying that it will be the end of Arcturus if people from Earth start showing up here."

Paul gritted his teeth, "They may be right, Cliff. You know how bad the Fed was getting when you were there. Well, the New Federation is a lot worse. They're doing forced relocations of thousands of people. They confine some people to reeducation camps, forcing them to accept a new way of thinking. A lot of people get arrested and then just disappear."

Cliff sighed. "Some of your people told me about it."

"I remember you predicted the coup. You also predicted that a military leader would rise to the occasion, and put a stop to it. I think that time is now, but I have to go back and be a part of it. That's partly what this mission is all about. G.J. and I have a plan. We had to get control of the Hanno to do it, and now we've got it. We can unite the colonies against the New Fed, but I'm thinking maybe there's a better use for the Hanno. She could be a formidable military force. If I could rally support, I could possibly topple the New Federation."

He sensed Cliff turn towards him in the cold glow of the alien moon. His brother didn't say anything for a moment, and Paul wondered if he would encourage him to take the lead in fighting the New Fed, or say he should support someone like General Hebert.

"I'm out of touch with all of it, Paul. I can't advise you."

"You won't have much time to catch up on the trip back to Earth. With this new ship, we can be there almost instantly."

"Paul, I wasn't planning on leaving Arcturus. This is my home now."

"What? You can't be serious." Paul spun to his left and squinted at Cliff's profile. "Have you gone completely fucking crazy?"

He heard Cliff chuckle. "I know it must seem crazy, Paul, but I feel like this is where I'm supposed to be."

"What about Dad? He's waiting to hear if you're still alive. He's waiting for me to bring you home, for Christ's sake. What about our sister, Abby? Cliff, you're coming back with me!"

"Mm, maybe I should go back for a while, but I'd have to return to Arcturus soon. I've got family here, too."

"What family?" Paul demanded.

"I've got a wife and a son here, Paul. They're in my house, in Desin, the capitol city. Her name is Etti. The boy's name is Paul."

Paul sat in the darkness, stunned into silence. His brother had an alien wife…and a son named Paul! His head reeled at the thought. He now had a half-alien nephew.

"You named him after me?"

"Yes. He's about four years—Earth years—old, and a beautiful child."

Paul didn't know what to say. A thousand thoughts spun out of control. A few days ago he'd hoped to discover that Cliff was dead and gone. Now, he couldn't imagine leaving him behind. He never imagined finding his brother with a wife and child—much less an alien wife and child.

The dim outline of the moon glowed through the hazy atmosphere, almost straight ahead and above them. It had changed position since they sat down.

"I'm out of sync," Paul said at last. "It's the middle of the night and I just woke up. I guess I should meet this family of yours. What should we do? Could I meet the…Elpastre, tomorrow, and then go across the sea to meet your wife and son?"

"I think so. Commander Aguire wants to have a meeting tomorrow, first thing. After that, I suspect the agents of the Old Rulers are going to try meeting with you before you can speak to Elpastre, but we could probably arrange an audience with the royal couple sometime tomorrow, then go to Desin-Arcturus."

"The capital city?"

"Uh-huh. The full name of the capital is Desin-Arcturus. It means the Heart of Arcturus."

"Their name for this planet is Arcturus?"

"Right. That's one reason we think they originally came from Earth. We've called this star Arcturus since the beginning of history. If they came from Earth, then they might bring the name with them. Their oldest myths speak of coming from another world through a magic tunnel. No one here even remembers that story, but it's in some of their oldest books. Gentry and Emerson went through their libraries looking for more information. These people kept good records of all sorts of things since the Flood ended, five thousand years ago." Cliff stood up and stretched. "Maybe you should try to sleep a little more. I know I could use some rest, too. We can continue in the morning. You've given me a lot to think about."

Chapter 51

"Thank you for your input, Commander Sirenko, but this is my call," Commander Washington repeated when she just wouldn't shut up. "Captain Poluka and Commander Aguire have been missing, as far as I am concerned, for the last sixteen hours. I'm going down there to see for myself what the hell is going on."

Viktoriya Sirenko pursed her lips, her normally sad-eyed expression tinged with obvious impatience. "Even though Commander Sheffield said that everything is under control, and he specifically said that no one should go down without clearance from groundside?"

Washington turned away to look at the planet out the window in his office. Sirenko already delayed him until the terminator slid across the village where El Toro had landed. With the sun up on that part of the planet, he'd have to drop in far to the west, and fly east in the atmosphere to the sun-lit side of the planet.

"Try to understand my position, Commander. The last time we heard from the Captain was just before they had a firefight. At that time, we had reason to believe that Aguire and his team were prisoners. We got no assurances that the aliens are friendly until after that action. Suppose they are hostile and Sheffield is being forced to say whatever they want. He sure asked for a hell of a lot of doctors all of a sudden, which I find disturbing, and all communication has been text-only bursts from Sheffield. There was nothing about the Captain's status except that he was unavailable, which is simply not good enough. I'm taking a security team down, and I have to go right now."

Viktoriya marched into the bridge when Washington left for the shuttle docks where 32 SP guards were waiting.

Commander Martensen had the watch, and was nervously drumming his fingers on the command desk when she entered.

"I'm trying El Toro again," he said before she could ask.

They waited a moment while Communications punched through a text burst on 625MHz, the frequency that seemed to work best with this atmosphere. This time they got an answer. It was Ensign O'Riley for a change.

"Let me send something," Viktoriya said.

Martensen slid out of the command chair. She sat down and typed a question for O'Riley.

HANNO: Should we send Lieutenant Swanson down?

The reply came back immediately.

EL TORO: I wish you could. Andre is dead. Don't worry. Nobody has a gun to my head. Poluka is in a meeting with the senior officers and the doctors. They will go see political opposition, then will see the King this morning. BTW, we have met twelve survivors from the Himilco including Cliff Poluka. They say most are still alive but not here right now. Everything is okay. Hanson is doing well and should be out of the hospital in a couple of days. Aguire is completely healed. The doctors here are amazing.

Before they could finish reading O'Riley's reply, a voice from the S-Bay announced that Commander Washington's four shuttles had just launched.

"Communications," Martensen barked. "Open a link to Washington."

Viktoriya nodded silently in agreement as she typed in another message.

HANNO: Be advised, Washington is on the way with four shuttles full of SP's. Poluka didn't com and we got nervous.

EL TORO: Could be bad. There is political situation here. Not all locals happy to see us. Armed troops will make us look bad. Will try alert skipper before he leaves.

Commander Martensen forwarded the text from O'Riley to Commander Washington.

Chapter 52

Popa Utirka called himself a lawyer. After all, that was his education and, for tax purposes, his livelihood, but he was really so much more than a lawyer. He was the confidant and councilor to the Grand Matriarch of the Old Rulers, Aylata Naray herself.

Utirka had a full staff of flunkies to take care of the day-to-day mischief Aylata insisted on inflicting upon the royal family, but today Utirka was handling the mischief himself because this was the turning point in history. Even someone as high and mighty as Popa Utirka would not be safe if the old bitch felt he screwed up somehow. Besides, if it actually worked, the rewards would be beyond price.

Popa Utirka's lip curled into bitter amusement thinking of the absurd prediction that the King of Earth would land at the pyramid. That was just another screw-up of Aylata's whining cousin, the senior psychic Mata Buray. The Himilco Earthmen had been insisting since the prediction was made that Earth did not have a king. All the psychics agreed the Earthmen were telling the truth, but the old hag whom Utirka served thought that things may have changed on Earth since the Himilco came to Arcturus.

He just wanted to spit when he thought of how much Aylata relied on her imbecile cousin for information. He had more faith in paid informants.

"They could have a king by now," Aylata had insisted. "After all, a monarchy is the only natural form of rule. In time, all great worlds must end up with a king—or a queen."

"So true, Grand Matriarch," Utirka had responded soothingly, switching on his false smile for Aylata and Mata, who both posed like patiently suffering victims of cruel fate, because they had been denied their rightful place as Arcturusian royalty.

Like all Arcturusians, the cultural memory of The Flood was

in Utirka's bones and he was afraid of the sea, yet he came by boat anyway. He crossed the Vodita by night, just hours behind Clifford Poluka, and here, in the village of Arvod, he found that the reports were true: Poluka's brother had arrived from Earth.

Without delay he found a meeting hall on the road between the hospital and the royal residence, and rented it from one of the locals. The owner unreasonably inflated the price when he guessed the magnitude of Popa Utirka's need, but Utirka paid and waited for morning.

He squinted out of the doorway at the procession of Earthmen coming down the street. Teki Koray, the second-ranking psychic on the planet, watched from the window. Teki would be invaluable. The administrators who ranked psychics judged Teki as second only because she wasn't the Matriarch's cousin. That old fool Mata, being the best, was sent to the pyramid and would take days to get back. That was much too long. If this starship captain could be persuaded to keep his people away from Arcturus, it would have to be now, before the royal couple can get him in their pocket.

It was a manageable group, alien though they were. Utirka would focus on Paul Poluka, just as Teki would. She had an elaborate set of signals and gestures to indicate covertly what the Earthman was thinking and feeling. Teki was dressed like a respectable official in a traditional long skirt and high-collared blouse, looking like the mistress of an estate or a businesswoman.

A wicked smile flashed across Utirka's pudgy face at the thought of stripping away Elpastre's rule, and of the nobles bowing down to a new ruler who would, in fact, be an Old Ruler!

Utirka could see the Poluka brothers, the younger one recognizable from his resemblance to Clifford Poluka, who was a familiar face in the capital. They had as much information about Clifford Poluka's brother as could be gleaned from ten years of snooping. The younger one was a warrior and, if the information could be trusted, was not quite as smart as his brother.

This military background was a strange thing to the minds of the average citizen, but Utirka thought he understood it. Ancient stories, passed down among the Old Rulers, about armies and wars told how they had once ruled by the sword, too, before The Flood. In a way, it was a natural extension of politics.

"Welcome, visitors from Earth," Popa Utirka called out as he threw the door open wide, and stepped out to meet the group. His translator (another strange idea on a planet where everyone speaks the same language) repeated his words in the visitors' language. A handful of boys from the guilds were recruited to learn Earth-speech when they began planning for this day. Most had been sent to the pyramid with the best psychics, so this boy—whose name Utirka didn't know or want to know—was the only one available when they suddenly had to rush across the sea.

He saw Clifford Poluka's eyes narrow in distrust. The younger Poluka seemed startled at the welcoming shout and, frankly, had a completely idiotic expression. Utirka suppressed the urge to laugh, and his confidence soared with the hope that Paul Poluka would turn out to be a fool.

Three others wore Exploration Corps uniforms, and three wore some other uniform. One of the others was a woman, which Utirka found confusing. These were soldiers, he understood, but he didn't know that a woman could be a soldier. Perhaps she was just a clerk in their army. Yes, that must be it. She would no doubt be taking notes.

* * *

After saying goodnight to Cliff last night, Paul Poluka sat in the dark thinking about how his brother had married an alien—and had a child with her. He tried to think of other things, like the possibility of getting medical help for his injured crewmen from the alien doctors, or how to deal with announcing their discoveries back on Earth. But his thoughts always returned to his brother's new alien family. He would have to meet them, of course, but how would he feel about them? How would their dad feel about having an alien grandson? It made him queasy. Some people thought he was prudish, he knew, but this was a lot to accept. Then, this morning, they sprang the big news on him.

Not only have men from the Himilco been making babies on Arcturus, but the king of this bloody planet wants a lot more Earthmen to do the same! Their race was dying. It was some sort of genetic-drift scenario like what occurred on Earth in many places after the Great Disaster. These aliens called it genetic fatigue.

Their population was decreasing rapidly. Conception was becoming rare, and the pregnancies that occurred usually ended in stillborn babies or birth defects. The answer? Get fresh genetic material—from Earth.

The whole idea was so...so...well, shocking, that he almost missed the caveat that the plan mustn't offend the sensibilities of the alien population.

What about Paul Poluka's sensibilities? Cliff laid it all out as if describing a recipe for Christmas turkey. Aguire he could understand; the man never had a decent family life. But his other officers just kept nodding their heads as if the whole idea was perfectly fine. Even Leroy Donno—a good, decent Southern boy—acted like it was some humanitarian act to bring hordes of men from Earth to copulate with alien women.

Poluka staggered along with the others to another meeting, still struggling to comprehend whether he was the only one who had a problem with this notion. Suddenly, someone shouted at them, and a swift translation followed, given by a boy who looked like he was maybe ten years old.

"Welcome, visitors from Earth."

The one who had spoken the alien language was a corpulent man with a repulsive face, overly large lips, and a bulbous nose. Through the young interpreter, he introduced himself as Popa Utirka, a representative of the Old Rulers. Poluka vaguely remembered that this meeting was on today's schedule. He dearly missed his pills and considered asking Doctor Moorpark to let him have a few, just to get through today.

They filed into a meeting hall. There was a round table surrounded by chairs, and a small group of aliens: five men and a woman.

Introductions flew by with Paul hardly noticing. He'd been warned that these were the bad guys, but they seemed so normal, so professional. It was like so many other meetings he'd attended in his years of service. He found himself sitting opposite the one called Utirka, an unblinking man with small, pebbly eyes, who spoke slowly and deliberately with a soothing baritone about the subtle differences between their worlds. The boy standing at his shoulder was so unobtrusive; he seemed to fade into invisibility as the translation poured out.

"Captain Poluka, we are honored by your kind attention to our concerns. No doubt you heard about the history of our world, but perhaps some of the finer details need consideration before you speak with our beloved Elpastre.

"Though some may describe us as being opposed to our leader that does not mean we are his enemies, or that we do not respect his sovereign rule.

"Quite the contrary, the Old Rulers are but one of many checks and balances of a complex culture. We have peacefully maintained our part in this civilization for thousands of years, and hope to continue for thousands more.

"However, contact with Earth now brings a danger that our civilization has never faced before. You see, we are different from your people. We have grown into a culture rich with ancient traditions and values after many thousands of years without war or the need for armies. We have always been one nation with one language and, except for some minor variations that give us no trouble, one religion.

"The Epoch of the Flood, which you have heard about, lasted for a thousand Earth years. During that time, we were forced to live in cooperation and harmony. After many generations, it became who we are.

"Your world has a very different history. Oh, yes, we know something of your world. Our psychics have had visions of your people, and have seen some of your history. Also, in ages past, we were visited by another race who traveled among the stars. They brought us news of Earth, and told us about your many nations, and your wars."

At this, Cliff sat up straighter and asked, "Are you referring to the Erosians?"

Utirka's eyes flicked to Cliff for a moment, and then returned to Captain Poluka.

"Your brother has heard of that ancient race. They do not come here, anymore. Perhaps they no longer exist. They, too, were a warrior people, Captain Poluka." Utirka leaned forward, fixing Paul with his stony eyes. "You are aware of Elpastre's thoughts concerning…interbreeding, yes?"

Poluka's head reeled at the news that there was another space-faring race, a warrior race, out here somewhere. His own memories of war came back in a jumble of images, and his own acceptance of a military lifestyle made him feel that this alien was casting judgment upon him. In a flash of insight, he understood that the asteroid field that killed so many of his people must be the handiwork of this other race. His imagination flared with how his own government would use such power, and how many innocents would die. He sensed Aguire on his right and Cliff on his left, each looking at him, waiting for him to respond. Their scrutiny was a vise tightening on him. Sweat was beading on his scalp and he wanted this meeting to be over.

"I've been told a little about what your king has in mind. I expect to learn the details when I meet with him."

The young boy behind Utirka swiftly translated Poluka's response into the alien tongue. The alien man glanced around at his associates before continuing. "Elpastre, our King, has been listening to a small minority who believe there is only one option available to our people. I assure you, many in our scientific community believe that our situation is not so desperate. In fact, there is a research center near the capitol city doing work that has great potential for completely solving this so-called genetic fatigue that is currently preventing our population from increasing."

"Popa Utirka," Cliff interrupted, "the population is decreasing. Many families have sick children due to genetic fatigue, and many young couples cannot conceive a child at all."

Utirka didn't take his eyes off of Poluka, or acknowledge that Cliff had spoken. "There is sickness in our world, just as there is in your world. Not all of it is due to genetics. Our leader, Elpastre, has been listening to council that would lay all of our world's difficulties on genetics. We have tried to persuade him to listen to other opinions, but…he is…narrow in his view. Some speculate that he is not fully versed in the intricacies of this branch of science and so is…mistaken."

Poluka hoped it was true. He truly didn't want to deal with this. It didn't escape his attention that Utirka was hesitant to criticize his king, or that the other aliens visibly tensed as he came close to doing so. Perhaps the "checks and balances" that Utirka mentioned weren't enough to keep the King from making an unwise policy.

Captain Poluka responded carefully. "Mister…Utirka, I understand that your world's medical science is quite advanced. We also have doctors." He indicated Doctor Moorpark and his associates. "They will listen to the scientific argument and give me impartial advice on this subject. For myself, I certainly hope that you are correct in believing that extreme measures are unnecessary."

Popa Utirka glanced at his companions again before continuing on a different tack. "Yes, I am sure you have only the most honorable intentions, Captain Poluka. This is why I am confident you will appreciate another aspect that we find disturbing.

"Our world has a tradition of marriage and…well…romance. Ideally, an Arcturusian woman first falls in love with a man, then marries, and then has a child. Some here find it…offensive…that a child would be planned and conceived as part of a genetic experiment. Indeed, this whole plan is not known to the general population because no one knows what the reaction would be, and…meaning no offense…your race is known for being violent. Many already feel uncomfortable having contact with Earth. The idea of producing children of mixed blood will be unthinkable, at least until we understand your people better."

Poluka was starting to feel better about this discussion. This man brought up a good point about how the common people would react to such a scheme. How will people react if their king suddenly decreed that aliens will impregnate their women? Poluka knew how he would react if the situation were reversed. Of course it would be disruptive to their society! The Protocols would probably prohibit even considering such a thing—he'd check on that later.

"And," Utirka went on, "perhaps we shouldn't rush contact. Our culture has a different way of looking at things—due to the differences in how our two worlds have developed. Don't you agree?"

"Yes, I can see that." Poluka felt his people turn to look at him again, but he no longer felt the vise squeezing him. He was sure of his footing now. He wondered if Cliff's view was colored by his own intimate relationship with an alien.

A knot twisted in his stomach at the thought of Cliff with that

331

alien female. How could his officers accept the proposal so easily? Could it be…were they all so eager to jump into bed with alien women? He looked right and left at his people. Aguire, Donno, and Sheffield now seemed less innocent in his eyes. This planet was too seductive on many levels. He felt an urgency to remove his people from this world before they gave in to their basic passions.

At least this alien, Utirka, had the proper concern for decency. Obviously, not all of these aliens had wicked intentions. Indeed, this alien king probably had good intentions as well. But perhaps not. He hadn't actually met Elpastre yet.

Each side exchanged more comments that were just reiterations of the same ideas, and Paul Poluka tried to assure everyone that he would keep an open mind while remaining mindful of the Arcturusian people and their cultural dignity.

* * *

Utirka thought it went well, even if the older Poluka did get a bit rude towards the end. He watched the Earthmen walk away to the royal residence, and knew that he would have a good report for Aylata Naray. A nervous presence at his side brought his attention to Teki, who also watched the departing group.

"So, Teki, your signals got a little confused there at times, but I think we were able to steer the alien away from Elpastre's plan."

"Yes, we did, I'm sure," Teki answered. "But it was frightening."

Utirka looked more closely at the matronly woman. She was smoothing her gray hair with trembling fingers, and her eyes were troubled.

"What is it?" he asked.

"The things that went through his mind while you spoke together…I didn't understand most of it. There were feelings that didn't match what he said, and images of horrible things…a war, I think…a real war." Teki's voice dropped to a whisper. "It was worse than I had ever imagined. It was like probing the mind of a madman, and it wasn't just him. The others had the most violent thoughts. When you spoke about them being a violent race, their soldiers remembered horrible things, and yet they were not horrified by the memories. They simply agreed with you, and accepted that they are violent. There was even a sort of…satisfaction…in knowing that they are proficient at violence."

Popa Utirka thought long about what she told him. A tiny seed of worry began to grow in his heart.

* * *

As soon as they were a short distance down the street, Major Rivers informed the others that someone in El Toro had been pinging them repeatedly during the meeting, but she hadn't opened a channel because it would have disturbed the meeting.

"Let's find out who's calling," Aguire said. "While we're at it, we may as well transfer the recording of the meeting, and have it relayed up to the Hanno."

"Paul," Cliff said. "I think that woman was a psychic. She kept making subtle gestures during the meeting. She was probably letting Utirka know how we were reacting to what he was saying, so he could adjust as needed to get us to respond in his favor."

Paul stopped walking, bringing the whole group to a halt, and asked Cliff, "Tell me, was anything he said false? Is it true that other alternatives may exist?"

Cliff's eyes widened at the accusatory tone. "I've heard other ideas, and I've heard why those other ideas won't work. Paul, what do you think of all this?"

Poluka began walking again. "I'm thinking that we need a medical opinion as well as a political and ethical opinion. This is a complex issue, Cliff. I can't reach any conclusions without looking at it from all angles. I think it was good to hear from these people, and what they said should be taken into consideration."

Cliff opened his mouth to speak, but Major Rivers cut him off.

"Captain, Ensign O'Riley says four shuttles are approaching from the Hanno. Commander Washington is bringing down a security force to find out why he hasn't heard from you. Their ETA is twelve minutes."

This was what Paul needed; he just didn't realize it until now.

"Signal Washington. Tell him to land his shuttles by the

hospital. We'll meet him there."

"Paul," Cliff said, staring intently at his younger brother, "we don't need a security force. We need to meet Elpastre."

"I'll send my apologies to the King later. Let's get moving, back to the hospital."

Chapter 53

"What's happening?" Bart Hanson croaked with a voice that hadn't spoken in days.

"You are in a hospital, and are being cared for by Arcturusian doctors. You will be fine."

Hanson looked up at a thin man with long, curly hair and an impish grin.

"Who the hell are you?"

Another man answered. "His name is William Emerson."

Hanson searched the faces around him to locate the new voice. One face seemed strangely familiar, especially the eyes. He blinked at it a few times and said, "Hello, Gentry."

Hanson was lying on his back, but felt that someone had rolled him over just moments ago. He moved slightly and painful jolts of sensation ran through the skin on his back and down his legs, as if he were on a bed of needles. The reason for this hypersensitivity became clear as Emerson translated for Doctor Pamm.

He had third-degree burns on over half his body. For two full days he'd been growing new skin, as well as nerve endings, under the supervision of Arcturusian doctors. He wasn't quite healed yet, but his condition was stable enough to revive him, and let him try walking a bit.

Hanson's attention was divided between listening to the doctor and looking at Lynda's brother. Gentry was a troubled fourteen-year-old the last time they'd met. Now he was 29, with an air of confidence and experience.

Lynda and G.J. were here, too.

"You look good. I'm glad to see you," Hanson told Gentry. "How's Aguire? The last I remember, someone was shooting at him."

"He had minor injuries, but he's recovered now," Gentry answered. He paused for a moment before adding, "He's back aboard the Hanno. Paul took most of the Earthmen back for medical and psychological tests. He thinks maybe this planet has affected some of his people."

"Affected, how?"

"Well, maybe corrupted is a more accurate term. Apparently, when the Captain found that some of the crew of the Himilco had gone native and married local girls, Paul felt that there was something...disgusting about it."

Bart was sure he hadn't heard correctly. He tried to sit up, but the sharp icicles grating his backside made him grimace instead.

"You've got to be kidding."

G.J. gave Hanson a wry grin. "It was the offspring that bothered him the most, I think. He didn't like the idea of half-alien children."

Gentry snorted a bitter laugh. "I wonder what he'd think if he knew about us."

Hanson shot a quick glance at Emerson but Lynda reassured him. "Everyone in this room knows that we're Erosian. Doctor Pamm has known about Gentry for years, and so has Emerson."

Emerson's impish grin widened. "Gentry and I spent many years going through ancient Arcturusian records looking for information about Erosians, but at the moment,"—his smile faded slightly—"we're more concerned with recent events. We need to bring you up-to-date on what's happened."

Doctor Pamm had a big lunch sent in for the whole group. Everyone enjoyed the local cuisine of soup and meat pies while taking turns telling what they knew.

Some of it was a bit sketchy because none had been there when the Captain ordered all Earthmen into El Toro, and back to the Hanno. Gentry, G.J., and Lynda had been in the village looking at how long-distance messages were sent using a beam of light aimed at the atmospheric barrier, and Emerson had been with Elpastre waiting for a meeting with Poluka that never happened.

Instead, four shuttles came screaming in over the village, scaring the hell out of the residents. The native people already expected Earthmen to be bloodthirsty savages, so it didn't help when Commander Washington appeared with 30 armed men and locked down the area, not letting anyone come or go from the hospital until Captain Poluka showed up.

"I've heard from the hospital staff," Emerson said. "The worst part was when Paul Poluka ordered the crew of the Himilco who were present to board the cruiser. They refused, so the security people took them by force. There were some injuries and even some weapons fired, but at least no one was killed. Still, it made one hell of an impression on the local people.

"He didn't take everyone though. A lot of those whom Commander Redbird sent down were off doing things when Poluka pulled this stunt. They're still here. He left Maria Rodriguez here, in charge of the pinnace, and he left Major Rivers and a couple others who might be good for security, but only female personnel. He seems to think the male crewmen are tempted and corrupted by their carnal nature, but women won't abandon their basic decency. Still, he only got 25 people rounded up.

"Rodriguez is supposed to have them stay in the pinnace when they show up until she can account for all of them, then bring them back to the Hanno."

"But why did he do it?" Bart asked.

"We're not sure," Lynda answered.

"Bart," Gentry said, "there's a lot more we could tell you, and we will, but first there are some people who would like to meet you."

A tall man entered the hospital room. He was lean and dignified, with straight, graying hair hanging down below his collar, and light, brownish-gray eyes. He wore a starched blue tunic and dark gray pants.

With him was an extraordinarily beautiful woman with cascading locks of long, black, curly hair, and large eyes so dark brown they seemed almost black, making her olive complexion seem light in contrast. She wore a billowy blue and white blouse, and a dark blue, floor-length skirt. Her timeless face made her age hard to guess, but Hanson estimated it at about 40 years.

Oppo Gunn, whom Hanson remembered from the forest, came in with them, dressed in his green uniform, and Major Rivers entered last, completing his party of visitors.

"Bart," William Emerson said, "I am pleased to introduce you to the King and Queen of Arcturus."

* * *

"Just what else do you want me to test for, Captain?" Doctor Payne asked.

"I'm looking for anything that could affect their judgment, perhaps some kind of mind-control drugs, or a virus maybe."

Jayne Payne pursed her lips and answered carefully. "If there's anything like that, we would have found it already. Since you brought it up, Captain, the pills you've been using are considered a 'judgment-affecting' drug, and Doctor Moorpark has scheduled you for a full physical examination."

Poluka's eyes widened, partly in surprise, but also in indignation. "I don't have time for that. Don't you realize that we have a crisis brewing?"

"Captain." Doctor Payne's tone snapped to a less amicable mode. "What I understand is that you see a crisis where no one else does, and that you have been using an illegal, behavior-altering drug. I also see that you've been making erratic decisions. My staff and I agree that you may, and possibly should, be pronounced medically impaired and unable to perform your job."

Poluka froze, except for his eyes, which whipped wildly around as if searching desperately for something. At last, he inhaled deeply and let out a gravelly, growling whisper. "You can't do that to me."

"If you do what you are supposed to, which is let us take care of your health, nobody would even consider it, Captain. But actually, I can, and I will if I believe you are a danger to this crew. You know it's the right thing—the only right thing—if you give me no choice."

Paul Poluka hesitated for only a half a heartbeat. "Very well, Doctor. I'll be back for an examination in two hours."

He spun on his heel, and was gone before she could unclench her trembling fists behind her back and wipe the sweat from her brow. She took a moment to compose herself.

This isn't the Navy, and the captain doesn't answer only to God, she reminded herself.

Still, there have been only a couple of times when a doctor removed a captain from command. Such an action would damage a captain's career, even if a subsequent investigation showed that his removal was unwarranted.

It would also damage a doctor's career even if it was warranted. If it was found to be unwarranted, the doctor would never practice medicine again, and might even spend some time in prison. Under the New Federation, she couldn't begin to guess what the consequences might be.

She ordered her face into a mask of professional calm, and briskly walked to where Clifford Poluka and Commander Aguire were waiting in another room.

"Well, gentlemen, I've spoken with the captain, and he's agreed to an examination in two hours. Now, getting back to our alien friends, tell me how this psychic thing works."

Cliff's face relaxed a bit, then he chuckled at the question about psychics.

"That was a tough one for us, especially before we had a good grasp on their language. But essentially, maybe one percent of the female population, and a smaller number of males, have varying degrees of abilities. For most of those who have any measurable talent, it's just uncanny intuition. There are some who can read minds, but it's a tricky business…too easy to confuse another person's thoughts with one's own…or to misinterpret thoughts. It's not the same for all of them. Some can get words from another person's mind. Some get images or emotions. Others may only get vague impressions."

"How do they get trained?" Doctor Payne asked.

"For at least several centuries—I'm not really sure when it began—they've had formal schools. Before that, they had elders who would give private lessons.

"There are other abilities besides reading thoughts. Some can see events from great distances. A few in their history saw events on Earth, but again, that was prone to misinterpretation since what they saw was out of context, in a culture they didn't understand.

"Another, less common, ability is to see the future. The highest-ranking psychic on Arcturus has this ability to some degree. That's how they knew the Hanno was coming, and even where some of the landings would be."

"So," Aguire said, "that's how they knew where my shuttle would land, but Oppo Gunn was sent by the King, not the Old Rulers. Doesn't the ranking psychic work for the Old Rulers?"

"Unofficially. The ranking psychic is a cousin of the Old Ruler's Matriarch, and predicted only one landing: that the King of Earth would land at the pyramid in the equatorial desert."

"That was Leroy Donno's shuttle," Aguire said. "But he's not the King of Earth. So, their best psychic screwed up."

A big grin grew across Cliff's expression. "Right, and I'll bet she's taking some heat for that right now. The Matriarch is a nasty old woman who doesn't forgive mistakes, even from her cousin."

"Maybe it's not such a big mistake," Doctor Payne said. Cliff and Aguire looked at her expectantly, and she explained, "The name Leroy comes from Latin roots—you should know that, José—it means 'the King'."

"Ah, that may be it," Cliff sighed. "Come to think of it, the name Donno is similar to their word for the planet Earth: Dona. So I guess Leroy Donno might be picked up by a psychic as the King of Earth.

"But the most important landing, from the local government's perspective, was my brother's. The Queen, Lapastra, is also a psychic. I think most people didn't realize it, until now. I certainly didn't. She knew the exact time and place of each landing. She also knew that there was no King of Earth. Furthermore, she was able to diagnose Bart Hanson from six thousand kilometers away when your own medical people pronounced him dead, and then she sent a psychic message to her brother Oppo that Hanson could still be saved."

"It's fantastic." Payne shook her head. "I've heard about people who claim to have abilities like this, but I never believed them."

"You know," Cliff said, "I think they originally came from Earth, thousands of years ago. Their own records claim they did. That also explains why many animals here are nearly the same as the ones on Earth. They've got dogs and cats, horses, llamas, cattle, sheep, squirrels, and so forth. The critters that are definitely different are the fish. Those, I think, are genuinely native. It's my theory that this talent became concentrated in their gene pool by their need to survive The Flood."

"That's another story I've just heard a little about." Doctor Payne said.

"They have no written records, and very few oral traditions, about anything before The Flood. Apparently they came to this world, maybe a million of them, when there was an ancient disaster on Earth. They were fleeing, and somehow got transported to this world. Their theory about the moon shifting its orbit makes sense. For about a thousand Earth years—around 70 Arcturusian years—their moon orbited very close to the equator, close enough to pull the ocean to one side of the planet. It was almost, but not quite, geosynchronous. From the surface it would appear to circle the world once every local year, which is about fourteen and a half Earth years. Its tidal influence caused the ocean to sweep across the surface at around eleven kilometers per day."

"So, they had to move ahead of the Flood constantly, at least eleven kilometers, every day?" Doctor Payne concluded.

"At the equator, yes, but further north or south they could move slower and stay ahead of the water. During those centuries, they forgot almost everything about who they were before The Flood, but developed a new culture based on their constant migration. The land ahead was always new—reformed by the sea—and the water could break through into a low area at any time behind them. They have stories about flatlands of maybe a million square kilometers that would flood without warning in a matter of days. To this day they have a cultural fear of the sea, and don't live in low-lying areas." Cliff turned to Aguire. "You may have noticed all the homes have a circle pattern on one side of the building. That's symbolic of the wheels that were on the wagons and carts they used during The Flood. It's just a traditional decoration today, but for a long time they really had wheels on their houses.

"You can imagine how anyone with psychic ability could help their chances of survival. Their technological progress was at a standstill during the Epoch of the Flood, but the families with psychics became more common as those without psychics fell to misfortune."

"Does Poluka—I mean, your brother—know all this?" Aguire

asked.

"Some. Why?"

"I think he already doesn't like the Arcturusians, and he's been getting paranoid lately. I can see a military advantage to these abilities. I'm sure your brother will see a potential threat, and begin to imagine the worst is already happening."

Cliff studied Aguire for a moment, and then nodded slowly. "José, I guess you've already figured out that I really love these people. I only want the best for them."

The commander shrugged. "I don't want any trouble for them."

"There's something else I need to ask," Doctor Payne said. "The Arcturusians healed Aguire and Hanson. Can they do something for the injured people we have here…the ones that we can't do anything more for?"

Jayne Payne usually oozed confidence in just about every situation. For the first time in all the years that he'd known her, Aguire heard a humble plea for help.

"Their medicine is more advanced than ours, but I can't speak for them," Cliff answered. "I'd like some of their doctors to come aboard to tour your facility and see if they could help, but I just don't know if Paul would allow it. And now that he's insulted the monarchy and terrified the hospital staff, I'm not sure they would come."

"Well, we've got to try!" Jayne Payne's voice cracked with emotion as she let her mask slip for a moment.

Aguire had seen her in the throes of erotic passion. He'd seen her furious, and sad, and giddy with mirth, but he'd never seen her vulnerable, until now. She was one of his dearest friends, but he sometimes overlooked how fragile she could be under her veil of professionalism.

"We should be able to convince Captain Poluka," Aguire said, "but can we convince the Arcturusians?"

Chapter 54

The tale of violent Earth warriors spread to nearby villages and cities. Nobles were arriving in Desin-Arcturus, the capital city, from even the farthest plantations. Concern and curiosity changed to fear and alarm when they heard the details of the encounter, which agents of the Old Rulers made sure everyone heard.

"At least they haven't heard what happened at Himeka-ar-Vod," Oppo offered. He kept his men quiet about the meeting with Aguire in the forest, and how the Earthmen had almost killed one of their own. Still, it was only a matter of time before rumors from the hospital made it back from across the Vodita Sea.

Elpastre turned from the window where he'd been watching the latest group of nobles arrive in their steam-powered cars. Even the technology of his own people was baffling to him; his strength was in history and philosophy, not science. He couldn't even hope to understand the Earthmen's technology.

"It's bad enough these Earthmen are an adversarial people," Elpastre spat. "But they've brought such awesome machines. Even if we meet them on their own violent terms, we can't begin to match their weapons or their flying machines."

"We can't," Lapastra agreed, "and we won't. The prophecy says that there will be violence, but not war. Our world will be saved as the prophecy foretells, but not by fighting the Earthmen."

Eeja Burr, who'd been sitting quietly, finally spoke. "The prophets were never clear on the details, but they didn't guarantee success…only a chance for success. If we don't try we will surely fail. And as for war, to us it's just a word, a concept handed down from the most ancient times. If it comes to that, we will be like the short-horns in the fields, ready to be slaughtered."

Elpastre pressed his lips tightly together at the reminder that action was required.

"Well," Oppo sighed as he looked over Elpastre's shoulder at the street, "if the Earthmen excel in some things, perhaps we exceed them in other ways."

"We do." Lapastra suddenly brightened. "We have better doctors. Even now, many people aboard their ship are thinking about this, and want the medical help that we can provide. I have an idea."

"What sort of plan are you thinking of, my love?" Elpastre asked.

She gave him a dazzling, almost wicked, smile. "My dear, the men have tried formal diplomacy. Now, it's time for subtle influence. In other words, it needs a woman's touch."

* * *

Poluka was so pissed off, he could hardly think straight. His first impulse was to have Doctor Payne arrested. His SP's would do it, but if he couldn't come up with legitimate charges it would only make things worse.

His next thought was actually sensible. He went straight to the gymnasium across from the Med Center and called Commander Washington. By the time his old buddy showed up, Poluka was sweating on a treadmill with the idea that any toxins in his body would work their way out faster with a little exercise.

Washington's meaty, ebony face frowned when he heard what Doctor Payne had said to his captain, but he didn't say that she was wrong.

"Listen, Paul. The doctors are playing this by ear. They know you screwed up with those pills, but they have no way of knowing how it's affected you. They're just being cautious and—let's be honest—they're trying to keep this all in the family so long as they can verify that you really are okay. I say, go along with it and get it over with."

Paul stopped the treadmill and wiped the sweat from his face. "You're right. And she's right. Oh, God, how I've screwed up. I passed out from fatigue in the middle of making contact with aliens…all because of those stupid pills."

He didn't say—or want to believe—that the 207 deaths in the Zone might also be due to his personal weight loss program, but he knew it might be.

"Listen, Alex, you know I'm concerned about what's happening back home with the Fed."

Washington nodded, "You want to be part of it…getting rid of the bastards."

"Yeah. That was my plan before all this alien shit came out of nowhere. Well, we'll do whatever's right about the aliens, then get back to Earth, and do what's right there. Some on this ship may not feel as strongly about it as we do. I was thinking of giving them a choice. They can be with us 100 percent, or we can drop them off at Tau Ceti. They can stay there until the dust settles if they don't want to be part of it."

"I guess that's okay, but let's talk again when the alien business is resolved."

Paul showered and put on a fresh uniform, then went back to the Med Center. A sort of peaceful clarity settled into him. The talk with Washington helped to put him at ease. He'd lost a lot of weight in the last couple of months, and he felt pretty good after the treadmill. No doubt getting off the zippies was going to help him feel healthier, too.

"Doctor Moorpark scheduled an exam for me," he told the clerk at the front desk. He hoped it would be Moorpark doing the exam. In fact, if Payne wanted to do it herself, he would insist that it be Moorpark. He had nothing against female doctors, but he preferred a male doctor for his own exam.

"Yes, sir," The young crewman said, and read a note on his monitor. "You'll be in 247. All the other examination rooms are booked. Doctor Moorpark will meet you there."

Poluka dutifully trod up to the second level and had to walk through the rows and rows of beds. Someone had pulled back all the curtains. He saw about a hundred people who were beyond hope of recovery before he got to room 247. It was depressing. It was also obvious. They arranged his appointment on the upper level so that he would see all these people.

"Good Afternoon, Doctor," he greeted Moorpark. "Please contact Doctor Payne, and tell her that I got the point. I will allow the alien doctors to provide services to our people under her supervision."

He got some satisfaction from the embarrassment on Moorpark's face, which verified that he was in on it, and that they'd thought they were being more subtle.

The examination revealed no problems. Moorpark asked about anxiety or irritability, and Poluka admitted to some of both.

"That's to be expected after a couple of months on zippies. It should clear up in a week or so. Until then, I can prescribe a mild tranquilizer if you like."

"That won't be necessary," Paul said, and hoped it was true.

He was ready to leave the Med Center when he got a call. They'd received a message from the pinnace. G.J. wanted to talk to Captain Poluka about scheduling another meeting with the Arcturusian government, this time aboard the Hanno.

* * *

Lapastra had a fine sheen of perspiration on her brow. Her husband couldn't recall another time when her abilities were taxed so heavily. Eeja Burr and Gentry Stokes waited with the King to learn the result of her effort.

"We were lucky," she said. "He was exercising when I touched his mind. The physical activity made it easier to influence him. He will accept the offer, now."

"I didn't know you could do that," Gentry said.

Lapastra gave him a tired smile. "Don't worry, Gentry. There aren't any others alive today that can do this. Very few in the history of my people could send, as well as receive thoughts. Even Mata Buray cannot come close to such a feat, and I rarely try this. I wouldn't try it now, except our need is so extreme, and Paul Poluka's own people have told me that he has become irrational."

"Lapastra," Gentry asked, "you have never been taught at a school for psychics, and your talents are hidden from everyone. How did you develop such skill?"

Elpastre answered for his wife. "She didn't need help developing the skill. She needed help to limit it. When she was quite young, her mother recognized her potential and hired an elder to teach her. You see, Lapastra comes from a noble family.

Men have always wanted wives with talent, and women want to marry men who have good positions in our society. It is only natural that noble families have a concentration of psychics. After hundreds of generations, some noble families have women of extraordinary psychic talent. In my Lapastra there is an especially potent concentration of ancestors, but her family was not prominent or wealthy compared to many nobles, and her lineage went unnoticed until now."

"Yes," Eeja Burr added with a distressed expression, "until now. People are beginning to guess that Lapastra has a special gift. The Old Rulers have already sent agents to the Hall of Records to reexamine the Queen's bloodline."

Oppo patted his shoulder and said, "You hate the idea of those vermin poring through the ancient texts, but it is their right. All have the right to the true historical record. It is a fundamental principle that makes us civilized."

"But they're doing it for an evil purpose," Eeja protested. Chroniclers like himself maintained the library for millennia, diligently adding to it as history unfolds. It galled him that political opportunists were using the huge repository of knowledge.

"But what about Captain Poluka?" Gentry tried to steer the conversation back to the immediate problem. "I don't see how getting doctors up to the Hanno is going to help us."

Again, Lapastra smiled. "When I said this needed a woman's touch, I didn't mean mine."

Chapter 55

Doctor Jayne Payne waited in the shuttle docks, way down in the belly of the Starship Hanno, while the whooshing of preheated air rushed through pipes and filled the pinnace dock. The dock door hissed open, and she marched through it behind Captain Poluka and Commander Aguire.

Cliff Poluka was here, too, along with representatives of a dozen different departments aboard the Starship Hanno. The officers wore dress-grays, and the Hanno was as clean and tidy as she'd ever been.

Jayne was nervous and unsure about wearing her Corps uniform instead of her usual doctor's smock for meeting alien doctors. Aliens didn't even exist until a few days ago, and now she was meeting alien doctors. It didn't help that she kept hearing they were superior to Earth doctors.

They got Hanson to grow new nerve cells, which is impossible. What else can they do? Will they see us as primitive? Thousands of questions bounced around in her skull.

The pinnace side-hatch slid open with a soft whirring sound and the ramp extended.

First out was an attractive young woman in a Corps uniform who smartly saluted. "Lieutenant Tully reporting, with Arcturusian representatives requesting permission to come aboard."

Captain Poluka returned the salute. "Permission granted. Welcome aboard."

The visitors seemed so human that Jayne had to keep reminding herself they were aliens. Even their clothes and hairstyles were not unusual. They spoke a melodious language that was not unpleasant, reminding her of some Mediterranean place—Italy—Greece—some place like that.

There were 22 doctors, and seven diplomats. Three former

crewmen from the Starship Himilco also came as interpreters, and introduced themselves first.

"I'm William Emerson, sir." A curly-haired man shook hands with Captain Poluka. "This is Hank Rodriguez."

A ruggedly handsome Hispanic man stepped forward and shook hands with the Captain.

"Oh, yes." Poluka smiled. "Maria's uncle, I believe."

"Yes, sir. I can't tell you how happy I am that Maria came on the first ship to follow us to Arcturus. After all these years, I'm so proud of how she turned out."

Next was Ivan Tershensky, a huge man in his sixties, with old scars on his face, and a wicked gleam in his eye.

"Tershensky!" Poluka stood up straighter. "It's an honor to meet you, sir."

Jayne got the impression of bold appetite for adventure, and had been attracted to such men in her youth, but was puzzled by how awed her captain was, until she understood that this was the man behind the Meduza legend, who had molded the character of the Exploration Corps in its early years.

Doctor Pamm was the senior Arcturusian physician. He was about the same age as Jayne, with thinning hair and a round face that smiled shyly during the introductions. The other doctors were quickly introduced along with their specialties, some of which, like "organ regeneration," "nerve bundle interfacing," and "synapse reordering," made Doctor Payne perspire with anticipation.

Both male and female Arcturusian doctors wore pale bluish smocks and pants which couldn't be more drab if they tried. Their hair was a bit longer than current Earth fashion, and the women doctors had theirs pinned up in neat buns behind their necks. Jayne noted, almost subconsciously, that their faces were attractive by Earth standards.

The plan was to tour the Med Center before the seven alien diplomats split off with the Hanno's senior officers for a private meeting. The doctors would remain in the hospital to determine which of the injured crewmen might be helped by alien medicine.

Jayne led the group through the extensive laboratories and treatment centers, explaining the purpose of each area to the Arcturusians. Captain Poluka stayed at the head of the tour, smiling and nodding as the perfect host, and wearing a mask of diplomacy that Jayne saw slip only once, when Doctor Pamm asked if they had any pediatric facility. Poluka's eyes scanned the group suspiciously for a moment until Pamm said that he was only asking because they had so many new childhood sicknesses they still hadn't found treatments for.

Jayne explained, "We don't normally have children on an exploration ship, and so we have no facility for pediatrics, though several of the ship's doctors do have training in the field."

Poluka's blandness returned, and Jayne glanced around at the alien faces, wondering if they'd noticed. That's when she realized that the women doctors were staying in the back of the group, away from Captain Poluka, and she finally noticed that they were the majority. Sixteen of the 22 doctors were women. She hadn't noticed at first because all seven diplomats were men, making the group as a whole almost evenly balanced between men and women.

The tour ended, and the diplomats went to the ship's library for their meeting. William Emerson went with them. The other two translators, Tershensky and Rodriguez, stayed with the doctors.

"Doctor Payne," Ivan Tershensky said before they went further, "would you mind if we freshen up before meeting your patients?"

They were shown to staff restrooms, where the alien doctors disappeared for a while, and Rodriguez chatted outside with Jayne.

"So, Mister Rodriguez, I understand the Himilco's doctor didn't make it to Arcturus. He died in the Zone, didn't he?"

"No, ma'am. He actually died just as we were leaving the Zone. He overdosed on tranquilizers. Doctor Hall was...was a good guy, but he didn't handle the discovery of aliens very well. I'd like to think the overdose was accidental."

"Oh, I didn't realize. I guess we should be watching for people on this ship who might not receive the news very well." She bit her lip and wondered if that was part of Poluka's problem. "So, you didn't have anyone with medical training, except the Arcturusian doctors, for the last ten years?"

"Well," Hank smiled, "I've had some training. I'm a dentist, and I doubled as Doc Hall's assistant."

"Oh, I didn't know your background. Of course, the Himilco

had a dentist."

The Arcturusian doctors came streaming out of the restrooms, first from the men's room, and a bit later from the ladies' room. The reason the women took a little longer was obvious when Jayne saw that they had applied some cosmetics. Their lips and eyes now had some attractive color, and their hair was down. Most of them were wearing modest, but very, nice earrings. They were no longer drab, but had an exotic, subdued beauty.

The unexpected transformation was too deliberate, and they'd waited until Poluka was gone to make the change. Before she had time to wonder about it, Ivan Tershensky explained.

"Doctor, if I may speak bluntly, your captain's got his head up his ass. Now, don't give me that shocked look. You know as well as I do that he's against allowing any romantic encounters with aliens simply because he thinks it's like having sex with animals. If you didn't understand that before, you will as soon as you give it a moment's thought.

"These people are human, Doctor Payne—just as human as you and me—and the proof of that are the 47 children the crew of the Himilco has fathered."

His disparaging comments about her captain triggered a defense instinct but, before she could react, the truth of his estimation hit her: the idea of mating with an alien disgusted Poluka, which perfectly explained how he treated his brother. Instead, she responded to Ivan's second statement.

"47 children? Well, yes, of course, I suppose that indicates we're the same species...at least, I think it does."

"Well, anyway. Emerson has just about proven from these people's own historical records that they came from Earth thousands of years ago. Now, they're a dying race, and only by having contact—and offspring—with our people can they be saved."

She'd already heard enough about this genetic fatigue from Cliff to comprehend the scientific issues. It wasn't just inbreeding, it was a sort of countdown for the species. A molecular strand in the genome, called an allele, allowed them to continue propagating, but, unlike other sequences, it changed with each generation, like a frayed string unraveling at the end.

Such a phenomenon had been known on Earth for centuries,

but it involved individual cells being able to reproduce: a typical cell in the human body would wear out and then divide to make a new cell about 80 or 90 times but, each time, it would lose a piece of the allele until there wasn't any left. Then, the cell died without reproducing.

Something similar was happening to the Arcturusians, and exacerbated by genetic drift; the effect of isolating a small population for many generations, which allowed certain inherited problems to become more prevalent when outside gene pools were cut off from the population.

The ship's database had case studies of genetic drift as recently as the last century on Tau Ceti, and as far back as a thousand years ago with Eastern European Jews. The principle was proven, but had never before manifested as something that could cause extinction.

Before the Great Disaster of the 22nd century, scientists on Earth mapped the entire human genome, but all that was lost now. Genetics was still a re-emerging science in the 28th century, but Doctor Payne believed the alien scientists were right. It seemed genetics was another science that the Arcturusians understood better.

She wondered why they'd brought sixteen attractive women onto the Hanno, until a wild thought occurred to her.

"Hold it! You don't expect these women to all get pregnant during this visit, do you?"

Ivan's eyes popped wide open. He started laughing and couldn't stop. Hank Rodriguez came to the rescue.

"No, Doctor. Elpastre's original plan was to set up an enclave for people from Earth to come and meet people from Arcturus, with the expectation that both men and women would choose to immigrate from Earth and assimilate into the local culture, as we have.

"It seemed like a workable plan until your Captain caused a diplomatic incident, which allowed the political opposition down on the planet to sour the idea in the minds of most people. It was never a broadly accepted idea to start with."

Ivan finally got his humor in check, and hastily explained to the Arcturusians what Jayne had said, which set off a chorus of giggles from some of the women, and made Doctor Pamm blush.

"Sorry about that, Doctor Payne," Ivan explained. "Your

question took me by surprise, but I suppose it did look that way. Actually, the weakness of the original plan is now clear. We need to convince your Captain Poluka from within his own organization, so, we brought two sets of diplomats, the ones that are with him now, and the ones," he gestured, indicating the Arcturusians doctors, "who will be meeting the crew. These really are all doctors. We simply brought a disproportionate number of attractive female doctors because, as the saying goes, you catch more flies with honey than with vinegar."

Jayne frowned at Ivan's smiling face. "Mister Tershensky, I was led to believe that these people would be helping our injured."

"And they will, Doctor, right now. Only, this way, word will spread that the Arcturusians are pleasant, nice people much more quickly than if we just brought cold, unremarkable-looking doctors."

Rodriguez was translating the discussion to the Arcturusians, and one of the doctors, an exquisitely gorgeous woman named Doctor Tahl, stepped forward with an earnest expression. The woman was a bit younger than Jayne, but projected professional confidence. She spoke and Rodrigues translated.

"Doctor, we will help your patients. Let us show you what we can do."

Right now, Jayne just wanted to see some results from their allegedly superior medical expertise. At the moment, they looked more like employees of a cocktail lounge than physicians, and Jayne wondered if they'd selected the best doctors to send, or just the prettiest.

They broke up into groups of twos and threes, quickly going from bed to bed, starting in the spinal injury section.

Earth medicine could only do so much when the delicate nerve bundle in the spine and neck was damaged, and there were 62 cases that Jayne's people were unable to treat beyond keeping them alive.

The Arcturusian doctors got a look at each patient's x-ray, which they regarded as a wholly inadequate method of diagnosis, and proceeded to use their own instruments. They'd brought tiny devices about the size of pill bottles that somehow detected the internal condition of a patient, and gave a multicolored text display that the doctors could scroll through.

Doctor Tahl used her device on an ensign with a broken neck. Rodriguez translated for her.

"This young man took an impact between the third and fourth vertebrae, which caused a three-centimeter fracture in the lamina of the third vertebra. A number of blood vessels were ruptured, and there was fluid intrusion into the centrum. Also, there is damage to the scalenus medius, which was not repaired."

The woman shot a quick, almost accusing, look at Jayne.

"We can't just repair this kind of damage," Jayne responded. The alien instrument was impressive, but they needed treatment, not diagnosis. "Look at this case."

She indicated another patient, and explained that the spinal bones were not damaged but the surrounding tissues on the left side of the spine were destroyed, causing a dramatic curve in the back that would eventually lead to more problems. Unfortunately, the tissue could not heal properly before straightening the spine by using a temporary metal frame, which would be held in place using pedicle screws.

"I don't know what pedicle screws are," Rodriguez said. "I can't translate it."

Doctor Payne took a piece of paper, and drew a picture of a vertebra, then showed where a metal screw attached to the bone. Doctor Pamm gaped at the picture and shook his head while sputtering a burst of alien protests.

"Ah...Doctor Pamm doesn't think that's such a good treatment," Rodriguez said.

"Then, what would the doctor suggest?" Jayne crossed her arms, and looked at the Arcturusian. Some of the staff gathered to listen.

Doctor Pamm made a lengthily statement, with a couple of interruptions from Rodriguez, who finally turned to Jayne and explained that there was a technique using "surrogate" bones that would hold new tissue while it grew within the body to replace the damaged parts. Then, all of the tissue would be reattached to where it belonged. Drugs would accelerate the healing so the patent recovers in about four days.

"I sort of shortened the explanation," Rodriguez admitted. "There are a lot of medical terms that just have no equivalent on Earth."

"Can we do this procedure here?" Jayne asked.

"No. This patient should be transported to a hospital on the planet."

There was a small commotion at the bed where Doctor Tahl was still working with the broken neck case.

"Doctor Payne!" a nurse cried out.

Jayne rushed to the bedside, where the patient was squeezing Doctor Tahl's hands with his own! His feet moved slightly with the effort.

"His grip is good," Ivan translated for Doctor Tahl, "but he needs better nutrition. Some soup today, and solid food tomorrow. You can let him try to stand the day after tomorrow."

The Med Center staff gathered around, babbling excitedly, and Jayne asked, "What did you do? This is impossible."

"Doctor Tahl repaired the damaged vertebra, and encouraged the fluids to escape from the centrum," Tershensky said.

"But how? I didn't see any treatment."

"The instruments they use for diagnosis can also be used for simple procedures, like this."

"Simple procedures," Jayne repeated numbly. She watched in fascination as the patient turned his head to look around. An excitement filled her that she hadn't felt since the first time she'd saved a life.

"Let's see who else can be helped right now," Jayne said, "and we'll make a list of all the patients who need to be taken down to the planet for treatment."

A nurse went to a com-console and informed Elisa Santino that Francis Braque was healed by alien doctors. When Elisa told the youths in the ship's laundry, they cheered so loudly that people came in from the corridors to see what the excitement was. Within an hour, hundreds of people had either called or come by the Med Center to see who else the aliens healed.

Chapter 56

The size of the Hanno awed the Arcturusians. In the ship's library the tens of thousands of paper books impressed them, but Joseph Redbird felt sure they didn't comprehend that most of the library was stored in computers.

He was a Cherokee Indian who never gave much thought to his heritage until he was a student at the Angola Pilot School and had exposure to cultures different from his North Carolina community. Upon returning home he began looking at the history of Indians, and how they'd been affected when Europeans first crossed the Atlantic.

Native Americans did pretty well after leading the world back from the brink of extinction following the Great Disaster of the Twenty Second century. But for hundreds of years before The Disaster, things had not been so good for his ancestors.

Now, he saw the possibility for history—the worst part of history—to repeat itself here at Arcturus. There were huge inequalities in technology, and cultural differences even more extreme than it had been for the Europeans and the Native Americans. At least the Indians had a concept of war in their culture. These aliens never had a war. They never had nations or borders, and they've always spoken a common language.

Redbird didn't expect them to survive much longer now that Captain Poluka had taken the role of Christopher Columbus. Before long, others will come, and either destroy them or absorb them into Earth's culture so completely that the Arcturusians would lose even their identity. He wondered if they would guess this outcome, and how they would respond.

The diplomats watched a slide show about Earth, prepared and narrated by Commander Redbird. He had a background in social and political science, and made such presentations before while doing political analysis for the Navy.

The slide show gave an extremely abbreviated history of Earth, focusing mostly on technological progress through the ages, with only the slightest mention of wars. Most of it showed what Earth has been like since the end of the Corporate War and the beginning of the old Federation. There was no mention of the recent coup or the New Federation. Redbird thought it would just confuse and alarm their visitors without providing useful information.

Five of the Arcturusian diplomats were nobles; Oppo Gunn, the Queen's brother; Eeja Burr, the royal chronicler; and the ministers of economics, science, and health.

Aga Ayab, the former captain of the Fledik was also there. The seventh diplomat was a very large man whom Commander Donno recognized as the senior bodyguard for Miyuree, the royal princess.

Oppo Gunn asked if the various nations on Earth still had distinct cultures under one world government. This started a round of discussion.

Someone pointed out that Commander Aguire's native language was Spanish, and that Commander Donno's cultural background was slightly different than Commander Sheffield's even though they have the same native language. Commander Sirenko said that she and Bart Hanson had different cultures and native languages, yet shared the same religion.

The guests absorbed it all in stride, until Commander Redbird said that his ancestors had stone tools when the Europeans, who had steel tools, came to America.

Captain Poluka interrupted Redbird. "Today's Native Americans are prominently represented in industry and finance. Any problems that existed are a thing of the ancient past."

"Yes," Oppo Gunn said icily. "The crew of the Himilco told us about the conquest of America."

Captain Poluka glared at his brother, who sat expressionless.

* * *

"I can't concentrate," Lapastra gasped in a foreign tongue. The King's best translators were on the starship, so they spoke the Erosian language while Bart Hanson was with them. Hanson was amazed that some Arcturusian nobles learned his people's language as a way of sending secret messages.

"We are losing Paul Poluka." Sweat beaded on the Queen's forehead like tiny pearls in the candlelight. "Oppo made an unfortunate comment, and Paul's mind became closed. The last thought I got from him was about leaving us to our fate…abandoning us to the genetic fatigue…unless we can find another way to save ourselves."

"He's not a god," Hanson grumbled from the couch in royal suite. He was struggling to fit his thoughts into the Erosian language, which he'd not spoken in years, and had never used for complex discussions. "There are other officers who will not forget—or abandon—your people. Help will come."

Elpastre felt abandoned already with his closest advisors aboard the Hanno. He was glad this Erosian was with them, and so full of hope. Yet, that was the earmark of the Erosians—to hope, and look optimistically to the future. Perhaps that had been their downfall.

Still, Bart Hanson was also from Earth, and understood those people, perhaps even better than they understood themselves.

"We can't wait for another generation, Bart," Elpastre said. "We have not yet lost the ability to maintain our culture, but we are declining. If we do not turn the situation around in the next few years, we will slip to numbers that cannot sustain our society. Soon, we will crumble into a barbaric existence. What took thousands of years to build will be gone forever."

"I can't reach him," Lapastra suddenly wailed. She hung her head, and trembled with frustration. "We…we must convince him to send the wounded. I must…."

Elpastre went to his wife and tried to comfort her. Hanson wished to do the same and almost rose from the couch, but the new skin on his back screamed for him to be still.

Then, he saw the tiny princess watching from the hallway with tears in her eyes as she felt her mother's distress.

Miyuree knew all about the Earthmen and the need to persuade them. Like her mother, she had special talents and little could be hidden from the child.

Hanson watched as Miyuree pressed her hands together as if in prayer and closed her eyes. Even without psychic gifts, he felt it; an irresistible force swept through the room and reached up to the heavens, up…to the orbiting starship. Elpastre felt it, too. It almost knocked Lapastra down and she had to hold onto her husband for balance.

"What have you done?" Lapastra whispered.

The little princess opened her eyes and smiled sweetly.

* * *

Commander Aguire thought his captain was getting back to normal, but halfway through the meeting Paul Poluka suddenly decided to send the wounded aboard the Hanno to the hospital in Arvod—right now.

The Arcturusian diplomats were as surprised as the Hanno's officers, but recovered instantly and said that the hospital could receive the patients at any time.

Aguire wanted to question the decision, but not in front of everyone, especially their guests. He sat quietly while Poluka made a call to Doctor Payne and got things moving. When Poluka returned his attention to the meeting, Aguire hoped that someone—Doctor Payne or Commander Washington—would have the sense hold up the operation until the meeting was over.

* * *

"Doctor Payne?" The nurse had to raise her voice over the excited chatter in the critical care ward. "The Captain is on the com for you."

"Doctor," Poluka said as soon as he saw her on his screen. "I've decided to allow patients to be transported to the Arcturusian hospital, assuming they can be safely moved, and cannot receive better treatment in our own facility."

This was too good. It made her suspicious. No competent officer would make such a decision without consulting the medical staff. She was now sure that her captain was not fit to command.

Glancing up from the com screen, she looked around the ward. Over 40 patients were sitting up, chatting with people. They'd been doomed to lay immobile for the rest of their lives before the Arcturusian doctors came aboard.

"You have?" Jayne struggled to maintain her professional demeanor. "That's...very good, Captain. I think I could put together a schedule for it right away."

"Just work it out with Lieutenant Townsend. He'll arrange the transportation."

"That's fine, Captain. By the way, the visiting doctors have already helped over a hundred patients. Some are completely healed."

"Healed? Of course they healed them. That's why I invited them here."

Everyone thought something was wrong with the Captain when he was rushing things. She supposed it was just the law of probability that sooner or later one of Poluka's crazy decisions would actually be a good one. She wasn't going to wait for him to change his mind. As soon as the com link closed, she opened another to the shuttle docks.

"Lieutenant Townsend, I have some transportation requirements. How many hospital gurneys can fit into the pinnace?"

The next call was to Hydroponics for more helping hands. Ensign Harper was still shaken from his last trip to the surface, and unwilling to lead his people back to the planet where he'd seen a fish destroy a shuttle and wild boar the size of buffalo, but his attitude softened considerably when he met Doctor Tahl and the other native beauties.

The list of patients grew to 180. Jayne called Townsend again to explain, and he actually came to the Med Center to see for himself what kind of situation was brewing.

Townsend lost his trademark composure when the first person to greet him was one of his own crewmen: a young woman that he'd worked closely with until the accident. The last time he'd seen her, she had a broken back and was scheduled to have her crushed legs amputated. Now, she expected to be walking in about a week—provided she gets treatment down on the planet.

Townsend sprinted back to the shuttle dock to get both the pinnace and El Toro ready to receive all 180 patients.

* * *

"What about the primitives on Earth?" Oppo Gunn asked.
"Primitives?" Aguire was completely at a loss.

"The people who live without modern technology, outside of your cities."

"You know about them?"

The conversation took an unexpected turn, but it made sense that the Arcturusians were interested in the millions of people who lived outside of the technology-based culture of Earth.

Much to Aguire's surprise, the officers of the Hanno, including himself, didn't really know much about the people of their own planet who lived on the fringes of society. What they did know seemed to satisfy the Arcturusians, and perhaps reassured them that Earthmen could coexist with cultures of diverse technological preferences.

At Oppo Gunn's prompting, Aga Ayab, who had first met Cliff Poluka in the Zone, gave an account of how his people built the Fledik.

"We'd love to hear about it," Chief Braun said. "The mix of technology has been puzzling us. How does a civilization that uses steam engines and crossbows build a faster than light starship?"

Ayab was happy to clear up the mystery.

"Our scientists derived the principal of permittivity-drive from a sort of quantum theory, instead of by studying time dilation, the way it was done on Earth. You see, we did not have your theory of relativity. We only learned of it when we met Clifford Poluka. Our steam engines and crossbows may not reflect our understanding of mathematics but, I assure you, we've known transdimensional mathematics for over a thousand years. We simply approached problems from a different direction."

"I meant no disrespect," Braun said. "On the contrary, I am impressed. Tell me, please, what is the hull of the Fledik made of? We've been having some difficulty analyzing it."

"That is a difficult material to work with. It's what you would call a chemical element," Aga Ayab answered. He looked at Cliff Poluka for help. Cliff nodded and continued the explanation.

"This was one of those things that took quite some time for my people to understand because it deals with subatomic physics. We had to develop a vocabulary before we could even discuss it with the Arcturusian scientists.

"There is a phenomenon where subatomic virtual particles pop into existence for a fraction of picosecond, and then self-annihilate. This happens all the time all over the universe, but here in the vicinity of the local sun an exotic particle that isn't supposed to exist in our universe reacts with helium. It becomes a new element which sort of freezes in time, keeping it from annihilating even though it shouldn't exist in the first place.

"The change in the flow of time at the subatomic level gives the metal its unique toughness. Any momentum that approaches the surface of the metal is reflected. A spaceship made of this stuff can withstand an asteroid collision because the asteroid feels its own inertia turned against it."

"An exotic particle?" Braun asked. "Like a quark?"

"More like a pentaquark. The Arcturusian view of subatomic physics doesn't exactly match up with our standard model. In fact, I'm sure theirs is a better model."

Viktoriya asked, "How do you make anything from this material if it's so tough?"

"The hull of the Fledik was not built." Ayab was rather proud that his people knew something better than the Earthmen, and it showed. "Rather, it was grown on a wooden form covered with a paste of organic material which is rich with this element. A special bacteria was placed on the outer surface of the paste, and it ate its way inward, toward the wooden form, digesting the paste and leaving purified, solid metal behind. This metal shell eventually became the hull of the Fledik. The wooden form inside was broken up and removed before the interior of the ship was assembled.

"There are no rich deposits of metal ore anywhere on the surface of our planet. We only began extracting meaningful amounts of metal from the soil in the last few centuries. Tons of soil and organic material is processed, yielding a spoonful of iron, aluminum, tin, copper, and other metals. Yet, it is being done because, for some things, we simply must have metal."

"Remarkable," Chief Braun said. "This explains why so much of the Fledik was made of glass. I never would have guessed you could get permittivity-drive without knowing about time dilation, but I see now that it can be done other ways."

Viktoriya commented, "Our chemists will want to hear more about this new metal, but I was wondering why you made such an effort, especially when metal is so expensive and you had no way of knowing what you would find in space."

Oppo Gunn became very serious, "We knew that your people were there, and that our people would swiftly fade into extinction if we could not make contact. The price of metal was irrelevant compared to the alternative."

This sobered the moment, and Aguire noticed that his captain appeared to be agitated. Poluka was frowning, and had the look of someone who was desperately trying to understand something. The Captain glanced at his watch and said, "Well, gentlemen, perhaps this would be a good time for Commander Sirenko to show our guests the Fledik. We have the ship here, in our SERFS work bay."

"You brought it?" Cliff exclaimed, and almost leapt to his feet while William Emerson translated for their guests.

Aga Ayab was speechless, and the others were thrilled to see their planet's first and only spaceship again. In SERFS much of the interior furnishings of the Fledik were strapped down to the deck of the cavernous work bay outside of the now-empty hull. The gravity was turned on, and there was breathable air inside the bay now. A handful of researchers were picking over the bins of debris.

Aga Ayab wept. Even Aguire choked-up as he recognized something in the man's reaction: being a spaceman isn't an occupation, it's who you are, and your ship isn't just a machine.

Captain Poluka took an urgent call from the bridge. The communication department had strict orders to redirect all his calls. Only Washington was authorized to interrupt the meeting.

Washington's ebony face peered out of the screen when the link opened, "Captain, did you authorize a medical evacuation?"

"That's right, Commander. Doctor Payne can send as many as she deems appropriate."

"But, Captain, they've filled both the pinnace and the cruiser with patients. This is a hell of a lot of our people. When Townsend called for launch clearance, I thought it was a goddamn mutiny. Shouldn't we plan for security escorts and send inspectors first?"

"How many is she sending?"

"180, sir."

Confusion, anger, doubt, fear, and absolute confidence rolled across Paul Poluka's features in a cascade of contortions.

"180," Poluka finally repeated.

"Yes, sir."

"Well...then...it's 180. Authorize the launch."

"Captain," Aguire had been listening. "Commander Washington has a point. It wouldn't hurt to hold up the launch until we put together an escort."

"I know that," Poluka snapped at Aguire, then to Washington, "I will call Townsend myself, Commander. Have...30 security people sent to shuttles. This meeting is almost over. We'll all go down together."

Chapter 57

"Hey." O'Riley stopped shuffling a deck of cards, and gestured out of the shuttle with his chin. "Looks like something's happening."

John Burke looked. Wagons loaded with bed linens, and groups of nurses were coming from the village. A teenage boy ran up the road in long loping strides, with a small canvas pouch on his belt. Instead of going straight to the hospital, he turned aside and ran to the shuttle.

Burke went to the port hatch to see what the kid wanted. The boy was lean and lanky, built for running, and wearing short pants, a sleeveless shirt, and a cloth headband.

He surprised Burke by snapping to attention and actually saluting before handing him an envelope while making a brief announcement in the local language. Before Burke could wonder what the kid said, he was off again running to the hospital with another envelope in his hand.

"I guess he's the mailman."

"What did he bring?" O'Riley asked.

Burke opened the envelope, and found a note from Lynda Stokes who was with Hanson and her father in the royal residence.

"Holy crap. We've got a shit-load of traffic coming. Poluka's inbound right now with the pinnace, the cruiser, and a bunch of shuttles."

O'Riley punched up com links to warn the handful of personnel who were scattered around the hospital and village. Burke dragged portable lights out of storage to designate landing areas.

Ten minutes later, the sun went down with the crimson aurora lightshow in the sky. The radio noise cleared up right as night fell, and a message came through from Poluka. O'Riley reported that all was in order, and all personnel on the ground were accounted for.

"Aye, sir. Most of them are right here, and there aren't any that I haven't communicated with in the last ten minutes." O'Riley stretched the truth just a bit.

"Very good, Ensign." Poluka sounded pleased—or maybe just relieved—that he hadn't lost anyone else. "A couple of shuttles will land first, followed by the pinnace, then the cruiser. They'll have doctors and patients. Give any assistance you can to keep things orderly. I am in the pinnace with the Arcturusian delegates. The other shuttles will do a high altitude patrol where they won't disturb anyone on the ground, but still be handy if we need them."

"Aye, sir. We'll have landing lights set up before you get here."

The link closed, and Burke said to O'Riley, "Strange. I wonder how Lynda Stokes knew they were coming when the only radio that can get a message from the Hanno is in the shuttle."

O'Riley tugged on his lower lip as he considered something. "Um...I've been meaning to talk to you about her. You remember when we picked her up at the alien wreck, and her gloves were damaged?"

* * *

"Well?" Popa Utirka growled at his junior associate, a clerkish man who would never amount to much.

The others in the meeting hall with Utirka paused in their conversations to look at the fellow. He shrugged noncommittally and continued decoding the unexpected message from the Grand Matriarch that came through the public laser service. Utirka wished that his associates hadn't been here when it arrived so he could evaluate the bitch's latest edict before having to entertain their moronic opinions concerning it.

They went back to their idle talk when the answer was apparently not forthcoming.

Utirka drained his wineglass and a girl, one of Teki's students, came with a bottle to refill it.

"Thank you, my dear." He smiled. Such a nice girl: always nearby if he needed anything.

The more Utirka considered it, the more certain he was that everyone, including himself, would be better off if Elpastre succeeds in his plan. But, in many ways, the Grand Matriarch was more powerful than Elpastre, and more dangerous.

Popa Utirka's ancestors didn't perpetually walk around the world as the common people did.

Four thousand years ago, the rulers rode in gigantic wagons pulled by oxen bred for that purpose. The caravan was a grand mobile city carrying thousands of the ruling class. Their word was law, and generations of peasants devoted their lives to serving them since the beginning of history.

Millions of common folk across the land had smaller, simpler wagons. The poorest carried their possessions on their backs.

It was a glorious time when everyone learned to live in harmony and cooperation under the benevolent guidance of the rulers. At least, that was the story the clan of the Old Rulers taught to their children, and it was mostly true.

Utirka knew the more complete version of history which told how the ancient rulers—his ancestors—took for granted their supremacy. Such arrogance allowed power to fall into the hands of the prophets when The Flood ended: arrogance not forgotten when the common people chose a king, and it became engrained in the culture that no member of the Old Rulers would ever rule again.

Popa Utirka could live with that. He was rich, and he was powerful. What was there to complain about?

It was the females, Utirka was convinced, who would never be satisfied. Aylata yearned to be royalty, certain that she deserved it.

The Grand Matriarch once dreamed of marrying into royalty, but when Elpastre married a raven haired beauty from an obscure family, Aylata turned all of her energy towards rising through the ranks of Old Ruler aristocracy, until finally reaching the top.

But it wasn't enough. She saw one more step to climb, a step that was stolen from her by the current Lapastra. Aylata's revenge would be to force the royal couple into giving their daughter to her son.

Foolishness. Madness.

Utirka was not young, and remembered other Grand Matriarchs whom he was truly missing, now.

"I've got it," the clerkish man said as if confessing to a

horrible crime. It made Utirka apprehensive as he took the paper and read the secret message.

"It says here," Utirka revealed to them, "that the Grand Matriarch has gathered loyal supporters who wish to defend Arcturus against the evil earthmen. Her supporters are crossing the sea now, and they are armed with hunting weapons"

"Armed!" one of the aristocrats cried. "Are we already infected with Earth's lust for violence?"

"The Grand Matriarch," Utirka continued, "instructs me to direct these—loyal supporters—into a violent incident with the earthmen so that even the most ardent supporters of Elpastre's plan will be shocked and horrified by how evil the earthmen are."

"I don't like it," one of them said.

"We must do as she says," another insisted. "We must remain unified or we will lose this opportunity to take back what is rightfully ours."

There was some agreement, as well as some dithering, but no one dared to say the obvious, that it was a barbaric idea. Even Popa Utirka, who was, he admitted to himself, the most intelligent person present, couldn't openly refuse to obey. He cursed the timing. They'd just learned from their psychics that Paul Poluka was returning, and bringing armed guards, otherwise, he might have been able to limit an incident to something insignificant.

"Well, then," Utirka sighed, "if we're all agreed, let us go to the port, and meet this boat."

He'd been thinking about Teki's insight about the Earthmen's thoughts, about how they find horrible acts of violence to be satisfying. The thought of provoking a warrior-world's wrath did not appeal to Popa Utirka.

* * *

"Darkness is coming," Eeja Burr murmured as he sipped tea with one of the royal guardsmen at a pleasant sidewalk café called The Crossroads in the seaside district of Arvod. There was always activity here between the planter's auction house a few blocks to the south and the theater across the street to the north.

"Indeed," the middle-aged guard said without really listening. He was watching for his niece, Inna, who should be along any time now. She was a good girl who adored the royal couple, but hid her connection to them.

Her parents were from a village south of the capital, but her uncle lived here in Arvod since he was a boy. People never guessed a connection. This made Inna a valuable spy, especially since Teki Koray, the number-two psychic, brought her and some other students to assist in the Old Ruler's bid to influence Paul Poluka, and Inna was able to overhear most of the Old Ruler's strategy.

The theater doors were opened all at once by ushers in black long-coats, preparing for the evening's performance.

Eeja preferred music, but it would be a drama tonight.

The guardsman wandered over to the ticket kiosk, as if interested in who was performing. Eeja stayed with him while well-dressed people gathered to buy tickets. An attractive girl brushed by them, slipped a note into the guard's pocket, and rushed past to a noisy pub where the younger crowd flocked.

"Don't look at her, sir," the guard whispered. "It's best if no one notices."

Of course, Eeja was a better chronicler than spy. He took the note and read it, then gave it back to the guardsman with instructions to deliver it to Elpastre immediately. As for himself, he began running to the sea.

* * *

Popa Utirka glared venom at the broad avenue as he led his group through the lamp-lit town. The residents of Arvod seemed carefree compared to the capital city's minions. The people across the sea in Desin-Arcturus had an active nightlife with far more diversions, but everyone here in this village seemed to enjoy it more.

Laughter and music came from a club near the theater, drawing Utirka's attention. Through the open door he saw a young girl dancing among the other youths. He walked a few more steps before realizing she was that schoolgirl whom he liked so much. It gave him unexpected amusement to think that, in the middle of all this serious business, the girl could sneak out for dancing. Oh, to be young.

Shouts came from somewhere ahead. Down near the water, a

bell rang wildly. The cause of the commotion became evident as yellow flames licked across a building at the pier and smoke billowed skyward. Men were dragging hoses to the long dock that stretched out to deep water. Barrels of cooking oil were burning, and had somehow leaked all over the pier.

A short distance out to sea, the flames illuminated a large boat. In a flash of intuition, Utirka guessed that the fire was deliberately set to prevent Aylata's scheme. Acts of sabotage were rare on Arcturus, but not unheard of. Usually, it took a mind like Utirka's to conceive of such an option.

A man running from the pier stopped when he saw them, and then slunk away into the shadow of the trees on the south side. Utirka's companions were fixated on the fire and didn't notice, but Utirka recognized Eeja Burr. A devious possibility occurred to him that would make the Matriarch's plan unnecessary.

"The Earthmen have attacked our people," He told his group. "Spread the word."

* * *

Maria Rodriguez came out of the cruiser and strode across the damp grass, casting a long shadow in the glaring floodlight.

"Captain, Commander Washington reports that his shuttles are circling as planned, 40 klicks above us and keeping a ten kilometer radius."

"Very good, Lieutenant."

"Sir, he also said they've spotted a fire in the village. It looks like a structure on the coast is burning. There's a lot of activity, too, firefighters maybe."

He noticed the distant bell, now. It had been clanking for a while.

"Well, it's a local matter. I don't think we need to—"

The landscape suddenly lit up from a sickly-yellowish fireball that blossomed in the distance, accompanied by a much larger plume of black smoke. Indistinct shouts wafted across the village from the sea, and Paul got the uneasy feeling that the timing was too much of a coincidence. He went into the cruiser and contacted Washington.

"I'm worried this may be political, Commander. You know, not all of the people here are happy with their King's plan."

"Could be their version of terrorism, I suppose," Washington speculated. His brow furrowed with concentration as studied the view from the belly camera. "That was a stack of containers on a pier that blew a moment ago. You probably saw it from there. It's not much heat, but it's spreading…some kind of chemical fire…oil maybe. I'd like to take a closer look. I can stay a hundred meters above them, and get more information."

"Do it," Poluka said.

* * *

Etti was an attractive young woman, and well known to the King and Queen. She stopped at the royal residence in Arvod with her young son, hoping to find her husband there. It was early evening and they'd been traveling for days to get here. The guard at the gate recognized the fair-skinned brunette and her travel-weary boy.

"Etti, I didn't know you were here in Arvod."

"We've just arrived with a group on the old highway. The others are getting rooms in town, but I wanted to see my husband first. Is he here?"

"No, but he'll be at the hospital." The guard shook his head. "Etti, he's been to the starship. He went up in the morning, and has just returned. I saw the smaller ships landing a few minutes ago."

Her heart beat faster. Her husband had been thinking about Earth for a long time; part of him wanted to go there, and she was terrified that he would. A flash lit up the buildings across from the gate, followed by a rumbling sound from the waterfront. Before she could wonder what it meant, the Queen herself appeared at the door wearing a riding skirt and bundled in a woolen cape. When she saw Etti, Lapastra squeezed the woman in a quick hug.

"Etti, I know you're tired but we must run to the hospital. There is no one else here that speaks the Earthmen's language. You must tell the captain to keep his people away from the fire. Don't ask…there's no time. Please, Etti, come. Come now."

The urgency in Lapastra's voice compelled Etti into motion, and it confirmed that something terrible was happening. She pointed to her son, and said to the guard "watch him", before running with her Queen and two more guards across the street to a lane that went towards the hospital. It wasn't far, but they still didn't get there before it was too late.

Years ago, she'd seen the wreck of the Himilco, but this was her first encounter with operational spaceships. There were six of them by the hospital. The largest was bigger than the boats that cross the Vodita, and vaguely shaped like a huge insect. The next largest was like a giant turtle. The four small ones matched the description she'd heard of the Earthmen's shuttles.

Such a quantity of metal has probably never been seen anywhere on Arcturus. The sheer wealth it represented was daunting, and the possibilities their presence represented were staggering: they could save her people, as the ancient prophecies foretold, or they could bring death and misery. Or, they could take her husband away to Earth.

She saw the Queen's brother talking to an Earthman who must be the captain she'd heard so much about. Etti wanted nothing more than to fold herself into her husband's warm embrace, but Lapastra repeated the warning she wanted translated as they approached.

Oppo saw them coming, and said something that made the others turn toward them. Worry showed on their faces, but her husband's eyes flickered with pleasure when he saw her. She had to hug herself to keep from throwing herself into his arms before giving the message.

"Lapastra says that none of the Earthmen should go near the fire."

The starship captain blinked at her and asked, "Why not? We already have a shuttle moving in to look at it."

A loud chirp, like a bird might make, came from a device the captain was holding. It was a small box that fit easily in his hand. A voice came out of the box, and Etti understood that it was a communication device.

"Damn. They're shooting at us. It looks like old-fashioned cannon—hey, we're hit."

"Retreat," the captain said with sudden decisiveness. "Get out of there. Acknowledge."

"We're listing…can't climb. We'll try for the shore."

Lapastra was speaking rapidly to Oppo, explaining something. Etti was distracted by all the people gathering, and couldn't catch what she was saying. Oppo signaled for his guardsmen to gather around him.

Another Earthman appeared and said, "Hello, Etti."

It was Gus Barret, one of the crew of the Himilco, whom Etti had taught to speak the Arcturusian language.

"They're going down," the starship captain said. "I've got to send security people to the waterfront."

Etti's husband put a hand on the man's shoulder and said, "The Royal Guards are going. If you must send your own people, send them together with Oppo's people, and Gus can go along as an interpreter."

Captain Poluka gave the order to his men. They left with the green-uniformed guards led by Oppo Gunn.

Finally, her husband gestured the captain's attention to her and Lapastra. "Paul, this is Lapastra, the Queen of Arcturus, and Etti Poluka, my wife."

Chapter 58

Elisa Santino got herself temporarily reassigned to the laundry and helped those kids grow up a little. She had many faults, but callous insensitivity was not one of them, and if there was one thing she couldn't stand, it was misery.

The young rebels in the laundry had given Ensign Francis Braque a rough time at the beginning, but when his neck was broken they became despondent and dysfunctional, because Braque was their ensign.

This bunch saw themselves as the unwanted and unneeded of the universe, fit only to wash dirty socks for people who were far above them, but Elisa never considered the laundry, or these kids, trivial. Every job, especially on a spaceship, was worthwhile.

Without really trying, she passed that attitude on to them.

When they saw her weeping at the com console, the laundry came to stop. Nothing else mattered when tears were streaming down her face.

She told them the alien doctors fixed Braque's neck. He was going to be okay.

The kids cheered and danced madly atop the washing machines causing such a raucous that people came in from the corridor and neighboring facilities to find out what had happened.

Being the only officer working in the laundry, Elisa gave them the rest of the day off and they all went to the Med Center.

Braque was already sitting up and getting his color back. Each of them found a moment to say thank-you to the Arcturusians who moved quietly from bed to bed, like ethereal, exotic fairies, casting healing spells on those who had given up hope.

"They're still at it," Doctor Moorpark whispered to Elisa, "Jayne took all the brain damage and eye injury cases down to the surface. These others stayed to fix everything else. Four of them are in surgery right now, showing us their techniques. By the way, the Captain doesn't realize that they're still here. We sort of let him assume they'd all gone back to the planet with Doctor Payne."

"Why? Wouldn't Poluka agree to let them stay and help?"

"We don't really know. We were stunned that he allowed us to take patients down there at all. But it was important for other reasons that they stay onboard. As long as they're here they can talk to people about their genetic fatigue problem. Poluka doesn't want to help them."

"But they don't need his help. They just need more contact with Earth. The mating part will take care of itself without Captain Poluka's participation."

"That's assuming the people on Arcturus still want contact after Poluka's done making us look like a bunch of savages. Apparently, he doesn't like the idea of mixed-race children…pretty weird attitude for the 28th century, but there you have it."

Elisa said goodbye to Moorpark and the laundry crew, blowing Braque a kiss which made him blush, before catching up with Debra Davis, whom she'd spotted leaving the Med Center.

"Hey, Debra."

"Hey, you off duty?"

"Yeah. Why?"

"I thought I'd go up to the bridge. We poor engineers don't get out much. Besides," Debra added conspiratorially, "Commander Martensen's got the watch."

"You have a thing for Martensen?" Elisa grinned, and followed her to the speedwalk.

"Tell a soul and I'll strangle you."

"Your secret is safe." Elisa giggled. "I had no idea."

"Anyway, I don't really know him. The Nordic beast will probably break my heart." She flipped her brown ponytail, and clutched her chest in feigned distress while fluttered her eyelashes. "Then I'll have to find someone else to be infatuated with."

"Who knows, maybe he'll be Prince Charming." Elisa said. She wondered how her relationship with Luther Braun would end, and it would have to end soon. He was incredibly nice, but…he's older than her father.

The Forward Section was dimly lit and quiet. It was the beginning of the night shift. Ensign Wong was running the S-Bay.

Henry Tran was hanging out with the techs in the I-Bay, unable to relax and call it a day after meeting aliens. Ensign Blossom Hill was at the pilot's station, scanning through old news stories in the database.

"Good evening, Commander," Debra said in her silkiest voice.

Martensen turned his head and smiled. "Hello, ladies. Is this a social call?"

"Definitely. We don't get up here often enough."

"It's quiet. The medical group landed half an hour ago, and our people got straight into treatment. It's miraculous what these aliens can do. I hope we can return the favor, and help them with their problem."

"What do you think of this genetic fatigue thing?" Debra asked Martensen. "I mean, if they're basically human and it's happening to them, could it happen to us?"

"I'm not sure I even understand what it is. I mean, is it just inbreeding, or is there more to it than that?"

Wong overheard and came out of the S-Bay. "They started with a few million people, right? So, after four or five thousand years they've completely homogenized their genes, and there's no one to marry that's not related. They've got genetic-drift problems, like we had on Earth after the Great Disaster."

Henry Tran joined the discussion. "It's a statistical problem. A man on Arcturus could find a woman who doesn't have a common ancestor within the last, say, five generations, but that ancestor had the same problem a century earlier, and it's been that way almost from the beginning. But, apparently, there's more to it…something like a countdown to sterility with each generation."

"Okay," Elisa picked up the conjecture. "But is it going to happen to us someday?"

Tran became pensive before replying. "It's not impossible. We should find out what the Arcturusians have learned about it."

"If they're all related," Wong wondered, "shouldn't they all look alike? I'm Chinese and I still have features like my ancestors—maybe not as clearly as my distant ancestors—but I probably won't be mistaken for a German."

"Appearance may not be an important indicator," Tran said. "I'm Vietnamese—maybe 50 percent—but I could pass for German. Maybe before the Disaster it was different. I've seen pictures of people from before the Disaster, and their racial features were really pronounced, a lot more so than nowadays."

Martensen leaned back in the command chair and looked at the planet through the front view port. "The Corps will need to send researchers and set up a permanent base on the surface. With ongoing contact, the genetic problem will gradually go away."

"If that ever happens," Elisa said softly. Martensen looked a question at her, and she continued. "This is a tangled mess. The monarch of this world wants contact, but he can't just command it. They've got complex social issues. People down there are concerned about the cultural and moral questions, not to mention the scientific considerations of introducing genes from Earth into their population. From what I've heard, there's also a power struggle brewing that may upset the foundation of their civilization.

"Then there's our side of the problem. We have a totally screwed up government that will look at these people the same way they see the primitives on Earth—that they should just let the New Fed run their lives and tell them what to do.

"Commander Redbird said that contact with Earth could be disastrous for these people, but none of us really got the point. I think I get it now. The New Fed may well decide to simply take this planet as a new resource, and justify ignoring the rights of the natives because they don't seem to be able to survive with our help. Besides, we have the military strength to just insist on whatever we want."

While she spoke, Ensign Hill turned from her pilot's controls, and stared at her with such intensity that Elisa felt that she'd somehow offended the girl.

"Ensign?"

Blossom Hill was the youngest officer on the ship. Her short stature and chubby-cheeked baby face made people not take her too seriously, but she stood up and spoke her mind as though the others didn't vastly outrank her.

"We can't just turn this over to the government. The New Federation lies, steals and murders every chance they get."

On Earth, no one dared say "murder" publicly to describe the New Fed's actions, but this girl was saying it now. Hill's hands curled into fists at her sides, and her voice quavered as she got louder. "They kill people every day to build the fantasy world they want—a world where they have absolute power—a world where they can treat us as slaves. All those primitives on Earth aren't dying because they're doing anything bad; they're dying because they don't need the government, and the New Federation can't tolerate anyone that doesn't need them.

"The people of Arcturus aren't going to be absorbed...or reeducated...to fit the model." Her words start coming in big, shouting sobs. "They're gonna be exterminated like cockroaches if we tell anyone about them. Right now, the only people who know they exist are here. If we go back and report about these people, it can only result in their absolute annihilation."

The techs in the I-Bay were like statues, watching the bridge. The S-Bay crew was peeking around the corner to see the commotion. Elisa's mouth hung open in shock at the diminutive girl's outburst, and the passion with which she delivered it. She gave a sideways look at Commander Martensen, half-expecting him to tear into Hill for it.

"As I recall," Martensen scrutinized the young woman with brooding eyes. "They murdered your parents."

Elisa blinked in surprise when he chose the same verb that Hill used.

Ensign Hill's eyes were overflowing as she nodded, "The coup...my mom was a captain in the Old Guard. She was the first one to die. After it was all over, they killed dad, too."

The Army's Old Guard traditionally protected the Capitol. There wasn't a single person left alive in the Old Guard. Family members were arrested—and quietly executed—just to keep things tidy. It wouldn't do to have hundreds of survivors that could condemn the new leaders and draw sympathy from the masses. Elisa wondered how Blossom Hill had escaped. But, of course, she hadn't: she was assigned to the Starship Hanno.

Lieutenant Buckmaster's voice cut in over the intercom from Communications.

"Bridge...We've got a shuttle down. They're under attack. I'm patching it through now."

Only Martensen reacted for a moment. His hands flew across his keyboard, and brought up a split-screen display of transcripts from several radio sources on the main screen. It showed the last five minutes of conversations that led up to the current transmission.

At the same instant, the relayed voice of Captain Poluka broke into the ambiance of the bridge.

"...all other personnel report to the pinnace."

The I-Bay techs began a vain attempt to see through the atmosphere, and Ensign Hill returned to the pilot's station.

A woman's amplified voice came through, and the scrolling transcript indicated it was Major Rivers. "We can see the shuttle. There's a crowd gathering nearby."

"Washington here. No one is hurt. I think we can get airborne in a few minutes."

"We copy that, Commander," Rivers came back. "Our local escort wants to move closer...get between the shuttle and the crowd."

"Copy. I see you."

"Poluka here. Rivers, ask Oppo Gunn why the boat fired on the shuttle, but avoid causing another incident."

"Yes, sir."

Elisa and Debra retreated to the back of the bridge as more officers began showing up. The report must have shown up on screens all over the ship. Even Major Doyle, the Army chemist, showed up.

He took a position in the back, with Elisa and Debra. Soon, there were a dozen officers standing around, anxiously waiting for more information. Doyle was the ranking Army officer onboard until Major Rivers returned from the planet, and Debra, who'd been reading the transcripts, quickly brought him up to speed:

"Apparently, a fire broke out on a pier. Commander Washington thinks it was arson, and took his shuttle closer to have a look, but a ship—not a spaceship but a sea vessel—opened fire on him with some sort of projectile weapon. The shuttle was hit, and went down on the shore. Major went in to give them some cover. They had to go with an escort provided by the local authority."

"An alien escort?" Doyle asked. "Alien soldiers?"

"Major, you really should read the daily logs. They don't have any army. These are guards—like bodyguards—for the royal family."

"The aliens have a royal family?"

"Jeez, Doyle, get out of the lab more often."

Rivers' voice came through again.

"Captain, things are looking ugly here. There are some people who are accusing us of setting fire to the pier. Someone's saying that Commander Washington fired on the boat, and the boat captain fired back in self-defense. The crowd is getting angry."

"Damn. Stay with your escort, Major. If they can handle the crowd, keep our people out of it. Get back to the hospital as soon as possible."

"Yes, sir."

"Washington here. We're flying. Major Rivers, you don't need to concern yourself with the shuttle anymore."

"Copy that. We are on our way back. The guards are staying with us."

Chapter 59

Paul Poluka deferred to Commander Washington on security issues, and to Doctor Payne on medical issues. In fact, he deferred to just about anybody who was willing to accept some responsibility. At Aguire's urging, the Captain got some sleep, and let others keep an eye on things through the night.

They didn't wake him in the morning. It wasn't until after breakfast and Aguire was informed that some of the patients could return to the Hanno, that the first-officer went to where Paul Poluka was softly snoring inside El Toro.

"Anything else happening?" Poluka asked when he was roused and heard the news. He rolled out of the bunk, and groped for his boots.

"It seems the King and Queen will have to go to the capital for a formal meeting with the nobles about further contact with Earth. It's not looking like he'll get much support."

"Okay," Poluka murmured. "You know, José, I've really fucked up everything. Even if the New Fed didn't already hate me, they'd still have my ass for how I've handled this mission."

"Captain," Aguire began, "you don't have to—"

"Bullshit. I've got 207 dead because I wouldn't listen to my officers. I disregarded good advice and needlessly sent six shuttles into danger, resulting in two crash landings and one destroyed shuttle. I screwed up the first contact with the only alien civilization we've ever found and created a political crisis for the alien government.

"I appreciate that you and the doctors have kept it quiet about the pills, but any investigation—and you can bet there'll be one—will show that my judgment was affected by a drug that I was using illegally. Even in the best of times, they'd have my head on a pole for what I've done."

Aguire didn't know what to say. Poluka was right. Finally, he asked, "Where did you get the pills, anyway?"

"I bought them from a primitive near my dad's farm in California. Primitives are called boxers there, because they build homes out of shipping containers at the edge of the city. This guy—a primitive—was selling hot-dogs from a push-cart on the street. I made some comment to him about being so skinny while he's selling food. He told me about zippies, and sold some to me. A few days before the mission, I went back and bought more."

"I thought you didn't like primitives."

"I don't, but I don't like being fat even more. Listen, what I'm getting at is that I don't think we'll even get a chance to report on this mission. We're all on the Fed's black list, and we're not supposed to survive this mission. Henry Tran analyzed some data from when we left the Solar System, and it seems that the convoy of ships we passed was probably General Hebert leading an attack on Earth."

"What? Earth could be under attack—right now?"

"Exactly, and we could be back there in a matter of days. A ship like the Hanno could make a big difference. This could be our chance to topple the New Federation, and restore some order. What to do about these aliens will just have to wait until the dust settles."

Aguire wasn't sure he heard right. Poluka wanted to go in on the side of revolution against his own government? It may be a bad government at the moment, but this wouldn't be another coup with limited bloodshed. This would be a real war.

Poluka's original plan, according to Chief Braun, was to act as some kind of coordinator, getting the colonies to unite against the New Fed. Aguire hadn't yet worked out if he liked even that plan. A direct attack against Earth's planetary defenses didn't take as much head-scratching; it would be suicide, especially when the problems may not even need a military solution.

He'd followed Paul Poluka's lead for the last eleven years, always confident that the Captain knew what was best. The confidence ended here.

On the lawn outside, Jayne Payne was waiting with Doctor Pamm, the director of the Arcturusian hospital. Both were in high spirits, and smiling through their exhaustion. Poluka gave the go-ahead to load 110 patients onto the cruiser. This time, the wounded walked on their own.

Despite his other worries, Aguire smiled broadly as a long line of men and women walked stiffly across the grass, dressed in the white linen robes provided by their healers. They were pale, and dazed perhaps, but far better than the vegetative state they arrived in.

Lieutenant Tully had a recorder, and caught the moment for posterity. Aguire stayed outside until El Toro disappeared into the western sky, racing to the night side of the planet, and then up to the Hanno.

"Tomorrow," Doctor Payne told Poluka, "the other 70 patients will be ready to go. We've gotten valuable knowledge from these people, Captain, and there's a lot more we could learn from them."

It seemed she wanted to say something more, but dared not to.

Doctor Pamm approached Poluka with Hank Rodriguez acting as his translator.

"Captain Poluka," Pamm said, "we are happy that we could provide our services to your people. All of us wish to continue working together for our mutual benefit."

"That is my wish as well," Poluka replied stiffly.

They went into the hospital together and reviewed what had been accomplished. When they broke for lunch, they got a surprise visit from a group of about 50 people that included at least 20 small children. They were wives, children, and some in-laws of the crew of Clifford's starship, the Himilco.

Everyone gathered where a buffet was hastily set up between the hospital and the pinnace. Lynda and her father joined Aguire, while Clifford Poluka introduced his brother to the group.

Some of the children were infants, and as cute as any babies anywhere. The oldest, Ivan Tershensky's boy, was about eight years old, and could speak some English and Russian. Maria Rodriguez met her two-year-old cousin, a round-faced girl with big inquisitive eyes. Hank Rodriguez's wife was a curvaceous beauty with silky black hair.

Paul Poluka was smiling diplomatically as each woman was introduced. Etti Poluka he'd already met, but when his sandy-haired, cherub-faced, smiling nephew was introduced, the Skipper surprised everyone by picking the boy up and wrapping him in a big hug. The boy loved it. Clifford's eyes got misty and he could hardly continue the introductions.

"I'm going to have to give up being a pessimist if this gets any better," G.J. said dryly.

"I know what you mean," Lynda agreed. "Where'd Gentry get to? He knows all these people. He should be here."

Aguire pointed. "Here he comes."

Lynda glanced to where her brother was approaching them before returning her attention to the next person being introduced: a sturdy looking young woman whose clothes seemed more nondescript and rustic than the others. She was good looking, but not beautiful, with a kind and honest face, and seemed strangely familiar, as if Lynda had seen her before, somewhere.

The woman had a girl about six years old, and a boy about seven that stood out because of their lovely turquoise eyes. Most of the people here had brown eyes of various shades. A few had bluish or hazel eyes, but these kids were different. In fact, they looked kind of like—like Gentry!

Lynda's own eyes popped wide open in sudden comprehension.

"Papa…Lynda," Gentry said, "This is Ella, my wife, Cassi, my daughter, and William, my son. He prefers to be called Willy."

Ella held her kids hands, and stood with apprehension in her hazel eyes while Gentry completed the introduction in her language. Lynda's intuition told her the woman had picked up clues over the years that there was something unpleasant about Gentry's relatives. She snuck a quick look at Papa, and confirmed he was frozen in shock. She stepped forward with a warm smile and embraced her sister-in-law.

"I am so happy to meet you," Lynda cried enthusiastically, while gently turning the woman away from Papa, giving him the instant he needed to take the hint.

The old man stepped forward, hesitant at first, a shy smile flickering before becoming a genuine grin that lasted the rest of the day.

Chapter 60

Bart Hanson poked his head into Aguire's office, and said, "All personnel are accounted for, Commander."

Aguire looked up from the computer. Lynda saw he had weary, red eyes.

She'd stayed with her brother's family all day yesterday, and started getting to know them. She found out why Ella seemed familiar when they first met. Ella was the first officer on the Arcturusian ship, and Lynda had seen her in the ten year old video that Cliff left in the thruster. This morning, Lynda was giving them some time to settle into their new quarters on the Hanno.

"All aboard who's coming aboard, Mister Hanson?" Aguire managed a smile.

"Aye, sir," Bart responded softly. "I guess it's for the best that they stayed behind."

"For now, anyway." Aguire pushed himself away from his desk and looked at Arcturus-4 through the Radglass. "I'm kind of surprised, though, that even the ones who didn't marry local girls don't want to go home yet. Some say they'll visit Earth later. At least Lynda's brother is coming with us."

"For now, anyway," Lynda said. "He'll want to bring his family back here. This is their home…and now his, too. At least I'll know where to find him."

"Yeah, I suppose that's true enough. Still, I'll bet it's a hard choice when you're an heir to the Stokes business empire."

"Oh, that reminds me," Bart added. "Cliff Poluka made a suggestion to the Captain about sending a gift to Elpastre, sort of like a goodwill gesture."

"A gift? What was it?"

"About ten tons of metal, mostly iron, copper, and tin ingots, but also some gold, silver and platinum. Cliff says Elpastre can distribute it among the nobles to foster some desire to see us return."

Aguire sighed, nodding his approval. There were hundreds of people aboard the Hanno who'd been given another chance because of Arcturusian medical expertise. Some metal was the least they could do in return.

"I guess we'll be leaving orbit soon. I better get to the bridge."

"You're exhausted," Lynda told him as they went together.

"Everyone is, I think."

They found Commander Washington at the command desk directing the retrieval of several pixie probes.

"I'd completely forgotten about those," Aguire said. "It's been just a few days since we deployed them to study the atmosphere…seems like a lot longer."

"Poluka's making the rounds," Washington told him. "You know, like he used to on the Livingston just before starting a voyage."

As if on cue, Poluka showed up then. Lynda's father and brother came in next and sat with her in the observer chairs. They'd left Ella and the kids in the library with Commander Redbird.

Washington wanted to meet with his staff. "We need to go over the reports on contacts with the indigenous people. There's something bothering me about all this."

"Something about the local politics?" Poluka asked.

"Actually, sir, it's their history—ancient history—I know we've got recordings of the official meetings where they told about their history, but I want to see if anyone's picked up any additional information through all the contact we've had. I don't even know yet how many of our people spoke with them, especially since we had their doctors aboard."

"I'm scheduling a meeting about it anyway. A couple of hours after reaching the Zone, we'll have everyone who's had any contact with the native people meet in the conference hall."

Maria Rodriguez was at the pilot's station sniffling quietly and wiping tears from her face.

"Captain?" Aguire said just before Poluka gave the order to break orbit.

"What is it, Commander?"

"With your permission, Captain, I would like to pilot the ship to our next stop."

This got a raised eyebrow from Poluka, but he caught the look of gratitude Maria gave Aguire, and understood that it was hard for her to leave her uncle behind.

"Lieutenant Rodriguez, if you have no objection, Mister Aguire will be driving today."

"No objection, Captain," Maria answered huskily, and moved from the pilot's station.

Aguire steered the giant ship away from the planet, and followed a meandering course the engineers had requested to record data about other planets in the system, and to collect some particles near the star. Major Doyle specifically asked for samples from the red giant's magnetosphere, and Chief Braun was making a project out of the innermost planet.

During all this, Captain Poluka was quiet, but focused on the ship's operations. Lynda was starting to appreciate just what a good actor Paul was—or maybe he was just good at compartmentalizing. Leaving Cliff must bother him as much as it pained Maria to leave her uncle behind. If they return to Earth he'll either be punished for how he discharged his duties, or join a civil war against his own government. Surely it must be distracting.

Three hours passed before the Hanno was clear of the star system. Papa whispered descriptions of the Hanno's capabilities, and told Gentry how Lynda helped with the starship's construction. Her brother listened, and kept looking at her.

Finally, Gentry said to her, "You would have made a marvelous engineer, but I'm glad you chose to study law instead." Lynda could see Papa was surprised, but there was no time to ask about it.

Poluka made his customary "Ladies and Gentlemen" announcement to the crew, and the steel armor closed the front window, cutting off the view.

The countdown reached zero and the navigation display blanked-out for a moment before showing the Hanno had moved one light-year towards Earth. The ramifications of the capability were daunting; they could travel to any colony anywhere—and to another—and another—all in a day's work.

At the very least, it would change how people felt about Earth, the home world of everyone, except the Arcturusians. If this technology existed when Vincent Batastia staged the coup against the Federation, everyone all down the trade route could have heard about it the same day, instead of months later. Their approval—or disapproval—would have been felt on Earth immediately.

The navigator announced, "We are now six light-hours from the center of the Zone."

"Excellent," Paul Poluka sighed with polite disinterest. "The master probe should be five and a half light hours distant. That's an eleven hour round trip for a radio signal. Mister Tran, please contact the probe. When we get some data to analyze, we shall consider sending new programming to the probes, and leave them to continue studying the field while we drop in on Earth."

"How long do you expect we'll be here, Captain?" Aguire asked.

"Oh, two days—three at most, meanwhile, the scientists and engineers can busy themselves with long-range observations. Maria, you may open the window."

The armor peeled back, exposing a view of Sagittarius ahead. Sol, their home star, was a bright point 35 light-years away. The asteroid field occupied about four and a half degrees in the field of view with the naked eye—about the size of a tennis ball held at arm's length, and looked fairly safe from this distance.

For most others, it was a chance for a little relaxation. Captain Poluka turned the management of the Hanno over to Commander Garcia, and then left for the Med Center to see how his people were doing.

Aguire turned to Lynda's group, and asked, "What do you say we all go to lunch?"

"Thank you, Commander, but we left Ella and my grandchildren in the Library." G.J. Stokes had a special ring in his voice when he said my grandchildren.

"We could meet them, and go all together to the aft cafeteria," Aguire suggested.

There were nods all around. As they strolled along the speedwalk, Lynda's father and Aguire took the lead, and chatted about possible improvements to the Hanno, such as adding more major corridors like Main Street, on other decks. Gentry and Lynda walked behind them.

Gentry asked her if she had close friends on Earth.

"Oh, you know," she answered. "There were some girls in college I hung out with sometimes, but I've really made some friends here, onboard the Hanno."

"Yes? Anyone special?" Gentry made a gesture that she didn't quite understand. She looked a question at him. He repeated the gesture, pointing ahead at Aguire, and raised his eyebrows. She felt her face heat with what must have been a record breaking blush, and shook her head vigorously.

Her face cooled by the time they reached the library. Cassi was leafing through magazines looking at pictures. Ella was sitting with Commander Redbird, who was showing little Willy how to select videos for viewing. They were in the middle of one about African wildlife, but didn't mind breaking for lunch.

"Would you care to join us, Commander?" Gentry suggested.

"Please do." Ella smiled. Her English was good, with a subtle, pleasant accent.

"I'd love to and, please, call me Joseph."

The lunch crowd was small, but it was still early. Some medical techs were there, and some people from CEFR, the ship's main power source. A group of tugboat pilots were having a meeting in a corner. Ensigns O'Riley and Burke were sipping coffee on the other side of the room.

The aft cafeteria was as big as the forward café—about 500 square meters—but had no windows. Instead, the walls were 3-D panoramas programmed with nature scenes from Earth. The current images were desert landscapes.

Lynda followed Ella through the serving line. She had become fiercely protective of her brother's wife and children. Gentry had always been miserable, at least since their parents separated, and his unhappiness drove him away—so far away that, for ten years, no one knew what had become of him.

He was truly happy now. She could see it in his eyes whenever he looked at his new family, or even when he talked about them. Lynda wanted to be close to them, and wanted them to feel good about her being close.

Gentry was a handsome man and, being also rich, he could have had any sort of wife he wanted on Earth. Lynda was sure he could have chosen one of the many beautiful women on Arcturus. Yet, he married a woman who was rather plain-looking. It could only be true love.

Papa was being uncharacteristically civilized, and totally charmed by his grandchildren. Gentry had been the first to bring up that business of Papa having him arrested and put in the mental hospital. He made it crystal-clear that he understood Papa's reasons and—though he thought it was a mistake—he forgave Papa, and held no grudges. Papa cried when he heard it, and since then there's been a carefree bounce in his step. He seemed years younger.

The kids got burgers and fries, which Gentry said were similar on Arcturus, though their potatoes were smaller and sweeter, and the burgers were served open-faced with beef that was more like buffalo.

Ella was wary, but everyone insisted that she sample everything. The kids were happy with the burgers and it was clear they intended to go back for dessert. Commander Aguire got an aromatic Spanish dish called paella. Joseph Redbird chose turkey with mashed potatoes. Lynda got the same as the kids.

"Doctor Stokes," Aguire said when Ella and the children went to look at the sweets. "I wanted to talk to you about our return to Earth."

"If it's about the reception we'll get from the government, I've been thinking about it, too. And call me G.J.."

"Did you know that General Hebert may have brought a group of small ships into the system just as we were leaving?"

G.J. frowned and rubbed his jaw. "Yes, I'd heard."

So had Lynda, but she hadn't given it much thought. At first, it didn't seem to affect them because their original plan was to go to the colonies down the trade route. Later, when she heard Paul was planning to return to Earth, they'd been in the middle of a crisis with the Arcturusians and there was no time to think about it.

Gentry looked back and forth between Aguire and his father. "Is this a problem? I wasn't told anything about it."

"The Captain has…suggested," Aguire said quietly, looking around the cafeteria to see if anyone was close by, "that he would favor using the Hanno to support General Hebert in an insurrection against the New Federation."

"What?" G.J. gasped. "The Hanno isn't a warship. Even a heavy-cruiser could destroy us. He should consult me before making any such plans."

Gentry shifted uncomfortably but said nothing. Behind him, Ella was 20 meters away with the children, looking at pastries, but Lynda saw her turn suddenly and give her husband's back a worried look. Lynda wondered if her sister-in-law had some psychic ability.

"I don't think we need a military solution," Aguire said. "It would make the Jupiter War look like a sideshow. We still have a democracy. It may not be working very well at the moment, but the new government can still be fixed using legal, peaceful methods."

"Oh, I doubt that, Commander, but I'm certain the Hanno should avoid any sort of combat. If we go to the Solar System, but stay far from Earth, we could learn what's going on and still be able to leave without getting involved. I think that would be the prudent thing at this point. After all, we do need to know what's happening."

"Agreed," Aguire said. "You know, since returning from the frontier, I've had my head buried in the sand concerning the New Fed. I'm trying to catch up now with all the changes. I should talk to Commander Donno."

"Why him?" Lynda asked. Gentry—still quiet—looked at Aguire expectantly.

"Because," Aguire answered, "he pays a lot more attention to the big picture—politically speaking—without having an axe to grind. He'll give me an unbiased evaluation. Besides, he's my best friend."

"I trust Commander Donno," Redbird added.

Ella and the kids returned to the table with a platter of desserts for everyone. She cast a worried look at each of them before sitting down next to Gentry.

"So," Lynda smiled at Willy and Cassie, "what did you choose for dessert?"

"Ice cream," Cassie held up a bowl as evidence. She had Gentry's face, and could speak a little English. Willie spoke only the Arcturusian language and looked more like Ella. He was named after William Emerson, Gentry's best friend. Cassie was named after Lynda and Gentry's mother, Cassandra.

Papa had said nothing about it.

"I should to do some catching up, too," Gentry said. "But I doubt if your ship's library will give the unbiased view that you expect from Mister Donno. Do you think I could just talk to some of the crew, and get their opinions about this New Federation?"

"You're perfectly free to talk to anyone you wish," Aguire answered. "But we will be leaving the Zone in a couple of days, and I expect at some point before then Captain Poluka will call all his officers together and tell them his plans. He'll need nearly unanimous support to take us into battle—especially against our own government. It may not be all that difficult for him. This entire crew is on the Fed's black list. They expected us to die on this mission."

"Yes, I know." Gentry grimaced. "My father explained it to me, though I didn't quite understand why the new government would have such a list, or why they'd actually kill people for being on it. I guess I've always been a bit naïve."

Ella was listening intently, but her attention suddenly shifted to someone approaching behind Lynda and her eyes narrowed in apprehension.

"Commander Aguire." The baritone voice of Commander Washington interrupted the conversation. Lynda turned to see him.

"Commander?" Aguire responded.

"The Captain scheduled a meeting to review our experience with the aliens." Washington noticed Ella and the children before adding, "I mean…the Arcturusians."

Ella's grip on Gentry's hand tightened slightly, and Gentry asked in an ice-cold tone, "May I sit in on this meeting, Commander?"

"Actually, Mister Stokes, you are invited, as is everyone who's had any contact with the…natives." Washington matched his coldness. "The meeting will commence at 0200 hours in the conference hall. If you'll excuse me, I need to see a few more people before then."

Washington crossed the cafeteria to where Burke and O'Riley were seated.

Redbird whispered to Aguire, "I disagree about democracy being the answer, Commander. I think a war will have to be fought sooner or later and, frankly, it scares the hell out of me. If you don't mind, I'm going to talk to Viktoriya. I value her opinion the way you value Donno's."

Gentry and Ella stayed in the cafeteria to speak with some people. Aguire returned to his office, and G.J. went back to his quarters with the kids. Commander Redbird disappeared towards SERFS.

Lynda had a hunch about the rules concerning authority in the Exploration Corps, and went to the library to check it out.

Chapter 61

The clamor of voices in the foyer surprised Aguire. Close to 200 people were clustered in groups as he emerged from his office. They were thickest down by the conference hall where the crowd was squeezing through the doors like sand through an hourglass.

Amid all the uniforms, he spotted G.J. and Gentry. Lynda was with them, but he almost missed her now that she was wearing a blue-on-gray jumpsuit and had her hair in a braided ponytail. She had no patches or insignia, but otherwise could have passed for a crewmember. He suppressed a smile and wondered if Lynda was considering a new career.

The hall was a small auditorium with tiered seating that slopped down from the smoked-glass walls of the foyer to a stage with a podium. The Captain was already there, arranging notes and greeting his executive officers as they took their seats.

Aguire sat next to Sheffield and watched the hall fill with the hundreds of people who'd met aliens. Like himself, many here had been treated by alien doctors for crippling injuries, but were now fit to return to duty.

Lynda, Gentry, and G.J. were in the front row with the Lieutenant Commanders. Donno arrived as Poluka tapped the microphone, producing a muffled thud-thud, and getting everyone to hush. Commander Washington hurried in at the last moment.

Meetings of this sort happen after every mission, though usually less formally, with only a handful of people, but this mission had been one screw-up after another, and no one kept good track of events since the first shuttle launch. From Aguire's perspective, it had all been horribly unprofessional.

"Thank you all for coming," Poluka said with his usual bland smile. "We will briefly review what we've learned of the Arcturusian people. I won't belabor the importance of the last several days. When we announce our discovery, it will be most helpful, and reflect well on this ship, if our information is complete and consistent.

"Each crewmember's report has been reviewed by a commander and combined into summaries. In the next few days, we will combine each commander's summary into a single document that will contain every significant observation made during this mission.

"At this meeting, each commander will present his or her summary to all of us, and point out any gaps in information that should be addressed. It may be that one of you has a missing piece of information without realizing it. It's also possible that some of you may spot a problem that no one else has noticed. There will be an opportunity for suggestions before the final report is drafted.

"Mister Tran will begin with brief overview of the planetary system, focused primarily on the fourth planet. This will be followed by the three commanders—Aguire, Sheffield and Donno—who first landed on the planet. Then, we will hear from Major Rivers and Commander Washington. Finally, Doctor Payne will talk about our contact with Arcturusian doctors, and their medical capabilities."

Tran gave a concise review of the physical attributes of the system with particular attention to the strange atmosphere of the fourth planet. He would have diverged to talk about the Zone, but Poluka said that could wait until the data from the robot probes were analyzed.

Sheffield's description of the shuttle crash, and the giant wildlife on the continent the natives call Navost-Fledik had everyone's attention, and he showed a short video of the gigantic fish that they'd spotted just before his shuttle was attacked by it.

At this point, Captain Poluka interrupted to ask Gentry Stokes, "What does the word Fledik mean?"

Gentry stood and answered, "Fledik is a species of bird which always migrates from west to east, probably as a leftover instinct from the Epoch of the Flood. However, the Fledik's eggs or babies have never been seen. The adult birds cross the continent where people live, and then continue across the sea.

"When they've circled the planet, they return to the west coast with new, young birds that were born on the other continent,

Navost-Fledik, which means Birthland of the Fledik.

"This is how the people first came to suspect there was another continent, and later a few explorers actually discovered it by sailing around the world in small ships."

"How long ago was that?" Poluka asked.

"Um...I think about a hundred local years ago...make it around 1500 Earth years."

"Fascinating. I'm looking forward to hearing much more of their history but, for now, we should continue with Commander Aguire's report."

Aguire went to the podium and gave a brief description of penetrating the atmospheric barrier and showed videos of abandoned farms and giant carnivorous plants. But it was his retelling of the encounter in the forest, and the alien guards' reaction to being fired upon, that had them riveted.

He commented on the shortcomings of the Hanno's shuttles, and suggested that future missions have rugged secondary vessels, perhaps a fleet of light-cruisers, like El Toro.

Donno's account of meeting the child princess was fascinating, bringing smiles to most faces when he showed a recording of the crowned girl's charming official greeting to the visitors from Earth. Aguire made a note to ask Gentry about the history of the monarchy which was crucial in understanding the politics of Arcturus.

Donno had some fabulous aerial pictures of the capital city which he displayed on the big screen, as well as images of the equatorial desert, the pyramid, and the village of Arvod. He concluded by announcing that a list was available on the ship's computer net of Arcturus's products and industries. He invited everyone to review it and to add anything they could think of.

Major Rivers gave a good overview of all activity from the landing in Arvod, up to the delivery of several tons of metal ingots as a gift to the monarch. She wrapped up her part of the presentation with an opinion about the inequalities between Arcturus and Earth.

"It is evident," she said, "that we should be cautious in making sweeping judgments about these people. There are obvious differences in technology and resources but, while we may have superiority in some areas, the Arcturusians are clearly more advanced in others.

"They have built a civilization with a lack of rich metal deposits, which took them on a technological path very different from our own, but even more than the lack of metal, I believe their early history of needing to cooperate, rather than compete, for survival has had the greater effect. Though they are arguably the same species as we are, they are truly alien in some ways. That is not to say they are better or worse, more or less advanced, good or bad. It simply means that we must not presume to understand their culture or their capabilities too quickly."

This got a murmur of agreement from the crew as the Major sat down, and Commander Washington went to the podium with pages of notes. Though Aguire was the first-officer, Washington had more years of service, and was the Captain's friend long before Aguire. The only reason Washington wasn't a first-officer—or even a captain—was because he didn't want it. He left the hectic mission operations in younger hands, and focused on the bureaucratic side of running a starship. On this occasion, he jumped right in with more energy than Aguire expected.

Washington's brisk review of his people's actions, and their contact with the locals was more like a police report than a sociological summary. He focused on how this discovery could benefit Earth. The mention of the attack on his shuttle (with what turned out to be a gunpowder weapon, using polymer projectiles, and designed for defending boats against the giant fishes of Arcturus) emphasized that it was "unprovoked and resulting from a volatile political situation, reminiscent of the days when Earth was ruled by warlords".

Aguire thought he was way of the mark with that assessment. Gentry was surprised by the comparison, too.

Washington concluded with, "There are a number of things we absolutely must know more about. This psychic ability some women seem to possess will have a tremendous impact on our future contact and will surely affect how our own society operates, just as it affects theirs, by giving advantages to those who control it, while placing those who don't at a disadvantage. The information we have so far indicates that only a small percentage of women have the ability—and we can't tell which women those are."

He glanced at Gentry Stokes, who stared back stonily, before continuing.

"Perhaps of even greater importance are their ancient records. We have woefully scant information—vague references and hints—concerning a vastly more powerful alien race called the Erosians. After studying what little we learned of them, I suspect these Erosians are responsible for the creation of the Zone. After running our data on the Zone through an analysis, I found its appearance may coincide with the date of the Great Disaster of the 22nd century."

The crowd stirred uncomfortably. Aguire, too, felt a stab of anxiety.

The Disaster happened in the distant past—six centuries past—yet still lingered in every person's mind as an apocalyptic horror, not as a prophecy that may happen someday, but as an historical fact that forcibly reshaped civilization after violently ripping it apart.

No one saw it coming or knew what caused it. The survivors learned over many years that something happened in the Chinese desert where all of the world's electric power was produced in those days. A seismic shock wave shook the world, destroying cities. The initial destructive force was felt around the globe within the first 24 hours. Power and communications went down almost immediately. It was years before people knew how bad it was.

Each group of survivors had its own name for the event, but eventually the history books would simply call it "The Great Disaster of the Twenty Second Century".

The Americas were the least affected and, even there, civilization crumbled without a world economy and electric power.

The climate was ruined for decades. Crops failed. Sickness and hunger killed many. Diseases, injuries, and other health problems not only went untreated, the knowledge of medicine almost disappeared in a single generation. By the year 2200, the population was down to 300 million worldwide. The Amazon Basin had some small cities and towns, but scattered villages were the normal communities.

Eight billion died in the first century, half of them in the first 24 hours.

Only the poorest and most technology-independent cultures continued seamlessly, though not entirely unaffected. Specifically, the native Indians of North and South America, who had been the most disadvantaged of peoples, survived the best.

Places already accustomed to harsh conditions, like remote cities in mountains, still suffered tremendously and their populations decreased, but the numbers never fell below what was necessary for passing knowledge to the next generation. Specific knowledge of science and technology was still lost or obscured because it wasn't actually used anymore. Some things were forever lost. Others had to be rediscovered.

The most fortunate communities reached out to others, and began to spread assistance. Memories of worldwide communications urged people everywhere to reestablish links, but they couldn't manufacture new high-tech devices. Things like computers were never made to last more than a decade, so in about a century mostly gone, and no one knew how to make one from scratch.

It was a low-tech world for centuries. Outside of the few towns and villages that were once great cities, farming communities sprang up, as well as brutal warlords. Outside even these rustic areas, nomadic hunter-gatherers roamed the wilderness making tools from chips of stone, and wearing animal skins.

The 24th century found mankind the way it had been in the tenth century, except they had radios linking people together, and stories of how things had been before the Disaster. Progress was steady after that, but the memory of the Great Disaster still affected them now that they were exploring the galaxy in the 28th century.

Commander Washington didn't have to actually say they might one day encounter aliens who caused the Great Disaster—out here, in space—to get his point across.

"The Arcturusians have a Hall of Records which we understand has meticulously stored everything they've learned since this Epoch of the Flood of theirs nearly six thousand years ago.

"By the way, they believe The Flood was caused by their moon shifting its orbit and ... a thousand years later...shifting again, ending The Flood. It's unlikely that this could occur naturally. Perhaps these Erosians were also responsible for the Arcturusian Great Disaster.

"If so, the Arcturusians should be happy to share information with us regarding the Erosians, but if they aren't," Washington said with another look at Gentry, "I believe we must use whatever means necessary to persuade them. This other alien race may be the biggest danger we—or any other civilization—will ever encounter. It behooves us to get as much information about them as we can as quickly as possible."

When he got to the "by whatever means necessary" part, there was some indistinct murmuring, some nods, and also some angry head-shaking. The phrase was common during the Jupiter War, and perhaps in every war. It conjured up images of returning to the peaceful people who had healed hundreds of their shipmates, and robbing them at gunpoint.

Jayne Payne didn't seem to notice the crew's reaction, and launched into a dissertation about Arcturusian medical skills that was overtly biased and obviously intended to foster support for helping the alien race with their genetic problems.

She rekindled everyone's gratitude and compassion for the Arcturusians. Aguire felt it was a good counter-point to Washington's doom and gloom speech.

Poluka wrapped up the meeting with a list of broad categories he'd like more information on. If someone had further information, they were directed to report it within the next few hours.

* * *

Lynda hadn't seen Gentry since she was eleven years old, and they'd both changed in immeasurable ways, but she still knew when he was angry, though his expression didn't show it. He didn't say anything until getting to Papa's quarters.

Ella knew, too. She was waiting at the door as if she'd felt his unhappiness coming down the corridor. She hugged him. He returned the embrace with an ease and familiarity that was foreign to Lynda. No one in her family ever showed much affection, except for Mama, but Lynda could hardly remember.

"And to think I didn't want Aguire on this ship," Papa growled. "I didn't think Washington would turn out to be such a bastard."

Gentry forced a strained laugh that sounded more like a gasp.

"He's just doing what he's supposed to do, Papa, putting his side before all else and, frankly, I don't blame him for fearing the Erosians. What little Emerson and I found out suggests that Erosians can be extremely dangerous."

His wife took him by the arm and guided him to a sofa saying, "You have not had time to talk about the Erosians. Sit, and talk about them now."

"Yes, Gentry, tell us what you've discovered," Papa said. "My own father never told me much."

The com pinged, and Lynda punched open a link from Bart Hanson's quarters. He said he wanted to come by and talk. He didn't need say it was about Washington's statements. He said Elisa Santino was with him, and she wanted to come, too.

Papa, standing outside the com-camera's view, shook his head resolutely, but Lynda just said, "I think that'll be fine, Bart."

"Lynda," Papa stood in his lecture pose and frowned at her when she closed the link. "I really wanted to hear about our people, and that woman, Santino…"

"Her name is Elisa, Papa. She's nice, and she's my friend. She knows we're Erosian. She saw me use The Gifts, and she knows that Gentry believed grandpa was an alien. The green eyes, the strength and speed, the superior intelligence, and the…odd behavior I've displayed my entire life was enough for her to figure it out, especially after finding the Fledik."

She hoped it wouldn't cause Papa too much distress but she was sick of secrets. Besides, he had a right to know who else was in on the family secret.

He studied her face and blinked a few times before asking, "How much does she know?"

"Almost as much as I do, which isn't much. Papa, she won't tell anyone," Lynda said.

Papa shook his head. "The more people that find out, the more likely everyone will find out, but if she figured it out, others will, too. It's becoming more imperative for us to find our people."

Gentry was about to add something, but there was a chime at the door. It was Bart and Elisa.

Elisa was introduced to Ella and the children. Gentry had the kids go play in another room, and the adults gathered in the sitting room. Gentry sat in the middle of the sofa with Ella on his left and Lynda on his right. Bart and Elisa took the short sofa, and Lynda's Papa eased himself into a big over-stuffed chair.

"I was at the meeting, of course," Gentry began, "and so was Elisa. She didn't go to the planet, but she met with Arcturusian doctors onboard. We were both concerned about what Commander Washington said."

"I was more than concerned," Gentry said. "Particularly when he suggested that the Arcturusians should be compelled to cooperate. The Hall of Records is a central part of their culture. Anyone can go there to look for any information. They strive to be sure all records are accurate and free of bias. It's not only the law, it's part of their religion to provide the truth to anyone who's interested. I'm afraid the Earth's government won't send a few polite researchers to browse through the Hall of Records. They'll send soldiers to cart it all away, and not let anyone—even the Arcturusians—have access to it."

Papa nodded his head slowly, deep in thought. "Yes...yes, they would. As a businessman I've done things like that, not caring about the fairness of it. That's the Earth way, to score all you can for your own side, and expect everyone else to do likewise."

"Like the bull and the matador," Lynda whispered so softly that no one else heard.

She never heard Papa talk like this. He'd changed since meeting his grandchildren, like a glacier that finally broke through some obstacle after ages of being stuck.

"It seemed wrong to me," Elisa said to Gentry. "Like an abuse of strength, but I had no idea how serious it would be for the Arcturusians. I was more worried about how you'd be questioned concerning the Erosians. Washington knows you spent a lot of time in the Hall of Records. Sooner or later, the government is going to consider you their expert—and expect answers."

Gentry smiled and shrugged. "There's not much I could tell him, but maybe I should explain what we've learned. I know you're aware of our ancestry, Elisa. I won't withhold anything.

"Erosians visited Arcturus at least 70 times in the last five thousand years. Just after The Flood ended, they appeared to the ruling priests, which was before they had a king.

"At least twice in the last two thousand years they've

contacted an Elpastre. There are records of ordinary citizens encountering Erosians, sometimes. The last such incident was less than 600 Earth-years ago, at almost exactly the time of the Great Disaster."

His listeners unconsciously leaned forward, completely focused on his words. Ella snuggled closer to him as he continued.

"From piecing together all the accounts, and learning how Arcturusians perceive things, we got an impression of the Erosians, and some of their history.

"As long as six thousand years ago, they already had a nation that spanned the galaxy. Their early history and origin are still a mystery to us. They were not one race, but diverse, interbreeding with races all over the galaxy. Apparently, there are a lot of other people out there. They had autonomous governments within the overall civilization, yet retained an all-encompassing identity.

"They were proud and arrogant, and other races were subject to their whims. They were not particularly cruel or insensitive to other races, but had the scientific and technical knowledge to enforce their will, and treated no one as equals.

"They were not infallible, however, and readily acknowledged it. They are known to laugh at themselves, and acknowledge their faults.

"Commander Washington guessed right about Erosians causing the Epoch of The Flood. They used Arcturus as a base for observing Earth, and had some sort of transdimensional portal that connected Earth to Arcturus about 5800 Earth-years ago. In some way, similar to how the Hanno works, they were able to join two distant points in space, and make them the same place. Ancient stories tell of a magic tunnel that people walked through from Earth to Arcturus.

"There was something happening on Earth at that time— some sort of cataclysmic event that caused people from Mesopotamia and surrounding areas to flee with whatever they could carry. They found the Erosian portal, and went through it. It's estimated that close to a million people passed through, and the Erosians didn't even notice. They were busy with other things, and left the portal unattended.

"They never told any Arcturusian how that actually happened. For some reason—we don't know why—they shut off the portal and moved the moon of Arcturus into a very low equatorial orbit just before leaving. They didn't realize for about another thousand years they'd allowed a million humans from Earth to get to Arcturus.

"That's when they again moved the moon—this time into an elliptic, polar orbit—ending the Epoch of the Flood, and then made contact with the native people. They confessed that The Flood was their fault, and apologized.

"The Arcturusians feel the Erosians were sincere, and they held no grudges, but believed the Flood was really part of the Creator's plan for them." Gentry looked into his wife's eyes for a moment. "They're like that. They are a people of hope and forgiveness."

"Gentry," Papa asked, "what has become of the Erosians? If we are Erosians, then they've been to Earth as recently as this last century."

"Ah, this requires some speculation. You see, they visited the Elpastre who reigned about 600 years ago. They didn't specifically tell him what was going on, but it was clear not all was well in the Erosian nation. Things were moving too fast—getting out of control—and the nation wasn't as solid as it once was.

"The record of that visit seems to hint that at least some Erosians wished to be outside of the mainstream of Erosian society and were looking for some place to go. Shortly—less than one Arcturus-year later—the psychics of Arcturus sensed the Great Disaster on Earth. They didn't know what had happened, except that billions died suddenly.

"For a time afterwards, Erosians landed on Arcturus frequently. They didn't come to make contact, but were seen in out-of-the-way places on the planet. Then, they were gone, and haven't been back so far as anyone knows."

Lynda took a deep breath, digesting the tale.

Elisa looked around at each of them before asking, "Gentry, did the Erosians cause the Great Disaster on Earth?"

"I believe so, but only because of the timing of their visit to Arcturus, and also because they're reckless and irresponsible. Maybe it was an accident, like letting a million people through the portal, but I think they probably did cause the Disaster, somehow."

"But that was hundreds of years ago," Papa said. "Where did

my father fit into this?"

"I think the Erosian nation reached a breaking point and fell apart, at least, in this part of the galaxy. They're so big; it would take hundreds of years for the whole thing to collapse. It's more likely it would just fragment into isolated pieces. Your father, and the others that came with him," Gentry said with a nod to Bart, "were looking for a safe place to go.

"By the way, the records indicate that we're not in the majority among Erosians, racially speaking. Most Erosians have a lifespan at least double what ours is. One of their achievements was genetic engineering. Many were engineered to eliminate weaknesses and enhance desired qualities. Our genetic lines were created to serve some specific purpose in society—I can't say what that purpose might be—but they wanted us to be easily distinguished from others, so they gave us bright eye colors."

"The Gifts," Lynda asked, "are engineered enhancements?"

"Strength and speed, yes, but not intelligence. We're not really more intelligent than Earth people, but we can focus our learning in a specific direction. Our family focused on scientific developments in the field of space travel, and we became good at it. We neglected to learn arts and social skills as a result."

"But," Papa protested, "We are smarter. Look at yourself. No one has ever understood transdimensional physics the way you do."

"I was raised with it, Papa," Gentry softly explained. "And I had a grandmother and mother who were both brilliant. They were chosen by grandpa and you because they had intelligence in their genes."

"What?" Papa's eyebrows climbed up his forehead. "Are you saying you got your brains from the human side of the family? What about my dad? He was pure Erosian, and he perfected permittivity-drive…and invented hundreds of new things."

"He didn't invent permittivity-drive, Papa—an Earthman did. He just made it work better, and his inventions were Erosian technology that he remembered. How many of your inventions were either derived from old Erosian technology, or invented with the help of very smart Earthmen working for Stokes Industries? Is your new engine design original, or based on something grandpa told you about?"

His father took a few puffing breaths and stared aghast at

Gentry for a moment before sagging into the chair. Lynda watched closely for signs another collapse. Doctor Payne never put much energy into finding out what was wrong with him, and now Lynda thought the doctors on Arcturus should have examined him. It was too late now, but maybe they could go back…after dealing with the situation on Earth.

There was some sort of struggle going on behind Papa's eyes. He'd always seemed immovable and permanent, but she'd seen him change when he met his daughter-in-law and grandchildren, and again after hearing Gentry forgive him. The changes in him, and in herself, thrilled Lynda with possibilities that were unimaginable just days ago. She held her breath, waiting for Papa to speak.

"Oh, damn," he said. "It's true. I'm not even sure I really understand how the new engines work."

Chapter 62

Aguire got the itch-on-the-back-of-the-neck feeling that someone was watching him. Joseph Redbird was looking at him from the doorway of the S-Bay.

"I'll be in my office," Aguire told Commander Garcia, who had the watch. A subtle head-jerk told Redbird to follow him.

"José, I just got back from SERFS," Redbird began when they got to the office. "Viktoriya, Sheffield, Chief Braun, and Jayne Payne were there. None of us are in favor of going toe-to-toe against the New Federation."

"I see." Aguire rubbed his chin, and wondered how fast the rumors were spreading. "I'm not in favor of it, either. I think we could do much better, both for ourselves and for Earth, if we head down the trade route."

"That's what Viktoriya and I think, too. Fighting's got to be done, but charging down the throat of the Navy with an exploration ship isn't going to work. Sheffield and Braun hate the new government, but are completely focused on the aliens now. They just want to go renegade, and concentrate on the Arcturus situation. I think half the crew would go along with that."

Aguire shook his head. "The scientific communities on Earth are the people best qualified to deal with the Arcturusians. That should be obvious after seeing how we screwed up, and any talk of going renegade is just nonsense. What did Jayne say?"

"Jayne Payne can't say what we should do, but she's convinced Poluka is completely nuts, and will try to have him relieved of command before we leave the Zone."

"She what?"

"She's got a consensus with the medical people, and she wants support from executive officers. Shit, José, I don't know what to do. I think she's right, but it's damn serious. Poluka will likely just lock us in the brig like he did to McGee."

"McGee? What happened with McGee?"

"Don't you know? Luke McGee went over all the records leading up to the asteroid collision and decided the Captain was criminally negligent. When his buddy Swanson died, McGee took it real hard and wants Poluka held responsible. He asked Washington to file charges against the Captain. He asked in his very loud and colorful way, right in front of a dozen other officers. Washington arrested him on the spot."

"When did this happen?" Alarms started ringing in his head. It was unimaginable that an officer could be arrested without Aguire being notified.

"When the alien diplomats were onboard," Redbird answered.

Aguire punched up the brig status on his screen.

"This says the brig is empty."

"McGee is there," Redbird insisted.

Aguire selected "Luke McGee" in the crew locator. A blinking icon appeared on the map right in the middle of the brig.

"Crap. He's been there for…what…three days? And I wasn't told?"

It hadn't occurred to him the Captain's actions were criminal, but maybe it should have. Aguire's head reeled with the implications of such a charge. By locking up the man who made the accusation, Poluka was digging his own grave.

"Washington's backing Poluka on this?" Aguire cocked an eyebrow in Redbird's direction.

"Definitely. The SP's are all hand-picked people loyal to Washington, and Poluka is the law. I tried to explain it to Jayne, but she seems to think everyone will have no choice but to do things by the book. She can't imagine him just saying no and getting away with it."

"Has Donno heard this?"

"Not yet. I wanted to get your take on it first."

"Well…I…I expect Poluka will announce his intentions shortly, hoping for support from his officers." Aguire's mind raced, trying to sort it all out. "I'll favor staying clear of Earth for now, but I still feel that an armed insurrection is not the way to fix the government. As for Doctor Payne, I'll go talk to her. Trying to remove Poluka on medical grounds will only destroy careers—his, hers and anyone else who gets involved."

Commander Redbird stared intently at Aguire before saying,

"It seems you're a lot like Doctor Payne—still trusting that things can be done by the book."

* * *

"Hello Elisa." Luther Braun smiled as she came into his office. He was leaning on the window, looking out at the Zone, or perhaps toward Earth. "Coffee?"

"No thanks. What's going on?"

Braun's face became pensive, making his age more obvious. She really liked him, but....

"Elisa, I'll get straight to the point. When you came to me in New Wichita, you needed a way to survive, and I accepted your affection while giving you that way, but...hell...I'm an old man. I'll always love you, but you need to be free of me, and I'll just go on being who I am. We both know there's no future to this relationship. It's time to just step apart, and be friends...if you want to be friends."

It was not unexpected, but Elisa marveled at how he'd chosen the right moment. "You are so good. You're right...and I do want to be friends, always."

"Good." Braun gave a sharp nod that betrayed how uncertain he'd been about how she'd react. "Then let's have a drink to celebrate our new friendship."

He poured two glasses from square bottle with strange markings etched into the smoke colored glass.

"This is Arcturusian wine—very good too. We collected lots of local products while we were there. They've got things that'll be in high demand when Earth finds out about them. Look at this."

He handed her a piece of white fabric made of intricate knots, the size of a handkerchief.

"It's beautiful. I've never seen anything like it."

"Something like it was common on Earth before the Great Disaster. Hardly anybody makes it anymore, and none as good as this. It's called lace on Earth. The Arcturusians have another name for it."

"Luther, what's going to happen to them?"

"The Arcturusians? They'll get screwed, probably. I intend to fight for their right to sovereignty, and do whatever I can to help with this genetic thing but, in the end, they'll get screwed."

"Help with the genetic thing? Luther, did you find an alien replacement for me?"

His startled look made her laugh. When he realized she was teasing, he blushed.

"Well, who knows, my dear? They've got a huge need for what I can provide," he snorted while dramatically hiking up his pants.

This time they both laughed.

"There isn't some way to make it work?" she asked, serious now. "So they won't be harmed by contact with Earth?"

"I don't see a way, but I'll keep looking for one. It'll take someone smarter than me, someone with resources that can defy the money-grubbers of Earth. There's money to be made from this discovery, and that's what usually drives space missions."

"Someone smart that doesn't need money—like the Stokes family, perhaps?"

* * *

Poluka allowed a tight smile of satisfaction while he reviewed the New Federation's military capabilities with Commander Washington. The more he thought about it, the more certain he was that it would work.

The old Navy didn't exist anymore. The New Fed gutted both the Army and Navy by executing their best people. The same went for every branch of every bureaucracy. Fear that someone might plan another overthrow made Vincent Batastia purge the government of competence from the top down.

"I think we're ready to inform the crew," Poluka said.

"And the ones who don't go along?" Washington looked sideways at the Captain.

"We'll drop them at Tau Ceti. This ship can be there in the blink of an eye, spend a couple of hours shuttling them down to the Planet of Industry, and be at Earth's doorstep a moment later."

"Let's do it."

* * *

The doctors waited until the Captain told his executive staff about General Hebert entering Sol Space, presumably to trigger an insurrection. It was just becoming clear that Poluka intended to take them into battle against the government when Doctor Payne made her own announcement. Everyone—including the Captain—was stunned.

True to form, Doctor Jayne Payne tried the by-the-book approach: to remove a captain on medical grounds, Exploration Corps regulations require three commanders and two doctors to agree. Doctors Moorpark and Payne went on record as determining Captain Paul Poluka was mentally impaired. Commanders Martensen and Sheffield stood by them. Jayne figured that since she technically held the rank of commander, she would also count as the third commander. Poluka didn't see it that way.

Washington must've expected some kind of trouble because armed guards swarmed into the conference hall within seconds.

"Well," Redbird groaned, "that certainly went well."

"I don't believe it," Aguire whispered. "I don't fucking believe it."

A dozen SP's marched from the conference hall with the two doctors and Commanders Martensen and Sheffield. Jayne Payne was shouting at the guards that they must follow the regulations. They ignored her.

"Commanders," Captain Poluka bellowed like an enraged bear. "This meeting isn't over. Return to your seats."

Another dozen SP's remained in the hall on each side of the stage. Washington stood with his fists on his hips, glaring at the group of 25 executive officers.

Aguire watched his captain, too shocked from seeing four officers—and friends—being marched off to the brig, to judge whether Poluka had just broken the law and was now ruling by decree.

His fellow officers squirmed in their seats with eyes flicking from Poluka to Washington—and occasionally to Aguire. They wanted leadership and they wanted things to make sense, but they weren't getting it today.

"Now hear this," Captain Poluka snarled, "I am disappointed—gravelly disappointed—by what just happened. Our nation is suffering under tyranny. People—our people—are being imprisoned and murdered. We have a moral responsibility to take action now that the opportunity has presented itself.

"Four of my officers have just shown they'd rather run from danger than join the fight against evil. They will remain in the brig until we reach Tau Ceti. There they will be shuttled to Ceti City along with anyone else who chooses to leave this ship before engaging the enemy." With a great effort, Poluka began to speak more evenly, though his eyes still had a mad-dog appearance, and a drip of spittle ran down his chin. "I will not force any member of this crew to join me in this honorable fight. Those who wish to sit out the war on Tau Ceti may turn in their insignia and uniform."

In a wrenching spasm of shame and guilt, José Aguire made up his mind: Captain Paul Poluka—his close friend—was insane. Jayne was right: he had to be stopped, but there was no procedure, no regulation, left to invoke. Jayne tried the only avenue, and it led to the brig.

Chapter 63

Elisa's friends in the ship's laundry tracked her down to tell her about the arrest of four officers. Somehow, they always seemed to hear things first. The laundry gang had no idea what it was all about. Neither did Elisa, but she rushed back to G.J.'s quarters. Lynda told her what Captain Poluka had in mind.

"Fight?" Elisa gaped at Lynda in horror. "Fight the Navy…with an exploration ship? Is he out of his mind? Never mind…don't answer that."

The tiny woman shifted from one foot to another, unconsciously running her hands over her uniform as if to smooth away wrinkles in the fabric. Bart was pacing and scratching his head, while Gentry sat bolt upright on the sofa, clenching and unclenching his fists. His wife, Ella, was tight-lipped and wide-eyed with suppressed alarm. Only Lynda's father seemed unaffected. He hadn't said much since learning that his alien genes didn't necessarily make him better than Earthmen.

"I can't understand why Washington is backing him on this." Bart Hanson looked around for answers, but no one had any.

Lynda ran through a list of officers in her head, trying to guess how many might support Paul Poluka. It couldn't be more than a handful, but she kept coming back to Bart's question: why was Washington going along with it?

"It is despair," Ella said quietly. "That's why he favors going to battle."

They looked at her, and she explained. "Washington's friend, Paul Poluka, will have no good future, and maybe since the Earth government wants everyone on this ship to die, he thinks none of us have a good future, but especially his friend Paul."

Bart slapped his forehead. "So, a glorious death in battle is the best option? Real nice of him to choose that for the rest of us, too."

413

The com chimed again: a public announcement—all officers were instructed to check their messages immediately.

"What's that's about?" Bart wondered.

"Well," G.J. grumbled from the soft chair, "you're a friggin' officer. Check your messages and tell us what it says."

"Oh, yeah." Bart punched his I.D. into the console. "Um, it's from Poluka to all officers. There'll be a public broadcast announcing that Earth may be at war now and, if that's the case, we'll be taking sides against the New Federation. There's some crap about duty and honor, then he says those who 'can't find it within themselves to join the good fight' will be dropped off at Tau Ceti. It goes on to say…oh, shit."

"What?" the others said in unison.

"Aguire's been relieved of command."

"He's on his way to the brig by now," G.J. mused. "I imagine it's going to get pretty crowded down there."

* * *

It was disheartening, but not surprising, that none of his fellow officers rose to join José Aguire when he said he would be the third commander necessary for removing Poluka from command.

His action might be enough to start crumbling Poluka's authority. All of the requirements were complete now: two doctors and three commanders—including the first-officer—were in agreement. Washington cursed him and had him taken away, but Poluka didn't even look at him or acknowledge that he had spoken.

It was as if a surgeon's knife finally separated them once and for all: a clean cut, but a permanent one. Whatever Paul Poluka's destiny was, José Aguire would not share in it.

Only the SP's could enforce his rule now, but they were sworn to uphold the Corps regulations and the laws of federal government. Some of them must surely be questioning the legitimacy of backing Poluka.

The brig was located near the 100 meter mark on the deck below Main Street. The SP's were silent but thoughtful on the ride down.

Even before the lift doors slid open, they could hear the

commotion. It was a fight. About two-dozen crewmen were crowded into the corridor throwing punches at each other, and wrestling on the floor.

The guards sprang into the melee to break it up. Aguire, as surprised as anyone, assisted by pulling apart combative pairs of crewmen.

"What the hell's going on here?" Aguire roared. Then, to the nearest guard, "Call for more security."

The guard obeyed. A moment later five more guards from the nearby brig charged into the fray. A few of the battling crewmen got thrown roughly to the deck. The others backed off with some shouting and finger pointing as to who started it.

When Aguire took charge and ordered the group to the brig for questioning, the guards seemed to forget they were here to escort him to a cell. Aguire brought up the rear to ensure none of the troublemakers slipped away.

One of the youths whispered to Aguire as they headed off towards the ship's jail. "Now's your chance, sir. Get to CEFR while there's still time to stop Poluka."

It took half a heartbeat to realize it was a set-up. The security guards didn't get it until five minutes later, when they found Aguire was no longer with them. They had a bunch of delinquents from the ship's laundry, but the commander had escaped.

The maintenance decks were a complex warren of passageways in the belly of the Hanno for moving heavy equipment between shops. With walls 70 meters apart, and the ceiling towering 68 meters above the deck, even whole shuttlecrafts could be hoisted through the lower decks without disrupting activity. A lone man running through the passages was hardly even noteworthy.

The intercom chimed high-low tones for a ship-wide announcement. Even without seeing him, Poluka's voice betrayed his unstable mind. The pace of his words alternated between rushed and halting, and there was a sort of defiant assertiveness, like a frail plea begging fate to prove him justified. But there was no hint of indecisiveness: the Hanno was going to war, and anyone who refused this "opportunity of noble purpose" would be seen as a coward. Poluka dressed it up in eloquent prose, but the unreasonableness of it shined clearly through.

People began scurrying through the maintenance decks now, looking for assurance that this can't be happening.

Aguire remembered his locater beacon and tore open the seam of his shirt to yank out the tiny transmitter. He dropped it into an electric truck and ordered it to the pod docks. The robotic vehicle rolled off toward the front of the ship.

Aguire followed the numbers painted on the deck until he got to the 50 mark. The maintenance area gave way to low-gravity bulk storage. Water tanks, 300 meters tall, loomed ahead, and beyond those would be air tanks. He started looking for a lift to get up to the aft OAC. He would bypass Main Street, and continue back to the 62 mark, just short of the end of the midsection. It was far, but he got to the Coherent Emission Fusion Reactor without running into security.

He wondered who set up his escape—and whether he should have escaped at all. Nausea wrenched his gut from what was happening to Poluka. The man he'd served and admired, the man who taught him how to be a leader and was like a father to him, was now his enemy.

A CEFR tech waited in the corridor and waved Aguire through. Inside, the Hanno's mighty power generator hummed smoothly. Half a dozen CEFR personnel were fidgeting in the control room. Elisa Santino, Bart Hanson, and Kern from the Tug Fleet were huddled around a control panel. They had com links open to Henry Tran in the I-Bay, and to Lynda Stokes in her father's quarters.

"Thank God, you made it." Santino's squeaky voice quavered slightly.

"Good of you to join us, sir." Hanson grinned.

"You set up my escape?" Aguire asked. "Why? What do you think we can accomplish."

"Poluka has been legally and properly relieved of command," Elisa said. "And that makes you the senior officer on this ship. As soon as everyone accepts that, it will become a reality."

"Aguire," Lynda said from the screen on the control panel. "Only the crew's confusion is keeping the Captain in command. As soon as it's clear that he's been relieved, he'll have to accept it, too."

He went to the screen and said, "He's also got...how many...200 security guards? It doesn't take many to control a ship."

"Speaking of guards," Tran hissed from another screen on the com console. He was hunched over a radar screen in the I-Bay, watching the activity on the bridge. "Washington just found out you're in CEFR. He's sending the barnacles to get you."

"Damn." Aguire turned to Hanson. "Get Santino out of here. I'll go with Kern up to Tugs, and slip outside with a work platform. I can get back in at Forward OAC."

Hanson was unhappy with the idea, and shaking his head, but he didn't have a chance to complain before a strong soprano cut in from behind them.

"That's a bad idea, Aguire."

The barnacles must have been nearby when they got the order. Major Rivers and at least fifteen others were already inside the power plant. The CEFR tech who'd been watching the hallway was cringing between two sergeants that were each twice his size.

One of the reactor techs leapt up to stand protectively in front of the fusion reactor, and shouted, "No weapons fire in here."

"I don't think weapons will be necessary," Major Rivers said soothingly. She was twelve centimeters taller than Aguire, and looked like she could lift him off the deck with one hand.

"I don't need a weapon." Bart Hanson's blue eyes narrowed as he stepped toward the soldiers.

"Hold it, everyone," Aguire barked. "Major, this is a Corps matter. You needn't be involved."

"Law enforcement aboard starships is part of our job description, Commander."

* * *

Only ten SP's manned the security center now. Nearly a 150 were stationed around the ship to keep order, and the rest were searching for Aguire.

Curses and taunts echoed from the detention cells where the laundry crew was confined, while the guards had to stand at attention by the front desk of the brig and endure a torrent of observations regarding their qualifications from Commander Garcia, who had a talent for scorching criticism.

He was in rare form. Standing nose-to-nose with the ranking

sergeant, Garcia screamed a description of the man's next tour of duty, which would involve a toothbrush and many, many toilets.

"To make matters worse," Garcia seethed, "I've just learned that the ship's Army contingent has found the escaped commander, and they're bringing him in."

The sergeant choked off a groan. Being bested by barnacles was worse than death.

With a titanic effort, Garcia forced himself to be civil for a moment when Lynda Stokes and her brother appeared at the security gate.

"It's our father," Lynda explained. "He's had another seizure. The doctors in Med Center are doing their best, but Doctor Payne treated him last time. I thought maybe we could talk to her about it."

"Of course, Miss Stokes, I'll take you back myself." Garcia flashed an automatic smile at her as he buzzed the gate open for them, then glared at the guards and quietly hissed, "And you may continue standing at attention."

The sergeant looked down the row of guards standing beside him, and wished he'd stayed in the Navy.

Just as Garcia disappeared into the brig with the visitors, Major Rivers and three of her non-coms showed up with a prisoner.

"I understand you lost something." The major had a smug grin. "Good thing you've got the Army to help you out."

None of the SP's offered any witty comeback, but the sergeant buzzed them through. His jaw muscles visibly bulged as he ground his teeth.

"Hey." One of the SP's spoke. "This isn't Aguire."

The sergeant looked and, sure enough, it wasn't even a commander. It was an ensign. He was about to laugh in Major Rivers' face for dragging in the wrong guy, but then he recognized Bart Hanson. He almost had time to be afraid.

* * *

"You're pretty good at that," Gentry said to Lynda. "You didn't kill him, did you?"

"He'll wake up with a headache." She gently lowered Garcia's limp body to the deck. Gentry helped place him out of the way so that no one would step on him.

Around the next corner were the cells. The prisoners fell silent when Lynda and Gentry appeared, not quite sure what was happening. Lieutenant McGee was in the first cell with five others and watched warily as they approached.

Martensen and Sheffield were in a cell with more kids from the laundry, and Doctor Payne was on the women's side with a couple of young women from the laundry.

"Lieutenant McGee," Lynda stepped up to the bars, "I never apologized for hitting you. Is there some way I can make it up to you?"

"You can get me out of here," he said. "Do you have the code to open this door?"

"I'm afraid not. We'll have to force it open."

"We've tried," one of the laundry youths said. "Even with all of us together we couldn't do it."

McGee's expression brightened when Bart Hanson come in behind them, but darkened again when he saw the barnacles.

"Don't look so glum, McGee," one of the soldiers laughed. "We're all in this together."

"You're not protecting Poluka?" McGee asked.

"Listen," Major Rivers said seriously. "All of you, listen. The Army is sworn to support the law and to take action when local enforcement breaks down. Captain Poluka has been relieved of command in accordance with regulations. The ship's police force is confused about who is in charge. Until further notice, I am assuming responsibility for enforcement, and Commander Aguire has ultimate authority on this ship. Now, let's open these doors."

Four soldiers, five laundry workers, Hanson, Lynda, and Gentry took hold of the bars and strained against them. McGee shook his head and muttered something about needing 20 more men, when the bars suddenly bent and the lock fell to pieces. He looked suspiciously at Lynda and Gentry.

"I accept your apology, ma'am." McGee suddenly grinned. "And I'm glad we're on the same side. What's the plan?"

* * *

As plans went, Aguire had to admit it was pretty bad. He was counting on Major Rivers to get control of the armory after springing Martensen and Sheffield from the brig. He needed more commanders to support his authority and, even more urgently, he needed to announce to the crew that Poluka was relieved of command. After that, he was sure the SP's would fall in line, and Poluka would have no choice but to surrender.

Unfortunately, Poluka controlled the Communications Center just down the hall from the bridge. Access to the intercom and computer net was locked down.

Aguire was in uncharted territory without rules and procedures to guide him, but Poluka had a knack for finding a way around any problem, despite the rules. Deranged or not, the Captain should not be underestimated.

A worker's coveralls, toolbox, and hardhat made José Aguire inconspicuous in the Infrastructure Control area. Activity there never slowed as teams worked to keep the ship's artificial environment livable. Anyone with a toolbox could pass through unnoticed.

Close to the dorsal "roof" of the starship, there was an airlock just ahead in the alcove, servicing the no-man's land between the inner and outer hulls and, he hoped, some pressure suits. A 20 minute spacewalk would get him to the forward OAC. From there he'd pick a route to the Communications Center, avoiding Poluka's police force.

A group of SP's spilled into the Infrastructure area from the lift ahead. Some went forward, away from Aguire. Five others started coming his way, looking at each crewman they passed. He ducked into the alcove, dropped the toolbox and dashed to the pressure suits hanging by the airlock.

* * *

"Step away from the console, Tran," Washington shouted. He had his weapon in his hand.

Tran stood up while tapping a button on the panel that would scramble his communication log. He left the I-Bay with a sigh of resignation.

"Commander?" Captain Poluka rose from the command desk with his hand on his own sidearm.

"The Army is working against us, Captain. Rivers just took the brig and the armory. Buckmaster tracked unauthorized messages between the brig and Mister Tran. He's been helping them."

"Get the bastard out of my sight," Poluka growled. "Ensign Hill, check the I-Bay to make sure we're clear for departure."

"Aye, sir." Hill jumped from the pilot's station to obey.

The girl's commitment was gratifying. Poluka was confident that most of the crew felt the same since, like her, many had lost loved ones to the new government's tyranny. He could see it in her eyes, the longing for pay-back.

"Sir," Donno called out. "Security has Rivers pinned in the armory, but they can't take control. The Army has the superior weapons now."

Donno was still following orders, but was clearly unhappy about Aguire being arrested. Poluka understood; he, too, found it disturbing that Aguire took the wrong side. Still, he'd have to watch Donno.

"Have the air supply to the armory shut off," Poluka snapped.

Ensign Hill called out, "Captain, security's located Commander Aguire. He's outside the ship in a pressure suit. He exited from Infrastructure Control. I've got a beacon from his suit."

Poluka stared out the window at the endless void of space. He hated what he must do next, but Aguire made his own choices.

"Are there any problems for our departure, Ensign Hill?"

She hesitated slightly. "No, sir."

"Return to your station, Ensign. We leave for Tau Ceti in five minutes."

She scurried to the pilot's station with a questioning glance at the Captain. Her hands trembled as she brought the engines up to a ready condition.

Washington returned after finding some place to lock up Tran. Poluka told him, "Aguire is trying to get into the Forward OAC through an airlock. Go down and wait for him, Alex. If he comes through before we leave the Zone, arrest him. If he doesn't—say a prayer for him."

The countdown reached the last few seconds. Aguire's beacon was still 200 meters from OAC. The countdown reached zero.

"Good-bye, old friend. Forgive me," Poluka whispered, then to Hill. "Ensign, activate the engines."

With tears in her eyes, she whispered, "God forgive me," and obeyed.

"Captain!" Donno screamed and rushed from the S-Bay. "You moved the ship? There was a beacon—someone was outside the ship!"

"Yes, I know. That was Aguire."

The horror on Donno's face stabbed Poluka down to his soul. He hadn't merely killed a friend—he'd left him drifting in spacesuit, waiting to run out of air in absolute solitude. It was a spaceman's nightmare. He began to feel the horror, and guilt, too, like a rot creeping through his bones.

His own decision to leave Aguire behind shocked him, making him slow to react when Donno lunged at him like an enraged beast.

* * *

Between the inner and outer hulls of the Hanno was a gap, a ghostly steel cavern nearly 20 meters wide, held open by steel struts. An unsightly mess of cables, pipes, and conduits crisscrossed the inner hull, and rows of life-pods dotted the surface near the accommodations section of the ship. Aguire opted for this route, and ejected an empty pressure suit from the airlock to drift away as a decoy. He wore another suit because the only air in this no-man's land was whatever happened to leak from inside the ship.

The gravity simulation rods inside the ship had a weird effect out here: each rod pulled compressed quantum space up through its center and out the top, where it then fountained out, and back around the outside of the rod in nearly parallel flux lines, returning to the other end.

Only a miniscule amount of quantum space was actually moved by the GSR's, and it didn't even cause optical distortion. The nature of space and time was not intuitively obvious to creatures who perceive only three dimensions. Even in the 28th century, when such technology was commonplace, most people didn't clearly understand how it worked. It was the flow of space outside the rods that simulated gravity, and one never experienced the space moving through the center of the rod, unless one happened to be passing by the ends of the rods—where Aguire was now.

It actually made it easier for him. He found a line along the ship where the struts were just the right distance apart, and swung between them like a monkey in a tree. When he was over the top of a GSR, he'd be on his inner swing—closer to the inner hull—and the GSR's fountain of quantum space would push him away from the ship. On the outer swing—closer to the outer hull—he was between GSR's, and the space would be flowing back towards the ship just as it was for people inside, and it would let him complete his swing with almost no effort on his part.

Someone would be waiting to catch—or kill—him in the OAC, but he couldn't get there anyway from this weird place that was neither inside nor outside the ship. He got in through a maintenance hatch.

It was faster and easier than his original plan. He stripped off the pressure suit, but his positive expectations crumbled when a burst of hysterical curses boomed through the passageway. It was a woman's voice, followed by the baritone shout of Commander Washington. There was a popping sound he recognized as weapon's fire. Memories of war came flooding back. His blood ran cold as he rushed to the OAC and crouched low to peer around the corner.

Anguished sobbing told him where to look. He found technician first-class Hilda Harris lying on the deck next to Commander Washington. Blood soaked her uniform from a wound on her belly. Washington was face-down with a pool of blood around his head. He was dead. The steel pipe that killed him was still in Hilda's hand. Washington's Aurora-5 lay next to his body.

"Oh, Aguire," Hilda gasped. "He said you were dead."

Despite her pain, she smiled. Then she was gone.

* * *

"My god, what have you done?"

Poluka turned to see who spoke before realizing it was his own voice. He looked at the plasma pistol in his hand, then down at Leroy Donno.

Blossom Hill jerked the belt from her trousers and tied it around Donno's leg above the knee. His right leg was destroyed, hanging together by a few chords of flesh. A smoky stench filled the bridge.

Poluka looked around. His lips moved, calling for help, but no sound came out. The I-Bay was empty now; the techs had fled. The S-Bay was still manned, but the Lieutenant Wong was just staring at him, and the others were hiding around the corner. Jack Trimble, the navigator, was on the wrong side of his station, as far from Poluka as he could get.

"Lieutenant Wong." Poluka spoke slowly. "Get some medics up here."

Wong backed up into the S-Bay without taking his eyes off Poluka.

Blossom Hill straightened up and turned to the Captain.

"We need Washington." Her voice cracked. "You can't do this alone, sir."

"Do what?" He really wanted to know.

She said, almost as a question, "Defeat the New Federation, sir."

"Yes, of course." Poluka forced himself to concentrate. "Washington should've been back by now. Go down the hall, and have Buckmaster page him."

"Aye, sir."

* * *

Aguire was not in a reasonable mood. He tried to not hurt anyone too badly, but he had to get the job done. He got Lieutenant Buckmaster down on the deck and securely tied to a pillar with a power cable along with two other engineers, then scanned through the logs to get some idea of what was happening.

Some of the SP's had changed sides already, but others still blocked the entrance to the forward section. A battle was raging just 50 meters away.

Major Rivers' team had injuries, but the SP's pinning them down gave up and fled to Main Street only to be caught between two groups led by Maria Rodriguez and Elisa Santino.

Other areas had signs of anarchy. The lifts and speedwalks were shut off, along with normal communications. Kern and his tugboat pilots were using helmet radios to coordinate medical services. Townsend had his shuttle dock people assisting anyone who opposed Poluka. Most were simply staying out of sight with no information about who was in command.

It was time for Aguire to tell them. He demanded the access code to the intercom. Buckmaster cursed him. Aguire picked up a very large, heavy wrench and squatted down next to the lieutenant.

"Listen, I know you think you're on the right side, Stephen, but I'm not going to be nice about this. I'm going to start knocking your teeth out until you tell me. If that doesn't work, I'm going to kill you, then try the same thing with your engineers. Hopefully, one of you will give me the code."

The swishing sound of the door spun him around. He lunged at the short figure that entered, and dragged a startled Ensign Hill to the deck, pinning her down.

"Where's Poluka?" he demanded.

"Aguire, you're alive." She was surprised but not frightened. A quick look at Buckmaster told her the situation. "The Captain is doing the right thing. We have to stop Batastia."

"Don't let your anger cloud your judgment, Ensign. Poluka's in no condition to lead an attack. If our government is bad, it will fall, with or without us."

"If?" Hill searched his eyes. "They murdered your friends."

He returned her scrutiny, wondering what she was talking about. When he didn't respond, she continued. "My mother was in the Old Guard. I grew up around men that talked about you. Remember Milián, Meder, and Jorge? They were my mom's best friends."

His first thought was that she was trying to confuse him with the names of the boys he escaped with from the orphanage, so many years ago.

It was another life, when he was someone else.

He had tried to contact them when he returned on the Livingston, but couldn't locate them. Now he understood why. When he joined the Navy, his childhood friends joined the Army. They'd been there when the old Federation fell. They fell with it.

"You knew them?"

"They were like family to me."

Chapter 64

"It's not just General Hebert anymore, sir," the Navy commander insisted. "There're partisan fighters springing up all over the planet. We've got reports of Navy cadets from the Angola flight school attacking our bases all over Europe, and the McConnell Spaceport is under siege. No traffic is possible there. All over the planet, people are defying government authority."

Admiral Higgs hushed the commander when Vice President Batastia entered the Operations Center with a group of bodyguards. The staff visibly tensed, and tried harder to look busy. Monitor stations all across the enormous room were manned with over 200 naval officers. Mostly, they were young and naïve, or experienced and already corrupted—like Admiral Fisher, who was supervising the tactical station.

Higgs wished Batastia would just stay at the Capitol. In fact, he wished Batastia was dead, but he dare not act on his wish or even show any sign of it. The top level of government had shrunk considerably in the last five days as Batastia saw traitors everywhere and had them eliminated.

When 200 small ships entered the Solar System seven days ago, System Traffic Control tracked them. The transponder codes indicated a mix of merchant cargo and passenger ships: not too unusual, except for the large number. Sometimes ten or twelve would travel together making a less tempting target for pirates, but 200 was enough to attract attention.

The small ships fell into the standard class-three traffic lanes, 20 million kilometers above the ecliptic, and behaved nicely until they got close to the high-orbital tracking stations. That's when they attacked, taking out most of the automated surveillance around the planet Earth.

That was the good news. At least now they knew where General Hebert was. They had time to move the home-fleet around to that side of the planet and make short work of the attackers.

But they didn't know where he was. The bad news was that these 200 ships were converted civilian ships—obsolete hulks fitted with missile launchers—a diversion for the real warships that came into the system from below. 50 light-cruisers, six heavy-cruisers, and nine personnel transports along with no less than 75 light-fighters approached the Earth's southern pole at high speed before splitting up to engage predetermined targets.

Before the Navy understood the danger, all nine transports descended through the atmosphere and disappeared. They might have been tracked all the way down if that bastard Poluka hadn't damaged the orbital tracking system as he left the solar system. As it was, Hebert managed to get perhaps 20,000 troops onto the ground, and nobody knew where they were until they began attacking key installations.

Still, it was like a gnat biting a bull, or would have been, if the government—and especially the military—hadn't been purged of experienced leadership to appease Batastia's paranoia. Then, to need major reorganizations due to Batastia having key people arrested right in the middle of the crisis made Higgs' efforts to coordinate a defense all but futile.

The result was a public perception of weakness and incompetence, followed by popular support shifting quickly to General Hebert. By the third day, the Vice President was asking about the military's capability to nuke surface targets.

The last thing Higgs wanted Batastia to hear about was partisan resistance. A lot of crimes burdened Higgs' conscience already. He wasn't about to consider a nuclear strike against people whose only crime was being sick and tired of the lies and oppression.

"Admiral Higgs," the Vice President said with a hint of hysteria. "I will speak to you…in your office."

Four of Batastia's guards went with them. Two checked the office for danger while one watched the door and another watched Higgs. As soon as the door closed, Batastia got right to the point.

"Higgs, I heard that some of the Navy turned against us, and the Army doesn't seem know how to stop civilian uprisings. Just tell me," he leaned close enough for Higgs to smell that the Vice

President hadn't bathed in quite a while, "are we losing?"

"Mister Vice President, if we let up for one moment, we could lose." Higgs followed it up with a way out before Batastia could become angry. "But we won't. There was a problem with the Navy, and I've dealt with it. I have direct control of planetary defenses. We now understand that Hebert is relying entirely on cutting off our control of communications. He thinks if we can't talk to the people, the people will turn against us. But he will fail in this. I've taken steps to ensure that we will never lose control."

"People?" Batastia's eyes narrowed into pure hate. He snarled, "What people?"

"Uh...the public...the voters." Higgs' hope of pacifying the man he now feared more than he'd ever feared anyone, was vanishing. He'd been Batastia's disciple in a quest to build a utopia, believing that this relic from the old Corporate State was the statesman who comes along once in a thousand years.

Now, Higgs finally understood. Batastia never cared about any of that. He only wanted revenge against a world that rejected the Corporate State and brought it crashing down. That was all this madman cared about for the last 40 years.

"The voters?" Batastia spat. "There are no voters. They think they're voters, but I count the votes. It's those fucking religious fanatics again. They were always the worst. A great man once called religion the opiate of the masses, but I call it the disease of the world."

"They will fail...this time...they will fail." Higgs put every ounce of persuasion into his voice. "Hebert went after the old telephone and radio infrastructure. He doesn't understand the new com-net. We still have control."

Batastia stared like a lifeless mannequin for a moment, and then seemed to become a different person. A smile spread across his face, and his eyes became childlike. It was spooky. Even his bodyguards were watching him instead of doing their jobs.

"Higgs...Higgs...you are my best...all those years ago...I saw it in you. Do you remember? You were the shining star at TerraPharm, and made us so much money."

Raised voices in the control center prompted one of the guards to poke his head out for a look.

"Hey, something big is happening," the man said.

Batastia led the way to the planetary defense screen. It showed less than a hundred red icons—all that remained of General Hebert's fleet—moving away from Earth. In the last few hours, Higgs finally got the Navy to use its superior numbers and equipment to push the enemy back. Only two light-cruisers and a dozen light-fighters were left of the enemy's real warships. A small hidden corner of Higgs' soul envied Hebert's valor, and the dedication he inspired.

"Admiral Fisher," Higgs called to the man whom he despised, but still needed, "do they pose any further threat to us?"

Fisher had a tendency to stammer under pressure, and Higgs watched with interest how the perverse man struggled to give a dignified answer while the Vice President's eyes were burning a hole into him. "N-no, sir. Only the cruisers could do any damage, and they might only hit one target before being destroyed. We can t-t-take our time chasing down what's left of them."

Higgs hid his thoughts behind an expression of grave concentration. He had an idea. It would mean leaving Earth, perhaps forever, and starting again somewhere else.

Since he was a boy, Higgs wanted to build a perfect world. He'd always assumed it would be on Earth, but this was the 28th century. He could go somewhere else. He'd known for days now, there would be no future for anyone in the Batastia regime. He already had his personal fortune liquidated and ready for a hasty escape.

"Well done, Admiral Fisher," Higgs said without meaning it. Any idiot could see the general's forces had exhausted their potential. "By the way, Mister Vice President, I've transferred Fisher from the Exploration Corps to the Navy, to replace an admiral who had to be executed."

"I see." Batastia was still staring at Fisher, whose pasty complexion took on an even whiter shade as he began to visibly sweat. "My secretary told me about you, Fisher. You've enjoyed the little perks reserved for the inner circle. She says you like the young ones."

Fisher looked like he might faint, which would have amused Higgs to no end, but if the cretin fainted now, it would reflect badly on Higgs.

"We're getting a report from the Jupiter TC," one of the officers announced. "A very large ship is entering the system at near-light-speed. They say it's bigger than a tanker."

"Track it," Fisher ordered.

"What could be bigger than a tanker?" Batastia demanded.

"Uh…well, a carrier or a destroyer could each look bigger on radar, sir," Fisher explained, "But of course, we've accounted for all such ships that are…."

"Damn it, Higgs," Batastia whined like a child. "You promised me this couldn't happen."

"It isn't happening, sir." Higgs thought fast. It couldn't be a warship, and the Corps ships didn't get that big, except for….

"It must be Poluka. He's returned…somehow."

He shot an accusing look at Fisher, who had assured them the Hanno would be a death-ship, never to be seen again.

"Poluka?" Batastia seemed mystified. "Why would he be here now?"

"What's their course, Lieutenant?" Fisher asked.

"They're in the major lanes…on the ecliptic…they'll have to begin decelerating in the next two minutes, or they'll overshoot Earth. Assuming they do, they'll be here in about 75 minutes, Admiral."

"Relay that to our fleet," Higgs ordered the officer. "And what is Hebert up to now?"

The young lieutenant wasn't a bad sort, even if he did get his position through nepotism. Higgs was considering taking the boy with him when the time to flee comes. He could use some help to build an empire somewhere else.

"Sir, I don't understand what they're doing. They're gathering into some sort of formation and holding position at 25 degrees ahead of Earth, 60 million klicks above the ecliptic and one-point-nine AU out. That makes them…one-point-one-five AU from Earth."

"There's no one close enough for direct observation," Fisher guessed, looking over the lieutenant's shoulder at the display. "Our ships are out of position. General Hebert might be getting ready to run for it, and get out of the system before we can finish them off."

"And that's exactly what we'll announce to public." Higgs managed a smile, hoping it would make him look more military. "I'll arrange a broadcast. In the meantime, perhaps we should divert some of our heavy-cruisers towards Poluka's ship. What do you think, Admiral Fisher?"

"I agree completely, Admiral Higgs, and maybe we should order them off—park them somewhere until the current situation is resolved."

"Well, let's contact them first, and find out what they're doing here."

"Sir?" The lieutenant looked back and forth between Fisher and Higgs, confused about whom he should be speaking to.

"What is it…Lieutenant?" Higgs wished he could remember the boy's name. He used to be good at names.

"The combatants are returning to Earth."

"What?" Higgs and Fisher blurted simultaneously.

"They're in a spear-of-battle formation and heading straight in."

Higgs really wished Batastia was not here, and he wanted to be somewhere else himself, like at home, having a cocktail and listening to music. He was tired of being an Admiral. Enemies never seem to take a break at convenient intervals.

"Alright, people." Higgs raised his voice to include everyone in the Ops Center. "We need analysis, and we need it now. What is General Hebert's objective, and how do we stop him?"

While they ran projections of the enemy's course against orbiting targets, Batastia went back to the office to make some calls to the Capitol. Higgs took the opportunity to sneak off to another office and made a call to his personal pilot. He wanted a courier yacht standing by to get him the hell out as soon as the time was right.

His escape plan got more complicated when a report from Base Security warned that an Army group was surrounding the Navy Ops Center, and the city police were now joining insurgents right here in the capital city. Higgs checked, and found the captain in charge of security was busy setting up snipers on the roof to keep the Army from getting in, while the Army was setting up snipers so no one could get out.

As long as it was a standoff, Higgs couldn't care less. The base was secure while there were men to defend it, and he would have the Army unit wiped out from above as soon as some of his light-fighters got back from engaging Hebert.

It was bad though. If the Army, some of the Navy, and now even police departments were turning against the government, it was truly over. This government would never survive, even if it makes it through the current crisis. Rule over the many by the few doesn't work if the many don't let it.

It wasn't until Hebert's ships got close and started adjusting for their final approach that someone figured out the target.

"They're going for a surface target—right here—or at the Capitol," the lieutenant blurted. "They could actually hit both targets. It seems Hebert's been communicating with people on the ground to help pick their targets. My guess is, they know the Vice President is here. We are the target, sir."

It was a last act of desperation. Hebert must know the city has surface-to-orbit weapons. The few who might make it through would have a slim chance of inflicting any meaningful damage. Having an expendable President as a figurehead had been a good idea, but the value of a disposable target only lasted while people were still fooled. Everyone now knew the New Fed was not really a republic, and Batastia was the dictator. General Hebert knew it, too.

"They won't go after the Capitol," Higgs mused aloud. "They aren't interested in President Garane."

Fisher scurried to the tactical station, babbling a hysterical string of orders to get every single Navy ship to drop everything and rush to save his life. Higgs would have stopped him, but Batastia grabbed his elbow and held him. The Vice President saw the disgust on the officers' faces as Fisher showed his cowardice and preferred to let him be the one to give the orders. Higgs turned away from both of them.

Someone called out, "We're getting a com from the Hanno."

"Put it through," Higgs ordered.

The bridge of the Hanno appeared on the big screen. A handsome young man with chiseled features stood in the center. His uniform was torn and bloodied, but he stood straight and proud. Higgs didn't recognize him.

"Navy Operations Center, this is Commander José Aguire of the Exploration Corps Starship Hanno. We've been monitoring your situation. May we be of assistance?"

"Commander," Higgs replied, "where is Captain Poluka?"

"I regret to report that Captain Poluka is dead. It was Poluka's intention to join this conflict on the side of General Hebert. He and those who supported his position are now either dead, or in the brig. The rest of us are here to fight for the New Federation.

We will be within weapons range of Hebert's forces in four minutes. We have missiles standing by."

Higgs signaled to have the audio cut before asking Fisher, "You know this asshole. Can we trust him?"

"I think he'll do as he's told," Fisher stammered.

"Then why was he on the black list?" Batastia wondered aloud with a sneer at Fisher.

"Admiral Higgs," the lieutenant shouted, "some of Hebert's ships have broken off. The rest are accelerating straight in. They're going to crash the ships into us at ten thousand kps. They'll destroy everything for a thousand kilometers in all directions."

"A suicide run?" Higgs marveled at the heroic commitment of the enemy, and doubted anyone on his side would make such a sacrifice. Then, the personal significance of the announcement sank in.

"Oh, shit." Higgs switched the audio back on. "Commander Aguire, we accept you offer of assistance. There is a group of ships making a suicide run on us. Would you be so good as to stop them as soon as possible?"

The Commander smiled, accentuating the chiseled lines of his face. "We see them, Admiral. Consider them stopped."

The link ended, and the planetary defense screen showed the Hanno moving to intercept. A cloud of new dots appeared, moving fast from the Hanno toward the enemy ships. The display numbered the missiles at 150—a mix of scorpions and hawks. The attacking ships numbered 82 of various makes. None were warships, which explained why a collision course was their only trick left.

Admiral Fisher's eyes bulged at the display. He staggered forward a couple of steps and his mouth opened in soundless scream.

"For God's sake, Fisher," Higgs snorted. "What is it?"

"What if…what if Aguire targeted us? The missiles and Hebert's ships are both coming right at us."

Higgs' eyes flicked back to the screen. Fisher's paranoia was maddeningly contagious. If the missiles overtook the ships and just kept going, they'd eventually slam right into the Earth.

"Tracking," Higgs spoke to the man monitoring trajectories, "where would they hit the ground?"

"The hawk missiles would hit the ocean, sir," The man said without looking away from the data. "If the scorpions turn in the next twelve seconds, they could probably hit us."

A notation on the screen indicated the ships would impact in 55 seconds. Higgs silently counted to twelve, and tried to ignore Fisher who was hopping from one foot to the other.

"There." Higgs glowered at Fisher. "They aren't turning. I just hope Aguire gets all of them. Maybe we should use the city's defenses, too. Fisher?"

"We can't target something moving at relativistic speed. We'd probably hit the missiles." Fisher was more composed now.

"What about those ships?" Batastia asked. "How do we know they're manned? Could this be a trick? It was awfully convenient of the Hanno to show up just now."

Higgs looked back to Fisher for an answer but saw no sign that one was forthcoming.

"What does tactical say?" Higgs said, inviting anyone in the group.

"Um." His favorite lieutenant dared to offer an opinion. "I'd say we can tell by their reaction to the missiles. Look."

The enemy ships had spotted the missiles and broke formation, trying to evade. A few began shooting particle beams at the oncoming missiles, destroying a couple of them. One actually swiveled around and fired its own missile straight back at the barrage from the Hanno. Two gave up the target and made a run for it in different directions, but they'd started too late.

Someone wailed from tactical, "They're ten seconds away from us."

The missile dots merged with the enemy dots, and both began to disappear.

The few remaining missiles either found the larger pieces of debris, or continued until hitting the Atlantic Ocean.

"We've got visual confirmation from the orbitals," the lieutenant sang out in jubilation. "The enemy is destroyed, and the last of the missiles has detonated. Hebert's two light-cruisers and his remaining fighters are heading away at high acceleration."

A cheer shook the room as the officers saw that they would live another day. Higgs savored the moment, but his plan to escape wasn't changed. The current government was still doomed, and the officers still here were either filth like Fisher, or temporarily confused about who the good-guys are.

"I'm safe," Fisher gasped. His expression was pure joy until his eyes slid from the debris pattern on the screen to where the Hanno's icon was blinking as it moved into an orbital parking position over the Capitol. His expression froze for a moment, and then scrunched up into a mean-little-boy look. Higgs found it fascinating, especially while noticing Batastia's face going through the same process, only more subtly.

"It seems the New Federation has a new hero, eh, Admiral?" Higgs chided.

"I...um...I'm not so sure, sir." Fisher tried to look authoritative—something he was never really good at—as he pointed an accusing finger at the Hanno icon. "Aguire's always been...a problem. Now, he's a loose cannon right over our heads. I suggest we hit him with our surface-to-orbit beam weapons without warning. Then, we can be sure he's not a danger to us."

Higgs struggled to keep from laughing. He knew Fisher was a coward and hated Aguire. He also knew Fisher placed zero value on human life, but he would have lost a bet to anyone who said Fisher could be stupid enough to display his true nature in front of so many officers and irreversibly lose their trust. How could anyone trust him if he would kill the very people who just saved his life?

"Nonsense," Batastia suddenly bellowed, making everyone, including Higgs, almost jump out of their skin. "We need a hero now and this fellow has just saved the world. I want to meet Commander Aguire as soon as that traitorous Army unit clears out. Get rid of them, Higgs."

Batastia's apparent lack of psychotic paranoia made Higgs suspicious. He ordered an aerial attack on the small Army force outside the base, but, before the light-fighters could even arrive, the Army left on their own when they learned of General Hebert fleeing the system.

Batastia got a moment alone with Higgs, and clarified his position.

"Listen, Higgs," the Vice President whispered, "invite this Aguire down to the Capitol, but only allow him to come in a shuttle with a few of his officers. In the meantime, have the Navy ready to fire on the Hanno if there are any tricks."

"What's going on, sir?" Higgs inquired uneasily.

"Our president has outlived his usefulness, and, with the support of a national hero—this Aguire—to back us up, we should be able to convince your precious voters that all the problems they've had are Arnold Garane's fault. Aguire will be our witness that Garane lost his mind and committed suicide. I've already put together evidence to show how every unpopular decision was made by the President."

Batastia was fooling himself. He'd never survive the fallout from this fiasco. It couldn't work—it just couldn't, unless...unless a lot of people besides Arnold Garane end up dead, and therefore unable to disagree with Batastia's version of events.

"I'll take care of all the arrangements," Higgs whispered back without a trace of mistrust leaking into his voice.

He had the idiot Fisher call the Hanno, but his own transportation to the Capitol he arranged himself. He would be driven alone by his own chauffeur who was also his pilot, and be light-years away before Batastia ever realizes he bolted. Fisher could ride with Batastia.

Admiral Fisher seemed to be taking a long time with the arrangements for bringing Aguire down. The difficulty was that Fisher insisted on watching video of the officers who were coming as they boarded the shuttle.

"What was all that about?" Higgs asked when the shuttle was on its way.

"I still don't trust Aguire, Admiral." Fisher had that annoying nervous grin on his face. "I wanted to be sure of who's coming. There's one in particular, Bartholomew Hanson, who should not be allowed off that ship."

"Hanson? The super-soldier from the Jupiter War?" Higgs scratched his chin. "He's on the Hanno?"

"And he's going to stay there," Fisher said. "Aguire's coming with Lieutenants Andre Swanson and Carolyn Tully. Stokes and his daughter will be coming as well."

"Do you know these lieutenants?"

"No, but I checked their records. They're nothing special."

* * *

"Where is Admiral Higgs?" Crush Skor, the capitol chief of staff asked Fisher.

"He is getting that renegade Army unit contained by Navy commandos."

Crush grunted and scanned the city skyline for signs of trouble as the shuttle descended from the east and set down on the landing pad behind the Capitol building.

Crush said to Fisher, "No one on the Hanno will dare attack once we get Aguire and Stokes inside where they can't be tracked by radio. You stay with Aguire. I have my own plans for Stokes."

Aguire came out of the shuttle, followed by Lynda, G.J. Stokes, and two lieutenants. Fisher couldn't take his eyes off Aguire who had changed into a dress-gray uniform, looking the part of the gallant hero, hansom and dripping confidence. Fisher grimaced at the thought of the Commander getting yet another medal. Higgs would probably promote him to captain, but at least Fisher would still outrank him.

A horrible thought occurred to him: What if Aguire gets promoted to admiral? He did just save Batastia's life. A way must be found to kill Aguire.

Everyone got scanned for weapons when they entered the capitol. The kitchen staff was hastily setting up a buffet reception in the East Wing. An odd mix of officials began arriving from unrelated departments and bureaus, everyone who hadn't gone into hiding, apparently, and was available on short notice.

Crush told Aguire's group, "I will inform the President that you have arrived, please help yourselves to the buffet."

G.J. whispered to Aguire after Crush and Fisher moved away. "A lot of these people are new. They didn't have these positions before we left Earth, but I recognize some names. They're cousins and nephews of Batastia's cronies."

"I can imagine what happened to their predecessors," Aguire whispered back.

Lieutenant Tully wandered over to the buffet and leaned over to get a better look at some pastries, while discreetly scooping up a handful of dinner knifes from the silverware bin and slipping them into her pocket. The other lieutenant stood between her and the nearest security thug.

A thin, grandmotherly woman approached Aguire and extended her hand. "Commander Aguire, my name is Prudence Rival."

Aguire shook hands with the senator.

The Senate was still a new idea for him. The old Federation had three branches of government: Executive, Judicial and Military. It worked perfectly for the first decade after the Corporate War. Then, like all political systems, the elite figured out how to play the system, and it was back to politics as usual. Eventually, it got so bad that even people like Paul Poluka turned against it.

Vincent Batastia took full advantage of public apathy and repugnance by staging a swift coup that didn't directly touch most people. He replaced the military branch of government with an advisory-senate that had much less power than the ancient senates of Rome and America, but seemed good to a downtrodden people.

Even someone as politically ignorant as José Aguire had heard of Prudence Rival. As a child during the 23 years of the Corporate War, she'd been called the Grenade Girl and later received a medal from the old Federation. 35 years later, the same Federation had her under house-arrest for sedition. When the New Federation took over last year, she was released, and her overwhelming popularity mandated a position in the new government. She has been a royal pain-in-the-ass for Batastia ever since.

"Pleased to meet you, ma'am," Aguire said. "Allow me to introduce Lieutenant Tully and Lieutenant Swanson."

The senator nodded politely to the elfishly attractive Lieutenant Tully, and the muscular Swanson who had incredibly green eyes.

"I understand, Commander, that you took it upon yourself to come to the assistance of the Navy."

"It's our privilege to protect our nation, Senator."

"Is that what you did? I'm told your Captain Poluka thought joining General Hebert would be protecting the nation."

"Captain Poluka was unstable, ma'am. He…started making irrational decisions during the mission even before we knew about the troubles here."

"About your mission, I thought you were going to Arcturus. Yet, you've returned after barely a week, months earlier than expected."

"Yes, ma'am. It's a complicated story. I'll be making a full report as soon as possible."

The Senator frowned disapprovingly, but not at Aguire. He followed her eyes to the door, where brown-uniformed Capitol guards with pistols on their belts had just arrived. Guards were at the other doors, too. A chill went through the guests, and conversation died.

Crush Skor returned with an announcement. "I apologize for the inconvenience, but there has been an incident, and the facility must be locked down for a short time. There is no danger and no need for concern. An explanation will follow shortly."

Aguire was asked to accompany one of the security thugs to see the President. Crush took G.J., Lynda, and the lieutenants somewhere else.

* * *

Maria Rodriguez looked back at Redbird from the pilot's station. "Everything okay, sir?"

"Just a typical day in the Corps, Lieutenant."

"Sir, why did Aguire ask Old Man Stokes to go with him? Wouldn't someone like Hanson, McGee, or one of the barnies be a better choice? For that matter, why Lynda Stokes and Tully? I know Lynda has a reputation for kicking ass, but she's a civilian."

"The invitation to meet the President was unexpected," Redbird answered. "Fisher insisted that only a few people come down with Aguire, and Bart Hanson could definitely not be one of them.

"I know Fisher," Elisa added. "He's paranoid, so Commander Aguire needed people that wouldn't be seen as threatening. Lynda is a martial arts expert trained by none other than Bart Hanson. Tully is—believe it or not—one of the best knife fighters around."

"But they won't let her take a knife in to see the President."

"Yeah, but at least they'll let her in. She'll have to improvise."

"How much help can Stokes be?" Maria wondered. "He's old and keeps collapsing."

"Oh, he's doing much better now," Elisa assured her. "And he's very resourceful."

"They're splitting up," Ella interrupted. "Aguire's going upstairs. The others are going down."

Lynda had guessed right about Gentry's wife. She had a psychic talent which was proving useful now that Aguire's personal radio beacon was shielded inside the Capitol Building. The Arcturusian woman sat beside Redbird at the command desk, staring out the viewport at the planet Earth.

* * *

Aguire was led past a dozen silk-suited men with radio ear-buds, endlessly patrolling the hallways. Aguire went to the corner office of the Vice President. Two more guards stood just inside the door of the elegant room.

"Commander Aguire." Batastia stood at his desk and spread his arms in a gesture of welcome. "Our hero."

His face looked like oiled leather, and his eyes were dark, deep caverns.

"Mister Vice President," Aguire said, "thank you for receiving me. Will we be seeing the President?"

"I'm afraid not." Batastia shook his head with grave solemnity. "It seems the President has taken his own life. I found out just moments ago, but I am not surprised. Like your captain, President Garane was becoming unstable. No wonder, after all the terrible things he has done. We've all been living in fear of what he might do next."

"I see," Aguire said slowly. "This will be quite a shock for everyone. What will it mean for our government?"

"I've been considering that very question." Batastia leaned on his expansive, polished-walnut desk. "I will have to assume the office of President, and you will be my champion. There is quite a lot of misperception among the people. Some seem to think I had a hand in Garane's flawed policies. You can do a great service by being our spokesman. The people will trust a hero with your exemplary record."

"I assure you, sir, I will do whatever is in the best interest of the nation."

A spasm of annoyance flickered across Batastia's face at Aguire's choice of words. "Very well, Commander, we will go to the pressroom to announce the change in government. I have prepared some notes for you to read to the...nation."

* * *

"A new government," G.J. repeated what he'd just been told. "But still under Vincent Batastia."

Crush explained again. "The old New Federation was under President Arnold Garane. All the problems with the government were Garane's fault. President Batastia will fix all that but he needs the cooperation of the big corporations. As the CEO of Stokes Industries, you will have a key role building a new, better world."

"How flattering." G.J. looked around the basement facility that seemed more like a dungeon than a conference room. The surveillance-proof design reminded him of his underground laboratory in Napa Valley, but the only experiments done here were for the science of torture. Lynda watched them from across the room where she waited with the lieutenants. Three guards stood by the door. A fourth guard stood behind Crush, who was sitting across from G.J. Stokes at a desk.

"And if I decline your kind invitation—what then?"

Crush's face hardened into a mask of pitiless coercion. He spoke slowly, as if talking to an idiot. "The new government may not be able to protect you—or your daughter—from political extremists. It would be…dangerous for you…if Mister Batastia's government does not do well."

Lynda's Papa looked directly at Lynda, locking his green eyes to hers, and then looked at the green eyes of the man calling himself Lieutenant Swanson. Papa winked at his son.

Crush wondered what the wink meant, but he never found out. G.J. Stokes suddenly moved faster than an old man should— faster than a human should—flying across the desk with a fist moving faster than sight.

The guard standing behind Crush blinked stupidly as blood and brains splattered across his uniform. An instant later, the old man's left hand closed on the guard's neck and snapped it like a matchstick. Lynda and Gentry took care of the other guards.

Tully had a handful of dinner knives ready to throw, but there were no guards left to kill. "Jeez, you people are fast."

"Comes from clean living," Gentry said. He went to the door. It was steel clad, and had a little square window. "One more outside. Do you think he'll open it if we push the buzzer?"

"Let's not bother him," Lynda answered. She checked the

441

time on her watch. "We'll open it ourselves. Is Ella still connected to you?"

Gentry nodded. "She knows everything."

"Will someone just kick the damn door?" G.J. said. "Lieutenant Tully, I suggest you cover your ears. There's going to be a mighty loud noise."

Gentry backed up and charged at the door, leaping up to hit it with both feet. When the door sprang out to the corridor, a boom shook the building. The guard standing on the other side became an integral part of the opposite wall.

Far above, in the orbiting starship, Ella informed Commander Redbird that the time was now.

* * *

"President Batastia is on his way to the pressroom," the Chief of Security informed all the capitol guards via radio before turning to a radar tech who was waving at him. "What is it?"

"The Hanno is launching shuttles, and they're heading our way. Hey, I think they just launched…oh, crap…it's a light-cruiser. I didn't know they had one of those."

The Chief of Security ran to the display. His eyes bulged at the swarm of spacecrafts accelerating towards the Capitol. He ran to the com link connected to the city's defense HQ. "Fire on that starship. Destroy the Hanno."

Another tech rushed over to him and blurted, "General Hebert's ships are approaching Earth."

"What the—? I thought Hebert's ships were destroyed."

"He's still got a couple of light-cruisers and some fighters. They slipped past the patrols and are two minutes out."

"Shit." The Chief looked from the radar display of the shuttles approaching from low-Earth-orbit, to the computer graphic of Hebert's ships screaming in at NLS from interplanetary space.

A message from the defense HQ confirmed they fired on the Hanno but without result.

"What's the problem?" the Chief demanded.

"They've tipped the ship up so the bow is facing us, making them a smaller target, and they put some kind of physical shield in the way. Our beam weapons can't penetrate it."

The tech watching the Hanno jumped up, knocking over his chair, and pointed a trembling finger at the screen. "They've fired a missile...my god ...it's an eagle."

"An eagle? Impossible," the Chief sputtered. "What's the target?"

"Navy Ops," the tech cried, "And they've launched another...going for surface-to-orbit defenses."

The ground shook as the first eagle "city killer" found its target a few klicks away from the Capitol. The Chief of Security ran all the way to his car and drove away. It was later speculated that his intention was to disappear before the government was completely overthrown. As he left the Capitol grounds, he ran into an Army Infantry platoon, and that was the end of him.

* * *

40 thousand kilometers above the Earth, the hull of the alien starship Fledik was holding position. Three mini-thrusters, hastily clamped onto it, kept it aligned between the weapons on the ground and the Starship Hanno.

"That was brilliant, Chief," Redbird told Braun, "I never would have thought of it."

Braun chuckled. "I can just imagine their faces when they let us have all four beams at once, and nothing happened."

Out the front window of the Hanno, the view of the capital city was eclipsed by the 300 meter wide hull of the Arcturusian spaceship. It was not enough to completely shield the Hanno, even with the starship pointed nose-down at Earth, but it showed up as the primary target on the groundside tracking system, drawing most of the fire. The massive particle shields of the Forward Section were sufficient for whatever energy got past the Fledik. There was some damage to the antenna towers, but repairs could wait.

"The last shuttle is away, Commander," Elisa Santino called out from the S-Bay.

"Excellent." Redbird crossed his arms. "Give me a link to General Hebert."

A squarish face with a six days growth of blond beard appeared on the front screen. General Hebert was on the flight deck of a light-cruiser. There were people packed in all around him. Everyone he had left on his ships when the Hanno arrived in the Solar System—nearly 300 people—were jammed into his two cruisers and a handful of light-fighters.

Aguire had contacted Hebert long before letting the Hanno be spotted by Jupiter Traffic Control. He'd made a deal with the general, and formed a plan. They'd taken the smart-machine circuits from the Hanno's electric trucks and installed them into 82 of Hebert's converted civilian ships, making them smart enough to fly unmanned on a suicide run that would scare the shit out of Batastia. Destroying the unmanned armada resulted in getting the Hanno parked right over the Capitol, where they could fire missiles at point-blank range.

"Commander Redbird, I trust your Commander Aguire is faring well in the Capitol?" Hebert asked.

Redbird shrugged. "He appeared on a broadcast with Batastia just as we hit the Navy HQ. They announced that President Garane committed suicide, and Batastia is the new president. The broadcast ended rather suddenly. Commander Aguire is separated from the others. We're counting on your infantry unit to take control of the Capitol. Have you heard from them, sir?"

"Just now, yes. My troops at the Capitol. Some of Capitol Security is still putting up a fight, but many are running. I'll be there at about the same time as your shuttles. I'd say we're going to win this one. My priority now will be to minimize casualties, but I will not allow Batastia to get away. There will be no negotiating if he's got your people hostage."

"Aguire and the others knew that when they went in," Redbird assured the Hebert. "My people won't hinder you, General. Get Batastia."

Hebert showed a boyish half-grin. "I aim to, Commander. Hebert out."

The image blinked off. Redbird sucked in a deep breath. Everything was moving so fast.

Chapter 65

Aguire lost track of Batastia when the first missile sent a rumbling tremor through the Capitol and a wave of guilt washed over him. He'd never been in this position before. He never ordered an attack that would end the lives of so many people who were just doing what they were told. During the Jupiter War, Poluka always had that responsibility, and the justification always made it seem…well…justified. Now Aguire understood that no matter how many lives his choice would save in the long run, it was still his order that killed those people today.

The brown-uniformed guards didn't know what was happening or they would have shot Aguire right then. As it was, they whisked their new president out a side door, and had a couple of beefy guards drag Aguire towards the basement. They got him between them, each with an iron grip digging into the flesh of his upper arms.

With a springing kick timed to the guard's gait, Aguire leaned back into their grip while launching his legs and hips into the air in a smooth, cat-like motion. The guards' automatic response was to become ridged, giving him all the support he needed as he pulled his knees in and completed a backward flip, wrenching out of their hands as his feet found the floor.

He followed up with a swift punch to the face of the guard on his right which sent the man reeling, but didn't disable him. The other guard leapt back, out of Aguire's reach, and jerked his weapon from its holster.

It would have been the end for Aguire had a stolen dinner knife not suddenly flown out of the stairway. It slammed into the left side of the guard's head and stuck there. The sudden agony of having a foreign object driven into his skull made his fingers squeeze reflexively as he reached for his head with both hands, forgetting that he had a pistol in one hand. The weapon fired just as he got it up to his own face.

Aguire spun to face the other guard, but he was already down with one knife in his neck and another where his right eye should have been.

Lieutenant Tully stood at the stairway with another knife in each hand. She was pale. Her breath was quick and shallow, but she gave Aguire a quick wink. On the stairs behind her were G.J., Gentry, and Lynda. All of them were flecked with blood, but it didn't seem to be theirs.

"Where's Batastia?" G.J. asked.

Aguire led them out the side door to a wide patio surrounded by a rose garden. There were smoldering bodies in brown uniforms on the pavement and an Army gunship hovering 20 meters above. Aguire raised his hands until the gunner waved at him.

"Aguire," a soprano voice called from beyond the garden. A dozen soldiers charged in, led by Major Rivers. "We're secure on this side. There's still some fighting in the West Wing."

Aguire gestured at the gunship. "Is this Hebert's Infantry?"

"Right. They hit the gates just after we launched. There's also a civilian group—armed to the teeth—marching from downtown, hoping to get their hands on Batastia."

"Do you have him?"

"No." Rivers seemed surprised. "Isn't he inside?"

They went around to the north side of the building. The shuttle Aguire arrived in was gone.

* * *

"Commander Redbird." Henry Tran raised his voice from the I-Bay. "Aguire's shuttle is heading west at high altitude, but Aguire's beacon is still at the Capitol."

An audio signal came from Major Rivers. "Commander Redbird, we're missing a shuttle."

"We see it, Major. Who's driving?"

"We think it's Batastia."

Redbird sprang from his chair and ran to the I-Bay to look at the graphic. The shuttle was heading due west. The speed was up to 20 kps—about as fast as it could go in the atmosphere.

"Don't lose him," Redbird told Tran, then, to Rivers, "It's

heading west, possibly toward McConnell."

"McConnell's blocked by some vigilante militia group," Rivers responded. "He can't land there."

"We'll track him, Major, but we need someone to go after him. All our shuttles are on the ground."

Aguire's voice came back. "Take the pinnace. It wouldn't be my first choice, but it's fast. We'll try to free up a light-fighter on this end, but it'll be a while."

"Will do, Commander. I'll keep you posted."

Redbird turned back to the command desk and found Maria standing in front of him.

"Sir, I'm the best pilot you've got."

"Right. Get down to the pinnace. I'll have people meet you there."

Elisa Santino called out from the S-Bay, "I'll find people and send them."

To a tech in the I-Bay, Redbird said, "Get me a link to the Director of McConnell Spaceport."

* * *

The shuttle docks were huge, steel caverns after all 40 shuttles and the cruiser were launched. Maria listened to the echoes of Townsend's people prepping the pinnace for launch as she waited. The first sent to join her was Commander Martensen.

"Glad to see you, sir." Maria gave him a big smile. "I've never arrested a dictator before. I hope you know the proper procedure."

"It's simple, Lieutenant. If he makes it terribly convenient, we take him alive so he can get a fair trial before he's executed. Looks better in the history books that way."

Ensign Jack Trimble showed up next and said he was her lookout officer. Then came Newhall and Harper with twelve crewmen from Hydroponics, bringing a long canvas bag that had HANNO ARMORY printed on it.

"Good idea," Martensen said. "What did you bring?"

"A bunch of plasma pistols," Harper replied, "some grenade launchers, and this."

He pulled out an Army-issue rotating gravity pulse weapon.

Martensen grinned. "That should do it."

Last to show up was Elisa Santino with a plasma pistol already on her belt.

"I may be short, but I know how to hunt," she said to Martensen's raised eyebrow.

The pinnace launched with eighteen aboard. Maria circled the ungainly vehicle around the tugboat group that was moving the Fledik back to the SERFS work bay.

Earth was 42 thousand kilometers ahead, filling about fifteen degrees of the view from the front window. A gibbous moon was off to one side. The sun was behind them.

Elisa took a seat behind Jack Trimble and looked out the starboard window at the damage to the Hanno's antenna towers caused by the capital city's beam weapons.

"Looks like the cable tray for the cameras got hit. We won't be getting images of the surface for a while," she told Maria.

"We'll find the shuttle with radar," Maria assured her.

"The shuttle's beacon just went dead," Trimble informed them, "but we've got it on radar. It's going straight for New Wichita. Its speed's down to five kps, but it'll be at the spaceport in fifteen minutes."

"So will we, Ensign," Maria said, and proved it by cranking the acceleration up to twelve gravities and holding it there for one minute. The frame of the pinnace creaked and vibrated as the inertia compensators strained to keep up.

Trimble's eyes got big and round as he watched Earth grow large in front of them. After crossing half the distance, Maria decelerated at the same rate until the planet Earth completely filled the view ahead and New Wichita looked like a shiny dot 100 kilometers below them. The pinnace hit the atmosphere at roughly 60 kilometers per second.

The hull temperature warning light was blinking as Maria slowed to a reasonable rate of descent, but she still had the nose pointed straight down, and Trimble had to force his attention from the oncoming planet to get a fix on McConnell.

"The spaceport is 200 klicks west, and 40 north of where you're going to slam us into the ground, Lieutenant."

Maria gave him a nasty look for his lack of faith, and adjusted the course. She got the pinnace flying level at 3000 meters altitude, just 20 klicks from the Spaceport. The ground-speed was down to five kps.

The com lit up with a link from the Hanno.

"Martensen." Redbird's face appeared. "I think I screwed up."

"How's that, sir?"

Redbird looked embarrassed. "I contacted the spaceport and asked to speak to the director. Before I confirmed whom I was talking to, I gave out more information than I should have."

"Why do I think this is going to be bad news?" Martensen asked.

"The spaceport is overrun with civilian militia," Redbird explained. "Some nut named Klein is in charge. I thought he was the director, and told him we're chasing down a shuttle that may have Batastia aboard."

"Did you say Klein?" Elisa asked.

"Yeah, does that mean anything to you?"

"It might."

Martensen looked at the radar and saw the shuttle entering spaceport's airspace. "Redbird, are these militia people going to start shooting at us?"

"Very likely. Watch yourself. We're trying to get them to cooperate, but don't count on it."

"Thanks for the warning, Joseph. We're about to get real busy. I'll call back later. Pinnace out."

"The shuttle's going low, Commander." Trimble punched in refinements to the radar and infrared data. "It's below the treetops. We've lost it."

Martensen studied the navigation display. "Drop our ground speed to 50 meters per second—altitude 800. When we get within a couple of klicks, drop the speed to around 20 meters per second."

Elisa scanned through radio signals, and almost screamed when a familiar voice came through on one channel. She cranked up the volume so everyone would hear.

"...no, no...there's no one else on b-b-board," Admiral Fisher said. "I'm coming from the shipyard in Texas—not from the Capitol. I just want to land and j-j-join the rebellion."

"Why's your altitude so low?" an impatient voice came back, "You get up where we can see you—then come straight in and land on the east tarmac. Don't get close to any buildings, or you'll be shot down. Understand, Admiral?"

Elisa's jaws clenched, and her hands knotted in the cloth of her uniform as she waited to hear the son-of-a-bitch's voice again, but there was no response.

"Where is he?" She glared at Trimble as if it was his fault they couldn't find the shuttle.

"Got him," the young navigator cried, and pointed out the window. "He's following the tree line almost at ground level. He's going around towards New Wichita."

Maria glanced out the window, and then at the radar. "I don't see him, but I'll take your word for it."

She pulled the pinnace around, and began moving west.

"Santino, call spaceport and tell them who we are," Martensen said. "Tell 'em we're in pursuit of...of Admiral Fisher. Deny knowing anything about Batastia. We don't want to encourage civilian involvement."

"Yes, sir, but if this Klein is who I think he is, it's Fisher that he wants."

The pinnace was fast, but not as maneuverable as the shuttle. When they got into the city they lost the tiny spacecraft as it zipped between buildings and under bridges. The streets were deserted but for occasional civilians scurrying through back streets and alleys.

"What about this Klein?" Martensen asked Elisa. "If he knows that Fisher is in that shuttle will he be coming after him?"

"Definitely. If this is who I think it is, Fisher murdered his sister."

"I see. Maria, get us some altitude, and put us over highway fifty-four. Mister Trimble, watch for any traffic from McConnell to the city. Maybe this Mister Klein knows where Fisher would go."

The pinnace hovered one kilometer above the prairie, right on the city limit. They had a striking view of the spaceport on the right, and the ruins of Old Wichita on the left. On the highway, a spaceport delivery van was moving west. Trimble measured its speed at a 150 kph.

"I didn't know they could go that fast," Martensen said. "It's got to be him."

The van took a side road towards the ruins of Old Wichita. There were small neighborhoods outside of the city, with big old houses dating back to the days before New Wichita was built.

"Stay directly above him," Martensen told Maria. "And,

Trimble, look for that shuttle. A lot of these houses are owned by the Spacemen's Association, and have landing pads. Fisher may have the use of one of them."

Elisa read a text message from the Hanno. "Hey, they say the fighting's over. What's left of the Navy's on our side now. Hebert is doing an announcement right now."

The news cheered them up, but Elisa couldn't stop thinking of Fisher. Even when he was running away, stripped of authority, he still intimidated her, still filled her with loathing.

"The van stopped at a house." Trimble zoomed in with the camera. "It's a big place—has a swimming pool and some outbuildings. There's a wall around the whole property."

"Switch to infrared," Elisa suggested. "See if anyone's home."

The image changed to show the heat pattern of the area. Trimble zoomed back out, and spotted something near the back of the house. It was warm patch of ground about twelve by five meters. At the corners were distinct outlines the shape of shuttle skids.

"He's been here and gone," Trimble concluded. "We're too late."

"Check radar," Martensen said.

"Aye, sir. There are six vehicles in the sky. These two coming from the west can't be him. Something small is circling the city—looks like conventional aircraft—probably police. There's one going south that's a possibility. But these other two are heading for Saint Louis. They both look like shuttles."

"Damn it. We can't chase all of them." Martensen scratched his head. "If Batastia's in that shuttle, why would he come here? Or, even if it's just Fisher, this is no place to run to…unless he needs something here before going somewhere else."

The com chimed with a link from Aguire. The screen showed him in the lookout pit of a cruiser.

"Commander," Martensen said with just a hint of reluctance. "The missing shuttle came to New Wichita and probably landed."

"Probably?" Aguire looked concerned. "I expect Batastia's looking for a way off the planet and didn't realize the McConnell is blocked."

"Understood, but we don't know for sure that Batastia's in the shuttle. We do know that Fisher is."

Aguire considered that news. "I seem to remember Fisher

going to the Galactic Bank just after he learned the Attorney General was assassinated. Maybe he was getting ready for quick get-away. Check with the Hanno to see if anyone knows Fisher's home address in New Wichita."

"I think we're there now, Commander."

"Excellent." Aguire nodded. "I'm enroute to your location. Our ETA is about 40 minutes."

When the link closed, Elisa said, "Fisher had an apartment downtown, but Admiral Higgs had a place out here."

"Our man is out of the van. Jeez, he's enormous." Trimble brought their attention back to the belly camera's view. "He's got a weapon—looks like maybe a hunting rifle—and he's climbing over a gate."

Indeed, a large man was struggling over the top of a wrought iron gate, and dropping into the yard. He reached through the bars of the gate and retrieved a long weapon.

"Look!" Maria pointed to the infrared screen. "Someone's there...by the far wall."

Trimble panned the belly camera to where Maria indicated. Obscured by an elm tree was a figure working hard at something. It became clear what was happening when the man threw a shovel to one side and got down on his knees.

"He's digging a hole," Trimble said unnecessarily. "Oh, I get it. The money Aguire was talking about. Fisher buried it. Why would he do that?"

"Because he doesn't trust anyone," Elisa said.

"I suppose we better go down and arrest him. Batastia may be in any of those buildings and, like Fisher, he won't trust anyone. He'll probably be armed, or even have some guards with him. Trimble, start looking for a landing site."

There was no place inside the walls big enough to set the pinnace down, so they opted for easing in on the side of the property with the most tree cover.

Each of them got a plasma pistol. A couple of the Hydroponics crewmen carried the grenade launchers, and Ensign Newhall got the job of blasting a hole in the wall with a short burst of rotating gravity pulses. Everyone stood behind him, poised to rush through as he hefted the RGP weapon and fired from the hip. Bricks vaporized, and a plasma flash set the bushes afire behind the wall.

Elisa held her breath as they sprang through the smoke and dust. Once inside, she saw the missing shuttle parked under a gazebo-like structure in the back.

A huge, muscular man with curly, black hair, a scraggly beard, and wearing tan coveralls came running out of the main house. Klein held an old-fashioned hunting rifle. His mouth hung open in amazement as Martensen ordered him to drop the weapon, but Martensen died at that moment as a burst of metal plasma burned a hole through his body from behind. The next to die was Newhall, who squeezed the trigger on the RPG as he took a blast on his left side. His weapon discharged into the sky, punching a round hole in a cloud overhead.

The others fired blindly towards the back of the yard, but hit no one. Fisher had gotten round behind them, and was at the hole in the wall with a pistol in each hand, rapid firing. Something exploded—one of the grenade launchers—and the fighting stopped.

Elisa was down, thrown by the blast and dazed. Her vision was blurred and she couldn't hear anything but a constant ringing. Someone was there, lifting her roughly, carrying her somewhere. Jumbled images got through Elisa's perception: Fisher's wild eyes and idiotic grin. He was talking—talking a lot, and very fast—but she couldn't hear him.

Then she was back inside the pinnace, lying on the deck by the airlock next to a plastic sack full of money. Her hearing was recovering now. Fisher cried out in fear and slammed shut the inner side-hatch. A face with furious eyes and a curly dark beard appeared in the window of the hatch.

"Motherfucker," Fisher screamed hysterically and stamped his feet, his voice rising a couple of octaves. "You goddamn motherfucker—damn you—goddamn you."

Klein beat the window with both fists, but it was armored Radglass—unbreakable. Fisher jabbed a button next to the hatch, and the outer door swung shut and locked. Klein was trapped in the airlock. Fisher suddenly giggled.

"I got you now, you bastard. I killed your whore sister, and now I'm gonna to kill you. I'll take you up to orbit and drop you out, you motherfucker."

Elisa sat up and started to rise, but a backhand slap from Fisher knocked her down again and put the taste of blood in her mouth.

"And you!" Fisher raved. "I'm finally going to have you, bitch."

"It's over, Fisher," Elisa gasped through her pain. "You'll never get away."

"No? Well, not in that stupid shuttle, but you were nice enough to bring me a pinnace. I'll find a spaceliner and get to the colonies, bitch, but before then, I'll finally make you beg for mercy."

He laughed and looked at Klein's face in the airlock window. "Just like I made his slut sister beg before I choked her. Ha! This bastard's been after me for weeks, but he ain't gonna get me."

He started laughing at Klein's enraged face and didn't notice Elisa roll over and start crawling on her hands and knees. When he turned back to her, she was right up against him. She shoved her tiny body against his legs as hard as she could, causing him to trip over her back and crash face-first onto the deck. She lurched to her feet and flung herself at a button next to the airlock. Before Fisher could stop it, the inner hatch opened and a giant of a man stepped through.

Chapter 66

"We've got sixteen dead, counting Fisher," an Army lieutenant reported to General Hebert. "There's no sign of Batastia."

"He wasn't in the shuttle when it landed here." Hebert shook his head. "Either he was never in the shuttle, or he got dropped off somewhere else."

"Ensign Tully is checking the flight recorder," Commander Aguire told him. "If Fisher dropped Batastia somewhere, we'll know shortly."

Aguire watched the soldiers bringing body bags from the cruiser and start putting his people into them. Martensen got bagged first. Next was Newhall, the young ensign who had gone to the alien planet with Aguire. Such a waste.

"Commander?" A sergeant approached Aguire. "Santino's in stable condition with no serious injuries, but Lieutenant Rodriguez and Ensign Harper need immediate evacuation to a hospital."

"Understood—can you get them in the shuttle? I'll fly them to New Wichita myself."

The soldier looked at General Hebert who nodded his approval.

"What about the prisoner?" Aguire asked before the man turned away.

"Klein? He's got scratches and bruises—some old, some new—but he's okay. He admits killing Fisher, but he seems…docile, now. Santino says Fisher raped and murdered his sister. She thinks we should let him go."

"General?" Aguire looked at Hebert.

"It's your call, Commander. I would have put Fisher up against a wall, anyway."

"Let him go, Sergeant."

As military activity cooled down on Earth, all personnel from the Starship Hanno were recalled to the ship. Aguire didn't want his people talking too much just yet. They were his people now. He'd made a vow to them, and they had pledged their service to him. Not to the government, nor to the Corps, but to him.

When he took the Hanno away from Poluka, he discovered it wasn't enough to have rules and regulations on his side. The crew of the Hanno simply wouldn't accept his claim to power just on the basis of procedure. They were not fighting just to survive, though that did account for a lot of motivation. They were fighting for beliefs. Each joined the Exploration Corps voluntarily for what they thought it represented, and they needed a leader who would be the embodiment of that ideal.

Many wanted to fight the New Federation, but not under a captain who would make their deaths meaningless.

Others were more concerned—even fanatical—about the Arcturusians: an entire civilization—an entire race—was facing extinction, and the aliens had endeared themselves to the crew of the Hanno.

In all cases, the officers and crew of the Hanno each stubbornly insisted that their beliefs were what the Exploration Corps was supposed to stand for. Aguire couldn't, in his heart, disagree with any of them. He did want to fight the New Federation, but only if the risk would have some meaning, some chance of accomplishing something.

He also knew, as an Exploration Corps officer, and as a human being, there was no excuse that could pardon him if he did not devote himself to the welfare of the alien people who were now at risk, not only from genetic fatigue, but also from the contact with Earth that the Hanno represented.

In the meantime, there was a government to rebuild. Aguire didn't really feel qualified to participate in the political decisions, but he knew someone who was.

"Is he up to it?" Aguire asked Doctor Payne.

It had been only four days since Captain Paul Poluka surrendered command to Aguire. He'd been confined to the Med Center, and was undergoing a combination of treatments that Doctor Payne and an Arcturusian psychiatric specialist came up with.

"Impossible to know for sure, José, he was almost catatonic when you brought him in, but you can talk to him now."

A hospital gown looked out of place on Paul Poluka, but so did the downcast eyes and gloomy disposition. He'd screwed up the mission; got people killed needlessly, made a fool of him, and shot his friend's leg off. At the apex of his shining career he'd screwed up everything.

"Good morning, Captain." Aguire tried to sound natural. He sat on a chair. Poluka sat on the edge of the hospital bed.

The Captain looked up as if he'd never seen Aguire before. "Good morning, Commander. Or is it Captain now?"

"Still Commander, at least for now," Aguire answered. "I've got a new job for you, sir, if you want it."

Poluka didn't respond, but waited to hear the rest.

"You've been told," Aguire went on, "about the fall of the New Federation. General Hebert is gathering leaders from around the world to put things back on track."

"On track? What does that mean?" Poluka roused himself out of disinterest. "Are they going back to how it was before, back to the old Fed?"

"It's possible, I suppose. I was never really any good at politics. I'm staying out of it."

"Hm, smart move. Smarter than most people. Most can't resist getting involved."

"I'd like you to consider being the chairman of the committee that will design the new government, sir. It'll be a temporary position, which will end when the new government takes effect. Hebert's already agreed to it.

"No one on Earth knows that you've had problems, sir. Everyone believes that you were in command of the Hanno this whole time, and that my story about you dying, and me taking control of the Hanno, was just a ruse invented by you to defeat the New Federation. Only Hebert knows otherwise, and he doesn't know much. He thinks you've been sick due to some toxic food from Arcturus."

Poluka squinted at him, and rasped in a hoarse whisper, "You're protecting me?"

"Yes, sir."

"Giving me another chance?"

457

"Yes, sir."

"Will I still have the Hanno?"

"No, sir. The Hanno is mine, now."

"I see." Poluka bowed his head. "Still, it's better than I deserve, isn't it? Why are you doing it?"

"I have no family, sir, except for my friends and, in the end, what else matters?"

"Indeed…what else matters?" Poluka looked up at him. "I had a plan worked out—thought about it for years—about how the Federation could be fixed. I'd like to try to make it happen, but then what? If I join this committee, what will I do later? Will I still be in the Corps?"

"I've been thinking about that, sir. Batastia's government killed the best and brightest in the Army and Navy. I think you would be just the person to rebuild the Navy. You could be the Admiral in charge of setting up and managing the command structure, and see to it the Navy becomes what it's supposed to be."

"That's a pretty good offer. I think I'll take it." Poluka finally smiled. It was a weak smile, the smile of a man who'd come to accept a fate he'd never planned on, but it was a smile. "What about the Arcturusians? I've been thinking about them, too. They were right about fearing us…our brutality. Two violent overthrows in as many years must horrify a people who've lived in peace under a benevolent monarch for…what is it…six thousand years?"

"I'm working on that." It was Aguire's turn to smile. "I can't turn my back on them. The Hanno can go to Arcturus and return to Earth in a matter of hours. We've already dropped off Donno and some others who need special medical help."

Poluka winced. "How is Donno?"

Aguire didn't try to soften the news. Poluka deserved to hear it the way it was. "Not much could be done about Donno's leg. The knee and lower leg couldn't be saved. Ensign Harper has shrapnel throughout his body that'll take time to remove, as well as ruptured eardrums that only the Arcturusians know how to fix. Maria Rodriguez had injuries that our doctors could handle, but why bother when the alien doctors can do it in days instead of months?"

"It's good that such doctors are available," Poluka sighed,

"and that they're compassionate to such a barbaric race."

"Well, I hope our barbaric race will eventually learn to behave better. We could learn a lot from those people," Aguire said. "I've reopened discussions with Elpastre, and worked out a plan. It isn't a great plan, but it has a chance of succeeding. I had to bring Hebert in on the secret and, to Hebert's credit, the General realized that he can't manage both the rebuilding of Earth's government, and the alien situation. He agreed to let me call the shots concerning Earth's policy on Arcturus, provided I can handle it. He warned me that if things start getting out of control, Hebert will step in and take over."

"I think you'll do fine, José, but what is your plan?"

"We're going to have it both ways. We'll keep the existence of the alien people a secret, at least for now, and yet still provide a way to genetically mix with people from Earth. This will be tricky. It'll require going ahead with your original plan, at least in part, by taking the Hanno away from the government.

"We will report that Arcturus has life, that it's dangerous, unpleasant life, and there's little in the way of valuable resources. That should keep the big companies from getting too eager. We will also report that people—descendants of a lost spaceship from the early days of distortion-drive—are living there, and have reverted to a pre-industrial society. That will keep settlers from guessing that the natives are actually aliens, at least for a while."

"Settlers? You're going to treat it like a frontier planet?"

"Sort of. General Hebert has agreed to stipulate for our new government—as a favor to me—that Arcturus will be declared off-limits, to protect the native ecosystem until it can be thoroughly studied by the Hanno, which will have exclusive jurisdiction in the entire sector. We will then unofficially encourage illegal settlement by individuals and small groups. The Arcturusian atmosphere will prevent anyone from easily getting information on the native population. Only a suborbital survey within the atmosphere will be able to even map the entire planet. No small operation can afford such an expense, and the people of Arcturus will be prepared for meeting newcomers."

"Clever, but it's a slippery tightrope to walk. I remember once writing in your performance evaluation that you were unimaginative."

"As I recall, you referred to it as 'a creative thinking barrier'."

"Well, you've found it within yourself at last." Poluka actually laughed now. "But, you know, the Corps still has a hierarchy that will want to have some say in Arcturus, and the government isn't going to want to give up the Hanno. How will you deal with that?"

"I'm going to get a good lawyer."

* * *

The title Elpastre did not make him a god. It did not make him infallible, or add any measure to his height. It certainly did not make him invincible. All it did was make him the King of Arcturus, and that was not enough. Not any more.

"My world has been governed by nobles and regional lords since the beginning of history, but the monarch's role has been mostly ceremonial with few exceptions. That is all about to change. I must become active and central in balancing the rights and sensibilities of my people against the immigrants from Earth who will take whatever land they choose."

Aguire listened to the translation. Elpastre, Lapastra and her brother Oppo were with them in the Hall of Records as they reviewed maps of Arcturus, to plan for the coming of pioneers from Earth.

"Your concerns are entirely justified," Aguire told him. "The first people coming will be few and not well equipped, but they will be unpredictable. I will do everything in my power to keep them on the uninhabited, north-east quadrant of the continent, but I can't watch everything they do. Sooner or later, they'll want to take a look at the rest of the planet."

"And my people," Elpastre said, "will do everything possible to keep from being noticed. It will seem like a great injustice to many, needing to hide from aliens on our own world, while they take our land, but to many it will be a great adventure.

A great adventure? Aguire hoped it would be nothing worse. The word underscored what a different way of thinking these people had.

"We should go, Elpastre."

They boarded the Hanno with a fair-sized group of Arcturusians. Lapastra remained on Arcturus, though she was invited to come, and even her husband couldn't understand her reluctance.

"I have imagined this since I was a boy," Elpastre confided to Aguire. "To see the stars that my people only know through ancient stories, and the world that legends tell us was our original home. When the Fledik launched, I wanted more than anything to be aboard her."

"Now you will see it all, Elpastre."

Aguire remembered the first time he'd gone to space, and couldn't deny Elpastre the same wondrous thrill. They made a scenic sub-light-speed pass by the Zone before jumping to a point where Sol was still a tiny, bright circle in the distance, followed by a ten-percent-light-speed entry past Saturn and Jupiter. The monarch's first view of Earth was magnificent.

Chapter 67

The people General Hebert brought together were a tough bunch. All were powerful in their own way, and what each one thought was best for the whole world was particularly good for that person's part of the world.

It took some fancy brinkmanship to steer the committee away from returning to the old Federation style of government, or from getting a new version of the Corporate State.

Poluka wanted a post-democratic republic like the old democratic republic of the United States with one major improvement: the House of Representatives would not be elected. They'd be drafted from the general population with a lottery, making the House truly representative. Even if an idiot was drafted, it couldn't be any worse than electing someone who actually wanted to be a politician. Anyone who refused to serve would be jailed for five years.

After serving a single term, a Representative who was popular could run for election to the Senate, or even the Presidency. It had some resemblance to the old Federation's system of advancement, but eliminated the military branch of the federal government.

Politicians hated the idea. They finally settled on a democratic republic that would be phased in over the next two years. Until then, the Continental Governors, together with the Advisory Senate led by Prudence Rival, would manage most of the planet's services. The Army, under General Hebert, would deal with global issues, including establishing the new government in a timely and orderly fashion.

"The interim government is going to need some watching," Hebert told Paul Poluka as they strolled Monument Avenue towards the Legislature Building. "Everything's moving too fast. The worst of the old regime is gone, but many people still in power had hidden ties to Batastia. The Continental Governors of Australia, North Africa, Asia, and South America haven't changed because they were clearly opposed to Batastia all along. In fact, they all suffered for their opposition, but were strong enough to survive the bastard's rule.

"South Africa, North America, East Europe, Russia, and the Pacific Islands all have new Governors, but we don't know much about them. The only ones I'm sure of are Russia and North America."

"They'll all be up for election in two years." Poluka said. "But they'll have an awful lot of power until then."

"True, but so will I. And you will, too. The Navy is still bigger and more powerful than the Army. We have to be sure its leadership puts the nation's interests ahead of the government's, and know the difference between the two. How you guide the Navy may be the single most important safeguard against getting another dictatorship down the road."

"I still have hopes for a post-democratic republic," Paul said as they turned a corner. "It's only a matter of time before the worst people learn to play the democratic-republic game. They always do."

"Everything is temporary, Paul." Hebert sighed. "Tomorrow, Aguire will face the interim government to make his case concerning the Hanno. Frankly, I don't see how he's going pull it off. I half expect to find he's taken the Hanno out of the Solar System by then, and turned renegade."

Paul didn't want to guess. Nothing turned out as he expected. Aguire was now the champion of the people, the great hero. He'd given Paul most of the credit, but it was Aguire that everyone praised—and he deserved it.

"We'll see." Paul Poluka shrugged. "Tell me, any word about the search for Batastia?"

Hebert's eyes narrowed. "No, damn it. The traffic logs show about a hundred small ships leaving Earth at about the same time. Most of Batastia's people bailed out when they knew they'd lost. Some of them we can get our hands on—and we will—but many just disappeared. Batastia was traced to a private yacht, and then to a Navy battleship in the trade route. The skipper and most of the officers on that ship were all his people. From there, we don't know where he went."

"And Higgs?" Poluka asked. "Any sign of him?"

"None. He may still be on Earth for all we know. By the way, we found out about something Higgs was involved in. It turned my stomach when I heard about this...."

Hebert finished the horrible story at the steps of the Legislature Building overlooking the Hudson River. Paul's disgust with New Federation boiled anew. He looked up at the granite building and swore he'd never allow such tyranny to take root again.

* * *

The next morning, Poluka was again on the Legislature steps.

"Good morning, Senator," he greeted Prudence Rival.

"Hello, Captain Poluka," she said warmly. "I never thought I'd be happy about getting more responsibly, but the senators who fled with the old regime won't be missed—not by me—even though the rest of us have to shoulder their load until the next elections."

"You're getting an early start today."

"Oh, that's normal." Senator Rival grinned. "The early morning is when we clean our offices."

"You clean your own office?" Paul couldn't hide his surprise.

Mrs. Rival chuckled and shook her head. "That's what we call it when we check for eavesdropping devices. "Batastia had our offices bugged regularly. The Continental Governors—well, some of them—have been doing the same thing."

"That's shocking," Poluka said, and he meant it. "That's got to stop."

"It will eventually. Oh, by the way, we don't clean the entrance foyer. The press has it thoroughly bugged. Be careful what you say in there."

"I will," he said as she continued to her office. "Thanks for the warning."

Limousines began arriving with Continental Governors. This would be a tricky bunch. He'd already met them while wrestling with the issue of redesigning the government.

Except for North Africa and South America, all of the governors wanted to delay phasing in the new democratic republic for several years, giving them more time to cement their own power base. If not for General Hebert's ability to unilaterally depose them for being assholes, they would still be arguing.

The Army and Navy would have a say in federal policy for now, and they were represented on the panel by four admirals and three generals. Hebert recused himself from the proceedings based on his connection to Commander Aguire.

The Exploration Corps did not have any specified role in the new government. Lynda Stokes had stridently opposed it, and eventually persuaded Poluka to avoid even discussing the issue with anyone. However, since the property of the Corps was the subject of today's hearing, six Corps admirals would sit with the panel in an advisory capacity.

The Exploration Corps admirals arrived in a single limousine. Poluka saluted as he met them at the curb. Admiral Lucille Montague's aged face showed apprehension except when she returned his salute. A warm glow filled her face as they locked eyes.

Aguire showed up with Lynda and her father. They all went into the chamber together. The spectator section was packed to capacity with over a thousand people. Lynda and G.J. were in the first row. Five rows back, Elpastre watched with Oppo Gunn, William Emerson, and Bart Hanson. 20 of Major Rivers' people had seats surrounding them.

Protocols were not yet established for these proceedings since the interim government didn't have a functioning judicial branch, and precedence for Aguire's claim to the Hanno were obscure. The hearing would be presided over by the Governor of South America.

Admiral Montague asked to say a few words before the proceedings began.

"Commander Aguire," she said. "On behalf of the Exploration Corps and, I'm sure, the entire interim government, I thank you for your actions, which resulted in driving out the vile regime that has plagued this world for the last two years."

There was some applause before Aguire responded.

"Admiral Montague, I appreciate such recognition, but nothing would have been possible if not for the leadership of Captain Poluka, and the devotion of the officers and crew of the Starship Hanno, not to mention the valiant efforts of the Army, and many civilians."

"Of course, Commander, but I believe you took an especially daring role in the events. With that in mind, and in light of your record, I am happy to announce your promotion to the rank of Captain."

The spectators rose to their feet with applause. The admirals and generals did the same. The Continental

Governors couldn't miss out on getting good press, and did likewise. Poluka clasped Aguire's shoulder, and said in his ear, "I think of you as family, too."

Aguire's smile was genuine when the press broadcast his image to the world.

At last, the room quieted and the Governor of South America brought the hearing to order.

Aguire's claim was read: that he would not only be in command of the Hanno, but his command would amount to personal ownership of the vessel. His claim was based on articles of the Corps Charter written in the days when many captains provided their own ships when they joined the Corps.

Several Corps admirals lamented what a loss it would be if the Corps were to surrender the Hanno's ownership, but stopped short of actually disputing Aguire's claim. One general pointed out that the Earth's military was now short on large vessels after the recent conflict. Some regional officials went further, and said that Aguire's claim was "misguided" if not entirely absurd.

"We are, of course, mindful of your recent heroism," the Governor of Western Europe noted. "And I am sure the Admiralty has a ship in mind for you, but I'm afraid, Captain Aguire, that the conditions these articles were written to address do not apply in this instance. In fact, now that I have studied the Charter of the Exploration Corps, I am appalled that such a document was ever written for any government agency. One of my first actions in the new government will be to propose a complete redefinition of the Corps."

At this point some of the governors nodded in grave agreement, while the admirals of the Corps looked aghast at the speaker. Some of the military leaders seemed surprised by the idea, too.

"We will leave that for future discussions," the Governor of South America interrupted. "Captain Aguire, are you prepared to present an argument for your claim?"

"Respectfully, Governor, I am." At least, he hoped he was. He'd been so busy with other matters, he'd left this battle for others to prepare. "My attorney will present my argument."

Lynda Stokes was wearing an ankle-length, blue pin-striped dress, and had her hair gathered into bun behind her head. Looking every bit the lawyer, she strode confidently to stand beside Aguire, and introduced herself. The appearance of the richest women in the galaxy had the press babbling ecstatically into tiny microphones, and a murmur rippled through the spectators.

"Ladies and Gentlemen of the interim government," she addressed the panel, "as the Governor of Western Europe has pointed out; the Corps Charter does not conform to accepted legal standards for government documents. It is relevant and necessary to understand why it was written this way. The Charter took effect when it was signed and ratified on the fourth day of August, 2755, but the Corps already existed prior to that date and, in fact, already had a charter that this new one replaced. This is referenced in the preamble, though it may not be clear if one is unaware of the origin of the Exploration Corps."

"Miss Stokes," Senator Prudence Rival asked, "do you have a copy of the previous charter?"

"Yes, Senator. I am introducing it as evidence, and the bailiff already has copies for the panel, but first, I would like to establish the legal status of the Exploration Corps."

"Please continue, Miss Stokes," the Governor of South America said.

"Yes, Your Excellency. The new charter was written to secure the Corps's survival, and prevent it from become a tool for political or commercial interests, though it did allow for consideration of the economic and security interests of the nation when missions were proposed.

"The original charter was written during the years of the Corporate State, and was signed by twelve people in the year 2745, though some believe the Corps was actually formed a year earlier. Precise records from those days are not available."

"Wait a moment." The Governor of Australia interrupted. "Do you mean to say that the Exploration Corps was originally an agency of the Corporate State?"

There was murmuring through the spectators. Every history

book written in the last 40 years portrayed it as a proud, patriotic moment in human history when the Corporate State was completely dismantled at the end of the war. The idea that one part slipped through unscathed was unsettling.

Paul Poluka suppressed the urge to grin. He looked up at Admiral Montague. She was a tough old girl, but she looked back at him with a twinkle in her eye. She'd guessed where this was leading.

"No, Governor, I'm not," Lynda answered. "The Corps was registered under the Corporate State as a trade association since it was a not-for-profit group dealing with specific technology. It was in no way a part of the Corporate State and, in fact, took an active part in the underground resistance."

"Indeed, Miss Stokes, that is quite interesting," Western Europe droned, "but the fact that it did not become a government agency until after the war does not seem to have any bearing on the issue of the Starship Hanno."

"But it didn't, Governor."

"Eh? Didn't what, Miss Stokes?"

"The Exploration Corps did not become a government agency under the Federation...nor under the New Federation...nor under the current government. The Exploration Corps has always been—and still is—a private organization. In fact, the Federation officially recognized it as such in a document written by the Judiciary 36 years ago, which guarantees the property and assets of the Exploration Corps will never be annexed by any federal or regional government. It's the same document that exempts the Corps from taxes. I have obtained a copy of it from the National Museum in Richmond, if you would like to read it, sir."

There was a moment of silence from the panel, but the spectators were beginning to buzz. The Governor of South America called for order before asking the bailiff to distribute Lynda's copies of the documents to the members of the panel.

The Governor of Russia had a question. "Are we to understand that Captain Aguire's claim rests on the idea that matters concerning the Exploration Corps are none of the government's business, and we should stay out of it?"

"I wouldn't put it that way, Governor, but the decision must be based on what is lawful, not what our leaders wish was lawful, as the Batastia regime did.

Paul Poluka watched their faces. Russia seemed amused by the comparison. North America was baffled. South America and Australia were stony and serious. North Africa didn't give a damn about the issue and was trying not to laugh, while South Africa, Asia, Eastern Europe and the Pacific Islands were hard to read.

The Governor of Western Europe was offended.

"Miss Stokes, you've brought an imaginative story to this panel, but I can assure you that the Exploration Corps is definitely under the jurisdiction of this government. As I said before, this charter is an absurd document. It will be nullified and a new charter shall be drafted by this government. I will make it a priority."

"Governor," Prudence Rival almost shouted, "I've heard nothing to indicate that Captain Aguire's claim is invalid. This government cannot—as Miss Stokes put it—rule by what we wish was lawful. If you have a rebuttal to the points she's made, we will hear it—after the counsel for Captain Aguire has finished her argument."

The Governor's face contorted with surprise as she scolded him. He'd been running much of Western Europe for thirteen years—surviving both the old and new Federations—and was not accustomed to public correction. A lemony sneer screwed up his face as he prepared a sharp retort for Mrs. Rival, but thunderous applause from the spectators slapped him back in his chair.

Poluka looked appreciatively at Mrs. Rival, and realized Aguire had an ally in this case. It was clever of her to remind the audience that this was all about Aguire—the hero who recently rescued the planet. The Governor of Western Europe, however, was going to be a problem. His career was on the brink, Poluka thought. If he apologizes, he could be in office for a while longer, but if he doesn't back off…

"Of course," Western Europe said when the noise subsided. "Miss Stokes, please continue."

He then whispered instruction to an intern who rushed off somewhere.

"Ladies and Gentlemen of the panel," Lynda resumed, "my client's petition may well be refused, but only by those who are lawfully authorized to make the decision. If we examine article 22 of the Exploration Corps charter, we find the conditions listed where a ship may be claimed by a captain. This article was invoked seven times that I am aware of, the most famous case being also the one involving the largest ship; the Starship Peregrine was transferred by the Corps to Captain Jeremiah Cronkite in 2759.

"The history books we've all read for the last 28 years tell how the famous explorer was given the ship, making it seem like the government bent the rules out of respect for the man. It makes a fine story, but the facts, as supported by documentation available from the National Library and the Exploration Corps Archives, show that Captain Cronkite submitted a petition to the Corps. The founding members, with the approval of a majority of the Admirals, then transferred title of the Peregrine," Lynda held up a copy of the charter, "in accordance with this document."

The Governor of South America interrupted, "You said that there are seven cases of precedence. Did you bring documentation of all of them?"

"I have, Your Excellency. Three cases are quite well documented. Four are a bit sketchy, but I brought what records exist."

"If I understand where your argument is leading, Miss Stokes, you intend to show that Captain Aguire meets all of the conditions required by the charter, and by precedence, yes?"

"Yes, Your Excellency, and that will conclude my argument."

"Of course. Since none of us have had the opportunity to become expert on these documents. I am going to ask you to wait until tomorrow before continuing. That will give us some time to study the evidence, which is necessary to make a fair and competent decision."

"Excuse me, Governor," Western Europe cut in. He was looking at the printout his intern just brought him. "The counsel has finished her argument suggesting this matter is entirely up to the Exploration Corps to decide, and the second part of her argument—dealing with the conditions for surrendering ownership of a starship—will only be relevant if the first part is valid. As much as we all admire Captain Aguire's heroic deeds, we cannot prolong this proceeding unnecessarily. I have some information that I think will settle this discussion. Perhaps I may now rebut the counsel's first theory?"

The panel had an informal discussion among themselves.

Aguire turned to Poluka and whispered, "I have no idea what's going to happen next. Did Lynda prepare for a rebuttal?"

"Wait and see."

Lynda did not object, and the Governor of Western Europe spent five painfully dull minutes giving long-winded praise to the Corps for all the discoveries and scientific advances made over the years, before getting to the point.

"The description you've given, counselor, of a non-government organization is not at all accurate. In fact, I can show you a chart of how the government has been funding the Corps in ever increasing amounts since the signing of the new charter.

"Just this year the taxpayers have put nearly a billion credits into the Corps, and in the last three years over two billion credits have gone into the cost of the Starship Hanno. I have exact figures here showing payments made to the Corps in each fiscal quarter.

"Now, as much as I'd like to see Captain Aguire rewarded for his heroism, I don't think we can simply give him a two billion credit ship that was clearly bought and paid for by the federal government."

The Governor looked up from his notes, not at Lynda but at the camera that was broadcasting the hearing. "I am very sorry to disappoint Captain Aguire, but his claim is in error, his request must be denied, and the interim government must get on to other business. It is unfortunate that the issue got this far. I'm sure a more experienced lawyer would have seen earlier that this would go nowhere, but I understand Miss Stokes got her license to practice law just this week, so it's not too surprising that she misunderstood the facts."

Poluka whispered to Aguire, "He can't publicly be an asshole to a popular hero, so he's being an asshole to the hero's lawyer. Won't help though—he just flushed his career."

"I believe those numbers are fairly accurate, Governor," Lynda responded. "But they fail to show that the Corps budget last year was over 20 billion, or that the cost of the Hanno was nearly eight billion. Clearly, the Corps does not rely on government funds to continue operating.

"Examination of every payment the government has made to the Corps will show that the funds were for specific missions of exploration, not for starships or for salaries. The government has never signed a paycheck for any member of the Exploration Corps, nor directly paid for any hardware that was not subsequently delivered to a government agency per a written agreement.

"In the case of the Starship Hanno, 750 million credits was supplied by executive order of the old Federation. The treasury records confirm this, and I have a letter addressed to the Exploration Corps Finance Department from the Federation Treasury explaining that the funds were a research grant for the new engine design and, as such, amount to a gift that does not imply any purchase or obligation to deliver a starship."

"A gift?" Western Europe bellowed. "Of three quarters of a billion? You must be joking. Something must be owed to the nation for that much money."

"No, Governor. It's much the same as the grant made to your Western Europe five years ago for researching ancient farming techniques. That was for the same amount, and did not provide the federal government with any tangible return, but enriched humanity for generations to come."

Guffaws of laughter echoed among the spectators, and the Governor of North Africa covered his mouth with a handkerchief. Aguire looked at Poluka, who quietly explained.

"Five years ago, this jerk wrangled a huge grant from the Fed for some nonsense that was just to pump money into his region and line the pockets of his friends. Lynda's just repeating the same words he used when he had to explain it to the press."

The Governor glared hatefully at Lynda, and finally asked through clenched teeth, "What about the other billion and a quarter of Federation money, Miss Stokes? That was not a gift."

"No, Your Excellency, that was a loan to subsidiaries of Stokes Industries. I have the original loan agreement here." She held up a document in one hand, and then held up another sheet of paper in her other hand. "And here I have a receipt signed by the current Secretary of the Treasury showing that the loan has been repaid in full as of yesterday morning. If you insist on having the grant money returned, we can do that, too, Governor, but the fact is, the Hanno is not government property."

The Governor of Western Europe opened his mouth as if to speak, then closed it and looked around at his colleagues for inspiration, but found none. He slumped down in his chair and mumbled something about needing time to examine the records.

The Governor of South America made a valiant attempt to stifle a smirk at his colleague's failure to make a swift end of Miss Stokes' case. "You seem to have a lot of cash Miss Stokes. Been saving your allowance?"

This brought a teetering of laughter even from members of the panel. Lynda allowed a small smile to cross her face.

"Actually, Your Excellency, Stokes Industries borrowed some of the money from the owners of Firehawk Industries, and the RadGlass Corporation."

The spectators didn't get it, but some members of the panel sat up straighter as they digested the implications of an alliance between such financial giants.

Poluka didn't know this was coming, and looked back at the spectators. Bart Hanson winked at him from five rows back. Bart was a major stockholder in Firehawk, and friends of his deceased parents owned RadGlass.

It's good to have friends with money.

* * *

The strategy for this moment was born in Lynda's subconscious during the struggle to take the Hanno from Paul Poluka when she'd been considering the legal issues surrounding authority within the Exploration Corps. Now, Poluka was helping her cement Aguire's claim to the ship. The irony was almost physical as they flew to Quebec in a mini-transport. She sat quietly and thoughtfully watched her companions.

"I knew you were a stockholder," Poluka was saying to Bart, "but I had no idea you had so much influence."

"My cousins actually own most of Firehawk," Bart responded. "And I have a big part of the Quebec Spaceshuttle Corporation. My father was an engineer there."

"I'm surprised you didn't go into engineering instead of joining the Navy."

Lynda knew Bart wouldn't answer too many questions, but what surprised her was that Poluka still hadn't guessed the truth, that aliens lived among them. He'd recovered remarkably from his mental illness, thanks to Arcturusian techniques, but the embarrassment, guilt, and shame still haunted him.

Elpastre and Oppo Gunn were on the flight deck looking down at Lake Huron, still awestruck at visiting an alien world. Aguire and Emerson were with them.

Chief Braun was chatting with an Arcturusian doctor who came along to keep an eye on Poluka, and to be available should the King of Arcturus need any civilized medical help. Lynda's brother and his wife were sharing in the conversation, too.

Elisa was talking quietly with Lynda's Papa, which was surprising in itself since they couldn't stand each other just a few weeks ago. Paul was joining them now. Bart was…was watching Lynda.

"What?" Lynda asked.

"You know where we're going?"

"To your hometown…for lunch."

Bart laughed. "Well, yes, for lunch, but we could have had lunch in West Point."

"We wanted a place where no one would be spying on us. Why?"

"The estate where we'll be landing belongs to the RadGlass Corporation."

"Oh, that won't make Papa happy. He's been trying to reverse engineer their technology for years. He never has anything good to say about them."

"That's because they're Blues," Bart said quietly. "Remember the photograph I showed you?"

The picture of the Erosians living on Earth.

"I remember."

"The baby in the picture was Sam—he's about 20 by now—and this house we're going to is owned by his grandparents. They don't live there but keep the house for business meetings." Bart stole a quick glance around the transport to make sure no one else was listening. "My grandparents will be there. I've spoken with them, and they want to meet you and Gentry."

* * *

Poluka shook hands with the elderly man whose eyes were as amazingly blue as Bart's. The man's charming wife also had very blue eyes. "Your grandson is one of the finest officers in the Corps, and a hero many times over."

"So I've heard," Bart's grandfather said with a peculiar accent. "We are very proud of him. Please, use this house while you prepare for tomorrow's hearing."

The "house" was a rambling estate with a two-story mansion in the center, and at least ten more buildings scattered across a wooded lot the size of a small village. There was a minimal, but professional, staff who attended to their needs. The elderly Hanson's provided a sumptuous meal for everyone. Afterwards, Paul got on the com net to monitor the political news. The others relaxed for a while.

Elpastre and Oppo Gunn disappeared for about an hour with Lynda, Gentry, and Ella. Chief Braun got nervous when he realized the King of Arcturus was gone, and found it curious to find their alien visitors had been visiting with Bart's grandparents, but he said nothing about it.

Towards evening they gathered under a gazebo for a light dinner. From there they could see the Sainte-Agnes-de-Bellecombe skyline, and Bart pointed out the onion-domed church where his adopted father was a priest.

"It's almost certain," Paul said, "that the government will have to leave it to the Corps to decide the issue, but almost certain isn't the same as definitely certain. The Governors—and some of the senators, too—won't want to concede that the Corps is a private organization. It's too much to let go of."

"Can they put pressure on the Admiralty to deny my petition?" Aguire wondered.

"Definitely, and they're doing it already. I got a short message from Prudence Rival saying she's been contacted by each of the Governors, and so have all of the admirals. There's a split among the admirals about which way your petition should go, but most of the Governors want the Corps to be under their authority regardless of what happens to the Hanno."

"Perhaps," Bart's silver-haired grandfather said with his exotic accent, "you should make sure you get the Hanno first. That would become a precedence the Corps can use to show they are autonomous. If you can make the government say—or even imply—that the Admiralty can make this decision, then the Admiralty could swiftly do so and Captain Aguire may then leave the Solar System, and the Navy will be able to refuse orders to stop him from taking the Hanno. The Corps will then have one less thing to distract them as they fight for their independent status. It will also inspire the public to see that the government cannot rule by decree, as Batastia did."

"If the panel follows the rule of law tomorrow," Lynda added, "they'll have to see things our way, because we're right."

"Somehow that doesn't sound like a guarantee," Aguire muttered.

"It's not," G.J. said. "These are politicians. Right and wrong have nothing to do with their decision."

"It would take only a small distraction." Bart's grandfather rubbed his chin. "Something that will keep the Governors off balance for few hours tomorrow, just long enough to miss their opportunity to stop the Corps from transferring the title of the Hanno."

* * *

Poluka took Aguire to the Legislature building just as the sun was rising in West Point.

"Why come so early?" Aguire asked. "The hearing won't resume for hours yet."

"It'll give us a chance to talk without being overheard," Paul lied. Since Aguire had never been good at lying, his plan would work better if Aguire didn't know what he was doing.

"Talk about what?" Aguire asked, his voice echoing along the granite columns as they entered the huge, vacant foyer.

"José," Paul stopped his friend in the middle of the giant lobby, "I've got to tell you something."

"What is it? Is something wrong?"

"General Hebert told me something yesterday, something…disturbing. The New Federation had something going on called The Perks. It was a system of perverse, decadent rewards for the favorites of the Batastia administration—very secret and very ugly. They had parties where every kind of pleasure could be satisfied."

"So, what did they do…get drunk and hire prostitutes?" Aguire sounded unimpressed.

"No, they got drunk and murdered people."

"What?"

"It turns out Batastia was a young man when the Corporate

State fell 40 years ago, and he was supposed to inherit the leadership of the State, or at least that's how he remembered it. He spent all these years resenting the Federation for taking that away from him, and this New Federation was his way of getting even. He didn't just want power; he wanted revenge on all the people who caused the fall of the State, and on the people who flourished under the old Federation.

"That's why he banned religion—because so many religious groups helped topple the State. And that's why he was so intent on getting control over big business—they'd replaced the old corporations that gave his family power."

"Okay." Aguire nodded. "I've heard speculation about this, but how do these Perks fit into the picture?"

"We got wind of this from Fisher's secret files that Santino hacked into. That led us to records of Admiral Higgs' activities which showed they'd been imprisoning people who would be abused, and later killed, for amusement. Batastia made a point of getting young women and sometimes young men who were the descendants of people he considered responsible for the fall of the Corporate State. When there weren't enough of those to go around, they would kidnap women from the primitives and make slaves of them."

Aguire stared at Paul with his mouth hanging open in total shock, but he wasn't saying anything. Paul poked him in the ribs. "Are you getting this?"

"Uh...yeah. My god...are you sure?"

"Oh, yes. Hebert's troops liberated a small prison that was exclusively for sex slaves. Some of the daughters of powerful industrialists were found there. Batastia wanted to punish them for being successful, and harming their families was his way of doing it. Records indicating who may have been participating in the abuse of these people are being analyzed now. Fisher was definitely one of them...and some of the former Governors, and...possibly...some of the current Governors."

"What? Some of these bastards may have been torturing innocent people for Batastia's amusement?"

Aguire looked like he was ready to kill any number of Governors.

"Hold on, José." Paul had to rein him in now, and let others take it from here. "We need to let Hebert handle this. When he gets all the information, he'll personally put the guilty parties up against a wall. I just thought you should know what was going on. We'll keep this just between us for now, okay?"

The hundreds of listening devices in the foyer of the Legislature Building provided news media groups all over the world with a fresh task this morning: to track down independent confirmations and background information in time to have hundreds of obnoxious reporters demanding answers from the Governors as they arrived a few hours later.

Everything Paul said was true, except the part about Hebert having information on which Governors had participated in the Perks. Hebert was frustrated in the lack of evidence, but he wouldn't be for long; he only had to wait and see who fled.

The Governors were completely flustered by the onslaught of questions and innuendo from the media, and in fear for their careers...if not their lives. The Governor of Western Europe did not attend the hearing. He and 22 other public figures from government and industry fled the planet within the next few days, but they didn't get far before Hebert caught up with them.

The panel dropped the ball concerning the disposition of the Starship Hanno. By that afternoon, the Admiralty convened separately to consider Captain Aguire's petition.

"You know, Paul," Admiral Montague said before the hearing began, "there's still no guarantee Aguire will win. The Governors had a valid point about handing over such an expensive ship."

"I know. But will they uphold the Charter, or make up their own rules?"

"The Charter will be upheld." She gave a sharp, no-nonsense nod. "But the conditions for transferring title of a starship are open to interpretation. I was going to have your promotion to admiral effective today, but the other admirals blocked it. They don't want you voting on this issue."

"Ah," Poluka pointed, "here come Captain Aguire and Miss Stokes."

The meeting was held at the Exploration Corps HQ in the capital. Only the Governors of South America and Russia still had enough wits to show up for it, though they would have no official role in the proceedings. They sat in the spectator seats with a few assistants. The public was not invited.

"Ladies and Gentlemen of the Admiralty," Lynda began, "we see from the precedence of the Starship Peregrine being transferred to Captain Cronkite how the conditions were met in that instance.

"He made a commitment to study a mystery of the universe that would—and did—take the rest of his life. The Peregrine was an ideal ship for his ambition of mapping planets, and he'd already proven himself aboard her.

"The cost of the Peregrine was largely paid by private donations specifically intended to supply Captain Cronkite with a ship—not to supply the Corps with a ship.

"There are clear parallels that apply to the case of the Hanno and Captain Aguire. He has proven himself aboard the Hanno, and he is committed to studying the Zone and the mysteries of Arcturus—including overseeing the sector to protect the ecosystem there. The cost of the Hanno—as we reviewed earlier—was not paid by the Exploration Corps except for some bookkeeping expenses. Most of the funds came from Stokes Industries, and a grant from the Federation. Stokes Industries fully endorses Captain Aguire's petition."

"Miss Stokes," one of the admirals interrupted, "we will consider the argument, but the new government will take steps to block our decision."

"Admiral, if the decision is made now, Captain Aguire can get on with his new mission immediately, and we can wait to see what the government has to say about it. If we delay, then the mission will probably never happen."

The admiral gave her a humorless grin. "You cannot ask us to make this decision, and expect an immediate answer, Miss Stokes. I am ready to vote in favor of Captain Aguire's petition, but not all of us are in agreement."

"Oh." Lynda blinked at him with that doll-like look. "I see there has been a misunderstanding. I apologize, Admiral, I thought it was clear that we are not here to ask the Admiralty to transfer the title of the ship."

At this, even Admiral Montague jerked upright in her chair. "If you're not asking for our approval, what are we here for, Miss Stokes?"

"Admiral," Lynda began to respond to Montague, then looked around at all the admirals. "Ladies and Gentlemen, this petition will be handled exactly as Captain Cronkite's petition was handled—by the founding members of the Corps, or at least those whom we can call upon."

At that, the side door opened. Two men entered and joined Lynda.

"Hello, Lucy," one of them said shyly to Admiral Montague.

"I'll be damned," she whispered huskily, "Hello, Ivan."

Ivan Tershensky stood with Luther Braun while Lynda brought the Admirals attention to the signatures on the charter, and affirmed that they were now looking at two of the founding members of the Corps.

Lynda said, "The charter states that the founders have the authority, and even the duty, to grant this sort of request from a captain. In the case of Captain Cronkite, it was the founders who made the decision. The admirals merely stated their approval. It is my hope that the admirals here today will also state their approval when the founding members transfer title of the Hanno to Captain Aguire."

"Wait a minute." One admiral stood up. His face was the image of indignation. "This is a mighty fine trick, Miss Stokes. I have to admit I'd never of guessed you could produce any founders, and I'll concede that the charter stipulates founding members, but this only underscores what the Governors were saying about the charter being poorly written. We won't always have founding members around."

Admiral Montague rapped on the desk with her gavel. "But we have two now, and we are bound to respect the charter...which is our legal authorization to exist."

The objecting admiral shook his head. "Two? We have two founding members of the original twelve. I'll tell you what...I'll go along with this if someone can produce just one more. Show me three founding members...and I'll accept it."

He crossed his arms and sat down.

"For that," Ivan said, "we'll have to go all the way back to the original charter."

Lynda got the photocopy of a handwritten document that was a single page in length. Scrawled across the bottom were twelve signatures which she read aloud, one by one.

The last name was Lucille Landess.

"Admiral," Ivan gave Montague a tender look, "Lucy, tell the admirals your maiden name."

Epilogue

The Captain rode in the back of the car and considered the technology that went into building the glass engine. It was different. An Earth engineer, restricted to using these materials, would have still tried to design it some other way. The engineers on this planet just had a different way to approach a task, and that's what it takes to solve unsolvable problems.

The steam-powered car dropped him off at the edge of the orchard where he could see the children playing. He walked the rest of the way.

There were already two thousand orphans here: children whose parents had been killed by the New Federation, mostly primitives, who had nowhere else to go. Batastia destroyed their families, their communities, and even the houses they'd lived in. Most were from the Rocky Mountains of America, some were from Europe. Another thousand would be coming in a few days.

In the side yard of the estate, he saw a woman turning fillets of meat on a barbeque.

"José," she called to him, and waved.

He joined her, and watched as she carved a morsel for him to sample. She was an attractive, fiftyish woman with sea-gray eyes, dressed in a clingy blouse and slacks that showed a figure many younger women would be envious of.

"Try this and tell me what you think." She handed him a piece of Arcturusian lamb, skewered on a long toothpick.

"Mm...yes, it's delicious." It was so perfect it almost melted in his mouth.

"Now, if I can just teach Lynda," she sighed with a wistful smile.

"I heard that." Lynda called out as she emerged from the house with her brother. "I am getting better, you know. I managed to make tea this morning without causing any injuries."

Lynda gave Captain Aguire a kiss on the cheek before hugging her mom and helping with the barbeque. Gentry and Aguire moved away from the smoke and looked out across the fields where children were playing.

The huge steam-cars were not common on Arcturus, but two more could be seen, still kilometers away, coming around the mountain from the east.

"Probably more nobles from the capital," Gentry pointed, "hoping to adopt a child from Earth. People from every province have been coming constantly since the first children arrived. Earth is going to run out of orphans, soon."

"Good." Aguire wouldn't mind if every last child who needed a family ends up on Arcturus. "There'll be settlers coming, too, maybe as soon as next year."

"Hm...that would be the Season of the Twins on the Arcturusian calendar."

"Cassandra seems happy here." Aguire changed the subject.

"She is." Gentry turned to look at his mother. "I'm happy to be with her again, and so is Lynda. You know, when our parents divorced, Papa kept taking us on trips. We went to Mars about five times, to the visitor's center at Alpha Centauri, and even to Tau Ceti once. It wasn't until I was an adult that I figured out that the trips were to keep her from seeing us. Lynda just found out a few days ago."

"You've forgiven him?"

"I have. Ella taught me how to forgive. Lynda's having some trouble with it but now that she's spending time with Mama I think a lot of wounds are healing. Mama may need more time, though. I think she feels that Papa never really loved her, that he married her just to get children."

Cassandra Stokes was a professor at the University of Mexico City, and came from a family of remarkable intellectuals. If such things were hereditary, Gentry and Lynda owed at least as much to their mother and grandmother as they did to their dad for being smart. Their father's mother had also been an intellectual, chosen by their grandfather to produce a brilliant son.

Aguire should have figured out on his own that the Stokes family was alien, but it wasn't until Ensign O'Riley brought his suspicions to him that all the pieces fell into place. G.J. didn't deny it when Aguire asked him. The question of Erosians would be another thing on the Hanno's list to investigate, but only a few would know about the aliens who were already living on Earth. Even General Hebert wasn't told about them.

The lunch bell rang and the kids began moving towards the yard, slowly, reluctant to abandon their games, and not worried about any shortage of food. If there was one thing this world had in abundance, it was food.

The last time he'd come to this world, Aguire discussed with Elpastre the possibility of exporting food to Epsilon Eridanus, the Iron Planet, and maybe wood, too, in exchange for metals. The people at the mining colony pay a premium price for goods from Earth, and would definitely appreciate another source.

Lunch was served by an army of elderly Arcturusian women, who also patiently taught the kids a new language and new customs. Aguire got a seat of honor next to the noble who owned the estate and was a close relative of the Queen.

Leroy Donno, who was adapting to his prosthetic leg, was already seated. The Admiralty offered Donno any assignment of his own choosing, but Aguire's old friend decided to retire from the Corps and take a position in the new government overseeing the policies concerning space exploration. This would be his last day on Arcturus for a while.

"Hey, buddy." Donno tried to smile at Aguire, but he'd been sullen lately, and smiled rarely.

"Hi, Donno. I made sure they gave you a good office. You'll be just down the hall from Senator Rival." Aguire watched his friend for any sign of enthusiasm.

"I guess I can live with that," Donno said. "Did Poluka finally move his fat ass out of West Point?"

"Uh-huh." Aguire sighed, wishing his friend could learn something about forgiveness, the way Gentry did. "He's at the naval training center in Portugal. He revived the old wooden ship program. Every new officer has to spend three months at sea, learning the old traditions, before getting an assignment to a spaceship."

"He must be very pleased with himself."

"He'll never leave Earth again. He's too ashamed of what he did, especially to you."

Donno thanked the native girl who brought him a plate of food, then looked coldly at Aguire.

"He would've left you to die, drifting alone 'till your air ran out. You should've killed him."

Aguire didn't know how to answer. He never wanted to kill Poluka. He would have, he supposed, if there'd been no choice, but never wanted to kill anybody.

Getting the Hanno was a mixed blessing. He would still have good people with him, but some of his best friends were going elsewhere: Donno would have an office at West Point. Paul Poluka was now a Navy admiral. Nigel Sheffield was promoted to Captain, and would be assigned to the new ship that G.J. Stokes was building specifically for studying the Zone, and Chief Braun would be joining Sheffield as the mission scientist. Even Bart Hanson would be gone. Bart's young cousin was missing, and he got put on reserve status with the Corps until he can locate the boy.

When Aguire noticed some of the native staff getting excited, he turned to see that the steam-cars they saw earlier pulling into the courtyard of the estate.

It was Lapastra, the Queen of Arcturus, with William Emerson and a phalanx of guards led by Pol Akwat, the lead bodyguard for the royal family.

The Queen got a warm greeting from the owner of the estate and she loudly praised his efforts to help the orphans, which pleased all the locals who lived there. Through Emerson, she greeted Aguire and said hello to the children, who didn't quite understand who she was, but understood enough.

"Captain Aguire," Lapastra said when they were sitting together. "It is almost beyond comprehension that your world has so many orphans and not enough families who are eager to adopt them. It is a sad thing, but perhaps we can erase some of this sadness."

"That is my hope, Lapastra. I was once like these children, but I chose to run away and live with a few friends in a gardening shed behind a cemetery. Of all the things I have done, bringing these kids here is what I feel best about."

Lapastra's dark eyes searched Aguire's profile as he looked at the children, trying to comprehend the alien man. "Captain, there is someone else who has nowhere to go. My friend, Eeja Burr, has become a fugitive on Arcturus. By attempting to serve this world, he acted rashly, and destroyed his career. My husband would have him arrested. It is my wish that you will take him with you, him and his wife."

Nothing could surprise Aguire at this point. "I will take him."

He would work out later what to do with the former royal chronicler. He might not be able to find a home for him on Earth, but there were plenty of other worlds, or Eeja could stay on the Hanno as a guest.

Earth was still an uncertain place. The new republic would be phased in soon, but the politicos were already jockeying for position, and the Corps may not remain independent. For a little while longer, Aguire would still make brief stops there, but he knew that would end soon. His home would be the Hanno, and the crew would be his family.

ABOUT THE AUTHOR

James Prescott presented the novel Between Earth and Arcturus as an audio podcast before putting it into print.

His career has been in space, military, medical, communication,and surveillance technology.

He now works in the field of atomic force microscopes and tends his garden in his spare time.